Praise for *Poseidon's Sword*

"An entertaining melding of fantasy and reality. Samantha Starr is a female character not to be trifled with." Donald Bain, author of the "Murder, She Wrote" series, Margaret Truman's "Capital Crimes" series, and "Coffee, Tea, or Me?"

"Move over, Indiana Jones, Samantha Starr is back in action! Throw in the quest for a doomsday weapon, a psychotic assassin, an underground Nazi cult, a secret Dragon Society hell-bent on helping their mysterious masters achieve world domination, hidden passageways with no apparent exits, a 727 airliner landing on an aircraft carrier at sea, Navy SEALs, and a Special Forces SAS lover who is tall, dark, and Scottish, and you have just another day in the life of "Danger Magnet" Samantha Starr!" Heather Ashby, author of the "Love in the Fleet" series

"Buckle your seat belt and hang on. *Poseidon's Sword* moves faster than a jumbo jet and has a cargo load of thrills. The chocolate-eating pilot and heroine, Samantha Starr, travels the world to unravel the eleven thousand year old mystery of Atlantis and discover its doomsday weapon as villains shadow her every move. An action-packed read with a little romance tossed in for fun, and one you can't put down." Susan Klaus, an award-winning author of thrillers and fantasy

"S.L. Menear has done it again with her second novel, *Poseidon's Sword*, adeptly intertwining mythology and modern day aviation. Add the beautiful Boeing 767 Captain Samantha Starr into the mix, and you have an action packed thriller that's hard to put down." George Jehn, author of "Final Destination: Disaster. What Really Happened to Eastern Airlines" and "Flying Too Close to the Sun"

"Sam Starr, or rather S.L. Menear, grips the reader once again in her second book of the Samantha Starr Series. In *Poseidon's Sword*, Menear develops strong characters and strikes out on another thrilling journey. The added treat is the backdrop of exotic locales. The reader, buckled up, feels the excitement of traveling with Sam as she fights her way out from evil. And there are plenty of villains. As in her first book, *Deadstick Dawn*, Menear throws the reader off until the very end. I'm ready for the third Starr." Fred Lichtenberg, author of "Hunter's World," "Double Trouble," "Deadly Heat at the Cottages: Sex, Murder, and Mayhem," "Obsessed," and "Retired: Now What?"

"S.L. Menear's second novel in her Samantha Starr Series picks up the action in full stride. Her multiple plot twists thrust Sam and friends into repeated danger and turmoil, keeping you on the edge of your seat, turning the pages as fast as you can. Great, well-developed characters earn your concern, and Ms. Menear's imaginative plot is without parallel. A Five-Star must read." George A Bernstein, Amazon Top 100 Author of "Death's Angel" & "Born to Die," the first 2 in the Detective Al Warner Series, and the psychological thriller "Trapped"

"Welcome back, Samantha! Author S. L. Menear has resumed the adventures of her unforgettable heroine, airline pilot Samantha Starr, whose new adventures excel in the Action, Adventure, Thriller genre. Menear merges well-crafted, thrilling action and brilliantly imagined characters into unpredictable plots as Samantha probes back into time to find Poseidon's Sword, a weapon of unfathomable power before it can be used to destroy the world. For those who enjoy reading inspired writing with roller-coaster suspense, *Poseidon's Sword* is a must-read." Tina Nicholas, author of "Affair In Athens" and "Condo Crazies"

POSEIDON'S SWORD

Book Two in the Samantha Starr Series

S.L. MENEAR

Black Stallion Publishing

Black Stallion Publishing
1281 N. Ocean Blvd., Suite 149
Singer Island, Florida 33404

Cover Design by Tim Pryor of Pryority Design Studio
Sword Design by Tim Pryor of Pryority Design Studio

ISBN-10: 1943264007
ISBN-13: 978-1-943264-00-1

For my beloved cousins,

Dick, Bob, Linda, Suzie, and Debbie

"Once you have tasted flight, you will forever walk the earth with your eyes turned skyward, for there you have been and there you long to return." Leonardo Da Vinci, 1452 - 1519

"If you wish to understand the universe, you must think of energy, frequency, and vibration. Electricity is all around us."
Nikola Tesla, 1856 – 1943

POSEIDON'S SWORD

S.L. MENEAR

PROLOGUE

IT WAS THE WINTER solstice in 8984 B.C., and time was running out for Atlantis.

The powerful nation clung to a small remnant of a huge continent. The sea had swallowed most of the land into deep trenches during cataclysmic earthquakes over the past ten millennia.

King Zoran strode off his longboat and gazed up at the glowing volcano looming behind the capital city as a strong tremor shook the island and rattled the docks.

He turned to General Xenos. "Take me to my airship."

Panicked citizens stampeded the pier where soldiers held them off.

"My men will escort you, Your Highness." The general signaled the airship floating twenty feet above the shoreline.

Zoran followed his soldiers to where the royal airship touched down. As soon as he boarded, it lifted off toward the white marble palace on the plateau above the city.

The king entered the cockpit. "Captain, do we have enough oxygen for a high altitude to escape the coming explosion?"

"Your Majesty, we have sufficient chemical stores for the oxygen generators to produce oxygen during our long journey, and the battery bank is charged with enough solar energy to heat the cabin and power the motors if we encounter cloudy weather."

The king's brows furrowed. "What about a massive ash cloud?"

"Ash will clog the motors and block the sun from reaching the solar panels. As soon as the queen boards, we must hasten from the volcanoes."

Zoran's expression brightened when he spotted a long-haired blonde, her diaphanous gown billowing in the breeze.

"The queen is on the landing pad. I will go to the entry door." He hurried aft.

Queen Aurora rushed up the ramp into her husband's arms. "Zoran, thank Poseidon you arrived in time!"

As his airship rose above the mountains, Zoran looked down on the volcano. Loud rumblings vibrated the rigid craft.

"At least we are together." Zoran held Aurora close as the flying armada fled his beloved island home.

Far below, the harbor area bristled like a beehive as terrified citizens rushed to board the longboats.

The airships climbed east from Atlantis above the mountains and caught favorable tailwinds.

The king's craft took the lead at twenty-thousand feet when a volcano on an island near Atlantis exploded.

"By our mighty god Poseidon, half that mountain just crumbled into the sea! The wave is higher than our pyramids!" The king watched in horror as the monster wave shot across the fifty miles to Atlantis.

A towering wall of liquid doom unleashed its full fury on the helpless Atlanteans. Everything below the high plateaus was crushed and buried undersea.

Cool water forced its way into cracks in the mountain and triggered a powerful explosion in Atlantis's pressurized volcano. The dome vaporized and formed a searing pyroclastic cloud that expanded with alarming velocity.

Deep in the bowels of the volcano, a chain reaction of

explosions created earthquakes on the ocean floor beneath the island, shifting the tectonic plates and collapsing the once mighty nation into the gaping jaws of a new undersea trench. The entire fleet of longboats went down with the island.

A small section of Atlantis high atop the western plateau behind the mountain was sheltered from the crushing wave.

The Great Hall of Records and Royal Library, standing along columned streets flanked by giant pyramids and sphinxes, sank into timeless perfection on the sea floor near the trench.

Aurora gasped and clutched her husband's arm. "Atlantis is gone!"

Zoran looked up as the enormous ash cloud swallowed half the airship armada.

"Captain, maximum speed! The ash cloud!" Zoran shouted.

The motors vibrated at full power as the royal airship struggled to outpace the dense cloud. One by one, the airships behind them vanished into hot swirling ash.

"The cloud is slowing." The king sighed with relief. "We might escape it."

"Any chance the other airships survived?" Aurora scanned the dark cloud.

"I doubt it. We should have seen them by now." Zoran stared into the darkness.

Two hours later, there was still no sign of the airships.

The king glanced around the main cabin where everyone waited in tense silence.

"We are the sole survivors of Atlantis, but do not lose heart. We have known for years this day would come."

King Zoran paused and looked into the eyes of his people.

"The secret enclave we built in the Himalayas will keep us safe until the appointed time. Remember the oracle's prophecy. Triplet goddesses of Sun, Moon, and Fire will activate Poseidon's Sword on the winter solstice eleven-thousand years hence, and our mighty nation will rise to rule again."

"Praise Poseidon!" the people said in unison.

Winter Solstice – 1992

FLIGHT ATTENDANT SUZANNE BERGLIND enjoyed the panoramic view at thirty-seven thousand feet over the majestic Himalayas after she carried two cups of coffee into the private Boeing 767's cockpit.

She handed the cups to the pilots. "Black with two sugars and one with cream and sugar."

"What a view! Is that Mt. Everest ahead in the distance?" She pointed.

"Right, it's just over twenty-nine thousand feet, easy to spot. I know you've only been working here a few weeks, but how do you like it, Suzanne?" Captain Peterson asked.

"I love it. They pay well, and I have lots of scheduled days off to work on my master's degree." She hesitated. "Uh, I don't keep up with the jet set, so I'm curious, what's the story with our bosses?"

"Ah, you mean Richard and Sheila Conor, the billionaire power couple with engineering doctorates from MIT?" The captain sipped his coffee.

The copilot nodded. "Yeah, they hold hundreds of patents for military software and high-tech devices."

"So far, they've been really nice to me," Suzanne said. "They seem decent and down-to-earth."

"And they designed this airplane's interior and the two survival pods in the tail section," the captain said.

"They're the sole owners of Gold Trident Industries. Nice, huh?" The copilot shook his head.

"I wonder how they came up with that name." Suzanne glanced from one pilot to the other.

"Mr. Conor told me he named the company in honor of his late father, Robert Conor, a Navy SEAL," the captain said.

Suzanne knitted her brows. "I don't understand."

"The gold trident is a symbol of the Navy SEALs, which began as underwater demolition teams. The seas are Poseidon's realm, and his weapon is a gold trident."

"Oh, right, makes sense."

Suzanne left the cockpit and heard the galley intercom chime. She picked up the handset.

"Yes? Bottles for the triplets? Right away, Mrs. Conor."

She prepared three bottles of baby formula, placed them on a silver tray, and hurried through the jumbo jet's spacious lounge, dining area, office, and two bedrooms.

The main cabin compartments connected through wide sliding center doors secured open during the day. A padded crib bolted to the floor in the aft bedroom cradled the Conor's daughters.

"I have their bottles ready." Suzanne set the tray on a table between leather club chairs.

"Thank you." Sheila unfastened the safety netting and handed one of the babies to Richard and another to Suzanne. She lifted the third baby into her arms and reached for a bottle.

Suzanne sat with the Conors and fed baby Blaze. "The triplets look identical except for their hair and eye colors."

"As you can see, Solraya has Sheila's golden hair and aqua eyes." Richard turned the blond baby toward Suzanne and smiled.

"And Luna looks like Richard with her black hair and deep-blue eyes." Sheila matched her husband's smile.

"Blaze is a mystery with flame-red hair and emerald eyes. No one in our family looks like her—must come from far down the family tree." Richard shrugged.

"Today is their first birthday." Sheila kissed Luna as her baby sucked on the bottle.

"How did you come up with such unusual names?" Suzanne rocked the red-haired baby.

"Actually, that's quite a story." Sheila glanced at her husband. "Should we tell her?"

He nodded and looked at Suzanne. "Please keep in mind we don't believe in mythology or ancient legends."

"Twenty-one months ago, I met a woman at a MENSA convention," Sheila said. "We discovered we both had occasional visions, usually of the future."

"Seriously? You can predict the future?"

"It's not like I have control over what I see or when I see it, but my mother has the same ability. That MENSA woman believed we were descendants of powerful women from ancient Atlantis."

"I'm working on a master's in ancient history," Suzanne said. "I read Plato's account of Atlantis—fascinating story. Just enough clues are scattered around the world to make Atlantis a tantalizing possibility."

Sheila nodded. "The woman took my hand and informed me I was pregnant with triplet girls. She said they would grow up to be as powerful as the Atlantean goddesses of Sun, Moon, and Fire—Solraya, Luna, and Blaze. And she predicted their hair and eye colors."

Richard broke in. "When Sheila got home, she took a pregnancy test that showed positive. We didn't buy into the goddess BS, but we liked the unusual names."

"So when my doctor told me I was carrying triplet girls, we decided to name them Solraya, Luna, and Blaze."

"Have you noticed anything unusual about them?"

Sheila exchanged a glance with her husband. "Every now and then, it sounds like they say real words, but we don't recognize the language."

Richard laughed. "Don't worry. Those words might be baby language. The important thing is they're healthy."

An explosion shook the airplane. The big jet yawed as a violent vibration shot through it.

The Conor's B767

SUZANNE SQUEEZED BLAZE AS she clutched an armrest and looked out a cabin window. "Oh, God!"

Fire, smoke, and debris trailed from the failed right engine.

Richard thrust baby Solraya into his wife's arms. "Quick, dress them in warm clothes and strap them into their survival pod! We might not clear the mountains on one engine. I'll check the cockpit." He rushed forward as the women sprang into action.

Suzanne glanced out the window again as she pulled on Blaze's insulated one-piece. "We're losing altitude, hurry!"

Turbulent air buffeted the aircraft as it skimmed the high peaks of the Himalayas. The women stumbled as they carried the babies to the little pod behind the aft bedroom.

When Suzanne leaned over to secure Blaze, the airplane banked sharply to the left and straightened. As she fumbled with the baby's harness, the interior lights extinguished. Silence.

Sheila's eyes filled with panic. "Sounds like we lost the other engine!"

Suzanne glanced at the control panel above the nearby aft jumpseat as she remembered her emergency training. "My panel is dark. That could mean we lost battery power too!"

Richard burst in. "The pilot said we flew into a dead zone. We're crashing! Suzanne, strap into your crew seat. We'll handle our babies."

"Richard, save our babies!" Sheila screamed.

Suzanne donned her uniform jacket and yanked down the crew jumpseat, which was on the aft bulkhead a few feet behind the two pods. She buckled the harness straps over her and pulled them tight.

Richard and Sheila rushed to secure their daughters in the pod designed to hold three infants and provide fifteen minutes of life support before the canopy opened automatically.

Sheila zipped her parka. "Hurry!" She handed Richard a parka as he closed the canopy on the babies' pod and rushed across the aisle to their pod.

Harnessed to her jumpseat behind the Conors, Suzanne watched Richard open their pod's canopy as an ear-splitting sound of screeching metal pierced the cabin. She looked up the aisle all the way to the cockpit door and saw the big jet's mid-section slam nose high into a razor-sharp peak that skewered its belly and broke the airplane in two.

An invisible force sucked out the warm air and replaced it with frigid low-oxygen air and swirling snow. Richard and Sheila vanished in a split second.

"Noooo!" Suzanne screamed as the front section holding the pilots plummeted straight down the steep slope. The back half carrying Suzanne and the babies, which had broken away from the front section ahead of the wings, catapulted over the peak and flipped end over end through the turbulent air—a nightmare carnival ride from Hell.

As the forward momentum shifted to a downward spiral, a wing caught the edge of a steep slope, and the aft cabin cart-wheeled from wingtip to wingtip down the murderous mountainside.

Suzanne lost consciousness in the thin air.

*****

SUZANNE WOKE AT A lower altitude as the aft cabin continued tumbling downward. She gasped when the babies' pod broke loose and flew out toward a distant green patch shrouded in mist. Then the tail cone carrying her hit a boulder, broke away from the aft cabin, and plummeted in the opposite direction.

Her heart hammered against her chest as the cold fist of fear squeezed the air from her lungs. She clamped her eyes shut and prayed the end wouldn't be painful as her wild slide down the mountain gained momentum.

The scraping of metal on ice gradually changed to muffled sounds of deceleration in dense snow. After several terrifying seconds, she no longer felt any motion.

Suzanne struggled to open her eyes, but they were frozen shut. She cupped her hands over her face and exhaled warm air until the ice melted. It took her a moment to focus when she opened her eyes. A shadowy figure loomed. Was it man or beast?

Feeling woozy in the thin atmosphere, she wiped water from her eyes and stared into the incredulous face of a man in his late twenties. She gazed around and realized the tail cone had slammed against a snow drift near what looked like a base camp for mountain climbers.

The man smiled and offered his hand. "Lord Colin Covington, at your service. Can you stand?"

Suzanne wiped the snow from her face with shaky hands. "I think so. I can't believe I survived." She shivered as she reached for him.

"Can't say I expected to meet a beautiful woman in a place like this." He grinned, unfastened her jumpseat harness, and pulled her from the wreckage. "What's your name?"

Her legs buckled, but Colin caught her and held her close.

"Suzanne."

Blood trickled from her scalp.

"You're all right now, Suzanne, I've got you."

"The babies! We must find them!" Her body shook as she focused on his face and fainted.

SEVERAL MEN CROWDED AROUND Colin and Suzanne.

Colin lifted her unconscious body in his arms as he spoke to the head Sherpa. "Call for help and look for babies. They might be in or near the tail cone."

He carried her into a warm tent where hot water boiled in a pot on a portable gas stove. He laid her on a cot and tended minor wounds on her head, arms, and legs after covering her with a wool blanket and applying an oxygen mask from a pony bottle.

Minutes later, she opened her eyes. He filled a mug with steaming water and added a tea bag, a spoonful of honey, and a shot of whisky. Colin smiled to reassure her as he propped her up with pillows and removed the oxygen mask so she could drink.

Shaking, she gasped. "The babies—"

"Relax, Suzanne, I bandaged some cuts where shrapnel must have sliced through your uniform coat and pants. Nothing serious." He lifted the cup to her lips. "Here, this will warm you. I'll hold it. Now, how many people should we be looking for?"

She sipped the hot tea. "Probably just the three babies. Their parents got sucked out at altitude." She sighed. "Thank you. I froze during my terrifying slide."

She took a few more sips. "No other passengers, just the two pilots and me." She bit her lower lip. "I doubt they survived."

"What happened?"

"We lost both engines and crashed. The 767 broke apart. It was horrible. The front half fell straight down a mountain."

She took another sip and fought back tears. "My employers were sucked out the aft cabin when the aircraft broke in two. Their babies may have survived, but the white survival pod they're in is small and will be difficult to see in the snow."

"It's most likely equipped with an emergency locator transmitter. The airplane will have one too. That should help find the crew."

"The ELT is in the tail section where I was. The pod's ELT might not work because we crashed in a dead zone. If the babies are there, no one may find them in time."

The head Sherpa entered the tent. "Help is on the way. How is she?"

"She's fine but worried about the others. They crashed in a dead zone."

The Sherpa's round brown face paled. "I have heard dark legends about the forbidden zone. Nothing electronic works there. Compasses spin. Those who venture there never return." His voice turned somber as he looked at Suzanne. "Sorry for your loss." He turned and left the tent.

Secret Enclave

THE SOUND OF SEVERAL splashes followed by a thud carried through the heavy mist to the king's ears.

He led a group of ten unusually tall men in hooded black robes and cautiously approached a strange egg-shaped object on the lakeshore.

"It is wet, as though it skipped across the lake like a stone before it slid into the sand," he said.

The king, wearing a gold crown imbedded with tridents and jeweled images of the sun, moon, and fire, bent over and opened the pod.

He straightened. "The Three have arrived!"

Warm fog swirled over the baby girls as they breathed fresh air.

The king spoke in a solemn voice. "On this winter solstice, the ancient prophecy has been set in motion. Our destiny is forevermore entwined with The Three. Twenty-four years hence our exile will end, and Atlantis will rise again when the goddesses of Sun, Moon, and Fire reach their age of full power and awaken Poseidon's Sword."

His bony fingers reached down toward the babies.

The king lifted Solraya above his head. "And the Golden Twin of the Sun Goddess will appear the year before the Sword and activate the Key. She will be a great asset to The Three. Praise Poseidon!"

"Praise Poseidon!" the men echoed.

The king's wrinkled face was filled with hope as he placed the little goddesses in a wooden hand carriage adorned with the same images as his crown.

The men lifted the carriage by its solid-gold, trident-shaped handles and carried the infants toward an obsidian pyramid towering in the eerie mist.

1

Craigervie, Scotland
September 28, 2015

SAS CAPTAIN ROSS SINCLAIR was unlike any man I'd ever known—laird of the Sinclair clan and a good, honorable man who served his country in the UK's elite Special Forces. I never thought Ross, who the prime minister of the UK had sent to kill me, would end up my boyfriend.

That was two months ago, and a lot happened since then.

Ever since my deadly encounter with an evil group of men bent on wiping out nine noble bloodlines and framing the Irish Republican Army, I'd been vigilant. One of their hired assassins, a former Spetsnaz soldier named Nicolai Vasiliev, survived a knife wound and a long fall into a river. I threw him into that river. Ross's soldiers killed the three men on Nicolai's team.

Revenge was expected.

Ross and I had sustained injuries almost seven weeks ago during the height of my Highlands adventure, which began during a month long August vacation in Scotland. That seemed like a lifetime ago.

Now our gunshot wounds were healed, my medical leave with Luxury International Airlines was about to end, and so was my steamy three-week stay with Ross. We were headed to an intimate farewell dinner party hosted by my mom's boyfriend, Laird Duncan MacLeod.

Ross drove his Aston Martin Vanquish on the narrow curving road to MacLeod Castle as I scanned the rock formations and bushes for possible attackers.

We passed under the stone arch emblazoned with the MacLeod coat of arms and followed the tree-lined drive to the imposing castle perched on a cliff overlooking the North Sea. Ross parked in front of ancient stone steps and maneuvered his six-foot-three-inch body out of the sleek sports car.

Ross strode around the car, opened my door, and pulled me close for a kiss. A brisk September wind swirled around his kilt and my cocktail dress as we climbed the stairs.

I squeezed his arm. "Thanks for wearing the kilt instead of your uniform. I like it when you dress like a Highlander."

"My pleasure, lass. Anything to keep that lust in your eyes." He chuckled.

"I wish we didn't have to say goodbye tonight, but you know I don't want to lose my airline pilot job."

"If someone had told me last month I'd be sad to see Samantha Starr leave Scotland, I'd have laughed in his face. Now I don't ever want you to leave." His deep aristocratic brogue kept my heart blazing and distracted me from thoughts of Nicolai.

The massive oak door creaked open, and my mom side-stepped around the butler.

"Good, you're here. Duncan's in the great hall." She smiled and smoothed her shoulder-length blond hair, looking elegant in her little black dress.

Ross hugged her. "Hello, Loren, and how are you on this fine Highlands day?"

"I'm not happy about leaving Scotland, but I plan to return soon. Duncan and I need more time together now that we no longer have to worry about my darling daughter." She hugged me.

"I suspect Sam's the sort of daughter you'll always have to worry about. Danger seems to follow her wherever she goes." He winked.

"Hey, that's not fair!" I punched his muscular arm as we entered the expansive foyer.

"*Really*? What about the two bombs that exploded on your 767 a couple of months ago?"

"That wasn't my fault."

"Then you came to Scotland and got caught in the middle of an international plot that could have started a war. We were both shot twice." He touched the scars on his thigh and shoulder.

"Now, now, children, behave!" Mom crossed her arms and smiled.

I couldn't help sounding defensive. "Our wounds weren't serious, just grazes, except for the through and through in your thigh. That took a little longer to heal."

"That's because I busted open the stitches when I rescued *you* yet again."

"Yes, but I rescued *you* when we first met, remember?" I grinned.

Ross raised an eyebrow, ignoring my distraction ploy. "What I remember is the psychotic assassin who wants to kill you. I wouldn't count on being safe until he's caught."

"Nicolai wants to kill you too. Maybe you should come to America with me."

"Sorry, lass, my commanding officer has other plans for me."

Mom's boyfriend sauntered into the foyer, and I reached out for a hug. As tall as Ross and sixteen years older, he looked dashing in his kilt ensemble with the MacLeod coat of arms on the navy blazer.

"Thank you for the bon voyage party last night with all my new Scottish friends and this farewell dinner for the four of us, Duncan."

"You and your mother transformed my boring retirement into a life of exciting adventure, like my days with the Special Air Service but with beautiful women." He smiled and kissed my hand. "Come along, I have your favorite wine."

He led us across the polished stone floor and into the great hall, an enormous dining room.

Heavy iron chandeliers and firelight from sixteen-foot high stone hearths at each end bathed the room in golden light. Centuries-old portraits covered the long walls. I recognized a portrait titled, Duncan MacLeod, 14th Laird of Clan MacLeod. His electric blue eyes and chiseled features matched the clan chieftain on the cover of my famous mother's most recent medieval romance novel.

A hand-carved oak table large enough to seat forty-four dominated the room. Place settings for four were clustered at one end. When we were seated, the butler poured red wine into four glasses.

"I'd love to see my daughter's sword again. You'll need to take it out of the safe anyway so she can take it home," Mom said.

I turned to Duncan. "Thanks for keeping it for me. Can Baxter bring it to the table?"

He summoned the butler. A few minutes later, Baxter returned with a long red leather case and placed it in front of me.

Inside was a hand-crafted sword with a jeweled hilt. Inscribed on the blade: Sir Lady Samantha Starr, First Knight of the Order of Boadicea.

"I sure never expected this when I decided to take a vacation in Scotland." I glanced around the table at the smiling faces and slid the box across to Mom.

She caressed the jeweled hilt. "It's so beautiful, a true work of art."

"It's well deserved." Ross leaned over to kiss the top of my head. "After all, you did save nine noble bloodlines and prevent a war in Northern Ireland."

I blushed. "Since that nightmare ended, I've certainly enjoyed my stay in beautiful Scotland."

"Where else would we find boyfriends who live in real castles?" Mom grinned.

"Aye, and Ross's castle has a moat." Duncan's eyes twinkled. "I heard he keeps crocodiles in there."

We laughed. A lavish steak Diane with steamed vegetables and new potatoes was served. The aroma of baked rolls filled the air. Wine glasses were kept filled with Opus One, my favorite blended red wine.

"Too bad your twin brothers couldn't stay long enough for this final dinner with us," Ross said, his deep-blue eyes on me. "I enjoyed sharing my military missions with them."

"Unfortunately, the Navy wanted them back. Matt and Mike told me they enjoyed accompanying your SAS teams." I couldn't resist another sip. The wine was so smooth. "They mentioned something about free drinks for life from the Brits."

Ross grinned. "Aye, they earned it when they saved my men from drowning in that downed helicopter in the North Sea."

2

THE TWO HOURS OVER dinner passed too quickly. Mom and I went upstairs to change clothes for the flight home.

After I pulled on my jeans and sweater, I packed my dress and walked across the hall to her room.

"Mom, there's something I've wanted to tell you, but we haven't had a moment alone. I think I had a vision on my flight to Scotland last month."

"Sam, honey, I warned you this happens to females in our family when they reach their mid-twenties."

"Yes, but I assumed it was another nightmare about Mark's murder because one of the boys in my dream looked like him. But there were nine boys, all alive, and later I found them in a cave like the one in my dream."

"Welcome to the club." Mom hugged me. "I'm glad you don't have nightmares about your little brother anymore. His murder was a long time ago, and it wasn't your fault."

"Maybe, but I can't help thinking I might have saved him if I'd been there."

"Please don't give it another thought, Sam. You can't change fate." She hesitated. "You probably don't remember my best friend, Sheila Conor. You were only three when she was in a plane crash in the Himalayas with her husband and triplet daughters. Their bodies were never found."

"I have a vague memory of her. I think I used to call her

Aunt Sheila."

"Yes, you did." Her eyes filled with sadness. "Sheila also had visions. We looked so much alike, people thought we were sisters. I remember thinking you and her blond triplet looked like sisters too."

Baxter knocked on the open door. "Ready to go, ladies?" He picked up our luggage.

I followed Mom down the stairs and into the great hall. A force drew me to the portrait that I knew hid the lever for a secret passage. My head tingled with strange energy.

"Duncan, I feel compelled to enter your secret passageway."

Mom nodded. "I feel a pull too."

He raised his eyebrows. "Which passage?"

I tilted my head and closed my eyes. "Not the one you and Mom used last month to the stables—the other passage that you told me leads down to the sea."

"That passage has steep curving stone steps down a hundred and forty meters. It's a long trek and a difficult climb back up. Sure you want to do this right now?"

Before I could answer, Duncan's stable boy entered and offered me a small gift-wrapped box. "Miss Starr, this is for you. It was delivered to the Highlander Inn."

Ross took it from my hands. "Not so fast, lass." He turned to the boy. "Who sent this?"

"Don't know, sir. It was left at the front desk." He stepped back and glanced at Duncan.

Ross lifted the box to his ear. "No ticking, sounds like liquid. Did you bring it here on your bicycle?"

"Aye, sir, in the front basket. It jostled a bit, but nothing broke."

Ross glanced at his former commanding officer. "Duncan, whatever it is should be stable. Best I take it outside and have a look."

"Steady as you go then. I'll keep everyone inside until you sound the all clear."

I ducked around Duncan to block Ross. "Toss it over the cliff or give it to Scotland Yard. No way am I losing you over some stupid box!"

"Don't worry, lass, I'm trained for this. Wait here." He gave me a light kiss and nudged me aside.

Duncan closed the door behind Ross, and I ran to the window. In the fading light, I watched him edge along the cliff and place the box on a boulder.

I glanced at Duncan beside me. "Doesn't he need tools for this?"

"He has a skean dhu. That should be sufficient."

"A what?"

He pointed to a knife inside his sock. "A dagger."

As if cued, Ross drew a dagger from his right knee sock. I held my breath as he slit the wrapping paper and opened the box.

He lifted something out and looked at it, then stood still for a moment. He placed it back in the box and made a call on his mobile phone before returning.

When he walked in, his expression spoke for him. His clenched jaw, the fire in his eyes—whatever was in that box wasn't good.

"Baxter, bolt the door and keep everyone away from the windows. Duncan, a word?" Ross walked into the great hall.

Mom and I waited in tense silence in the foyer with the butler, maid, and stable boy. Ross and Duncan soon returned.

"Duncan and I agreed you and Loren should see this even though it'll upset you. We want to impress upon you the gravity of the situation so you'll remember to be careful when you return to America." Ross held up a glass jar full of clear liquid.

A human eyeball floated inside.
One word was written on the lid: SOON.
I gasped. "Nicolai's here!"

3

"NICOLAI SENT THIS AS a scare tactic." A hard tone laced Ross's voice. "Remember, he tried to cut out your left eye before you flipped him over the cliff."

"How could I forget? If Charlie hadn't buried a knife in Nicolai's back—"

"Oh my God! That monster wants my daughter's eye!" Mom couldn't stop looking at the bobbing eyeball.

Duncan pulled her close. "We'll protect you and Sam."

My heart raced and my gut twisted as I flashed back to the scar-faced giant holding a combat knife an inch from my eye.

"Why aren't we getting weapons? He could be right outside the door!" My voice was an octave higher as I glanced from Ross to Duncan.

"Baxter went to the armory when he saw the jar. Here he comes now." Duncan nodded in his direction.

Baxter, a former SAS soldier under Duncan's command, was carrying a duffle bag that looked heavy. "Shall I set it on the table in the great hall?"

Duncan nodded. "Aye, we'll hand out the weapons while we wait for Ross's men."

"I called for a Super Lynx with a combat team. We'll remain inside the castle until they arrive." Ross checked the magazine on an MP7 submachine gun he lifted from the bag.

Mom and I accepted Glock 19 pistols with extra magazines.

I inhaled, switched to pilot mode, suppressed my emotions, and focused on Ross. "Where do you want me?"

"The weapons are just a precaution, lass. Chances are Nicolai had someone else deliver that package. He's nowhere near here."

"Yeah, well, it sure feels like he's nearby." I glanced around the great hall.

"I warned you, Nicolai's keen for revenge. You bested him, lass. He won't let that stand."

"So why didn't he come after me the past three weeks at your castle?"

"Scotland Yard, MI5, MI6, Interpol, and the FBI are hunting him, and he may need time for his wound to heal. He's probably hiding out." Ross wrapped his arm around my shoulders.

It wasn't long before a helicopter circled and landed on the lawn. Ross jogged outside and conferred with his men. They spread out with their weapons drawn and searched the castle grounds.

Ross entered and nodded at Duncan. "The area's secure. Sam and Loren will fly home tonight as planned, but the Lynx pilot will take them to Edinburgh Airport, instead of you driving them."

Ross turned to me, his eyes filled with concern. "I'll accompany you to the airport now and have one of my men drive my car to the base. Keep a sharp lookout for Nicolai when you get home."

"The psychotic giant from hell hasn't forgotten you, either." I raised an eyebrow for emphasis.

Duncan consoled Mom, holding her close. Fear widened her moist eyes.

"Loren, as much as I'll miss you, it's best you and Sam leave Scotland and take care when you arrive home. I want to hear from you every day." Duncan kissed her and escorted her to the Super Lynx helicopter.

I said my good-byes to the butler and cook as my luggage was loaded. Ross and I boarded the helicopter.

Mom was already seated. As we flew off, I gazed down at MacLeod Castle, and memories of my Highlands adventure flashed through my mind.

A half hour later, I stood by the corporate jet and kissed Ross goodbye. "I'll fly back and see you next month, and in the meantime, I'll be careful. You do the same. Boyfriends like you are impossible to replace."

"Call me when you land." Ross gave me a passionate farewell kiss.

Mom and I boarded the Starr Corporation's G650 and took off for Palm Beach, Florida.

4

WHEN ROSS ARRIVED BACK at the 23SAS outstation in Dundee, his mobile phone rang, and caller ID indicated it was Sam's brother, Mike.

"Hello, Mike, your mother and sister are on their way. Did you get the watch?"

"DARPA was happy to help protect our famous heroine. The public loves her on both sides of the pond." Mike sounded pleased.

"DARPA?"

"Defense Advanced Research Projects Agency. SEALs are usually first to try out their new military weaponry and gear. DARPA saves our butts. Good thing they got permission to make the watch for Sam."

"Aye, I think our governments decided it would be better to protect her than to deal with the bad PR if they let her get killed."

"The device looks like her DOXA diver's watch with all the same features plus a GPS locator that broadcasts her location and an emergency signal button. Let's hope she won't ever need it."

"Nicolai sent her a gift today—a jar with a human eyeball inside."

"That sick sonofabitch! Did you see him?"

"No, someone else must've delivered it. Best give Sam the

watch as soon as she lands in Florida, and don't tell her we're tracking her. Let her think the signal only activates if she presses the emergency button." Outside the hangar, Ross gazed at the boat traffic as a brisk wind churned white caps on the Firth of Tay.

"You know my sister well. I gave the watch to my brother. He'll meet her plane. I have to leave for a mission. Matt will send you the GPS tracking code on your secure email. We'll keep Sam safe."

"Aye, your SEAL teams and our Special Forces are deployed in enough places worldwide to cover most of her destinations. I'm counting on our military intelligence networks to locate Nicolai so we can nail the bastard before he gets to Sam." Ross tried to conceal the worry in his voice.

"Has MI5 found evidence linking Nicolai to Lord Sweetwater?"

"No, the phone call Sam overheard after the ceremony at Buckingham Palace came from a burner phone. Sweetwater claimed the call was from an undercover informant who sold him info on arms deals. He said what she actually heard was, 'Nico lied,' not Nicolai. It's her word against his. No proof."

"My sister isn't likely to forget the sound of that psycho's voice. If she said it was Nicolai, I believe her."

"MI5 is keeping a close watch on Sweetwater. No sign of Nicolai so far."

"He'll stay off the grid until the international effort to capture him loses steam. Every chance we get Matt and I will warn Sam not to let her guard down."

"Good, she needs to remember Nicolai's a formidable opponent."

"Yep, a psychopath with the skills of a professional assassin is about as bad as it gets. Stay in touch, Ross."

5

LORD EDGAR SWEETWATER, A billionaire arms dealer with a penchant for vengeance, paced in front of the massive marble fireplace in the mahogany-paneled study of his country manor near London. The aroma of burning wood blended with the subtle scent of leather-bound books.

Sweetwater held a mobile phone to his ear. "A sunken temple in the Aegean Sea between Crete and Santorini? Did you find a gold statue of Poseidon? ... Good."

"We found scrolls that describe a powerful weapon invented by scientists in Atlantis called Poseidon's Sword. It's supposed to be inside an obsidian pyramid approximately one hundred feet high. Our archaeology expert thinks it was their doomsday weapon."

"I'll fund whatever you need for the search. Find that weapon." He stopped pacing and ended the call when his bodyguard entered the room.

"Lord Sweetwater, Nicolai has arrived," the muscular man in black said. "Should I bring him in?"

"See to it your pistol's ready before he comes in. He's six-eight, all muscle, and his wounds are healed. The man's a professional assassin and former Spetsnaz. Ever since that blond Yank and the Scottish boy nearly killed him, he's been on edge, barely controlling his rage."

Sweetwater walked around his desk. "And send some men

in with him."

"You can count on me, sir." The bodyguard thumbed off the safety and pulled back the slide on his semi-automatic pistol, chambering a round with a loud click. He slid his weapon into the shoulder holster and spoke into a tiny radio microphone attached to his left sleeve. "Bring Nicolai to the study with four guards."

Sweetwater sat behind an imposing hand-carved mahogany desk that dwarfed his short portly body. The Russian assassin wouldn't want to abide by his new plan. If Nicolai's rage took over, the situation could become deadly. His bodyguard positioned himself six feet behind the guest chair opposite Sweetwater's desk.

The Russian giant entered with Sweetwater's security team. Despite his size, Nicolai moved with cat-like grace. He sat opposite his host as the security escorts formed a semi-circle behind him.

"I hope you kept out of sight. MI5 suspects you're working for me, but they have no proof."

Nicolai focused his sinister, almost-black eyes on Sweetwater and absently rubbed his left index finger against the jagged scar on his cheek.

"*Da*, no one saw me enter. I am healed and ready to fulfill contract. I will kill blond American *sooka* and her SAS lover first, slowly and with much pain. Their left eyes will add new colors to my collection, aqua and deep blue."

Sweetwater fidgeted with the Montblanc pen on his desk. "Uh, about that, no one wants to see them dead more than I. Samantha Starr ruined a perfect storm of vengeance that I had planned for fifteen years. I'll never have an opportunity like that again."

"Yesterday, I sent her gift. She will fear me and know I am coming for her."

Sweetwater straightened. "What did you give her?"

"Eyeball in jar filled with alcohol." Nicolai smiled and sat back.

Sweetwater sucked in his breath. "Who delivered it? Can he be traced back to us?"

"Man from small village in northern England delivered package to Highlander Inn and then met me in Aberdeen. I killed him, dropped him in North Sea. No loose ends."

"Good. I want revenge, not a prison sentence." Sweetwater relaxed.

"I understand. Which body parts would you like? I am skilled with knife."

"I want her to suffer the emotional distress of feeling like helpless prey as she's hunted the next few months, always looking over her shoulder and wondering when and where. No peace of mind. My men will inflict non-lethal wounds to keep her in constant pain."

Sweetwater allowed himself a smug smile. "When she's with the Scottish brats in Orlando in December, you'll capture them and bring them to my secluded island in the North Sea. Then our real fun will begin."

Nicolai inhaled and clenched his ham fists. "I will kill her family and SAS soldiers from base in Dundee now. I must act before Loren Starr and her sons leave Scotland."

"Let's have a drink first. I have your vodka." Sweetwater rang for a servant. "Zyr for my guest and Glenglassaugh for me."

When the drinks were served, Nicolai drained his glass in one gulp. "I must go. Arrange for helicopter to drop me near MacLeod Castle. I will eliminate Starr family and Laird MacLeod tonight."

Sweetwater drank half the whisky in his glass. "No, Nicolai, I can't risk MI5 connecting me to that." He hesitated.

"Samantha and her mother and brothers have left Scotland."

"When?" Nicolai's face reddened, emphasizing the long purple scar on his left cheek.

Sweetwater steadied his voice as he glanced at the security team. "Her brothers left the day after the ceremony. She and her mother left last night."

He pressed on. "Listen, we need to keep a low profile and let the aftermath fade before we make a move. I'm not willing to risk my future for instant gratification. Be patient, Nicolai. I promise we'll have our just revenge in good time."

Nicolai crushed the empty tumbler in his hand. Shattered glass and drops of blood fell to the polished oak floor. The loud clicks of slides racking on pistols commanded his attention. He sat still as his eyes filled with rage.

The scent of whisky, blood, and fear permeated the silent room.

Sweetwater spoke softly, "Two million pounds sterling if you wait three months."

"I must avenge my team. I am Spetsnaz!" Nicolai roared.

"Every law enforcement agency is hunting you. I own an island in the Caribbean. You can hide there. I'll supply you with young women, vodka, anything. My jet's ready." He spread his hands on the desk, ready to signal the guards.

The seething Russian towered over the desk and bored his dark eyes into Sweetwater. "Five and we have deal."

"Five. The limo will take you to the airport where you'll board the jet in the hangar. Make a list of everything you want on the island and give it to the pilot. Remember, you're a professional. We're in this for the long game."

"*Da.*" Nicolai walked out with the security team.

Sweetwater's bodyguard holstered his weapon. "Sir, if you don't mind my asking, why not hire someone else and eliminate the unstable Russian?"

"A professional assassin driven by a lust for vengeance is a powerful weapon, damn near unstoppable. He'll succeed where men motivated by money alone might fail."

Sweetwater sipped his whisky and smiled.

6

NICOLAI PACED THE TERRACE as he spoke to Lord Sweetwater on the satellite phone. "Island is hot and boring. When do I leave?"

"Patience, Nicolai. You've only been there a week. Kill something. There's plenty of wild game in the center of the island."

"I prefer two-legged prey. Young dark meat. Arrange steady supply. I enjoy hunting and carving, adding to eye collection." Nicolai downed a shot of vodka.

"The island manager will take care of it. In the meantime, let the women relieve your tension."

Nicolai looked west over the sea toward Florida. "When will your men begin fun with American *sooka*?"

A warm breeze rustled the palm leaves hanging above the Russian.

"I have a team on Palm Beach watching her condo. The games will begin soon."

"Make sure they save her for me. I have special plans." He pulled out his Spetsnaz knife and impaled a coconut.

7

IT HAD BEEN A week since I left Scotland. I spent my free time practicing with my Glock 26 at the shooting range, sparring with tae kwon do black belts at a martial arts center, and catching up on stuff at my Palm Beach condo while I waited for the FAA to approve the medical paperwork to return me to flight status. The feds assured me I'd be cleared by the end of the week.

I called my mother. "Hey, Mom, how're you doing? Seen a big scar-faced guy?"

"I'm fine, no sightings of Nicolai and no visions. What about you?"

"No Nicolai and no important visions. Just small stuff, like seeing a raw egg full of blood before I cracked it so it wouldn't ruin my cookie batch—nothing like the first vision about the boys in the cave."

I withheld last night's vision about men in a black SUV firing at me. That would worry her. "When are you leaving for Scotland?"

"In about twenty minutes. I can't wait to see Duncan again. I think I really love that man." She sounded wistful.

"Duncan's a great guy, and his castle is fabulous. Give my colt lots of hugs. I miss my cute little Zeus. I hope he grows up to be like Argus."

"Duncan says he's getting bigger every day. I'll give him

lots of loving and hug Ross too."

"Thanks, Mom. Have a safe trip and remember Nicolai's still out there somewhere."

I climbed aboard my red Ducati Diavel motorcycle and adjusted the mirrors. Ross and my twin brothers had warned me to remain vigilant, but perhaps Nicolai had decided not to pursue me in America.

Nothing unpleasant had happened since my return, except for unwanted attention from another turn in the fame barrel.

In case I was wrong about Nicolai, I racked the slide on my Glock 26, slipped it into the holster in the small of my back, and thanked God for Florida's License to Carry and Stand Your Ground laws.

I rode my Ducati over a bridge connecting Palm Beach to West Palm Beach and headed west through the city toward Interstate-95. When I glanced in my mirrors, I saw a black SUV with tinted windows pull behind me.

It looked like the one in my dream, but it wouldn't be able to keep up with my nimble bike darting around cars and cutting through spaces too narrow for four-wheeled vehicles.

As I weaved through traffic, checking my mirrors for the SUV and hoping a cop wouldn't catch me, the black monster drove on a sidewalk to bypass traffic.

It was coming for me.

My heart raced as I considered my options. If I could make it to the expressway, I could lose them with my bike's superior speed and handling. That seemed better than trying to ditch them in heavy traffic and stop lights.

A mile before the on-ramp, a freight train approaching the intersection threatened my escape. The traffic gates were down, and only three vehicles separated me from the hunters.

Sunlight reflected off the SUV's windshield and obscured whoever was chasing me.

I cut around the railroad gate and felt the road vibrate from the freight cars as I shot across the tracks and accelerated to the interstate entrance. The SUV swerved around the vehicles in front, crashed through the gate, and cleared the tracks a second before the train crossed the intersection.

A bullet pinged into the pavement next to me as I turned for the on-ramp. My heart rate skyrocketed. I hugged my bike and leaned into the curve as I raced for the ten-lane super highway.

8

IN SECONDS, I ACCELERATED to 140 mph as I zipped around traffic. The Ducati felt smooth and stable.

My brain shifted into overdrive as I increased my distance from the SUV. *Did they have a way to track me, or had they spotted me during surveillance?*

I stopped behind a large sign on an overpass beside an exit ramp and waited. Squealing tires alerted me to their approach as the driver slammed on the brakes for the late turn to the exit.

In case they had tracked my cell phone, I dropped it on the road below the overpass and pulled out my Glock. When the SUV passed my hiding place, I shot a hole in the right front tire. The driver lost control, and the vehicle flipped onto its back and skidded off the curving exit road.

I holstered my Glock and raced south on I-95. When I exited on Lantana Road, I didn't spot anyone following me.

Lantana Airport was a few miles west of the interstate. I pulled around to the flight-line side of the building and parked near the small flight school and pilot shop.

The roar of airplanes coming and going was comforting as I removed my helmet, took a deep calming breath, and unwrapped a piece of chocolate. Trembling, I dropped the wrapper as I popped the candy into my mouth. I had to chase it several feet in the wind.

The chocolate melted on my tongue and soothed me. I returned to my bike, pulled out the emergency burner cell I kept in the tail bag, and called my brother, Matt. He was scheduled to leave NAS Jacksonville in a few hours on a Navy transport bound for Naples, Italy, where he would catch a flight to the aircraft carrier *USS Lawrence Lee*.

"Hey, Sis, how's it going? Do you like your new DARPA watch?"

"I almost pushed the emergency button about twenty minutes ago. Thought I'd better talk to you and decide what to do next." I tried to sound calmer than I felt.

"Are you okay? What happened?" Matt's tone was all business.

I briefed him about the black SUV. "I'm at the airport in Lantana now. I'm supposed to give a lesson."

"Take the student. They can't find you while you're airborne. I'll make some calls and arrange for armed men to meet you when you return. They're former SEALs Mike knows who own a local high-end security company. They may bring the FBI into the loop. You'll know them by the code words, Danger Magnet."

"Nice code. Is that your idea of humor?"

"You know me, anything to cut the tension. Be careful, Sis, and say hello to Bart for me."

"Thanks for the help, Rodeo." I liked using Matt's fighter-pilot call sign. "I hope they nail Nicolai and end this. I'm tired of being a target. I had my fill of that in the Highlands. Stay safe."

When I entered the flight school, a stocky average-height man in his sixties looked up from behind the counter. His Texas drawl distinguished him from the northeasterners living in Southern Florida.

"Howdy, Sam, or should I say, Your Knightship?" He

bowed and grinned.

I smiled. "Cut the crap, Bart. It's good to see you." I handed him my helmet and glanced around the empty room.

"Someone took a shot at me on my way here. I can't guarantee they won't come looking for me. Would you rather book another flight instructor?"

Bart reached below the counter and pulled out a Remington semiautomatic shotgun.

"I can handle my end of things. No need to leave."

"All righty. Matt says hello. He's arranging for armed men to meet me when I return from the lesson. Ask them for the code words, Danger Magnet."

Bart laughed. "I love your brother's sense of humor, even in tense situations. His twin acts the same way."

"Yep, they're a barrel of laughs. So where's the student with the big emergency?"

"Well, now, here's the thing. He has a private pilot license and way too much money."

"Let me guess, he bought an airplane that exceeds his piloting ability by a country mile, and he's too rich and arrogant to accept his limitations. Sounds like a dangerous guy."

"Now don't go gettin' your panties in a bunch. I convinced him to take spin trainin' with you so he doesn't kill himself when he plays fighter pilot." Bart hesitated and cleared his throat.

"Uh, there's one other thing. Sometimes he freezes on the controls in sticky situations. I had to punch him in the face once. Almost broke his jaw. He's afraid to fly with me now."

"Geez, Bart. I thought we were friends. What the hell?"

"Sam, I wouldn't have asked you to train him if I thought for one second you couldn't handle him. Besides, I knew you'd get a major charge out of flyin' his airplane. Truth be told, we're all wanna-be fighter pilots at heart." He grinned and winked.

"He's waitin' by his airplane right out there." Bart pointed out the window.

A shiny black Italian-built SIAI Marchetti SF260, like the one in the Bond movie, *Quantum of Solace,* glistened on the tarmac in the bright sunshine.

9

A MIDDLE-AGED MAN of average height and thinning hair stood next to the fighter/attack/trainer airplane. He wore a gray flight suit with important-looking patches sewn on the upper front and sleeves. The one-piece jumpsuit was unzipped halfway down his chest, revealing three heavy gold chains on bare skin.

I focused on the airplane. "Do I see machine guns mounted on the hard points under the wings?"

"Yep, he spent a fortune on that airplane," Bart said. "A U.S. senator buddy helped him get the permits so he could keep the wing-mounted guns. It's that plane from the 007 movie. He bought two thousand acres in Southern Florida so he can play military pilot and blast away at ground targets. I figured you'd want in on that deal."

"You figured right. Sign me up." I headed for the door. "Come out and introduce me."

A few minutes later, we stood by the sleek Italian fighter known as the Ferrari of reciprocating engine aircraft. Underneath the glass canopy, side-by-side seats featured dual controls with sticks. Unlike most airplanes, the instrument panel was designed for the pilot to fly from the right seat with the copilot or instructor pilot on the left side.

Bart turned to me. "Sam, meet your student, Grant Garrison." He looked at the man. "Grant, this here's Samantha

Starr. She'll give you spin training."

"I saw you on TV. You look even better in person." Grant ran his eyes over my curves and paused a bit too long on my breasts. "Whoa, Bart, how am I supposed to concentrate on flying with a gorgeous babe like Samantha sitting next to me?" He flashed his million-dollar smile at me.

"You're not a playboy when you're on my clock. I expect you to obey rule number one of Sam's flight instruction." I looked into his eyes with a don't-mess-with-me frown.

He stopped grinning. "What's rule number one?"

"Never touch the flight instructor."

"Any other rules?"

"If I tell you to do something in the airplane, do it immediately and ask questions later. Handle the controls as if you're playing a rare Stradivarius or making love to a sensitive and delicate lady. In other words, learn to have what is known in the pilot world as good hands. That pretty much covers it."

"So, if I'm good in bed, I'll be a good pilot?"

"You can learn to apply the same skills to flying, but there's a vast difference between *thinking* you're good in bed and *being* good in bed. I'll know the truth as soon as I see how you handle the airplane." My smug smile warned him he couldn't fool me.

Grant looked worried. "Damn, Bart, what are you trying to do to me?"

"I'm tryin' to keep you alive so you can enjoy your new toy. Swallow your pride and do what the lady says." Bart nodded in my direction, turned, and walked to the building.

"One more thing, Bart said your wing-mounted weapons are operational. Is that true?"

"Don't worry, I have federal permits for them. My firing range is southwest of here."

"Great, but the weapons aren't loaded now, are they?"

"I keep the system fully loaded, but there's no danger of accidental firing. The arming switch has a safety cover. I'll show you where it is." Grant pointed to it.

We did the preflight inspection, climbed aboard, closed the canopy, and taxied out for the engine and control checks before takeoff. During the takeoff run and climb, it became obvious Grant was no Don Juan in the boudoir.

He yanked back on the stick, and the Marchetti leaped into the sky at too steep an angle. He over-corrected with forward stick, and my body rose up against the five-point harness. The turn away from the traffic pattern felt jerky and abrupt. I noticed his fingers had turned white from his firm grip on the stick.

"I have the airplane." I took my control stick and rudder pedals as Grant released the controls on his side.

Flying the airplane gave Grant a break and distracted me from the SUV incident.

"Sit back and relax while I fly us to the practice area. If you're tense on the controls, the airplane will respond stiffly. Close your eyes and pretend you're a world champion Formula One driver. Every move you make in your race car is accomplished with a smooth, fluid motion as you finesse your way around the race course. The car becomes an extension of your body as you speed over the pavement and hug the corners." I watched his face as the tension melted away.

He smiled and opened his eyes. "I feel calmer. What would you like me to do now?"

"We're at 4,500 feet, so we have plenty of recovery room if you mess up. I'd like you to practice turning right and left so smoothly that I won't be able to feel the turns."

I surrendered the controls to Grant and closed my eyes. "Don't forget to check for traffic before you turn. Start with shallow-banked turns. Increase the bank angle after you get the feel of it. Remember to ease back the stick to maintain altitude in the turns."

I tried to focus on the sensations transmitted to my body by the airplane's movements and forget about the men hunting me.

Mike's SEAL buddies will protect me.

I felt the familiar vibrations at the moment of stall from loss of lift, opened my eyes, and watched the nose fall through the horizon. The monoplane entered a spin to the left.

The ground spun beneath us as we corkscrewed downward at 1500 feet per minute. My student froze with a deer-in-the-headlights look on his face. Every second brought us closer to death.

I pulled the throttle back to idle. Unable to wrest the controls from him, I employed my virtual sex flight instruction method.

I slid my right hand along the inside of his left thigh—*better than dying or stabbing him with my great-great-grandmother's giant hat pin*—and yelled, "Grant, stop! You're squeezing me (*the control stick*) too hard, and I'm falling off the bed. Quick, let go and stretch out your right foot (*full right rudder*) to catch me. Good. Place your feet on either side of me (*neutral rudder*). Much better. Relax your hands. Good. Slide your left hand up over my right breast (*full throttle*) and pull me close to you with your right hand (*stick back*). Ummm, much better."

We were out of the spin and regaining altitude. Disaster averted with no bloodshed.

I glanced at Grant. His mouth and eyes were wide open.

I squeezed his knee. "Level off here and throttle back to cruise power."

"What happened? I remember tensing up when the airplane stalled. Must've passed out. I dreamed we were having sex." He wiped his sweaty hands on his pants.

"It wasn't a dream. You froze on the controls during a spin. I had to do something drastic, or we would've died." I pulled out a large antique hat pin from my bag. "If my virtual sex method had failed, you'd have been screaming and pulling this out of your thigh."

He looked horrified.

"Hey, it's better than our airplane becoming a dirt dart."

"Damn, woman, I hope you never have to stab me with that thing. Sex talk is a much better way to go." Grant leaned away from my hat pin against the right side rail.

"Relax, Grant, I only stab students as a last resort." I gave him a friendly jab with my right elbow. "I'd hate to get blood on the Italian stallion."

He grinned, straightened, and puffed out his chest. Then he looked confused and turned to me. "I'm not Italian."

"I'm talking about the airplane."

"Oh." He slumped down.

I checked my watch. *When would the security team arrive at the airfield?* "Don't worry, we'll practice stalls, spins, and recoveries until you overcome your fears and feel comfortable with the maneuvers."

I put the hat pin in the map compartment.

Grant covered his left thigh with his hand. "First, I think we should deal with my fear of giant hat pins."

10

A MUSCULAR MAN IN his thirties walked into the flight school and smiled. "Good afternoon, my name's Rick Brown. I'm interested in flying lessons. What kind of airplanes do you use?"

Bart moved from behind the counter and extended his hand. "I'm Bart Branson. I own the place. We use four-seat Cessna Skyhawks for primary instruction. Are you looking to get a private pilot license?"

"Yes, but I have some questions. Which side does the student sit on?"

"Licensed pilots normally sit in the left seat, so that's where the student sits to get used to it."

"I'd like to see what the trainers look like. Can you show me one?"

"See that blue-and-white high-winged airplane over there?" Bart turned to a window and pointed at a Skyhawk parked about sixty yards to the right on the ramp.

Rick snuck behind Bart and clubbed him on the back of the head with the butt of his pistol. After Bart collapsed, Rick dragged him behind the counter and zip-tied his hands behind his back. He stepped over Bart and scanned the flight lesson schedule until he found the entry for Sam's lesson with Grant in the Marchetti.

Three burly men joined Rick in the flight school.

"Good thing we've been monitoring her calls all week. She's here, teaching a student in his SF260, whatever that is. They're due back in five minutes," Rick said to the men.

"I'll google it. We need to know what the airplane looks like." He tapped it into his smartphone. "Here's a picture of it." He held it out for the men to see.

Sam's voice came over the UNICOM frequency on the radio behind the counter. "Marchetti Two-Six-Zero-Golf-Golf is on short final for Runway Two Seven."

Since the airport lacked a control tower, the flight school monitored the radio frequency used by all the air traffic at their uncontrolled airport. The pilots announced their positions and intentions so that everyone could operate safely in an uncontrolled environment.

Rick pointed at one of the men. "Get the SUV and be ready to pick us up on the flight side. She's landing now."

He racked the slide on his silenced pistol and waited by the window. The two men behind him did the same.

"I'll shoot her in the right shoulder. We'll leave after we confirm I hit her." Rick watched the Marchetti taxi to the parking ramp near the flight school.

11

I SCANNED THE RAMP as Grant taxied from the runway. *Where were the men Matt had promised?* Maybe they were luxuriating in the cool air inside the flight school.

"Grant, I'm expecting a security team to meet me here. Approach slowly and park well back from the building, just in case." I strained to see inside.

"Just in case what? Why do you need a security team?" Grant looked worried.

"On my way to the airport, someone shot at me. They didn't follow me here, but I want to be prepared anyway. Just in case."

"Are *they* your security people?" Grant pointed at three men exiting the flight school as he shut down the engine.

The lead man drew his weapon and fired. The bullet pierced the Plexiglas windshield and slammed into Grant's right shoulder.

I started the warm engine, pushed in the throttle, and turned away from the building. I aimed for an open area west of the main ramp.

"I'm bleeding. The bastard shot me! Sonofabitch, my windshield!" Grant's face was ashen.

The gunmen jumped into a SUV and raced after us.

"Grant, I hope to hell your wing guns really work!" I lifted the safety cover and armed the weapons.

I looked over my shoulder, spun the airplane into firing position, and peppered the SUV with bullets. They swerved, and I kept turning so the guns would remain on target. The firing angle was only a few feet above the ground, but it was good enough to destroy their tires and hit the gas tank.

The men jumped out the far side of the vehicle moments before it exploded. I turned on the radio while I waited for their next move.

"Sam, Team Danger Magnet has arrived. Hold fire while we flank the shooters. Acknowledge."

"Roger, Danger Magnet, hurry! Marchetti will hold fire. Call for paramedics. My student is wounded." I looked back at the flight school and saw a black Hummer racing toward the burning SUV.

Grant's face was pale and sweaty, and blood soaked his shirt. I pulled off my shirt and folded it into a square to press against his wound.

He looked at my bra through dilated eyes. "Nice." He passed out.

The gunmen were left with no cover and surrendered after a brief firefight with the team in the Hummer. I secured the Marchetti's weapons and taxied to the flight school.

A fire truck and an EMT vehicle rounded the building as the propeller stopped turning. I secured the cockpit and waved to the paramedics.

Soon Grant was on a stretcher with an IV bag plugged into him. He woke and looked at me.

I stroked Grant's hair. "I'm so sorry you got hurt, but thank God your badass airplane saved our lives. I'll pay for the damage." I kissed his cheek.

"That was my first time in combat. You were so calm." Grant's voice was weak.

"Probably because I experienced plenty of combat in

Scotland two months ago. Besides, I always remain calm in dangerous situations when my brain defaults to airline-pilot mode."

The paramedics loaded him into the truck and drove away. I turned and faced Bart and six military-looking men. The prisoners were cuffed and corralled against the Hummer nearby.

I saw blood on Bart's shirt. "Are you okay?"

"Just a goose egg on the back of my noggin. Shouldn't have let him get the jump on me." He rubbed his head.

I smiled at the team. "Gentlemen, thank you for coming to my rescue."

"You made our job easy, pinning them down with those wing-mounted weapons. Matt didn't mention you'd be armed with heavy artillery." A team member grinned.

"My brother didn't know about the Marchetti's guns."

A tall dark-haired man stepped forward. "I'm Tim Goldy, team leader. We're waiting for the FBI to arrive and take custody of the kidnappers. Notice I said *kidnappers* so the feds will have jurisdiction." He winked. "I suggest you go inside and get a nice new T-shirt from Bart, not that I'm not enjoying the view."

The mid-afternoon heat, fire fight, and explosion had jarred me into forgetting I was shirtless. My body still vibrated from fear.

I was in too much shock to be embarrassed, and my floral satin bra resembled a bikini top anyway.

Now that the shooters were in custody and Grant was in good hands, I craved a big glass of Opus One with a chocolate truffle.

12

TWO DAYS HAD PASSED since my encounters with the gunmen. After double-checking the exterior doors and windows in my Palm Beach condo, I sat up in bed with a Joseph Badal thriller on my lap and a Glock 26 under my pillow. *Was Nicolai coming for me?*

The Bonnie Banks O' Loch Lomond rang out on my cell. Ross was calling.

"Sorry, lass, I was out on a mission and just got your messages. Are you all right?"

I gave him an update. "The kidnappers refused to talk to the FBI, but they were overheard arguing about shooting the wrong person. The shooter expected me to be in the right seat where instructors sit on most training flights."

"Sounds like he aimed to wound, not kill. Is your student expected to recover?"

"Grant will be fine, no permanent damage. Hc's already bragging to his buddies about his aviation combat experience."

"I doubt real combat pilots, like your brother Matt, would appreciate that."

"No kidding! There's an old aviation proverb: Piloting a fighter does not a fighter pilot make."

"Aye, so true. Now what about the man who hired the shooters? Have they identified him?"

"Yesterday, my attackers were being transferred to a

federal prison when their transport vehicle was forced off the road. A heavily armed assault team shot the guards and escaped with three prisoners. The man who shot Grant was left behind with a double tap to the heart and head."

"Whoever hired him doesn't tolerate mistakes. Nicolai or Sweetwater may have been behind the attack."

"The feds and local law enforcement haven't found the assault team and escaped prisoners."

"What's being done to keep you safe?"

I glanced out the window. "Feds are watching my condo. They want me to stay put, but I hate this. I feel like a prisoner in my own home."

"I doubt the kidnappers will make a move on you with so many police looking for them. They may have given up for now and left the country. When's your next flight with the airline?"

"I'm on standby call. I hope I'll get sent somewhere far away until things calm down." I sighed. "I miss you."

"I miss you too, lass. Let me know if you get assigned a flight. If you end up in Europe, I'll try to meet you on the overnight."

"That would put a smile on my face. I'll text you the moment I know where I'm going."

We rambled on with small talk. It was reassuring to hear his voice. When we hung up, I felt better and reflected on my airline pilot career.

Six months ago at twenty-six, I upgraded from copilot to be the first female captain at elite Luxury International Airlines. Unlike other commercial airlines, their Boeing 767 jumbo jets were outfitted with posh interiors and stocked with gourmet foods and drinks. Showers enhanced four of the twelve elegant lavatories.

Although 767s were designed to hold 181 to 409 passengers, Luxury International's 767s held only 100 passengers and had a spacious lounge mid-cabin. On their ultra-class airliners, the wide overstuffed leather seats fully reclined. Ten flight attendants provided extravagant service.

Working would help distract me from worrying about Nicolai and missing Ross, but Ross called often, and we planned to reunite at least once a month. Neither of us wanted the romance to end, even though an ocean and busy careers separated us. I fell asleep fantasizing about my handsome Highlander.

GOOD THING I LOVED being an airline pilot. When my phone woke me from a sound sleep at six in the morning, I was reminded of the US Navy's slogan, "It's not a job. It's an adventure." That described my occupation too.

"Crew scheduling calling for Captain Starr," the harried male voice said.

"That's me. What's up?"

"We need you to fly a charter with celebrities from LAX to the Dubai International Film Festival. Captain Martin and Captain Whitmore car-pooled this morning. A garbage truck hit their car, breaking Martin's foot and Whitmore's arm. We've already used up our other reserve captains for sick calls. Can you help us out, Sam?"

"Sure, how many days?" I jumped out of bed and pulled out my suitcase.

"Two weeks. You'll stay overnight in Los Angeles, then fly to Hawaii, Hong Kong, Delhi, Aqaba, and Dubai with activities planned for each."

"Isn't Aqaba at the southern tip of Jordan?" I asked, interrupting.

"Yep, I hopped a flight there last year and took a tour of Petra. Why do you ask?"

"It would be more efficient to go to Dubai first and then on to Aqaba."

"Right, but the celebs need to visit Petra before they attend the film festival in Dubai. After three days in Dubai, the return trip will go through Paris and New York. All in all, a fun-filled adventure with movie stars. A relief pilot will join your crew in Hawaii. Please get here ASAP!"

"Okay, I'll be on the airplane in thirty minutes. Bye." I punched the phone off and leaped into the shower.

Packing was a breeze. I could get a fast turnaround on laundry service at every foreign stop.

As I left my parking garage, I stopped next to the FBI car. "I'm leaving on a two-week trip around the world. I'll check in with your office when I get back."

"We'll follow you to the airport and escort you to the airplane."

It wasn't a suggestion.

13

FIFTY MINUTES LATER, I was on the takeoff roll at Palm Beach International Airport. Living fifteen minutes from my home base was a bonus.

After I leveled off at cruise altitude, I turned to my copilot. "Hey, Lance, I want an autographed copy of your upcoming novella about our explosive flight a few months ago. It's bound to be a best seller."

"Consider it done. Are you still dating that Special Air Service captain?"

"Yes, I saw Ross about two weeks ago. How's your love life now that you're a hero airline pilot?"

Lance's sense of humor and Texas drawl always entertained me.

"My dance card's full, but I'll always make room for you. That long-distance thing with your Scottish bad boy can't last. Long dry spells between over-the-pond rendezvous has to be tough. At the very least, let me take up the slack between visits." He grinned and winked. "It'll be our secret, scout's honor."

"Uh huh, like *anything* ever stays secret in our little airline. I just smile at a coworker, and it's on everyone's radar in a millisecond. If half the rumors about me were true, I'd be the most sexually satisfied woman on the planet."

"You could be if you gave me a shot."

"*Right,* it's a shame you suffer from such a lack of confidence." I laughed.

Lance was tall with a shitload of swagger—handsome and seductive. I wasn't about to let myself fall prey to a testosterone-induced brain fog that would cloud my better judgment.

I smiled at Lance. "You're a fun guy, but I do have to work here."

"Oh come on, I can keep a secret. If I'm lying, you can kick my sorry ass into next week with your tae kwon do black belt."

"If you lie to me, I'll kick your ass into the great beyond. Then I'll spit on your grave."

Lance grinned. "So, you're thinking about giving me a shot."

"Talk about a one-track mind. I'm talking about putting you in the ground, and you're still thinking about sex. Unbelievable." I laughed. "Reminds me of when our 767 was in flames as we stood in the pouring rain, and you suggested we engage in a night of adrenaline-charged sex at the hotel."

"Why not? We're both single. We could have fun together. Think about it."

Instead, I thought about Ross during the long flight, but couldn't keep the kidnappers out of my head. *They couldn't possibly know where I'll be for the next two weeks, could they?*

A beautiful blonde met Lance outside of baggage claim at LAX. Good for him.

While I waited for the crew bus, I scanned the area for potential kidnappers.

14

THE NEXT MORNING AT eleven o'clock, I greeted our passengers from the cockpit doorway. All three celebrities arrived with large entourages, including hairdressers, makeup artists, personal assistants, wardrobe coordinators, and others in the movie industry.

First to board was a short stocky photographer loaded down with camera bags. "Oh my, a woman pilot! Still don't see many females up front, even in this day and age. Uh, I mean, uh, you can fly me anytime, sweetheart. Wait, I didn't mean that in a sexual way ... unless you wanted me to. Geez, this political correctness crap is going to get me killed. God bless Amelia Earhart!" He saluted and rushed into the cabin.

A petite curvy blonde was next. I recognized her as actress Carlene Jensen. She flaunted a Texas accent and a snarky attitude.

"Oooo, a female pilot! You go, girl. Right on! Where's your copilot?"

I stepped aside and pointed at Lance.

"Oh, yummy!" Carlene stepped around me. "What's your name and where're you from, handsome?"

"Lance Bowie from Fort Worth, ma'am," he said in his deep drawl.

"Dibs on the Texan hottie!" Carlene shouted at everyone.

"What part of Texas are you from, Miss Jensen?" Lance

asked.

"Darlin', you're looking at the 2010 Ladies' Pistol Champion from Austin, and please, call me Carlene. We'll get to know each other real good in Hawaii." She winked and sashayed down the aisle in her five-inch stilettos.

The women in Carlene's entourage flashed Lance big smiles as they followed her. His face lit up with a grin as big as his home state.

I waited until the ladies were out of earshot and glared at Lance. "Gird your loins, cowboy. I expect you to behave like a professional."

"No problem, Sam. I'll give the women smooth flights and keep 'em happy on the layovers." He winked and grinned.

He was in hog heaven, and all I could envision was the slaughterhouse waiting for us in Chief Pilot Rowlin's office back in Palm Beach.

A tall lanky actor cruised through the entry door and stopped cold when he saw me. "Damn, woman, what you doin' in that pilot uniform? You messin' wit me? This ain't funny. Everybody knows Rod Rogan has a crazy fear of flying, girl."

I sighed and pointed at Lance. "Relax, Mr. Rogan, we'll keep you safe."

Rod's personal assistant poked him. "Fool, that's the chick what landed the bomb-damaged jumbo jet in June. She's badass. We good, brother."

"Right, I knew that. Just kidding, sweet lady. When we get to Hawaii, come to my suite and we'll party." He waved sheepishly and headed for the cabin.

A muscular British actor with a buzz cut sauntered in. Jack Stone looked like he believed he was the hero he played in action roles.

"Hey, baby, join me for drinks in my suite when we get to Honolulu." He winked and clicked his tongue as he strode past.

More women flirted with Lance during boarding. He flirted back, of course.

I waited until the women were well past us and turned to Lance again. "Don't mess with those high-maintenance females and their hair-trigger egos. They'll devour you and burn your entrails. It won't be pretty. Trust me."

"You'd better bunk in my room and protect me from those evil vixens. After all, you're responsible for your crew, *Captain*." He winked and slid into the right seat.

"I'd rather deal with an engine fire on takeoff than play chaperone for this group." I called the senior flight attendant to the cockpit. "Tawnee, see to it your cabin crew maintains their usual high professional standards."

"Did you check out Jack Stone? OMG, what a hottie! He asked me out for our Honolulu layover. I love his sexy English accent."

"Uh, Tawnee, did you hear what I said about professional behavior?"

"Absolutely, our usual high standards. Got it." She giggled and skipped into the cabin.

I shook my head and looked at Lance as I slid into the left seat.

He snorted with laughter. "This is one time I'm glad I'm not the supreme aircraft commander. Good luck, Sam, you're gonna need it."

He adjusted his seat and called for our clearance. Then he sang, "You Give Love a Bad Name," as we waited for the passenger service agent to close out the flight.

Lance was enjoying my angst way too much. Ah, but payback can be a bitch. I had plenty of time to plot my revenge during our multi-day flight schedule.

I pulled out my new iPhone and texted Ross, explaining I'd be jetting around the world for fourteen days and hoped he could meet me in Paris. The passenger service agent gave us the final count and closed the door. I switched off my cell and slipped it into my flight bag.

It wasn't long before we taxied out to the runway, blasted off for Honolulu, and landed several hours later.

Landon, a junior flight attendant, sat next to me on the crew bus and whispered, "Jack Stone initiated Carlene's hairdresser into the Mile High Club in one of the aft lavs. Later, he cornered Inga, the new flight attendant from Sweden, and bragged about his roles as a super hero. His fourth double Scotch finally sent him to dreamland."

"What about the rest of the passengers?"

"Half of the people in the celebs' entourages drank themselves into temporary comas. Rod Rogan and his personal assistant battled each other in a video game until Rod's Xanax put him to sleep."

"Any problems with the feisty little actress?"

"You mean Carlene Jensen? She got a little drunk and entertained the passengers with a one-hour comedy routine. Hilarious. Then she sang "Girls Just Want to Have Fun." Her voice is divine.... Nothing too crazy happened, but you should keep your guard up around Jack Stone. What a player."

"If the celebs have their way, our stay in Hawaii may turn out to be quite challenging."

15

KEEPING MY CREW OUT of trouble overnight could prove difficult. We were booked at the same Waikiki hotel as our passengers.

Lance was next door, and I pretended not to notice the connecting door. The flight attendants' rooms were on my floor—more temptation for Lance. No wonder he ate so many energy bars. I assumed the celebs were on the upper floors in the lavish suites.

I took a quick shower and slipped on a floral sundress. My waist-length hair took about ten minutes to dry with the blow dryer installed in the bathroom. I decided to go with straight hair rather than crank up the curling iron.

My electric-blue stiletto sandals matched my dress, and the four-inch heels jacked up my five-foot-nine frame to an impressive height. I'd tower over most of the Hawaiian women.

Loud knocking interrupted the finishing touches on my makeup. When I opened the door, a tipsy celeb walked in.

"Hey, Blondie, where's your dreamy copilot?" Carlene Jensen asked with slurred speech.

"Lance isn't in my room. Why don't you go down to the front desk and call him?"

"Why on Earth isn't he with you? You're not one of those carpet munchers, are you?"

"I have a boyfriend, but he's not Lance. How much have

you had to drink?"

Carlene sashayed past me, peeked in my bathroom, and grabbed the phone. She demanded to be connected to Lance Bowie's room.

Her voice turned sugary. "Hello, handsome, ready for our big date?" She listened and answered, "I'm in the captain's room. Where're you?" She hung up the phone and opened the connecting door.

Lance's inner door was open. He swaggered in with a wolfish grin. "We'll leave these open for later. Ready to go, Sam? Better keep an eye on your copilot. No telling what this lovely lady has planned." He winked.

Carlene grabbed his arm in a possessive stance.

I couldn't miss the challenging look on his smug face. "Uh, well, maybe I'll tag along until after dinner. Let's go."

I grabbed my key card and handbag, then slammed the inner door and locked it.

Lance pretended not to notice. He helped Carlene navigate down the hall to the elevator. I followed behind, watching her weave and bump against him. She squeezed his left butt cheek and giggled like a school girl.

The British actor was in the elevator looking ready for action. He focused on me. Oh boy, it was going to be a long night.

Carlene shoved me into Jack. "There you go, Jack, your date for the luau. Have fun."

Jack put his arm around me and locked eyes with Lance.

When we stepped out of the elevator, my cell played the tune for "Loch Lomond."

I turned to Jack. "I have to answer this—my boyfriend. He's a captain in the British Special Forces."

I noted a taken-aback look in his eyes. Score one for a *real* action hero.

"Ross, it's good to hear your voice. Did you get my text?"

"Aye, lass." His baritone brogue always made my heart race. "I'll meet you in Paris if I'm not out on a mission. Military assignments are impossible to predict. Where are you now?"

"Hawaii, flying to Hong Kong tomorrow night. Then stops in Delhi and Aqaba before we backtrack to Dubai for the three-day film festival. After that, I'll be in your arms in Paris for twenty glorious hours."

"I hope so. Be careful and call me before you leave for Paris. I miss you, lass."

"I miss you more. Give Zeus a hug for me and stay safe."

"Your mother's staying with Duncan and cuddles that colt every chance she gets."

"How's the romance going?"

"Duncan's quite smitten. They look happy together. I must go. Bye, lass."

I turned and found Jack standing behind me.

He took my arm and guided me to the waiting limo. "So, who's Zeus? That doesn't sound like a Scottish name."

"Zeus is a baby stallion. My mother's boyfriend is looking after the colt for me in Scotland until he's old enough to travel overseas. His sire saved my life a week before he was born, but that's a long story."

When I slid onto the back seat of the Hummer stretch limo, I noticed Carlene was sliding a hand along Lance's inner thigh.

Jack seemed miffed I wasn't fawning over him like that. I didn't want to offend him by explaining I preferred real men to those who played them in movies. When I spotted our ten flight attendants rushing to climb into the limo, I moved forward so they could crowd around Jack. Problem solved.

When we arrived at the luau site, my cabin crew kept Jack occupied while I blended into the crowd and made my escape. I froze when I thought I saw one of the men who attacked me in Florida standing by a palm tree. I felt a hand on my arm and turned.

"Hey, you're the pilot chick. I almost didn't recognize you out of uniform. Come and sit with me and Rod." Rod's personal assistant led me to a long front-row table on the beach in front of the luau stage.

I glanced back, but the suspect was gone. Rod Rogan lounged on an overstuffed cushion facing center stage. Nodding at me, he patted a cushion on the sand beside him. His assistant sat across from us.

"Hey, you that pilot babe what flew us here. Damn, girl, you look hot in a dress! I brought some blow." Rod glanced around furtively. "Want a snort?"

"No thanks, my boss would fire me in a New-York minute. Zero tolerance, you understand."

"Yeah, it's like The Man is always stepping in and spoiling our fun. Have a glass of Cristal. It's my favorite bubbly."

I accepted a glass of Champagne as Jack sauntered up with all ten of our flight attendants.

Good luck avoiding the inevitable cat fights. Maybe I should give crew scheduling a heads-up in case we need a few replacements.

Carlene and Lance took the empty seats next to Rod.

Lance glanced at me. "Primo seats for the show. Well done, Commander!" He grinned and saluted.

"I live to serve you." I raised my glass in salutation.

"In my dreams." Lance raised his bottle of Kona Longboard lager. "Cheers!"

Soon the feast was served, and bronze-skinned girls in grass skirts rocked their hips in perfect timing to the drums and music. Everyone was in a festive mood as the Champagne and rum punch flowed.

After the meal, the dancers dragged Jack, Rod, and Lance onstage and fastened grass skirts over their jeans. The hula dancers must've thought Lance was a celebrity because of his movie-star good looks. As a laid-back Texan, he always went with the flow.

I deluded myself into thinking the evening might turn out okay after all. Then a Polynesian fire dancer joined the hula girls and drunken actors on the stage. His performance was going smoothly until he twirled his double-ended torches and tossed them into the air.

Rod pushed him aside and caught one. When he tried twirling it, he lit Jack's grass skirt on fire.

"Fire!" Rod yelled. He dropped the torch and ran off stage.

Lance shoved Jack into the sand between the stage and the luau table and smothered his skirt with sand. The flight attendants helped, and the fire was out in seconds.

Rod ducked behind Carlene and me.

Jack glared at Rod. "Clumsy imbecile! Why can't you be more like your character in our action movies?" He looked like he wanted to punch Rod until the flight attendants started fussing over him and smothering him with kisses.

I grabbed a waiter. "Tell the limo drivers to pick us up in five minutes."

Soon our group was headed back to the hotel. When we exited the limos, I stepped behind an enormous urn and waited for everyone to disperse.

Checking my escape path, I spotted the man from the luau who looked like one of my attackers in Florida. He glanced around the lobby and entered the bar.

I took an elevator up to my room, bolted the door, and congratulated myself on avoiding the kidnappers from Florida and also uncomfortable situations with the actors.

It could be a long two weeks.

That night, I dreamed about three women standing back-to-back atop a giant black pyramid. One of them looked like me. Later, I dreamed men armed with MP5 submachine guns chased me through a jungle.

When I awoke, I decided on an activity that would avoid unpleasant situations from my dreams.

Surfing at crowded Waikiki Beach seemed like a safe choice.

16

THE SOFT WHIRL OF an electric fan blended with clicks and whirrs from a bank of computers and sound-recording devices. A stocky middle-aged man wearing wire-rimmed glasses pulled off his headset, pushed back his chair, and stretched in the dimly lighted room.

His lone coworker sat hunched over a keyboard, too focused to notice him, so he tapped him on the shoulder.

"Looks like that's all for now. I'm going outside for a smoke. Want a coffee?" he asked in a Scottish accent as he pocketed his glasses.

A young sandy-haired man with bad skin and muscles bulging against his T-shirt swiveled his chair toward the older man. "I'd rather have an energy drink." He gave him a handful of change from his pocket. "Thanks."

The older man walked down a long hallway and through a heavy metal door into the cold air. He pulled out a mobile phone and hit a preset number.

"Where is she?" an impatient sounding Lord Edgar Sweetwater asked.

"Hawaii. Her charter flight leaves for Hong Kong at ten this evening Hawaiian time. After a brief stay, she'll go to Delhi and Aqaba, and then spend three days in Dubai for the film festival. Her return trip stops in Paris where she plans to meet her boyfriend." He pulled out a pack of cigarettes.

"Excellent. She won't expect anything to happen during her trip around the world. We've been careful to let her see only the team in Palm Beach. They ruined her peace of mind. Soon, she'll never feel safe again."

The spy closed his phone and lit a cigarette. The moist Dundee air felt frigid on his face. He exhaled and watched the smoke swirl toward the nearby harbor and military base. How much longer could he operate under the noses of the British Special Forces without being discovered?

Lord Sweetwater was a hard man who rewarded success but dealt harshly with failure. He wanted to conclude the mission while it was still in the win column.

He squashed his cigarette and carried it into the lavatory to be flushed down the toilet. Back in the hallway, he rubbed the coins with his handkerchief, dropped them into the soda machine, and punched the button for the energy drink with his elbow.

After handing the cold can wrapped in his handkerchief to his young coworker, he opened an alcohol wet-wipe packet and wiped down everything he had touched that day.

On his way out after donning gloves and wiping the doorknobs, he flushed the tiny paper packet. He repeated the same ritual every day before he left work.

His vigilance had kept him out of jail and alive. He intended to remain a survivor in this dangerous occupation, unlike his coworker who was not old enough to realize the genuine possibility of his imminent demise. Inexperience and overconfidence might seal his fate.

17

I HEADED FOR THE surfboard rental shack on Waikiki Beach. It was the usual picture-perfect day in Hawaii, eighty degrees and sunny with long glassy waves rolling in like a machine had made them. I chose an eight-foot surfboard with enough flotation for easy paddling and headed out past the breakers.

A minute after arriving outside the break, I caught a six-foot wave, cut a hard right, and crouched down as the crystal-clear water curled over me and cradled me near the open end of the tube. I looked down through the wave to the coral-covered bottom fifteen feet below.

A warm salty mist caressed my face as the water roared around me. The wave closed out on the aft end of my board and fired me out the tube like a cannon ball. Supercharged from the rush, I executed a switchback maneuver, followed by a right turn, and rode the wave until I kicked out twenty yards from shore.

I paddled out past the break again and waited for my next ride. Every wave glistened like a tube of turquoise glass. They rolled past in an endless parade of perfection.

I caught another six-footer. Racing across a rolling liquid powerhouse as clear as air filled me with euphoria. I tucked inside the curl and waited for the slingshot effect when the wave closed behind me.

After shooting out and whipping my board around in a

sharp left turn, I cranked it back right and ripped up and down the face of the wave as it whisked me toward shore.

"Ahoy, surfer girl! Ride that board over here." From the beach, Lance waved me in.

I turned, rode toward him, hopped off in the shallows, and lugged the board onto the beach.

"Nice bikini. You look good in Hawaiian-print Band-Aids." Lance gave me a wolfish grin.

"For your sake, I hope you didn't call me in just to admire my bikini." I thrust my hands onto my hips.

"I already admired your bikini with my mini binoculars. I want you to go snorkeling with me in a secret cove. I rented a scooter and gear for two, bought a disposable underwater camera, and packed a delicious picnic lunch. The concierge told me the fish and coral there are spectacular, and it's unspoiled by tourists."

"Sounds nice. Too bad we can't scuba dive. Our flight leaves too soon. We'd get the bends." I squinted in the sunshine.

Lance pointed at his scooter. "How about it, surfer girl?"

"Okay. Hand in my surfboard while I rinse off the salt and comb out the tangles in my hair. Good thing we only had one drink last night. I bet the celebs are dealing with major hangovers."

"They probably won't wake up until early evening. That gives us a day off from babysitting duty. Let's *carpe* the *diem*."

"Roger that." I handed him my surfboard and headed for the beachside showers.

Five minutes later, I was toweled dry and wearing a short beach dress over my wet bathing suit. My hair was slicked back into a long ponytail.

"A mini-dress and flip-flops aren't exactly sensible attire for riding a scooter, so please be careful," I said.

"Aye, aye, Captain, no wrecking allowed. Now climb aboard and hug me tight." Lance patted the seat behind him.

We putted along the road to Diamond Head on the Vespa.

I leaned in to Lance. "I hope this wussy scooter can make it up those steep hills."

"We won't break any speed records, but we'll get there. The secret cove is a few miles past Hanauma Bay."

I glanced around. No men with MP5s. Simply wonderful.

An hour later, we dipped into the sparkling waters of a secluded little cove. The sun penetrated the clear-as-air water and illuminated the multi-colored coral reef. A school of brilliant blue and gold fish darted past us and circled back to check us out.

Lance grabbed my hand and pointed down to the left. A neon-green eight-foot moray eel meandered between coral formations ten feet below us. I froze.

The eel shot forward and swallowed his unlucky prey. A nearby blowfish inflated like a prickly balloon. Frightened fish scattered every which way in a kaleidoscope of color.

Something shiny reflecting the sunlight caught my eye. I broke the surface and turned to Lance. "There's something I'd like to check out down there, but I don't want to tangle with the green monster. Look big and scary so the giant eel stays away from me."

"Don't worry, Sam. Moray eels only attack when cornered. The big fella won't hurt you."

"Yeah, well, my fear of snakes goes all the way back to the Garden of Eden. That eel looks like a big-ass snake. I learned in my college marine biology class that morays don't grow longer than four feet, so excuse me if I don't believe this one won't attack in open water."

Lance grinned. "All righty then, I'll convince the critter I'm bigger and badder, even though he's got almost two feet on me." Lance inhaled and dove straight down waving his arms.

I held my breath and dove to investigate what looked like a gold coin inside a hole in the coral.

Lance waited for me at the surface. "What did you find?"

"I'm not sure. Could be treasure."

"I already found my treasure." He pulled me close and kissed the nape of my neck.

A jolt of energy tingled down my spine. *Damn my unfaithful hormones.* "Whoa, cowboy, this filly is taken."

"The Great Kahuna made Hawaiian waters neutral territory for people in relationships. Think of this as a no-harm/no-foul zone where you're free to enjoy life without consequences."

Although Lance was insanely hot, I wasn't about to do anything that would ruin my relationship with Ross.

"Geez, that was the most creative BS I've ever heard. How do you think up this stuff?" I splashed him.

"I'm a man of many talents. You should let me give you a private demonstration."

"Let's start with your underwater photography skills. I'll dive down and point at the gold. The flash should keep the eel away." I sucked in a deep breath and swam down fifteen feet to a coral wall.

I turned and pointed at the hole with the treasure.

Lance snapped several pictures. When he signaled thumbs up, we rose to the surface. He treaded water beside me. My body had its own built-in Mae West life preserver, so floating was effortless for me.

"Did you see something gold and shiny in that hole? Let's try to get it out." I dove back down to the reef.

Lance followed me and used a stick to poke around the gold. A tiny piece of coral broke off and revealed part of the face of a gold Rolex watch with a gold band.

I couldn't hide my excitement when we surfaced. "We found a men's Rolex!"

"Looks like it. No telling how long it's been there. Even if it doesn't work, the gold's worth a lot. Too bad my hand's too big to get it." He studied the spot from the surface through his mask.

I grabbed a floating four-foot branch and handed it to Lance.

"We can use this to scare away anything hiding around there. I don't want an eel biting my hand when I reach in to pull out the watch."

"You're planning to reach inside the hole?" His eyebrows lifted.

"Yeah, but not until I know it's safe."

He wielded the branch like a sword. "Okay, wait until I clear the area."

I gave Lance a head start before diving behind him.

He poked the stick in the hole, and a lone clown fish darted out. He signaled OK.

I reached inside and gripped the watch. Just when I thought I couldn't hold my breath any longer, it pulled free.

The big moray streaked past me as I kicked for the surface behind Lance.

18

AFTER A FEW GASPING breaths, I pulled the mask atop my head to inspect my prize.

"Rolex Submariner!" I waved it in front of Lance.

"Hot damn, woman! Every trip with you is an adventure. I would have been content with a little snorkeling, a nice picnic in this secluded cove, and maybe an afternoon delight to complete a perfect day. Then you find a freakin' gold Rolex!"

"Correction, *we* found the freakin' gold Rolex. Things have definitely improved since our explosive adventure in June and my Highlands vacation in August."

I handed it to him. "Take it. I know you love scuba diving as much as I do."

"I'll give this watch a good home. It's far better than my Seiko." He secured it on his wrist. It fit perfectly and displayed the correct time.

He shoved the Seiko dive watch into his zippered pocket. "Wow, thanks, Sam." He hugged me and planted another kiss on my neck.

"There you go again, trying to get me in trouble with Ross." I laughed and splashed him. "Let's go back to the beach and have lunch."

We swam to shore, toweled off, and relaxed on a beach blanket. While Lance studied the Rolex, I studied him—his broad shoulders, wash-board abs, and muscled physique. No harm in looking, right?

He turned his liquid-green eyes on me. "I'll have a local jeweler verify it's genuine."

He opened the picnic basket.

"Hungry?" He offered a sandwich. "Chicken teriyaki."

"I love the teriyaki sauce in Hawaii, which is good because they put it on everything. Thanks." I took a bite and savored the sweet tangy flavor.

We dined in silence. I stared out at the cove. *Are more treasures hidden there?*

"Earth to Sam, come in, please." Lance pressed a cold water bottle against my left arm.

"Sorry, I was daydreaming about whether or not there are more goodies out there." I took a sip from the water bottle. "I guess no one found the watch because this isn't a well-known dive spot."

"Or you're incredibly lucky when you're not busy being a danger magnet. It's God's way of compensating you for your harrowing adventures." Lance faced me stretched out on his right side with one hand propping up his head.

"Or maybe moray eels are like dragons and collect shiny stuff. He'll be angry we stole his stash." I leaned back on my elbows and glanced at Lance.

Texans and Scotsmen rang my bell big time. Both had sexy accents and tended to be confident manly men, like Lance. *Is he about to make another move?*

I froze when I heard car doors slamming. *Had the kidnappers tracked me somehow?* Loud rap music made me think otherwise. Then I spotted a group of teenagers setting up folding chairs and coolers forty yards to my left.

"Damn the luck." Lance looked crestfallen. "Have I mentioned how much I hate teenagers?" He took a long draw from a cola can.

I pulled on my beach dress and turned to glance at the teens. Three girls had stripped naked and were giggling as they splashed each other in the shallow water. They motioned for the boys to join them.

They chugged their beer before yanking off their swim trunks.

Lance glared at the naked youths. "This is so unfair. Why is God mocking me?"

That's when I noticed a bush was obscuring a sign with bold letters spelling **NUDE BEACH**.

"Well, aren't you the sneaky one! This is a nude beach, and *you knew it*. There's no way the concierge wouldn't have mentioned that. This wasn't about snorkeling and a picnic. You tricked me!" I snatched up the basket and stomped off to the scooter.

Lance strolled up a few minutes later, avoiding eye contact, and secured the blanket, masks and fins, and basket on the scooter.

He sighed and straddled the Vespa. "Climb aboard. We'll talk about this later."

I wanted Lance to believe I was steamed so he wouldn't try anything back at the hotel. I was determined not to cheat on Ross, and I didn't want to be forced into a no-win situation where turning down Lance would create cockpit tension for the next two weeks.

We had too much time to kill. Our flight wouldn't depart until late in the evening, and it was only two in the afternoon. I had to be strong.

No more alone time with Lance.

19

THE DRIVE BACK TO Honolulu led us over some steep terrain. As we crested a high point, a black Hummer ran us off the road. Lance managed to stop short of a cliff where water rushed from a culvert beneath the road and carved a narrow path through the thick foliage.

I was about to tell them off when I noticed MP5s slung over their shoulders as three men exited the vehicle. They were the same gunmen from the Florida attack, minus the murdered one.

Lance must have seen their weapons. He scooped me up and leaped into the white water. We vanished into the depths of the jungle before the gunmen reached the scooter.

Lance held me on his lap in an effort to protect me from whatever rocks we might encounter in the shallow water during our rapid descent down nature's waterslide. The cool water splashed our faces.

I squinted against the spray as we sped downward. It felt like we covered a long distance in seconds as my heart pounded against my chest. I decided this might be a good time to test the emergency button on the dive watch DARPA had given me. Our thrill ride ended with a ten-foot drop into a small secluded pond.

When we surfaced, Lance pointed at where we could climb out of the water. "Hurry and swim over there."

I grabbed our rubber-thong beach shoes floating nearby. Lance pulled himself up onto a flat rock and lifted me out of the water.

I handed him his beach thongs. "Let's find a fast way out of here." I glanced at the waterfall and slipped my feet into the flip-flops.

"Stay on the rocks so we don't leave footprints while we find a way through this jungle." Lance ran ahead, leading me into the trees.

A minute after we pushed through the thick foliage, I heard a loud splash in the pond. My gut tightened.

"Did you hear that?" I whispered.

He frowned and looked around. "If I boost you up into that palm tree, can you bonk the gunman on the head with a coconut on your first try?"

"Even if he stood right under the tree, I'd probably miss. Maybe you should wait in the tree and let me be the bait. I can't throw, but I can kick butt with tae kwon do."

"An automatic weapon beats martial arts. He'll shred you to pieces long before you get close enough to hit him."

"That maneuver in the Hummer was meant to knock us off the road, not kill us. They're the men who came after me in Florida. I'm their kidnap target. They'll want to eliminate you so it'll be easier to take me. You should shimmy up the tree."

"What if there's more than one? A lucky hit with a coconut will only work once." He glanced up the tree.

"I don't think they'd risk sending more than one man down that kamikaze water ride."

Lance hesitated, thinking. "Could be the other two are coming down a different way to cut off our escape. We need to get that first guy's weapon." Lance started up the tree.

"I'll act like I have a sprained ankle and say you ran to get help." I sat and leaned against the tree.

Seconds after Lance settled near the top of the tree, a wet burly man holding an MP5 submachine gun stopped in front of me. He looked surprised to see me just sitting there.

"Hands on your head! Good. Where's your friend?"

"I sprained my ankle. He went for help. No telling how soon he'll be back with the police and paramedics." I rubbed my ankle and winced in mock pain. "Why'd you run us off the road?" I pretended not to recognize him and bit my lip as though trying not to cry.

He looked around and frowned, like he was unsure what to do. "Can you walk?"

"No, that's why my friend left. I can't go anywhere unless you carry me."

"Get up." He pointed the MP5 at me.

"If you're here to kidnap me, I won't be worth anything dead. You're going to have to help me walk." I reached for his hand.

He stepped closer. "You won't be kidnapped today." He pointed the weapon at my shoulder joint. "This bullet's a message from—"

A coconut crashed on his head a second before Lance landed on top of him. I grabbed the MP5 as Lance knocked him out. Two loud splashes in the pond jolted me.

Lance focused on the automatic weapon I held. "Do you know how to shoot that?"

"I had experience with MP5s in Scotland. The shoulder strap's a lot stronger than it looks." I checked the magazine and slung the strap over my shoulder. "Sounds like his buddies followed him."

Lance frowned at the unconscious man. "He was going to shoot you."

"Let's get out of here. I think we need to bear left to intercept the road." I rushed through the jungle.

Lance ran close behind me. I worried we were making too much noise, thrashing through the heavy foliage. I ducked behind boulders and searched for a path upward.

Lance stopped next to me and caught his breath. "I'm not used to chasing after women who run faster than me. Why'd you stop?"

"All three men from the Hummer are down here. Let's climb up to the road and escape on our scooter before they realize where we went." I turned and climbed up the steep hillside, working through stubborn foliage with Lance's help.

Soon we were hiding in the bushes near the highway shoulder. We listened for the men. When we didn't hear anything, we made a run for our scooter.

I paused by the Hummer. "I'd like to shoot out their tires, but the gunfire would draw them back here."

"Too bad they didn't leave the keys." Lance ran to the scooter and started it. "Climb aboard, Sam. Time to haul ass!"

I jumped on the back, and we zoomed past the Hummer.

Moments later, I glanced back and saw the gunmen burst from the jungle and leap in their SUV. No way could we outrun them.

"They're coming! Look for a narrow side trail. Maybe they won't be able to follow us." I scanned the sides of the road as the Hummer roared after us.

Just when I thought we were about to become road kill, a Navy Seahawk popped up from behind the hill. The helicopter allowed us to pass under it and then hovered low in front of the Hummer.

Lance pulled behind a big boulder so we could watch the takedown.

Our pursuers found themselves facing the business end of a hellfire missile ready to launch.

Honolulu Police Department cars raced up the road and

surrounded the SUV.

The gunmen surrendered and were taken into custody as the helicopter climbed and turned.

Lance and I saluted as the Seahawk flew past.

"Thank God for the Navy." I took a deep breath. "Good thing their base is only about a five-minute flight away."

Lance looked puzzled. "How did they happen to be here and know to block that Hummer?"

"Uh, that would be me. I signaled them with my watch." I tapped my DARPA watch.

Lance laughed, and the tension in his face relaxed. "If anyone else had told me that, I'd think it was BS, but you I believe." He shook his head. "Let me guess, your twin brothers in the Navy had something to do with that watch."

"Actually, it was a governmental decision between the US and the UK, but my brothers helped."

"So it was decided letting you get killed would make for bad PR on both sides of the pond."

"Something like that. Lucky me, huh?" I noticed his cuts and scratches. "Our jungle fun took its toll on you. You're bleeding."

Lance looked me over. "So are you, but nothing serious. Just a few cuts and scrapes."

The police officer in charge walked over.

A former Air Force fighter pilot, Lance took a deep breath and remained calm as he shook the officer's hand. "How did you know to come?"

The cop nodded at me. "She signaled the Navy. SEAL Team Nine zeroed in on her GPS location and called us to arrest the gunmen."

"Officer, I'd like to thank you and your men for coming to our rescue." I smiled and shook his hand.

"I'll take that." The officer reached for the MP5 slung over my shoulder.

"Oh, right, we took this from one of the bad guys." I handed it to him.

"The paramedics will take care of your wounds, and then we'd like to ask you a few questions." The officer led us to an EMT truck as lights flashed on HPD cars blocking traffic.

Although we were safe, adrenaline still hummed through my veins as I tried to relax and drop my heart rate. My hands shook as the paramedics made short work of dressing my minor wounds.

I'd left my cell phone in the hotel room. Ross would know I activated my emergency signal.

I didn't want him to worry, so I borrowed a cop's cell and fired off a text: *It's Sam. SEAL Team Nine rescued me. I'm OK, don't worry. More later.*

20

AFTER INTERVIEWS WITH THE police, we arrived back in our rooms at 5:30 p.m. Our flight was scheduled to depart in four and a half hours. I bolted my door.

A long hot shower soothed my tension. I considered a nap, but I was too pumped up. A call to Ross went straight to voice mail. *Must be on a mission.*

A soft knock on the connecting door caught my attention.

I pulled on a sun dress and opened the door.

Lance looked serious. "Sam, I've been thinking about what happened. It might not be over. I doubt the men in the Hummer were the masterminds behind the attack. We may encounter worse adversaries in the Middle Eastern countries on our itinerary. Maybe you should call in sick and fly home."

"Screw that! I may as well quit my career and lock myself in a vault. I'll steer clear of you if you're afraid to be around me." I started to walk away.

Lance grabbed my arm and turned me around. A pounding noise interrupted us. The sound came from my door.

"Ignore it and they'll go away." He tried to pull me against him.

The knocking grew louder.

I slipped free, checked the peep hole, and opened the door. Carlene shoved me aside and rushed to Lance. She was surprisingly strong for her tiny stature.

Lance's eyes widened. Before he could react, Carlene yanked his arm, pushed him into his room, slammed the connecting door, and locked it.

I stood frozen. It had all happened so fast.

Lance must've spent some time in Carlene's room last night. Just as well.

I felt like I was still vibrating from leftover adrenaline. Chocolate would take the edge off. I popped a dark truffle into my mouth and savored the sweet flavor as it melted.

I dressed in running gear, ran a hard thirty minutes on the treadmill in the hotel's exercise room, and took another shower, this time cold.

Where was Ross? I needed to hear his voice. Even though I had known him a short time and could only see him once a month, he was worth waiting for. I called him again.

Ross answered and fired out sentences. "I was out on maneuvers. Just received the message you activated the emergency button, and SEAL Team Nine responded. Then I saw your text. What happened? Are you all right?"

When he took a breath, I said, "I'm okay." I briefed him on the three men.

"What about Nicolai? Did you see him?"

"No, just the men who came after me in Florida, minus the murdered one." I paused. "I miss you, Ross."

"I miss you too. Please be careful, especially at your next destination. We don't have any assets in Hong Kong, and neither does the US."

"The police detective said someone from the FBI would call me after they interrogate the prisoners. It might have been unrelated to Nicolai, but the guy who tried to shoot me in the shoulder said it was a message. Lance knocked him out before he could name the sender."

"Maybe Lord Sweetwater sent them. I don't trust him." He

sighed. "Call me if you learn anything about the men who attacked you. I wish I could be with you right now."

"Me too. I can't wait for Paris. And watch out. Nicolai might come after you first."

"I hope he does. Then I won't have to worry about you. Take care, lass."

21

"BLOND *SOOKA* ESCAPED BECAUSE your men are amateurs. They were supposed to shoot her in non-lethal area and leave her bleeding. Instead, all three are in jail. They will ruin everything." Nicolai smashed his empty vodka glass on the stone terrace.

"Relax, the lawyer I hired said they haven't said a word. He'll bribe prison guards to take care of them," Sweetwater said.

"Island is boring, and I am tired of waiting. Let me take her."

"We've been over this. We'll terrorize her for a month or two, then back off. When she thinks she's safe, you'll deal with her and the two Scottish brats when they meet in Orlando, but not a minute before. Are we clear?"

"Let me send Russians after her. They are more efficient."

"Nicolai, Interpol is hunting you. Any Russian involvement will jeopardize our plan. I'll handle this."

"Then hire better men!" Nicolai tossed the satellite phone onto the hammock. "Damn Brit!"

22

I STOOD IN OUR Honolulu flight operations center and checked the paperwork for our charter flight to Hong Kong. I hadn't seen Lance since Carlene invaded. I assumed he was doing the walk around—inspecting the outside of our Boeing 767.

An FBI agent called and said the men from the Hummer were more afraid of their employer than our justice system. They refused to talk.

Pete Winston walked up with a big smile. "Hey, Sam, I'm your relief pilot for the next ten days. Should be fun. I heard what happened at the luau." He laughed.

I gave Pete a friendly half hug. "It's good to see you again."

"What do you have planned for Hong Kong—a delicious dinner prepared tableside by a chef with a blow torch?" He grinned.

"Very funny. Wait until you meet the passengers, especially Carlene. You may end up providing relief duties outside the cockpit. I think she wore out Lance earlier tonight."

"Now that you mention it, Lance was walking funny when I saw him a few minutes ago." Pete hesitated. "So, uh, how good looking is she?"

"She's Carlene Jensen, the movie star." I tried to keep my tone neutral. "It would be nice if at least one of my copilots would stay out of trouble. That ship already has sailed for Lance. Can you be the sensible one?"

"Don't worry. I'm happily married with a baby due soon."
He patted my back and chuckled. "Try not to take your job so
seriously. Loosen up a little."

"Easy for you to say. The captain gets blamed for
everything the crew does regardless of whether I'm involved in
the questionable activities. Not so fun. You'll change your tune
when you're promoted to the hot seat one of these days."

"You're paranoid because crazy shit happens to you a lot. I
heard about the men who attacked you and Lance. What was
that about?"

"They're the men who attacked me in Florida last week."

"Good thing they're in jail now, thanks to the SEALs. That
reminds me, are you still dating the SAS badass?"

"Ross and I see each other once a month. I'm hooking up
with him in Paris for the overnight layover." I patted his back.
"Congratulations on the baby. When's it due?" I picked up my
flight papers and walked beside him to our airplane.

"Right after I get home. Sure hope it doesn't come early."

"All my friends and relatives with children said their first
babies were late, so don't worry." I stepped into the cockpit and
slid into the left seat.

Pete stowed his bag in the crew closet in the back of the
cockpit.

Lance was seated to my right in the copilot's seat. He
looked busy programming the flight computer.

Pete eased forward and tapped his shoulder. "Hey, I hear
you've been getting a lot of action. Want me to take the first
shift so you can rest?"

"Hell no! The crew rest seat is in the front of the cabin. I'm
hiding from Carlene. If I were you, I'd seriously consider sitting
on the cockpit jumpseat." Lance turned and looked at Pete,
avoiding eye contact with me.

Pete stood in the open cockpit doorway. "You're

complaining about a beautiful actress in your bed? Seriously?"

As if on cue, Carlene walked to the doorway. "Ooo, another hot pilot! Are you coming with us, handsome? I hope you're replacing that switch-hitter, Captain Sourpuss." Carlene was too short to see me with Pete blocking her view. She craned her neck. "Where's Lance?"

Pete turned to me with a big grin. "Wow, Sam, sounds like I missed a lot last night. Next time you play for the home team, can I watch?"

If the fire that flashed from my eyes could kill, Pete would have been incinerated. He stepped aside so Carlene could see me.

"Sorry to disappoint you, Miss Jensen, but you're stuck with me for the duration." I shot her my don't-mess-with-me look.

"Oh, I was just kidding, Captain. You're doing a great job. Now, which copilot is coming back to the cabin with me?" She looked from Lance to Pete.

I was tempted to send Lance back to teach him a lesson. I glanced in his direction.

"Do you want to sit in the cabin for a while, Lance?" I asked sweetly.

"I can't. I have that re-qual thing I have to complete. Sorry, Carlene." Panic flooded his eyes.

I couldn't pass this up. "What re-qual thing, Lance?"

"Uh, you know, my international overwater requalification seat-time requirements because I flew too many domestic flights. I'll need to stay up here all the way to Hong Kong to make up the time." He shot me a pleading glance.

Lance had squirmed enough.

"Oh, right, the international overwater re-quals. There's no getting around those, FAA mandated and all. Sorry, Carlene." I gave her a not-really-sorry smile.

Carlene looked up at Pete. "That's okay. I'll have plenty of time to break in the new guy. You only need one up here with you, right Captain?"

Pete interrupted, "She needs two copilots on long flights like this. That's why I'm here, an FAA requirement."

"So she gets to keep *both* of you? That's hardly fair." Carlene's frown quickly changed to an evil smile. "Don't worry, boys, we'll make up for it in Hong Kong." She winked and left.

Pete didn't seem to notice the tension between Lance and me during the long flight to Hong Kong as we discussed antique airplanes, fast motorcycles, and favorite sport cars.

According to the senior flight attendant, nothing too drastic happened in the passenger cabin. The passengers were their usual loud rambunctious selves, using the mid-cabin bar as party central.

Several hours later, most of the passengers didn't notice the landing as they slept.

23

A DANK CELLAR IN an abandoned Hong Kong tenement reeked with the scent of burnt flesh, blood, and fear.

A tall man with spiked blond hair grasped pliers and ripped off the last fingernail on the screaming man's left hand. He spoke English with a German accent, "I will ask again, where is Poseidon's Sword?"

The Asian man had been stripped to his undershorts and bound to a metal chair. He took a deep breath. "Stop—I talk," he said in a weak, tremulous voice before his eyes rolled back in his head.

The German injected the unconscious man with a stimulant and waited until his bloodshot eyes opened. "Must I use the blowtorch again?"

The prisoner's eyes bulged from panic and the agony of numerous third-degree burns along with his bleeding fingertips. "No, please, I talk." He coughed. "Water."

The German poured bottled water into the prisoner's mouth, spilling it down his chest and onto burned spots, causing him to gasp and choke. He pulled away the bottle, waited until he recovered, and tipped the bottle to his lips again.

The prisoner gulped down the water, paused, and inhaled.

"Survivors of Atlantis live in secret mountain enclave. They have Poseidon's Sword." He paused, trembling. "For two thousand years, they have kidnapped orphan boys and trained them for Dragon Society they created." His chin fell onto his chest, and his eyes closed.

The German doused the man's head with water and slapped his cheek. "Keep talking."

The prisoner gasped, slowly raised his head, and opened his eyes.

"Boys brought to enclave blindfolded and raised to eighteen." He gulped air in short, shallow spurts as he struggled to focus. "Boys blindfolded again when returned to world and given missions." He coughed. "I was one of those boys."

"Good. Pity you did not speak sooner. You could have saved yourself from the blowtorch and pliers. Now, what sort of missions?" He studied the Asian's face for signs of deceit.

"Long before my time, many sent to construct secret underground chambers at powerful dragon-current intersections." He paused and took a deep breath. "Chambers hold information for Golden Twin and triplet goddesses of Sun, Moon, and Fire. Some chamber doors designed to open by their touch, others require key." His voice weakened. "Pendant keys for doors are hidden in historic structures built over intersections of dragon currents."

"What is to stop someone else from finding and using a pendant key?" the blond man asked.

"Keys only work for powerful women of Atlantean descent." He paused and licked his lips. "Combined power of triplets is foretold to be unequaled."

The German stepped closer. "Where *are* they?" He splashed cold water on him.

The prisoner gasped and shuddered. "Dragon Master said he received his final instructions twenty-three years ago. He was told Golden Twin would come this year." The prisoner's eyes were wild from the torture.

"*When*?" the German's tone betrayed his growing impatience.

"Before winter solstice."

He knew that to be true from reading the ancient scrolls. "What is *your* mission?"

"Help Dragon Master."

"And *his* mission?" the German stepped closer.

"Find Golden Twin and give her key to Poseidon's Sword."

He crossed his arms and glared. "And if he does not find her?"

The prisoner shuddered in fear. "Return key."

He clenched his fists. "*How* can he do that without knowing the enclave's location?"

"*They* will find him."

He lifted the prisoner's chin. "What does the key look like?"

"Only Atlanteans and Dragon Master know."

He sighed in exasperation. "Where is the key *now*?"

"In new curio shop." He coughed. "Hundreds of unusual items there, but none look like key."

He grasped the prisoner's shoulders. "How does the Dragon Master expect the Golden Twin to find his shop?"

He grimaced. "She will be drawn to shop by powerful dragon currents."

"Describe her." He had seen drawings of the triplets from an ancient scroll and knew the Golden Twin was supposed to be identical to the blond triplet.

The prisoner blinked hard. "Mid-twenties, golden-blond hair, aqua eyes, and beautiful delicate features. Atlantean crystals light up when she touches them." He hesitated before barely whispering, "Abandon quest. You cannot wield Poseidon's Sword."

Frustrated, he focused on the Asian's eyes. "Think again. I am Werner Voss, a member of the Black Sun. Our Nazi forefathers searched the world for powerful artifacts to benefit our cause. Our leader will know how to use the weapon. He has mastered the power of the Vril, or, as you say, dragon current. Now, tell me the exact location of the curio shop, and I will release you."

Werner was skilled at discerning the truthfulness of his torture victims. It was obvious the prisoner had surrendered his will and lacked the strength required to formulate believable lies. He jotted down the address the man cited and called one of his team members on his mobile.

"Check the address and verify the curio shop is at that location. Call me when you know." Werner hung up and waited.

Thirty minutes later, he received a call from his comrade. "Is it there? ... Good."

Werner pulled out his combat knife and slit the prisoner's throat without a blink. He left the dingy cellar and ordered his team members to take turns watching the shop. They reported a sign on the door announced the new shop would open the next day.

On opening day, Werner focused his binoculars on the curio shop and pulled out his mobile phone. His height allowed for an unobstructed view over most pedestrians.

"The Dragon Master has opened a shop in Hong Kong. My source said he's expecting the Golden Twin and will give her the key to Poseidon's Sword. We'll capture her and the key."

"Werner, remember the prophecy. We need her to activate the weapon. See that she is not harmed."

"*Jawohl*, Master. Your commands will be obeyed."

Werner slipped the phone into his pocket as he continued

watching the storefront. He ran his hand through his spiked blond hair.

Failure was not an option.

24

WITH HONG KONG UNDER communist control, I thought I'd be safe from armed kidnappers. My room in the Lotus Blossom Hotel overlooked the bustling harbor. I couldn't wait to walk the streets, shop, take a junk to Kowloon, and dine in a floating restaurant, but I needed to catch up on my rest first.

I fell into a deep sleep and dreamed about an unusual shop on a narrow side street in Hong Kong. The elderly shopkeeper had a Fu Manchu mustache. Another vision.

The phone woke me.

"Rise and shine, Sam. We need to escape the hotel before the wild ones wake and come looking for us. We'll meet you in the lobby in thirty minutes." Pete sounded chipper.

"Correction, *you* need to escape, not me. And what did you mean by *we*?"

"Lance and I. And I have it on good authority that Jack Stone is hot for you. We *all* need to escape before they shift back into party mode."

"Okay, see you in thirty near the main entrance doors." I jumped into the shower.

Lance and Pete whisked me out the door the instant I walked up.

"Hey, Lance, get any sleep last night? Never mind, I don't want to know." I laughed and shook my head.

"You were right about Carlene. That vixen's an evil man-eater. I need my captain to protect me for the rest of our trip."

"Me too," Pete said. "I think she's coming for me next."

"*Really*? Am I supposed to believe my big strong copilots can't fend off a five-foot-nothing actress? Seriously?" I stood with my arms crossed.

"That woman's a nuclear-powered sex cat from Hell. And she has the claws to prove it. Sharp teeth too." He pointed at a bite mark on his neck. "I prefer to hunt my prey, rather than *be* the prey."

"Yeah, that randy actress will have to capture fresh meat elsewhere. I'm saving myself for my lovely wife." Pete glanced back at the hotel. "Let's keep moving."

"Fear not, gentlemen, your captain will protect you." I looped my arms through theirs as I strolled between them. "I'm looking for a narrow side street with shops."

"There are shops everywhere in Hong Kong. Is there something in particular you want?" Lance asked.

"I'll know when I see it. It's an unusual little shop." I glanced around. "It might've been on an alley."

"An alley? Is our favorite danger magnet leading us into another exciting situation?" Lance glanced at Pete. "I don't think there's a SEAL team in China, Sam."

"Relax, boys, we're just going shopping. What could possibly go wrong?" I grinned and urged them onward.

After walking several blocks, I felt a tingling sensation in my head and an urge to turn left. I recognized the street from my dream. "This way, guys."

I turned down the dark one-lane street and scanned the shop windows. Halfway down the block, I found the curio shop and stepped inside. Lance and Pete followed.

An old man with a Fu Manchu mustache bowed in greeting. "Solraya Twin, Dragon Master welcomes you." His right forearm sported a tattoo of a dragon clutching a gold trident in its claws.

He seemed happy to see me, almost like he was expecting me.

I didn't know what Solraya Twin meant or Dragon Master. Did he recognize me from news stories or was this was about something else?

"Uh, did you say, Dragon Master?"

He nodded. "Head of Dragon Society. I am honored." He bowed again.

The store was dim, deserted, and eerily silent with a musty scent infused with incense.

I stepped closer to the old shopkeeper and bowed, reciprocating his polite gesture.

He smiled with a sweep of his arm. "Please to look around."

Statues, sculptures, idols, carvings, stuffed cobras about to strike, unusual china, and hundreds of antique oddities with embedded crystals covered the shelves.

I felt drawn to a beautiful hand-blown glass dragon perching on a crystal globe on a bottom shelf. When I pulled it out, I saw something behind it that made my breath catch. It reminded me of one of my dreams in Hawaii.

I set aside the dragon and pulled out the strange item behind it. The base was an obsidian pyramid with a diagram on one side, a map with trident symbols on another side, and strange writing on the other sides. The peak of the pyramid was flattened with a solid-gold disc holding three female statues standing with their backs to each other facing outward. They were crafted from white moonstone and held crystal pyramids.

One statue was adorned with long hair made of gold, aquamarine eyes, and a gold diadem inlaid with blue and yellow topaz gems. She could have been my twin. I felt a chill.

When I wiped dust off the crystals, I saw visions of an advanced ancient civilization on an island surrounded by an azure sea. A massive white marble palace, bordered by giant pyramids and enormous sphinxes, dominated a high plateau behind a sea-level city encircled by three canals. The outer canal joined the harbor where longboats were moored.

What was this place?

Two words of a strange language I shouldn't have been able to understand repeated in my head.

Then everything went black.

25

I WOKE ON THE floor in Lance's arms with the obsidian piece clutched against my chest and the crystal pyramids glowing brightly. I felt woozy as Pete kneeled beside me.

"Are you okay, Sam?" Pete looked worried. "The crystals lit up like flares, and you kept repeating a couple of words we don't understand. What the hell?"

Before I could answer, the Dragon Master stepped from behind the counter with a submachine gun. He crossed the room to us.

"Solraya Twin, you go now. Very dangerous here." He turned when four Nordic-looking men entered.

We were still on the floor when the old man opened fire on the men. Three collapsed in a staccato storm of bullets as they drew pistols with silencers. Their stray shots shattered glass figurines on the upper shelves behind us.

Broken shards showered the room. The fourth man took a bullet in his right shoulder and dropped his pistol before he escaped out the door.

Silence enveloped the shop like a heavy shroud.

The shopkeeper made a call on his mobile phone. In what seemed like seconds, four young Chinese men with dragon tattoos rushed into the shop, whisked the bodies into a van, and drove off.

Pete's hand shook as he pulled me to my feet. Lance stood

up beside me and sucked in his breath. I trembled all over. No one spoke. Wide-eyed, we checked each other over but only found tiny cuts from broken glass.

I was surprised the shopkeeper looked calm.

"I don't know what happened with this thing, and those men looked a lot different than the ones who attacked me in Hawaii," I said in a shaky voice.

My hands trembled as I stepped forward to return the odd object to the old man.

"Thanks for saving us." I bowed, and so did he, but he wouldn't touch the black pyramid.

Confused, I looked at him, full of questions.

"It is yours." He glanced at the door. "Dragon Society wait many generations for this day. Take it," he instructed. "Your destiny lies hidden in one teardrop on cheek of time, in rose-red city old as time. Follow dragon current and beware Vril wielded by Black Sun." He pointed at the door and ushered us out. "You go now. Hurry!"

I was still in shock. "What about the police?"

"No police! Go quickly." He locked the door behind us.

I felt like a character in a movie playing in fast-forward. We rushed down the narrow street and turned onto the main road toward the hotel, constantly scanning for the fourth gunman in the crowds.

I spotted a shipping office and ducked inside with my treasure as Lance and Pete followed me. I gasped for breath as I tried to slow my heart rate.

"This is too valuable to carry around. I'm sending it to someone I trust."

They guarded the door as I approached the counter.

"Can you pack this in a small wooden crate with lots of padding? I don't mind paying extra."

While the shippers gathered packing materials, I snapped

pictures of the pyramid's strange map, diagram, writing, and statues.

Then I filled out the paperwork to send it to Harvard Professor of Antiquities Ben Armitage, my former teacher and dear family friend. I wrote a detailed note in shaky handwriting and asked Ben to keep it secret and locked up, except when studying it. I asked him to text me if he discovered anything about it.

"Uh, miss, you want turn off lights before we load in crate?" a young Chinese man asked.

"Um, just a minute." I motioned Pete over and whispered, "Do the crystals feel hot?"

"Why don't you touch them?" he whispered back.

"There's no telling what'll happen if I touch it again. Don't be a wuss." I raised an eyebrow with a challenging look. "I need to know if it's hot. I don't want to put a cargo jet at risk."

Pete sighed with trepidation and haltingly touched a glowing crystal with his index finger. He shrugged. "It feels cool." He tested the other two with the same result.

"So? You turn off lights now?" the impatient employee asked.

"No, the lights will go off automatically. Go ahead and crate it." I smiled and pushed the black pyramid toward him.

I didn't know if the lights would go out, but at least they weren't producing heat.

Soon after I paid, a truck pulled up and loaded the packages waiting to be flown to the United States. Security problem solved.

Lance and Pete hovered near the door. Both had served as military pilots in combat, trained to remain calm in dangerous situations and continually assess their opponents.

"The old shopkeeper knows a lot more than what he told you," Lance said, peeking out the door.

Pete huddled close. "What do you know about that weird pyramid thing?"

Lance turned for my response.

"In Hawaii, I had a dream about something that looked like the pyramid from the store, except it was huge, and three real women were standing on it. My dream at the hotel here had glimpses of the alley, curio shop, and the old shopkeeper."

Pete looked surprised. "Are you saying you have dreams that predict the future?"

"The women in my family line start having psychic visions in their mid-twenties, usually relating to something in the future. Mine started a few months ago. Please don't go telling everyone at work about this. It's personal, and I know I probably sound like a freak."

"So, when you were in that trance, what did you see?" Lance asked.

"I saw an island with strange airships flying around and colorful longboats in the harbor. The city looked ancient with huge pyramids and giant sphinxes. I shouldn't have been able to understand the two foreign words you said I repeated, but somehow I did." I stared out the window.

Pete glanced at Lance, then at me. "So tell us, what were the words?"

"Poseidon's Sword. Sorry, don't know what it means or why I heard it." I leaned back and sighed. "Maybe we should google it and Dragon Society, Black Sun, Vril, and dragon current."

"We should go back and ask the old guy. I bet he knows." Pete looked determined.

I hated having more questions than answers. *How did the shopkeeper know me? Was it because I resembled one of the statues?*

"Pete's right. I'm going back and demand some answers.

The Dragon Master said the Dragon Society has waited many generations, so he must know everything about the black pyramid."

Lance looked like he was ready to tie me to the copy machine. "What if the last gunman is waiting for us in that dark alley? I'm sure he's not happy about his men getting killed. Maybe he brought reinforcements. We're unarmed. I don't think we should go."

"You're forgetting the survivor was wounded and dropped his weapon. He's probably in a hospital, but I'll hide my hair in your baseball cap and wear sunglasses and your windbreaker, just in case. He'll expect two men and a woman, so I'll go alone."

"The hell you will! If I can't talk you out of this, I'll follow behind you and guard your six." Lance's fighter-pilot lingo meant he would guard my back, the six o'clock position. He shot me his alpha-male glare to communicate arguing wasn't an option.

"And I'll walk ahead and scope out the area." Pete headed for the curio shop.

After donning Lance's cap and windbreaker, I walked a reasonable distance behind Pete with Lance tailing me. It had been forty-five minutes since we left the strange shop.

Fifteen minutes later, I saw Pete turn into the alley. By the time I reached the end of the block, Pete had walked back to me, looking shocked and confused.

26

"THIS *IS* THE RIGHT street, isn't it?" he asked. "You're certain?" Pete's face was pale.

"Yes, what's wrong?" I asked as Lance joined us.

"Come and see for yourselves." Pete led us down the alley.

We stopped and stared at the spot where the curio shop had been. The store was empty, the windows were partially boarded over, and the shopkeeper was nowhere in sight.

I knocked, but no one answered. I felt like we were in an old episode of *The Twilight Zone*. We walked back to the hotel in silence.

All the stress from our weird violent day triggered a familiar craving. I bought a small bag of dark chocolate squares from the hotel gift shop.

"I suggest we go to my suite and discuss everything," Pete said.

Lance glanced around the lobby. "I agree. We can order dinner from room service and lay low while we figure this out."

I popped a chocolate in my mouth and let it melt as I nodded.

We didn't encounter any of our passengers on the way to Pete's suite on the eighth floor. Pete pulled out a chair for me at a table in front of the windows overlooking the harbor. I scanned the room service menu and handed it to Lance.

Pete called in our orders and handed us bottled water from

his mini bar. "How good do you think the hotel security is here?" he asked after taking a sip.

"This is a five-star hotel. The security must be good," Lance said. "I doubt the last gunman will come here, but we should be careful."

"What if those gunmen had nothing to do with us?" I asked.

"Yeah, right, Miss Danger Magnet," Lance said with a roll of his eyes.

"Sorry, Sam, but Lance has a point." Pete nodded at Lance.

"After what happened in Hawaii, I understand why you think they were after me. But open your minds and think about where we are—the land of the Triads and Tongs. Could be those men were shaking down the shop owner. He seemed to be expecting them. Remember how he opened fire without a word? He must have known them." I looked from Lance to Pete for their reactions.

"The gunmen weren't Asian, and the shopkeeper was expecting *you*. His expression was obvious when he saw you walk in." Lance looked smug. "He used the words Solraya Twin twice. I don't know if it's a name or something in Chinese."

"What if he thought I was the twin of someone named Solraya and that's why he gave it to me?" I bit my lower lip. "This is bad. I have no way to return it if it wasn't intended for me."

"Relax, Sam." Pete patted my hand. "Remember how it lit up when you touched the crystals, and you saw visions while you held it? Nothing happened when I touched it. I don't know what Solraya means, but that black pyramid was definitely meant for you."

Room service arrived, and Lance pulled out his smart phone to google the terms I'd suggested as we ate.

"Nothing on Poseidon's Sword. Google says Poseidon

wielded a gold trident. Vril is Earth's electromagnetic energy. The name came from a science fiction novel, *The Coming Race,* written in 1871," Lance said.

"The gunmen were tall with blond hair and blue eyes. Definitely not aliens," Pete said.

"That book may not have been about aliens. What else did you find?" My gut turned.

"Black Sun is a Nazi cult started during World War II. Not much info on the Dragon Society. They're believed to be an ancient secret society of experts on dragon currents. Dragon currents, also called ley lines, are paths of concentrated electromagnetic energy that crisscross the Earth and intersect in many places around the world."

Pete frowned. "So how do we decide which one to follow?"

"Wish we had a map that shows dragon currents." I scrolled through the pictures I took in the shipping office. "There's a map on the black pyramid, but this picture's too small to see where the trident symbols are located. I hope Professor Armitage figures this out for us."

Lance narrowed his eyes. "What the hell have you gotten us into, Sam?"

"Wish I knew." I looked at their worried faces. "Might all be a coincidence."

Lance and I locked eyes. Another adrenaline-charged day with the hot Texan.

"Um, I think I'll go to my room and call Ross. I'll see you guys out front at pick-up time." I rushed out the door before Lance could follow me.

I ducked inside my room, sat by the window, and hit Ross's number on my cell. Damn, voice mail. I left a message that I was in Hong Kong and missed him.

Adrenaline from the day's events made me feel wired. I changed into workout clothes and headed for the hotel gym to burn it off.

An hour later, I returned to my room soaked in sweat and ready for a shower.

27

PROFESSOR BEN ARMITAGE OPENED the front door on his hilltop home in Marblehead and accepted the package sent by Samantha Starr. The documents indicated the crate had been shipped next-day air from Hong Kong, which was possible because the package had crossed the international dateline into the previous day during its long journey.

Ben carried the crate up to his newly built study over the garage, set it on his antique Chippendale desk, and walked downstairs to get a crowbar from the tool chest.

A few minutes later, he pried open the wood slats and pulled out the obsidian pyramid. As he sat in front of what he thought might be an artifact, he looked into the face of the gold-haired statue.

"What have you sent me, Sam?" Ben mumbled as he ran a hand through his thinning gray hair. He read Sam's letter, and his mind reeled with cryptic terms and possible explanations.

Statues look like her, especially the one with the gold hair. Glowing crystals, visions of an ancient civilization, and "Poseidon's Sword." Shopkeeper referred to himself as Dragon Master of the Dragon Society, called her Solraya Twin, warned her about the Black Sun and Vril. Told her to follow the dragon current.

Ben knew many ancient structures were built at ley line intersections. His fingers danced over the keys on his laptop as he selected an archaeology website for professionals to research Poseidon's Sword, Black Sun, and Dragon Society.

Ancient scrolls mentioned tales of a doomsday weapon called Poseidon's Sword, but gave no details except that it was rumored to be a massive obsidian pyramid.

Not much on either group. Black Sun and Dragon Society are secret organizations. Could secret societies and ley lines be connected with this unusual piece?

Ben stared at the small crystal pyramids held by the statues.

Still glowing, so they must have a function. This is more than a work of art.

Lost in thought, he gazed out the window at the picturesque harbor below. Sailboats tethered to their moorings bobbed in the autumn breeze. Determined to discover the strange object's secret, he touched the crystals. They felt cool. Next he studied the gold-and-jeweled diagram on the side of the pyramid with the blond statue facing him. No clues were evident.

He turned the black pyramid around to its map. Accurate drawings of the Mediterranean Sea, European coastline, and Atlantic coastline of the United States, including the Gulf Coasts of the US and Mexico, were carved into the obsidian, and the borders were lined with gold. Gold tridents were placed near Santorini, in Egypt, the Himalayas, the Yucatan, off Cuba's northeastern coast, and near Bimini. Major cities were marked with jewels.

The most unusual aspect was a large land mass in the Sargasso Sea where no land existed. It was marked with a gold trident bordered by gold pyramids and labeled with an eight-lettered word in a language he'd never seen before.

Ben turned the pyramid to check the two sides covered in the strange language. No help there.

Gold-haired statue has a seven-letter name carved into her belt and a sun image by her feet. Black-haired one has a four-letter name and a moon image. Redhead has a five-letter name and a fire image. Might be from an era when people believed in gods and goddesses. Could be the goddesses of Sun, Moon, and Fire. Sam looks like a twin of the Sun Goddess. Solraya has seven letters.

Assuming SOLRAYA was the name carved into the gold belt on the Sun Goddess, Ben found letters corresponding to the L and A in the four-letter name for the Moon Goddess.

L _ _ A. He surmised her name was LUNA. The same two letters were no help in naming the Fire Goddess, *_ L A _ _*. *Maybe I can figure out the word on the map.* Matching the letters A, L, N, and S to the unknown land mass, *A _ LAN _ _ S*, he guessed the eight-letter word was ATLANTIS.

My God! Have I found the lost continent?

Excited, he turned the black pyramid back to the diagram, but he couldn't discover how the artifact functioned. No pictorial instructions or symbols. The diagram's images of the three goddesses seemed to match the actual statues. He looked closer and noticed the positions of the jeweled diadems in the images were a quarter turn clockwise ahead of where the diadems were on the statues' heads.

The height of the entire artifact was twenty-five inches.

Unlikely something this small would be dangerous.

He placed his right thumb and index finger on opposite sides of the blond woman's diadem and gently twisted it a quarter turn clockwise. Her hinged fingers released the crystal pyramid. Ben placed it in the square slot in front of her feet. The slot tilted the tiny pyramid enough to make the tip point above her head.

He repeated the procedure with the other two statues. When all three crystal pyramids were inside the slots, they glowed with blinding brilliance. In seconds, bright beams from the tip of each pyramid shot up and merged above the statues' heads. The merger formed an eye-searing laser that fired up through the ceiling and roof, leaving two-inch diameter holes with flaming edges.

Ben shielded his eyes and froze. He dared not move the black pyramid. The powerful laser would burn down his house. He tried to turn back the gold diadems, but they were locked.

Don't panic! He studied the diagram. The tiny crystal pyramids depicted were actual diamonds embedded in the obsidian. He steeled himself with a deep breath and pushed his right index finger against one.

The blazing crystal in front of the blond statue popped out of the slot and landed back in her hands. Her fingers closed around it as her diadem rotated back to its original position.

The moment the crystal left the slot, the laser stopped. Ben pushed the other pyramid-shaped diamonds on the diagram. When all three crystals were locked in the statues' hands and their diadems had rotated back to their normal positions, the brilliant lights extinguished. The scent of ozone lingered.

Ben gasped and realized he'd been holding his breath. With the laser off, he sighed in relief. But it was short-lived as the shriek of the smoke alarm assaulted his ears. He ran downstairs to grab the full-size CO_2 extinguisher in the garage workshop. The fires in the ceiling and roof were small, but the smoke alarm had triggered the security system, and now his phone was ringing.

Ben ran up to his study to answer the phone. "Yes, this is Professor Armitage. There's no fire. My cigar lit some paper in the waste basket, but I took care of it. Sorry to bother you.... Yes, thank you."

Better to put out the fire before anyone noticed.

How would I explain it? Good thing I live alone.

He pulled the cord for the drop-down stairs to the attic and walked to the tiny fire. The handheld extinguisher smothered the two-inch flaming holes in the ceiling and roof and cooled the seared edges and singed fire-proof insulation. Ben plugged the openings with a foam sealant and called to arrange permanent repairs.

Thirty years of studying antiquities and ancient civilizations had taught Ben the importance of keeping secrets. He opened his large wall safe and placed the artifact inside. It barely fit. He locked the safe and swung the hinged painting of the Great Pyramid back into place.

The room smelled like burnt wood. A smoky cloud hovered near the ceiling.

He typed a text to Sam: *Artifact is powerful weapon, possibly from Atlantis, and could be small prototype of Poseidon's Sword. Burned holes through my ceiling and roof. I'm OK. Fire is out. Statues may be goddesses of Sun, Moon, and Fire—Solraya, Luna, and don't know name of Fire Goddess. Artifact locked in my safe. Keep secret.*

He opened the windows to air out the smoke, then retreated to his den and pulled a bottle of Macallan from the oak cabinet. He poured a double measure of the Scotch whisky and drank half of it in one swallow.

Ben finished his drink and poured another. He swirled the whisky and thought about all that power locked away above his garage.

Well, crisis averted.

He'd run some tests to determine the artifact's age as a starting point for his research, but he'd have to use the university research lab late at night so no one would see him.

28

WERNER SAT ON A wide leather seat aboard the private Gulfstream jet as it parked on the ramp at the Indira Gandhi International Airport near New Delhi. Filled with regret, he ignored the pain in his shoulder from the bullet wound, picked up the satellite phone installed in the armrest, and called the Master of the Black Sun. The line connected, but the man on the other end said nothing.

"I take full responsibility for what happened in Hong Kong," Werner began in an unsteady voice. "I am unworthy of your forgiveness, Master. The burden of my failure weighs heavily upon me."

"On me also. Fix this."

"*Jawohl,* Master."

"Where is the key to Poseidon's Sword?"

"I don't know. I was wounded and barely escaped with my life."

"I hope you know where she and her companions went."

"After our doctor tended my wound, I hired a local artist to draw her picture based on my description and sent men with copies of it to all the best hotels. The doorman at the Lotus Blossom Hotel recognized her."

"Good, did he give you her name?"

"She and the two men are pilots with Luxury International Airlines, Captain Samantha Starr and First Officers Lance

Bowie and Pete Winston. They're working a round-the-world charter."

"Solraya's twin has an interesting surname. Did the hotel doorman see her carrying that artifact you saw her with in the shop? The key must be inside it."

"She and her copilots had nothing with them when they returned to the hotel, and they didn't have any extra luggage when they departed the hotel for the flight to Delhi."

"Perhaps she took the key and left the artifact behind. What is your plan?"

"I bribed a ticket agent who handles Luxury International's flights through Hong Kong and secured a copy of their itinerary. The agent thought I was a fan of the movie stars on the flight. Captain Starr is scheduled to accompany the celebrities on a private night tour of the Taj Mahal."

"The Golden Twin is following the prophecy to the mausoleum. Sounds like an ideal place to kidnap her. Leave the others unharmed. We don't want to draw too much attention."

Werner rubbed his bandage. "My best men are preparing the ambush in Agra. I will ensure the jet is ready to depart when they arrive with her. How are the renovations progressing? Will the chamber be ready?"

"The pipe for the gas-fired flame is being installed in the vault. Take your time and do this right. She must arrive unharmed. Once she is secured in the chamber, she will tell us everything we need to know."

"As you wish, Master."

29

I GOT A TEXT from Professor Armitage during the ride to the Star of India Hotel. Lance was seated beside me, and I trusted him with everything except my womanly virtue. He'd risked his safety on my weird shopping expedition in Hong Kong, so I figured he had the right to be included in whatever facts I learned about the artifact. Pete too.

I nudged Lance and showed him the text.

Lance stared at the message. "It sure didn't look like a weapon. I wonder what it does."

"He said it set his house on fire, but he didn't explain how."

I typed back: *How does weapon work? Be careful. 4 gunmen attacked me in Hong Kong shop. Dragon Master killed 3, but 1 escaped and may be looking for artifact. He could be from group called Black Sun.*

Lance focused on me. "Solraya's the Sun Goddess on the pyramid? That means the Dragon Master thinks you're the goddess's twin, especially because your touch activated the artifact."

He grinned. "Hot damn! My captain's a real goddess. When we check in, I'll stop by your room so you can demonstrate your divine powers. It'll be our secret." He winked.

I laughed and shook my head. "You don't give up, do you?"

"Hey, a man can dream, can't he?"

The crew bus stopped in front of the hotel at 10:00 a.m. local time, and we checked in. After a late-night departure and morning arrival amid more time changes, we were ready for a good rest.

I pulled Pete aside. "I received an interesting text from Professor Armitage. Let's meet Lance for dinner, and we can discuss it then."

"What about the celebs? Won't they see us in the restaurant?" Pete looked concerned.

"Tawnee said the VIPs plan to rest up before the excursion to the Taj Mahal late tonight. They're worn out after their big party in Kowloon, plus more drinking on the flight. Unfortunately, we're mandatory chaperones tonight, but the Taj will be beautiful under the full moon because the marble is translucent."

I picked up my key card and headed for the elevator. "I'll see you in the restaurant tonight at six."

EIGHT HOURS LATER, I joined Lance and Pete at a corner table in the hotel restaurant. A large potted plant obscured the view of our table from the entrance.

Our thirty-six-hour layover in Delhi allowed for moderate consumption of alcohol up to fifteen hours before flight time, a company policy stricter than FAA regulations.

A waiter was ready with pen in hand. "What would madam like?"

"I'll have lamb chops and a glass of the house Merlot. Also, a bottle of Evian." I smiled and pulled out my cell to check for messages.

Pete ordered next. "Chicken curry with the house Chardonnay."

"I'll take the baked Salmon and a Jaipur Lager," Lance said

in his Texas drawl.

He turned to me after the waiter left. "I heard the celebs aren't having dinner until eight tonight. Why so late?"

"Haven't you noticed they're vampires? The full moon won't be over the Taj until midnight. They'll sleep until early evening, slowly rise from the dead, and have dinner in their suites before they launch for the Taj in a luxury bus with a bar, bathrooms, and waiters."

"I did notice one has vampire-like tendencies." Lance shook his head.

"Don't forget she bit you in Hawaii." Pete feigned concern. "We'd better check your teeth to see if you're growing fangs."

"We have to go with them tonight." I raised a brow. "Is it too late to purchase Kevlar vests?"

My iPhone chimed for an incoming text message. Professor Armitage again.

I read aloud, "*Artifact carbon dated approx. 11,000 years old. Map on pyramid matches one found later in Minoan kingdom, except Atlantis and symbols on pyramid map not on Minoan map. No maps that accurate again until 1800s. According to ancient legends, Poseidon's Sword was a doomsday weapon created by scientists in Atlantis. Possible prototype too small for mass destruction. More later.*"

"Whoa, woman, you found an eleven-thousand-year-old weapon that still works? Dang." Lance shook his head in amazement. "Every trip with you truly is an adventure!"

"I checked to see if dragon currents or ley lines, as the Brits call them, have any connection to unusual artifacts. Turns out ancient temples, medieval churches, Stonehenge, and other significant sites were built at the intersections of ley lines." I sipped the Merlot.

"How did they know where the ley lines intersected? They didn't have electronic sensors." Pete shook his head.

The waiter approached with our meals.

"Whoa, that was fast." Lance leaned back to accommodate the waiter.

He looked at Pete. "They didn't have EMF interference back then like we do now with all the modern communication signals and other electronic devices. Maybe they *felt* the dragon current." Lance took a bite of salmon.

"More important, how do *we* locate the dragon current and follow it to what I'm supposed to find?" I was eager to begin the hunt.

"I thought you already found it. Isn't that what the pyramid thing is?" Pete asked.

"Maybe it's a prototype for a much larger weapon, like the professor texted. In my dream, the black pyramid was a hundred feet high, and the three women standing on top were real." I slipped a forkful of tender lamb into my mouth.

"Yeah, but that could have been a vision of the ancient past, like what you saw when you rubbed the crystals. I don't recall any reports of discovering a giant black pyramid in the modern world." Lance took a long pull on his beer.

I had an idea. I texted Professor Armitage.

"What are you doing?" Pete asked.

"I texted the professor and asked him to compare dragon currents with where the trident symbols are located on the map. The Dragon Master implied the pyramid artifact and dragon current would lead me to what I seek."

"And what do you seek, fair maiden?" Lance asked with a wave of his hand.

"I seek enlightenment. I haven't a clue why the Dragon Master gave it to me or why it lit up when I touched the crystals. Is my destiny tied to the artifact? Who were the men with the guns? Why did the store disappear after we left?" I shook my head.

"I don't know if my pyramid dream was a vision of the past or the future. All I know is my other dreams were about the future."

30

A YOUNG MAN WITH an acne-scarred face waved in the dimly lit room to a middle-aged man wearing earphones. He grinned and pointed at his computer monitor.

When the older man removed his headset, the young man said, "We just hit the jackpot, partner. Look at these texts between Samantha Starr and Harvard Professor Ben Armitage. This takes the saying 'Two birds with one stone' to a whole new level."

The older man stood behind him to read the monitor.

"This changes everything. I must notify our employer. Looks like all the money he spent on this state-of-the-art spyware has paid off in spades." He exited the surveillance room.

The brisk breeze blowing across the Firth of Tay chilled the spy as he gazed toward the SAS base, took a drag from his cigarette, and hit a number on his mobile phone. Exhaling smoke into the damp air, he heard the sharp voice of his employer.

"What do you have for me?" Lord Edgar Sweetwater asked.

"Your expensive spyware is paying off. We gathered some interesting texts. Samantha Starr found an artifact in Hong Kong that may be a small working prototype of Poseidon's Sword. Someone named Dragon Master gave it to her before he gunned down three of your men. The fourth man escaped."

"I didn't send men after her in Hong Kong. Tell me about the weapon." Sweetwater sounded excited.

"She sent it to Harvard Professor of Antiquities Ben Armitage." He briefed him on the findings.

"Are you certain it isn't Poseidon's Sword?" Lord Sweetwater sounded breathless.

"The scrolls found in the sunken temple described an obsidian pyramid the equivalent of one hundred feet tall. The artifact she found is small enough to carry—too small to destroy cities like the weapon described in the scrolls."

"Continue monitoring her communications. Learn as much as possible before I send a team to steal the prototype. Excellent work!"

"May I make a suggestion?"

"Your expertise is one of the reasons I pay you."

"Miss Starr and the professor have agreed to secrecy concerning the search for Poseidon's Sword. Why not let them do your work for you? Have your men shadow her and protect her while she searches for your prize. The professor can use his vast resources at Harvard University. Once we know where it is, your men can take her prisoner. Keep her alive until you're certain you have everything you need to activate the weapon."

"Where's the prototype?"

"Inside Armitage's safe. Once they locate Poseidon's Sword, you can send a team to retrieve the artifact and kidnap the professor. You may need him to operate the weapon."

"I want to know who was after Samantha. She's mine. I'll protect her until she finds the weapon."

"Aye, we need to know who your competition might be. She mentioned a group called Black Sun. I'll check them out."

"Stay on it. Expect a big bonus deposited in your account tomorrow. Well done!"

The spy smiled as he opened the heavy steel door to the

building.

His work held a place of major significance now. If he handled this right, he could soon be rich enough to retire with a lifestyle better than an Arab prince.

31

MY CREW, A PHOTOGRAPHER, the three celebrities, and a few women in their entourage exited the luxury bus in Agra. We climbed aboard an electric trolley that whisked us through the western gate and parked in front of the long walkway to the spectacular Taj Mahal.

A full moon lit our way, and a reflecting pool the length of the walkway shimmered as the translucent white marble mausoleum glowed like a giant pearl.

A light breeze carried the scent of jasmine incense as crickets punctuated the silence. The property was closed to the general public.

A perky young tour guide from England named Hollie gave a brief speech and ended with, "The main spire on the central dome combines the horns of the moon with the finial point to create a trident shape. This beautiful mausoleum has won global recognition as the greatest single monument to love— 'One teardrop on the cheek of time,' according to poet Gurudev Rabindranath Tagore."

I froze and glanced at Lance and Pete. They were staring at me.

Lance scanned the area and whispered, "Didn't the Dragon Master tell you your destiny lies hidden in one teardrop on the cheek of time?"

"Yes, that was the first part. Could mean I'll find a clue

inside." I tried to sound positive, but my stomach churned.

"Yeah or you could find armed attackers waiting for you." Pete clenched his jaw.

I felt a strong pull to the Taj Mahal as its majestic reflection sparkled on the water. I reminded myself to look for trident symbols inside.

"Guys, I really want to know what I'm supposed to find in there."

Carlene snagged Lance's arm. "I'm stickin' with you, handsome." She edged up against his side. "Lead on, big guy." She smirked at me.

Lance rolled his eyes. "Stay sharp and don't stray from the group, Sam."

April, a young woman in Carlene's entourage, latched onto Pete with a death grip. "Dead people are in there. Could be scary. You'll keep me safe, won't you?" She pulled him forward.

Poor Pete looked like a cornered rabbit, ready to bolt.

Rod took my arm and strolled with me toward the famous mausoleum. I decided he was far better than having to deal with a randy action hero.

Four of our flight attendants flanked Jack. The other six had lost interest. *Smart.*

We admired the exterior of the Taj and how the semi-precious stones inlaid in the marble sparkled under the full moon. When we entered, the glowing opalescent outer walls and ceiling lit our path through the surreal interior. The polished marble floor amplified the clacking of Carlene's stilettos.

I pulled out the military night-vision binoculars/camera Mike had given me for my birthday. As I scanned the peak of the central dome ceiling, I found a tiny gold trident that blended into the mosaic and would have been impossible to see without my special binoculars, even in the daytime.

The trident glowed a little brighter than the surrounding mosaic. *Why would the trident have been included in the ornate ceiling built in the mid-1600s?* My integrated night-vision camera didn't need a flash as I snapped pictures of the dome and nearest wall.

Tiny gold trident symbols spaced in six-foot increments led from the dome to the wall on my right. The last one on the wall was six feet above the floor where I stood. When I reached up and touched the gold trident, my hand tingled, and a three-inch square compartment sprang open.

The tour group gathered around the sarcophagi in the center of the building and didn't seem to notice what I was doing.

I felt inside the compartment and pulled out a square gold pendant embedded with a trident beside a diamond pyramid. When I touched the tip of the pyramid, it lit up like a halogen bulb.

The marble compartment snapped shut and blended back into the wall. I touched the gold trident on the wall again, but the compartment didn't open.

Now what?

I hid the lighted pendant in my leather shoulder bag and took pictures of the area with the hidden box.

"Hey, Captain, why are you taking pictures of the wall? The tombs are way cooler." Rod pointed at the two sarcophagi.

"Those are fake. The real tombs are beneath these on the lower level. These prevent people from walking over them," the guide said.

"Let's head below and check it out. I bet it's dark and spooky down there. No telling what we'll see," Jack said and grinned when Rod looked panicky.

"No way am I going down there! I've seen the movies. The brother always dies first." Rod's eyes widened with fright.

"Relax, Rod, I'm sure Lance and Pete will protect us." Carlene winked up at Lance as she snuggled against him.

"That's not included in the tours, and it's very dark, especially at night." The guide stepped closer to our group.

Jack used a deep, authoritative tone. "Madam, this is a VIP tour, and we're not afraid of the dark. You have an approved lantern, so show us what's down there."

The flight attendants seemed to swoon over his take-charge attitude.

"Too bad your rules don't allow us to use our cell phone lights," Carlene said.

"Sorry, according to India's rules for site preservation, your phones and all lights except mine must remain off. Now stay close together." The guide motioned us forward. She headed for the stairs and switched on her light.

Probably shouldn't mention the glowing pendant in my purse. Hard to explain.

I hooked my arm through Rod's and followed Jack and his groupies down the stairway. Our footsteps echoed as we descended into the dark crypt.

The room was almost the same size as the area above but much darker with a chill in the air. The lantern illuminated only the center where the guide stood by the two stone sarcophagi. The remainder of the chamber looked like the Netherworld.

As we gathered around the tombs, the dark corners came alive.

A disembodied, German-accented voice resonated on the stone walls. "Everyone on your knees! Foreheads against the floor, hands behind your backs. Now or we kill you!"

Adrenaline surged through my body as I realized the emergency button on my DARPA watch wouldn't work below ground.

"I warned everyone not to come down here. Nobody listens to the brother," Rod hissed.

"Silence!" a German-accented voice shouted.

I knelt between Rod and Jack and felt Rod trembling against my left side. Large hands bound my wrists together with a plastic tie wrap. A few minutes later, a strong man yanked me to my feet with one hand and held me in front of him.

Another man threaded a rope through the lift rings on the tombs and through everyone's bound arms. He secured them to the heavy stone sarcophagi. Two men pointed silenced pistols at the captives. I counted four armed men.

"If anyone yells or tries to escape, I kill everyone," a cohort said as my captor dragged me up the staircase.

When he took me outside, his men joined us, and the moonlight revealed little about them. Tall in combat fatigues, they wore black balaclavas covering their hair and faces. *Were they working for Nicolai, or were they connected to the men who attacked the Hong Kong shop?*

The leader searched me. "What's this?" He hung the pendant around my neck and took pictures of me with his camera phone. "Come." He shoved me.

The men led me down a long side path bordering the gardens. Trees and bushes cast shadows in the eerie silence. Even the crickets were quiet.

My heart pounded as my mind raced. I struggled to devise an escape plan.

The leader walked point while two men flanked me, and another walked behind us. They hadn't left a man behind to guard the hostages.

Sixty yards from the Taj Mahal, I heard *phuumfh*, *phuumfh* on either side of me.

The men flanking me fell backwards with bullet holes in

their chests.

I dived onto the ground a second before the leader's head exploded. He landed with his bloody head just inches from my nose.

The man behind me collapsed too. I couldn't see or hear the shooter.

Trembling, I remained prone and prayed the shots had come from a British sniper who somehow knew I'd been taken.

32

I WAITED FIVE TERRIFYING minutes. When I heard crickets again, I risked sitting up and looking around. The expected laser dot on my chest never appeared. My breath came in fast spurts, like I had run a 100-yard dash.

I couldn't use the night-vision binoculars hanging around my neck because my hands were cuffed behind me.

The pendant's light illuminated the immediate area. A knife strapped to the belt of the dead man on my left solved my problem. Cutting the plastic cuffs with my hands behind my back wasn't easy, but I succeeded without stabbing myself.

After putting the brilliant pendant in my purse, I pushed the emergency button on my watch and scanned the area with the night-vision binoculars. No one was visible, and nothing moved.

I clipped the sheathed knife to my jeans, gathered the handguns, and shoved three in the outer pockets of my big purse and one in the small of my back. Then I pulled off the balaclavas, revealing fair-skinned men with blond hair.

After turning on my iPhone, I took a few quick pictures of their faces and bodies. Then I called the emergency number to summon local police in case a SAS team wasn't coming.

With a pistol in my right hand, I rushed back to the Taj to rescue my passengers and crew. Their fifteen minutes in pitch-black darkness must've felt like an eternity.

I heard sobbing as I crept down the stairs. My people were more important than India's strict rules against lights in the Taj, so I pulled a halogen penlight from my purse and pointed it at the sarcophagi. I was right. They'd been left alone.

"Don't worry, it's Sam." I took a moment to catch my breath. "I'll have you free in a minute. Stay still while I cut the rope and plastic cuffs."

"You okay, Sam?" Lance asked.

"How'd you get away from the kidnappers?" Carlene asked.

"Shut the hell up and let her cut us free before the gunmen return. I want out of this ghost hotel." Rod sounded panicked.

Several of the women were crying.

"I'm fine, and they aren't ever coming back."

I severed the rope and pulled it away from the captives. Then I cut the zip ties, starting with Lance, Pete, and Carlene. I handed them pistols.

"Stand guard while I cut the others loose."

"Hey! Why'd you give a weapon to Carlene instead of me?" action hero Jack Stone said.

"She's from Texas." I gave her a confident nod. "And she's a pistol champion."

"Don't you worry none, honey-buns. Daddy taught me to shoot flies off a watermelon at thirty paces." She moved the slide to see if there was a bullet in the chamber and grinned at Jack.

When everyone was free, I faced them. "I understand you're upset, but you need to be quiet until we get out of here. Dry your eyes, blow your noses, and come with me."

The teary-eyed guide relinquished command. "Thanks for rescuing us. I'll follow you, Miss Starr."

I led them up the stairs to the outside and scanned our escape route.

"Follow me to the western gate and keep a sharp lookout.

The police should be here soon." I inhaled and tried not to think about the four dead men and who killed them.

While Pete and Carlene flanked the group, Lance guarded the rear. Fifty yards from the gate, I heard a Super Lynx helicopter approaching fast. Moments later, it hovered in front of us.

"It's the SAS!" I tried to shout over the thundering rotor blades. "Everyone sit down and put your hands on your heads. Weapons on the ground!"

The helicopter pilot blinded us with a spotlight and landed. Soldiers rushed out with submachine guns and surrounded us. Their commanding officer approached me.

"Sir Lady Samantha Starr?" he asked with a British accent.

"Please, call me Sam." I smiled. "Thanks for sending that sniper to shoot the kidnappers."

"What sniper?" He looked confused. "We just landed."

"Four men kidnapped me and left everyone else tied up in the lower level of the Taj. After the sniper shot my captors, I took their weapons and ran back to rescue my people. We were on our way to the gate when you landed." I stood and handed him my handgun.

He looked me over and paused on the sheath clipped to my jeans. "Give me the knife. Who has the other weapons?"

His eyes focused on me with a fierce intensity. Ross was a pussycat compared to this guy.

"Two men and a woman have the weapons." I pointed to them, and his men collected the pistols. "I called the local police."

"I know—they're searching outside the gates. Show me the dead men." He summoned one of his soldiers to accompany us while the rest guarded the group.

I led them to the scene of the murders. The bodies were gone. The SAS commander gave me a scary angry-alpha-male look.

Damn, I broke rule no. 1 of my dad's rules for a happy life: Never anger an alpha male.

"Uh, apparently a clean-up crew took the bodies, but the blood is still here." I pointed to where the bodies had bled out. "Look, I took pictures of the dead men for identification."

He sent my photos to his mobile phone. "Explain to me again exactly what happened here."

Could his eyes get any more intense? He looked scarier than my kidnappers.

Once more I recited the sequence of events. Searching for signs of deceit, he stared at me like I had just arrived from a distant planet. Finally, he sighed heavily and called someone on his SATCOM.

I listened while he relayed my story.

I heard him ask, "Is this possible, sir?" He looked surprised at the response he received. Then he looked at me. The angry-alpha-male glare vanished. In fact, he looked amused as he handed me the phone.

"Hello?" I said, not knowing who was on the other end.

"Sweetheart, what the bloody hell are you involved in *now*?" Ross asked.

I stepped away from the soldiers for privacy. "Um, well, I'm not sure. I found an ancient weapon."

I explained what happened in Hong Kong and what my professor friend had discovered.

"The men who kidnapped me tonight looked and sounded German. Nicolai may not have sent them. They might be part of a secret organization called Black Sun. Please keep that and the ancient weapon to yourself for now. Sorry I don't know more. I miss you." The last sentence was a lame effort to appease him.

"Damn it, lass! It's hard enough trying to protect you from

Nicolai. Now you have a new group after you. I may have to lock you in my castle until all your enemies forget about you or are dead."

"That could be fun if you're there with me." I tried to lighten the mood.

Ross sighed. "Where are you going next?"

"Aqaba, Jordan. We're taking a tour of Petra with three celebrity passengers."

"Petra's a perfect choke point for terrorists. Stay the hell away from there."

"We'll have armed security. Jack Stone is tight with the king. He'll keep us safe. I'm supposed to accompany the passengers on all the tours." I tried to sound calm and confident.

"Lass, we don't have assets in Jordan. Now that we know you have unknown men hunting you, the wise move would be to call for a replacement pilot and fly to Scotland for an extended leave of absence at my castle." Ross sounded tense.

After my discovery inside the Taj Mahal, I was determined to pursue my destiny, despite the danger. An unseen force was driving me.

"Don't worry. I'll be fine now that the bad guys are dead. Thanks for sending the team. Love you." I knew the L-word would give him pause and ended the call before he could protest.

I handed the SATCOM to the SAS commander and kissed his cheek. "Thanks for coming to my rescue. Sorry I wasted your time."

He looked taken aback. "Right. Let's get your people back to the hotel in Delhi. We'll accompany you on the bus." He led me back to the group.

Lance walked up to me. "Sam?"

"Um, everything's under control. The soldiers will

accompany us to the hotel."

"Let's go." The SAS officer herded us through the gate and down the lane into the bus.

We had a brief delay while local police detectives took our statements on the parked bus.

Many of the women sat beside soldiers and continued sobbing. Everyone looked shell shocked as they settled in for the long bus ride.

Lance sat beside me. I waited until no one was looking to show him what was in my purse. The pyramid-shaped diamond on the pendant was still glowing.

His eyes widened. "Where—"

I touched his lips and whispered, "It was hidden inside a secret wall compartment in the Taj. Don't say anything about the artifact we found, or this pendant, or the Black Sun. We don't want to open a can of worms. I texted Pete with similar instructions."

"Darlin', the worms are already out of the can." He whispered, "High-adrenaline sex later?"

I glanced over my shoulder. "Shouldn't you be sitting with Carlene?"

Lance threw his head back against the headrest and sighed.

33

WHEN WE ARRIVED AT the hotel, the SAS officer questioned everyone in a conference room. He took notes for the written report he would send to the director of Special Forces. Lance, Pete, and I left out any mention of an ancient weapon, pendant, or Black Sun.

When the soldier finished, I spoke to the group. "We need to discuss whether it's wise to continue this charter flight around the world. I understand if you'd like to cancel the trip and return home, and I apologize if I had anything to do with what happened tonight."

Several people raised their hands and said in unison, "We want to go home."

April, the woman who had held Pete's hand earlier, stood up. "I vote we go home."

Jack Stone stood up. "It's not that simple. We're under contract."

"Jack's right," Carlene said. "I've never broken a contract, and I don't intend to start now."

"I have a solution," Jack said. "Non-essential personnel may return home. Some hair, makeup, and wardrobe people, along with the cameramen, must stay on. We'll need you for the Petra shoot and the Dubai Film Festival. You can get us ready in the hotel rooms and stay there."

Jack looked at the stocky cameraman who had snapped

pictures at the Taj before the ambush. "Sorry, Hal, but we'll need you for the shots in Petra."

"Jack, why can't you cancel the Petra tour?" Hal blotted sweat from his face and neck, even though the room was cool.

"The king of Jordan is financing our next action movie. He insists we take a private tour of Petra and provide him with PR photos of Carlene, Rod, and me on site. One does not refuse a king." Jack maintained an adamant tone. "But don't worry, the king's a personal friend. I'll see to it he assigns men from his Royal Guard for our protection."

"Jack's right," Carlene said again. "We have to fulfill our contracts to keep the funding for our movie sequel. The Royal Guard will keep us safe."

Rod looked too traumatized to speak.

"I'll see if I can arrange for another captain to replace me in Aqaba in case I'm the reason for the attack." I thought it was the right move, but I knew my airline was running short of captains and might not have a replacement.

"Hell, no! We're keepin' you, Captain Starr." Carlene gave me two thumbs up. "We want the best. I read about how you saved the bombed airliner."

Rod snapped out of his stupor. "Damn straight! We want a badass pilot. You have to stay."

"I appreciate your confidence in me, but you should know our airline has plenty of brave, highly skilled, badass pilots. Our chief pilot tops the list."

Jack stood with his hands on his hips and looked at me. "You may be a kidnap target, but so is every actor in this group. The king will keep us safe in Jordan. We have plenty of time to arrange for extra security in Dubai and Paris. You're the captain we want on our flights. Case closed." He crossed his arms and nodded at Carlene and Rod.

"Okay, I'll stay, but I need a list of everyone going home so

I can make the travel arrangements."

I gave the group my room number and told them to pass the word along to those not on the Taj Mahal tour. Jack stayed behind to help me.

An hour later, everything was handled. The three movie stars, their personal assistants, and one hair, makeup, and wardrobe person per star would continue on, along with two cameramen. Except for one photographer, the others would not be required to attend tours or events with the actors. The non-essential people were issued tickets to return home on a commercial flight.

"Jack, I suggest substituting a smaller aircraft for the remaining flight schedule. It's hard to justify the cost of a jumbo jet for seventeen passengers," I said.

"Nonsense, the king's personal airplane is a 767, so he'll have no objection to us keeping our luxury 767. Besides, we need to stay on schedule. I'll see you onboard." Jack nodded and returned to his room.

FAA regulations required a minimum of one flight attendant for every fifty seats on a commercial airliner. Our aircraft had a hundred seats, so I sent six of our ten flight attendants home and kept four to ensure first-class service for the seventeen passengers.

After we exited the crew bus at the airport, I gathered my crew in the operations lounge for a briefing before the flight to Aqaba, Jordan.

"Tawnee, Inga, Landon, and Arial, I want to thank you for volunteering to continue on. The actors would like the pilots and at least two flight attendants to accompany them on the Petra tour, but you don't have to go if you don't want to."

"I've always wanted to see Petra. Jack said the king will close the site to everyone not on our tour. Soldiers will keep us safe. Count me in." Tawnee smiled with confidence.

"I want to go too," Inga said.

"That means Arial and I can relax at the hotel pool and work on our tans." Landon looked pleased.

"That covers the cabin crew." I glanced at Lance and Pete. "What about you guys? You don't have to go on the tour. I'll babysit the movie stars."

"A stroll through a giant necropolis sounds fun to me. I'm going." Lance grinned and nodded.

"Kidnappers wouldn't dare attack a tour group guarded by the king's soldiers. No way am I missing this little adventure. Hell, we might even end up with cameos in their movie." Pete gave Lance a high five.

I smiled at my six crew members. "All right, let's give them a pleasant flight to Aqaba." I led them out to our Boeing airliner.

Forty-five minutes later, we were airborne for Jordan.

34

THE OLDER SPY READ the printout his protégé had handed him. "Excellent work. I'll call the boss with an update. Want an energy drink?"

"Aye, I've got some extra coins here. Get yourself a coffee."

The older man waved him off. "Thanks, but I'm buying. Keep up the good work. I'll be back in a few minutes."

He walked outside and lit a cigarette. A light rain blew across the Firth of Tay as he huddled under the overhang of the one-story building. He took a few long drags and exhaled little clouds of gray smoke into the brisk, wet air.

This job's a bloody gold mine. Must find a way to keep the big prize for myself.

He pulled out his mobile phone and hit the number designated LES.

Lord Edgar Sweetwater answered on the second ring. "What have you learned about our competition?"

"The men who came after Samantha in Hong Kong and Agra may belong to a secret organization called Black Sun."

"Who are they?"

"I did some research after Samantha sent a text to Professor Armitage warning him about them. Key members of the Nazi leadership established Black Sun around the time of World War II. Some members are reputed to have mental control over Earth's electromagnetic energy, which they call

Vril, a word they took from a sci-fi novel. After the war, they went underground. Their goal is world domination. They must want Poseidon's Sword."

"Did they try to kidnap Samantha because she had the prototype?"

"Aye, they probably think she's the key to locating the ancient weapon."

"Then let's make sure they don't get her. Keep feeding my strike team intel on her activities and schedule so they can stay ahead of the Germans."

"Good thing your men are shadowing her. The SAS team was late to the party in Agra."

"I don't count on the SAS for anything except buggering up my plans."

"They don't have anyone in Jordan; neither do the SEALs. The Black Sun may try to grab her at Petra. I suggest you have a team ready and waiting before she arrives."

"I'll take care of it." Sweetwater hung up.

The spy finished his cigarette and smiled.

After this job, I'll retire in luxury.

35

"THE FUEL TRUCK WILL be there tomorrow morning. It broke down on the way and had to be towed and wait for a part." The Jordanian Air Force general used an apologetic tone.

"This is bad. We want to be gone before the soldiers arrive with that VIP tour."

"You know you can trust me. I believe in your cause. I have always given your flights a military designation and safe passage."

"Yes, but if the soldiers see our airplane—"

"Your command center is safe. The aircraft is parked on the opposite side of the mountains from Petra. No one will see it."

"We trust you to make it so. Keep the faith. *Allahu akbar.*"

The general slipped his cell into his pocket and entered the Jordanian Air Force's command center. He had to be careful. If the king discovered his treachery, his military career would end along with his life.

36

WERNER PACED INSIDE THE Monastery, a dark tomb carved high into the mountain in Petra. With great trepidation, he stepped outside into the sunlight and made a call on his satellite phone.

Master's voice sounded cold. "The Supreme Master has expressed his disappointment. Have you discovered who shot our men in Agra?"

"No, but it may have been a sniper from the Dragon Society. I have a team following their movements now. They have not sent anyone to Petra."

"And you are certain the Golden Twin remains unharmed?"

"*Jawohl*, Master."

"What I must do next pains me. The Supreme Master has ordered this disciplinary measure to remind you of the importance of your mission."

"Master, have mercy on me."

A sound like a tornado roared through Werner's phone as it vibrated in his hand.

"Your failures brought this on you."

Werner felt a tingling sensation across his cheek that abruptly became a searing pain. He screamed as his eardrum ruptured, and blood poured from his nostrils into his mouth. He dropped to his knees, clutched the phone to his ear, and endured the fate he knew he deserved. As the pain ebbed, he heard Master's faint voice.

"Proceed with your mission."

Werner collapsed onto the stone terrace, blood dripping from his nose and ear.

37

I SIPPED HOT TEA in the elegant restaurant of the Hotel Royal in Aqaba with Lance and Pete as we studied the brochure for Petra. "Ross was right about the entrance being a perfect choke point for an attack. It's so narrow the visitors have to walk between towering rock walls for almost a mile."

"Uh oh, look at this." Lance pointed at the brochure. "The king had better send a small army with us."

"Why?" I looked at what he was pointing to. "Damn!"

"Jack Stone assured me we'd have the royal regiment at our disposal." Pete took a sip of steaming coffee. "What's wrong?"

"The brochure describes Petra as 'a rose-red city as old as time.' That was the second part of the Dragon Master's advice about finding my destiny."

"Great! Just when I thought we might have a fun day." Pete shook his head.

Despite the danger, the urge to discover my destiny was strengthening. *Will I need my new pendant in Petra?* "Surely the Royal Guards will prevent another attack."

"It's a long drive from here. I hope soldiers have been assigned to guard our bus too." Pete held up the map to point out our route.

"I heard Jack say it's a bullet-proof bus." Lance signaled the waitress for a refill.

"Well, this is shaping up to be another fun-filled excursion," Pete said. "Maybe they should hand out submachine guns as we board the bus."

"I wish we could've left earlier, but there's no chance of that with our night-owl celebs. Good thing it doesn't get too hot this time of year," I said.

Lance and Pete exchanged conspiratorial glances before Lance turned to me.

"Sam, you know we think the world of you." He hesitated. "Pete and I have talked this over and agree you should call the chief pilot and arrange for someone to replace you in Dubai. If we were the only ones involved, we'd tell you to hang tight, but it's not right to put the passengers and cabin crew at risk."

Pete hastened to add, "We're worried about you, seems like a lot of bad people are out to get you. Let Mr. Tall, Dark, and Scottish protect you in his castle until you get a handle on who's after you and why."

"Guys, I owe you an apology. I never should've allowed this to go so far, but the actors insisted I stay on the trip, and I was eager to learn more about my connection to the artifact and the pendant. It's like a powerful force is driving me. Sorry, I'll call Jeff now."

I called Chief Pilot Jeff Rowlin's office on my cell.

Jeff's secretary, Ruth, answered. "Sam, Jeff had to renew his carrier landing qualifications on a ship in the Mediterranean. He's a fighter pilot in the Navy Reserve and will be gone for a week. Can someone else help you?"

"Um, no, I'll talk to him later. No biggie. Have a nice day, Ruth."

I glanced from Lance to Pete. "Jeff's on an aircraft carrier in the Med for landing re-quals. I'd rather not get into a complicated story with his secretary or crew scheduling. Better to call in sick in Dubai. We'll have three days there, plenty of time to send a replacement captain."

Lance nodded. "That'll work. Now let's focus on keeping you safe until we get to Dubai."

"Thank you. I'm sorry you got dragged into this." I ran my index finger over the trident affixed to the gold pendant and avoided touching the diamond pyramid that had stopped glowing. "I wonder who this was meant for."

"Judging by what's happened, I'd say you." Lance slipped his right hand under the pendant hanging from my neck to study it.

A jolt of energy shot through me when he touched my skin. I shivered and our eyes locked. *Damn.*

Focused on the brochure, Pete missed our inappropriate moment. "Well, at least we won't have to contend with the usual high-pressure salesmen in the Petra souvenir shops, Bedouins selling trinkets, and camel jockeys selling rides. The king ordered the shops closed. He's keeping everyone out of Petra to ensure our security."

"Thank God for small favors. Have the king's guards arrived?" Lance glanced outside.

"I see soldiers standing by the bus. I hope that's not all of them." I counted eight.

A soldier dressed in a crisp uniform adorned with gold braid and medals approached our table. "Excuse me, I am looking for Captain Starr." He looked at Lance and Pete.

"I'm Captain Starr. What can I do for you?"

He lingered on Lance and Pete for confirmation that I was indeed the captain. They grinned and nodded.

"Uh, Captain Starr, I am Captain Mustafa of the Royal Guard. I have been assigned to provide security for your group in Petra. How many people are on the tour?"

"Two flight attendants, two copilots, and I will accompany the three celebrities and their photographer. The rest of their entourage and two flight attendants will remain in Aqaba." I handed him a list of everyone going on the bus. "How many soldiers are coming with us?"

"You will have eight of Jordan's finest Royal Guards." Captain Mustafa glanced at the list. "You may board the bus now." He strode back to his men.

Lance frowned. "What are the chances those pretty boys in their fancy uniforms have ever seen real combat?"

"The Royal Guards are considered the most professional soldiers in the Jordanian Armed Forces." Pete shook his head. "But it looks like they're expecting a cake walk with plenty of photo ops."

"They have MP7 submachine guns and Browning sidearms. If things go south, we may have to *borrow* them." Lance slid his chair back and stood.

Pete and I stood as Carlene strolled up in knee-high riding boots, tight breeches, a low-cut top, and a pith helmet, as if she dressed for a safari movie.

Lance gave her the once-over. "I hope those boots are comfortable because we'll be walking a lot today."

"Don't you worry your handsome self none, sweet cheeks. These boots are custom made and soft as a baby's bottom." Carlene slid between Lance and Pete, reached behind them, and gave their buns a playful squeeze. "Feel free to reciprocate." She giggled.

I picked up my shoulder bag and headed for the bus. Inside, Jack was seated with Inga, the Swedish flight attendant. Hal, the photographer, sat beside Tawnee.

Rod waved and patted the seat next to him. "Hey, Captain! Ready for a fun trip?" He raised a bubbling orange juice. "Care for a mimosa? It's made with Cristal."

"No, thank you, I need a clear mind in case we encounter any surprises today." I stowed my bag in the hat rack and sat next to Rod.

I heard loud giggling as Carlene boarded with Lance and Pete.

A white-coated waiter stopped by my seat. "Would madam like a beverage? We'll have hot croissants ready in a moment."

"Evian water, please." I saw the tour guide board when the waiter walked away.

Captain Mustafa checked that everyone was aboard before sitting in the right front seat. "Driver, you may proceed," he said in a loud, commanding voice.

The tour guide keyed the microphone. "The bus ride is approximately one and a half hours. There are two lavatories in the back behind the galley. A full brunch will be served. Also, snacks, picnic dinners, and two liters of water have been packed in individual backpacks. It is important to keep hydrated while walking. I will pass out the backpacks when we arrive at Petra. Relax and enjoy the trip." He sat opposite Captain Mustafa.

I texted Ross: *We're on the bus on the way to Petra. Eight soldiers from the Royal Guard are aboard. Petra has been closed to vendors and other visitors. I'll contact you when we get back to the hotel. Miss you.*

Rod entertained me with jokes and descriptions of scenes from his new action movie as we drove on the desert highway north to the ancient city that had been carved into solid rock two thousand years ago.

"The movie ends when my badass cop character runs out of bullets and lays some kung fu on the bad guys," Rod said. "Jack and I rescue Carlene, who plays the president's daughter. She's strapped to a nuclear bomb that Jack defuses with two seconds left on the timer, saving Los Angeles from a fiery end. Cool, huh?"

"Way cool." I gave him a high five, thinking he must be a

great actor because he was nothing like his character in the movie.

It was 11:30 in the morning when we arrived at the legendary entrance to Petra.

38

I SHOVED MY HANDBAG into the backpack the guide gave me and slipped it over my shoulders. He gathered us in a semicircle while Captain Mustafa sent two soldiers to check the entrance path.

"We will enter Petra through a long, narrow gorge that slices through the mountain." The guide pointed at where the soldiers had entered.

"It is called the Siq. You will notice that it slants gently downward as it curves through the beautiful, rose-colored sandstone. Take your time and enjoy the lovely tableau of natural images on the towering walls. We will proceed as soon as Captain Mustafa gives us permission," the guide said.

Lance leaned in and whispered, "Would you believe neither of those dickwads looked up when they entered the Siq?"

"I noticed. Forget about the colorful patterns along the way. Let's hurry our people through the choke point. They can admire the massive façade of the Treasury after we exit the gorge. We'll be in an open area where we can scan the rocks."

I looked up at the imposing mountain standing sentinel over the Siq. It was an ideal place for attackers to look down on unsuspecting tourists and launch an ambush.

The advance soldiers trotted out of the entrance and assured their captain all was well. Mustafa waved us forward as he led the way with soldiers walking in front and behind us.

The gorge was dark and silent. Faint light penetrated from the narrow opening overhead.

Carlene's snarky Texan accent echoed off the rock walls. "Ooo, it's dark and creepy. Stay close, honey buns." She latched onto Lance's arm.

The group proceeded slowly, frequently stopping to study the colorful designs that flowed over the rock walls. Hal took lots of flash photos.

Tawnee squeezed Pete's arm. "It's so dark. Hope there's no snakes or scorpions on this long trail."

Pete glanced up and answered in a loud voice. "No, but we'd better hurry along before a giant camel spider drops down on us. I heard they have webs up high stretched between the walls where we can't see them."

Women within earshot started a stampede, dragging the men with them. We passed through the Siq in record time. *Kudos, Pete.*

The soldiers rushed to retake the lead when Carlene and Tawnee pushed past them with Lance and Pete. Hal stopped shooting pictures to join the rush.

Rod jogged beside me. He kept looking up for spiders while I searched for snipers.

Jack tapped him on the back. "Rod, why are we running?"

"A shitload of big-ass camel spiders are up in webs, waiting to drop on us. Could be hundreds of 'em. We got to get outta here!" His voice raised two octaves.

Inga and Jack bolted around us and left us at the tail end. Two soldiers lagged about fifty yards behind us in a fast walk.

Rod grabbed my hand and pulled me into a run. "Hurry! Stragglers are always the first to die!"

It was all I could do to keep up with Rod's long legs. That man could turn on the speed. We burst into the sun-drenched clearing and gasped for breath.

The magnificent mausoleum known as the Treasury towered before us. Visions of *Indiana Jones and the Last Crusade* filled my head. I pulled a water bottle out of my backpack and took a long drink.

The guide caught his breath and looked at our group like we were from Mars. "You certainly are a lively group, but you must pace yourselves, or you will be too tired to complete the tour. And drink plenty of water. The desert air is quite dehydrating." He wiped his brow and pointed.

"Our first stop in the ancient necropolis is this tomb believed to be the resting place of a Nabatean king. It is called the Treasury because the giant urn at the top was rumored to be full of gold coins. Bedouins who fired bullets at it eventually realized it was made of solid rock. Visitors are not allowed inside the Treasury, but since this is a special VIP tour, you may enter." He led the group up the steps.

Lance and Pete slipped away from Carlene and Tawnee and stood beside me. They shot annoyed glances at the guards.

"Those guards are focused on watching the women. They're about as useless as tits on my daddy's prize bull." Lance shook his head.

"We should each stand near a soldier throughout the day so we can grab a weapon if we need one." I turned to Pete. "Brilliant tactic with the camel-spider BS."

Pete grinned. "Whatever works. It got us out of the Siq in a hurry." He looked around. "There are hundreds of places to hide in this town. Germans with guns could be anywhere."

"Pete's right. I don't think an entire regiment could defend us here. The enemy would have too many options. They could easily ambush us almost anywhere inside Petra with all the narrow paths, caves, open tombs, cliffs, and gorges. I have a bad feeling about this." Lance thrust his hands on his hips.

I nodded. "Captain Mustafa isn't about to accept suggestions from us. If we tell him we don't feel safe here and want to leave, he'll take it as an insult."

Pete turned to Lance. "Sam's right. We're stuck here for the day. No way will the soldiers lose face by letting us call the shots."

"I don't have a cell signal, so I assume the emergency signal on my watch won't work either. Not that it matters. Ross told me the SEALs and SAS don't have teams in Jordan. We're on our own."

"Then let's get this show on the road and hope for the best." Lance walked into the Treasury.

After inspecting the cool interior, we followed the guide outside and walked along the Street of Façades. I looked from side to side, expecting men to jump out from the dark tombs. The awe inspiring beauty of the ancient city was eclipsed by my growing sense of danger.

Carlene strolled up, clutching Lance's hand. "This place is more awesome than the little Grand Canyon in southwestern Texas."

I faced her. "Thanks again for helping us out at the Taj. Can I count on you if those Germans show up here?"

Carlene's smile evaporated. She glanced around with a look of concern. "Do you really think they might come here? Why would they do that?" She looked up at Lance.

Lance's facial expression was all business. "Same reason as last time, whatever that was. The soldiers aren't here for show, but they may as well be. If men like the ones who attacked us in Agra try again here, we might have to fend for ourselves. We could use an experienced shooter."

"Darlin', I don't have a weapon, do you?" She glanced from Lance to me.

"Our plan is to stick close to the soldiers and *borrow* their weapons if necessary. I know it sounds lame, but we don't have a lot of options. These fancy boys don't exactly inspire confidence." I nodded toward three soldiers leering at the pretty flight attendants.

Tawnee and Pete joined us as we continued through the vast site, posing for photos along the way.

After five hours of touring the necropolis and posing for pictures, our group reached the wide-open temple area in the central part of the city. We waited for an hour as Hal shot more pictures there.

Finally, the guide led us to tables and benches.

"We'll stop here for a nice picnic dinner. Your meals are in your backpacks." The guide pulled off his backpack and sat on a bench.

The group settled down at the tables, and Hal snapped pictures of everyone eating and chatting while I stepped away to find one of the chemical toilets. I used one among the rocks on a curving path near the picnic area.

When I exited the toilet, I heard the staccato blasts of automatic weapons reverberating off the towering mountains.

39

EARLIER, LANCE WHISPERED TO Carlene, "Maybe we should've sat with the soldiers. They're at the outermost tables where their weapons are beyond our reach." He caught Pete's eye and nodded at the Royal Guard.

"Relax, sugar, I don't think anyone will bother us way out here." Carlene patted his knee.

While the soldiers were occupied pulling food from their backpacks, commandos sneaked in from the rocks behind them.

Lance looked up from his meal too late. "Look out! Get under the tables!" He pulled Carlene down and crouched over her.

The intruders fired their MP7s into the back of the Royal Guards' heads before they had a chance to respond. In seconds, all the Jordanian soldiers were dead.

Pete and Tawnee ducked under a table. Jack, Inga, and Rod followed their lead. The tour guide panicked and tried to run away, screaming in his native tongue. His head exploded in a hail of bullets.

Hal, in the midst of snapping photos, made the mistake of pointing the camera at the attackers. He was shot before his finger could press the button.

Tawnee screamed and rushed to help Hal. A dark-haired beauty, she fell dead beside him with a bullet in her forehead.

Silence descended upon the group. Nobody moved. The desert air hung heavy with fear.

Men speaking German to each other interrupted the morbid stillness.

"Come out slowly, hands on heads," a man said in a heavy German accent.

The tour group eased out from under the stone tables. Five men in desert combat fatigues with Kevlar vests pointed automatic weapons at everyone. The commandos removed plastic zip ties from their cargo pockets and secured their prisoners.

The leader scanned the stunned group and focused on blond-haired Inga. "Are you Captain Starr? Answer or be killed by Black Sun."

Inga shook with fright. "No, she, uh, st-stepped away to the toilet."

"Which toilet?" The leader glared at her.

"I, uh, I don't know. I think she went that way." Inga nodded to her right.

The leader turned to one of his men. "Find her."

40

HIDDEN IN THE ROCKS, I watched the bloody scene in horror. Eleven dead, including one from my crew. I had to do something. I saw the leader send a man in my direction.

I need his weapons.

The element of surprise was my best ally, so I perched on a boulder where I could jump on him when he rounded the corner. I lifted a heavy rock that required two hands.

When the German commando walked past my hiding place, I pounced on him from behind and smashed his head. The sickening sound of his skull cracking open made me cringe.

Bone shards and brains splattered the rock as he landed on his face. Blood spread around his head like a crimson halo.

I took a few deep breaths and swallowed the bile rising from my stomach. Mike's account of the first time he killed someone during a SEAL mission flashed in my head. *"Taking a human life changed me forever."*

God, now I understood what he meant. Although I was justified, this violence would haunt me. I didn't have the luxury of contemplation. Time was critical.

I clipped his pistol holster to my belt at my right hip and his sheathed knife on my left. After slipping the MP7 strap over my shoulder, I dragged the body behind the rocks and covered the blood-soaked sand.

Someone would come looking for us. I returned to my vantage point and saw three men fanning out for a search while the fourth guarded the group.

My plan was to create a diversion so I could run in and rescue my people.

Someone else did it for me.

I turned around and found two Germans flanking me, their weapons ready to fire.

Two loud shots echoed through the canyon.

The men fell backward with massive bullet holes in their heads. I grabbed their submachine guns and another knife and ran for cover.

As I snaked through the rocks, looking for a spot to launch an attack on the soldier guarding the group, I heard him shouting, "Shots fired. Four men missing. Target not with group. What are your orders?"

A voice crackled over his radio, "Secure the target. We must take her alive and unharmed. Eliminate the others."

The other searcher returned to the picnic area. I wasn't expecting their next move.

The two commandos bolted down a path behind the picnic tables and vanished.

I took my chances, ran to Lance, and cut his plastic cuff and then Carlene's. I gave him a knife and handed the pistol to Carlene. Pulling out my other knife, I rushed to free Pete and the others.

"Pull on your backpacks and grab the guns. Hurry!" I shoved the dead soldiers' weapons into the hands of the terrified actors and my crew.

Lance pointed. "Let's go for the high ground. The stairs to the Monastery are that way. Follow me!" He ran into the narrow trail leading to hundreds of stone steps.

I turned to ensure everyone in our group was with us. Inga

froze in fear. Jack's male protective instinct must have kicked in because he grabbed Inga's hand and yanked her forward. Carlene was right behind Lance and Pete, and Rod ran so close to me I almost tripped over him.

The steep climb to the massive mausoleum loomed ahead. Our adrenaline surged. We leaped up the steps, taking two at a time. As we climbed higher, the incline and exertion slowed our pace.

I looked behind us and spotted two commandos following at a distance.

Lance stopped. "I see two Black Sun soldiers at the top." He turned and noted the two men below us. "We're trapped with no cover."

"Maybe not." My head tingled like it had in Hong Kong. I spotted a trail near the holy spring and felt a force draw me there. "This way!"

I led the group through a narrow cleft in the rock face. Thirty feet back, it dead-ended. I rubbed my hands over the rock, hoping for a miracle. My right hand found a soft indented area full of dirt that made my hand tingle like it had at the Taj Mahal when I found the pendant. The spot was six feet up.

"We're trapped! They're coming!" Rod shrieked.

"Quiet, I'm working on a solution." I spoke with a confident commanding tone to calm everyone. "Just a few more seconds."

I dug out the dirt with my fingernails. The sun glinted off a gold square about the size of my pendant. Outlines of a trident and inverted pyramid were recessed inside it.

I wiped the square with my shirtsleeve and pushed the pendant into the gold square.

It fit perfectly.

A grinding noise preceded a solid-rock door opening inward beneath the gold square. I peeked inside down a long passageway. Gun shots and men shouting behind us made the decision for me.

"In here. Hurry!" I waved everyone into the passage.

Carlene's pith helmet fell off as people jostled her running for the entrance. She yanked Lance's hand. "My hat!"

"Forget it!" Lance dragged her into the passage.

I pulled the pendant out of the door lock and rushed inside. The stone door closed behind me. We were now in absolute darkness.

Another dark tunnel like the one in Scotland. Damn.

41

SWEETWATER'S STRIKE TEAM WAS perched atop a plateau in Petra known as the High Place of Sacrifice. Using binoculars and sniper scopes, they scanned the stone stairs leading up to the Monastery mausoleum.

"Looks like we killed all the Black Sun. Samantha's group ran into a narrow gap in the mountain near the holy spring. They haven't come out yet." The team leader turned to his best sniper. "Can you see them on your scope?"

The sniper adjusted his range. "No movement near the cleft. According to our site map, there's no other way out."

"Stay on it." The leader of Sweetwater's mercenaries stood between the snipers.

Ten minutes later, the leader scanned the ancient city one last time. "All right, gentlemen, let's head for the chopper. We'll fly over the holy spring on the way out and verify Blondie is safe with her group."

The strike team climbed into a sand-colored Bell 206B Jet Ranger and flew over the stairs to the Monastery. The chopper hovered above the narrow crevasse.

One of the team's snipers adjusted his scope as he searched the area. "I see a pith helmet on the ground at the dead end. No tour group. No Samantha."

"She must've found a hiding place in the mountain. The threat has been neutralized. Best we bug out before the king sends his army to look for them." The leader tapped the pilot. "Let's go."

42

EARLIER IN THE TOUR bus, Ahmed woke in his reclined driver's seat to the sound of distant gunfire. Thirty minutes before, he had awakened from a sound sleep thinking he heard gun shots. But when he listened, there was silence. He assumed it had been a dream and fell back to sleep. Now he realized the shots were real.

He rushed outside and heard a few more shots. Then silence. He reached into his pocket. No mobile phone. *Must've left it in the charger.*

His heart pounded as he strained to listen. He focused on the entrance to the Siq, expecting the tour group to come running out. Instead he heard the thundering blades of a helicopter. He glimpsed the sand-colored chopper for a few seconds before it disappeared behind a peak.

Ahmed bolted for the bus. The chef and waiter were snoring in the back. They wore ear buds connected to MP-3 players.

"Wake up!" He stood in the aisle between them and tapped their heads.

The men looked confused. They pulled out their ear buds and checked the time.

"What? Did we oversleep?" the chef asked.

"I heard gunfire inside Petra. Give me your phone. I must call for help."

"We do not have phones. Only the guide and driver may carry phones. Use yours." The waiter looked annoyed.

"I left mine at home in the charger." Ahmed ran to the driver's seat.

He drove into the nearby village of Wadi Musa to a café. The proprietor looked disappointed when he exited the bus with only two men.

Ahmed ran to the owner. "I need your phone. My tour group is under attack in Petra!"

The shocked man pulled his phone out of his pocket. "Take it. What can I do to help?"

"Find the village policeman. The attackers have guns." Ahmed called 191 and was connected to the nearest big city, which was Aqaba. "I am the bus driver for a private VIP tour. They were alone in Petra when I heard many gun shots. I saw a helicopter fly away. None of my people came out."

The village police officer ran inside with the café owner. "Tell me what happened." He glanced from Ahmed to the two men with him.

Ahmed finished his emergency call and said, "I brought nine VIPs to Petra for a private tour. The guide and eight soldiers from the Royal Guard accompanied them."

"Ah, so that is why the site was closed to vendors. Go on." The local policeman stood with his hands on his hips.

Ahmed repeated what he had just told the Aqaba police. "I didn't have a phone, so I drove here to call for help." He glanced at his coworkers for support.

They nodded in agreement.

"What will the Aqaba police do?" The lone police officer looked concerned.

"They are sending police cars from Aqaba and soldiers in helicopters. The soldiers will arrive first. I was instructed to wait here. It will be at least forty-five minutes before the soldiers arrive. Are you going into Petra?"

"I must not abandon my post. The armed intruders may come to my village." The cop wiped his brow.

Ahmed called the tour company. His boss said he would call the king's office.

43

HIDDEN INSIDE THE MONASTERY, Werner had seen his men shot with lightning-fast speed. They fell off the steep cliff steps into the rocks a few hundred feet below.

Who attacked us?

He scanned Petra with powerful binoculars and spotted the strike team on a high perch opposite the Monastery.

Bastards!

Werner waited until he saw the killers fly away in a helicopter. He made a note of the tail number.

Her group disappeared near the holy spring. Must find her.

He headed down the stone steps in the dark shadow of the mountain as the sun dropped behind the summit.

Halfway down, he stopped by the holy spring and listened. No sounds of people. He crept into a dark narrow cleft, expecting to see frightened people huddled against the mountain. Instead, he saw a solitary pith helmet.

Werner shined a flashlight on the rock wall and spotted the gold square. He scrolled through pictures on his mobile sent to him when his men captured Samantha at the Taj Mahal. Her pendant resembled the square in front of him.

Must be the key that opens this mountain. She truly is the Golden Twin.

Trying to beat the arrival of the king's soldiers, he hurried to his Humvee hidden in a dry river bed to begin the grim task of collecting his dead comrades.

A half hour later, he returned to the river bed with his headlights off. Wearing night-vision goggles, he vanished into the night with his macabre cargo.

44

I TOOK A DEEP breath. *Don't panic.* In Scotland, young Charlie had talked me through my claustrophobia when we crawled through that dark tunnel cave. Now I had six people depending on me.

I could really use some chocolate.

My group pulled out their cell phones to illuminate the area. I rubbed the diamond pyramid on my pendant and slipped the chain over my neck. The diamond lit up like a halogen lamp. I pulled off my backpack and took out a small halogen flashlight and my night-vision binoculars from my handbag.

"Okay, we're safe in here. I have the key." I checked faces for signs of panic as I slipped the NV-binoculars' strap around my neck. "Turn off your cell phones and save the battery in case we get a chance to use them later."

Anxious faces stared back at me. Inga had a death grip on Jack, and Rod looked panicky. Carlene was plastered against Lance and Pete. Everyone huddled in shock.

"Captain, are we trapped? I don't want to die in here." Rod's voice was shaky.

"We're okay. Let me squeeze past you and check our escape route." I slid sideways along the rock wall and barely made it past everyone.

"I can't believe we lost Hal and Tawnee," Carlene said,

sniffling. She pulled a tissue from her pocket.

"The murder of our people, the tour guide, and the soldiers was horrific, but we have to put it out of our minds for now. We'll grieve later. First, we have to survive." I sighed.

My light revealed a narrow passage that seemed to stretch into infinity. I had never been good in dark closed spaces. Venturing into the mountain seemed way too scary. I realized my judgment was clouded by claustrophobia and the shock of having seen people murdered, especially the one I killed.

"What do you guys think we should do?" I glanced from Lance to Pete.

Lance spoke first. "We should follow this passage and see where it leads. It's only a matter of time before those Black Sun bastards blast their way in here and come after us."

Pete nodded to me. "I agree. A rock wall won't stop them for long. A few well-placed explosives and they'll be in here. Let's forge ahead."

"Do we have any spelunkers here?" I searched their faces.

"I've explored many caves around the world." Jack's deep British voice resonated in the stone passage.

"Good, you know what dangers to look for. Come up front with me." I waved him forward.

Jack recovered as he switched to his action-hero persona and swaggered up to me. "Right, ladies and gents, stay close together and proceed slowly."

"Wait, we need to secure the weapons. A gunshot could ricochet off the rock and kill somebody." I shined my light on the group. "I want everyone, except Carlene and my copilots, to sling the submachine guns across their backs."

Jack had a defiant look in his eyes. "I served in the Royal Navy. You can trust me with a weapon."

"Have you seen combat?"

"No combat, but I'm a damn good shot. Hardly ever miss."

"I'll count on your help if we come under attack."

I watched Lance and Pete help Inga and Rod sling their weapons behind them. "All right, let's go."

I shined my light down the infinite passageway. Our group of seven walked as close together as possible. Reflected light off the smooth rock walls and ceiling provided dim light while our path was bathed in the bright light of the flashlight and pendant.

The passage was so narrow we had to walk single file in many places. Jack stayed close to me and kept an eye out for danger signs.

As we ventured deeper, I felt like I was suffocating as the walls seemed to close in on me. My heart raced, and I felt short of breath even though we were walking down a slight incline. Claustrophobic panic hovered in the back of my mind.

Get a grip! Can't let my group see me lose it. Slow, deep breaths. Charlie would love this. If a twelve-year-old can do this, so can I.

It wasn't long before some members of the group started whining.

"How far are we going? My feet are tired," Inga said in a heavier Swedish accent than she normally used.

"What if there's no way out? We're going deeper into the mountain." Rod sounded scared. "We could get lost and starve to death. Or maybe we'll die of thirst. I want some Cristal."

Carlene surprised me. "Settle down and stop your whinin' right now. Our captain figured out how to open the mountain and save us. She'll find the way out."

"Carlene's right," Lance said. "In fact, we don't want a fast exit. We want to put plenty of distance between us and our enemies. Better to come out far from Petra."

"Uh, Captain," Jack said, "where did you get that pendant that opened the door?"

"A curio shop in Hong Kong," I lied.

"Don't worry about the details." Pete spoke in a reassuring tone. "We're safe now, and every step is taking us further from our attackers. Sam will lead us out of here when the time's right. Keep going."

Screw my claustrophobia! These people need me. No way will I let them down.

The sound of running water grew louder, and the passage opened into a large cavern. A waterfall flowed into a twenty-foot wide pool that fed a stream. The path narrowed as it curved around the pool. The air felt warm and moist from the falling water.

I signaled a stop. "This is the same fresh water that feeds the holy spring. I read about it in the Petra tour book. It's a hot spring, but the water's pure. We should refill our water bottles."

I slipped off my backpack and pulled out two one-liter bottles. One was empty, the other less than half full. I stretched out on my belly to fill them.

After everyone was finished, we rested. The fruit in our backpacks tasted refreshing.

"Since we don't know how long we'll be on our own, we should ration our food. Save as much as possible. We'll have plenty of water from the underground stream." The water amplified my voice as the high cavern eased my claustrophobia.

The path angled up as it circled the pool. Jack led the way and stopped halfway around. "The path is too narrow ahead. We'll have to switch our weapons and backpacks to our chests and walk sideways."

When I slipped my pack and MP7 over my ample chest, I realized balance could be an issue for the women. "Everyone hold hands until we're past the water."

Jack led and held my left hand. Lance was on my right. The women positioned themselves between the men so each could hold a man's hand. We side stepped toward the open area at the far side of the pool.

Before we reached the wide floor, Carlene screamed.

The wet rocks under her leather soles had caused her to slip over the edge. The same thing happened to Inga a second later.

"Lance, help!" Carlene yelled.

"Pete!" Inga squeezed his hand and kicked her feet against the vertical lip.

"I've got you, and Pete's got Inga. Up you go, Carlene." Lance gripped her hand and hoisted her onto the ledge.

Pete yanked Inga up before her feet touched the water. The group waited for the ladies to recover.

"Lance, darlin', I owe you big time. Thanks for savin' me." Carlene tried to kiss him, but he was too tall, and their packs got in the way.

"You're my hero, Pete." Inga squeezed his hand. "Now let's get the hell off this ledge."

Soon we all faced a new problem. Beyond the high cavern, the path split into three passages. Each looked endless in the dark. I took a deep breath as my mind searched for a solution.

"Shit, what the hell do we do now?" Rod said.

"Look for a trident symbol. It may be carved into the rock floor, a wall, or up high." I shined my flashlight on every surface of all three entrances.

"I don't see no tridents!" Rod shouted.

"Why are we looking for tridents?" Carlene asked.

Everyone looked at me.

"Because the key that opened the mountain has a trident. Could be another trident marks the correct passage. Move to one side so I can take in the big-picture view." I eased back to the edge of the pool and shined my light above the openings.

I studied the cavern ceiling. *What am I missing?* Then I saw it. I sighed with relief and pointed.

"We're taking the trail on the right under that stalactite that looks like an inverted trident. They don't normally form like that. It has to be our sign." I walked into the passage and waited for Jack to join me.

"Sure hope you're right about them tridents," Rod said.

We walked deeper into the dark mountain. I had no idea what might lie ahead, but anything seemed better than what we had left behind. Navigating the dark passages distracted them from the violent encounter with the Black Sun.

A strange scuffling noise came from the passage in front of us.

"Everyone stop and be quiet. I heard something." I listened.

"What is it? I don't hear nothing," Rod said.

"Shut the hell up and listen." Jack turned and glared at him.

My light faintly illuminated numerous four-inch yellow objects on the ground twenty yards away.

"I'm going to point my light behind me so I can scan the area ahead with the night-vision binoculars."

I soon realized what was scrabbling toward us: a horde of deadly yellow scorpions.

I forgot I was an airline captain as my screams echoed in the dark passageway.

45

WHEN THE KING HEARD about the attack, he sent elite paratroopers from the Royal Guard. They floated into the dark, ancient city in the early evening, fifteen minutes after Werner disappeared into the desert. Wearing night-vision gear, the jumpers converged on the open temple area in the center of the necropolis.

The major stowed his chute and addressed his men. "I want Saeed and Khaled on point with me. Wal and Yaseen, take high positions." He nodded at the rest of his team. "You three, cover our six. Check in every five minutes."

His men moved in silence through the stone ruins. The major approached the picnic area and ducked behind a rock. Bodies littered the ground.

He switched to infrared and spoke into his throat mike. "Eleven bodies in the picnic area near the temple. Weak heat signatures. Must have been the first killed. Meet me behind the rocks near the picnic tables." He noticed eight of the dead were wearing Jordanian military uniforms.

Royal Guard soldiers approached from several directions.

The major studied the remains of his eight soldiers. "Looks like they were killed with double taps to the head. Someone took their weapons." He scanned the ground around the tables.

"Sir, the VIPs must have been kidnapped. I found the tour guide's body. It's over here face-down near the snack hut.

Multiple head shots. Same with the photographer and a woman over there." The soldier pointed at the bodies.

"Check the pictures on the camera. Maybe he took shots of the attackers." The major made a call on his SATCOM. "We have eleven bodies—eight soldiers, a photographer, a woman, and the tour guide. What's the ETA for the dogs? Good. Area is not secure."

He turned to his men. "Dogs in thirty. Leave the dead. The police will deal with the crime scene. We must find the tour group. Let's move." He stowed his satellite phone and followed the trail to the Monastery steps.

Thirty minutes later, the major received a radio call. "Sir, dog teams have arrived."

"Lead them to the picnic area. Maybe they will pick up an escape trail. Keep me posted."

The major and his point men began climbing up the stairs to the Monastery tomb. He soon heard excited barks. He looked back and spotted dogs racing up the steps.

One of his men spoke into his headset. "Sir, the dogs found a place near the picnic area where more than one person bled out. The blood soaked into the sand by some rocks."

"No bodies?" The major watched the dogs approach.

"No corpses, but lots of blood. Enough for two or three people. The dogs are following a trail that seems to lead to the Monastery."

"The enemy could be hiding there with the tour group. I want five men with me. I'll hold back the dogs. Get here double time." The major gestured to the handler to stop.

The handler yanked the leads and halted. The dogs sniffed and barked at a spot nearby as he shined a light on the step. "Looks like it could be blood. I'll mark it for the forensics team."

When the three backup soldiers arrived, the major and his

men urged the dogs up the steps. Near the side trail for the holy spring, the dog team found another bloody spot.

"This blood could mean tour members were wounded while climbing the steps. Not enough blood to indicate mortal wounds," the soldier said.

"Unless the wounds caused them to fall off the stairs to their deaths. Call the other dog team to search the rocks below." The major looked down into the dark shadows.

It wasn't long before the major received another radio call.

"Sir, the dogs have found several places where bodies bled out on the rocks," a soldier reported.

"How many places?" The major hoped it wasn't the seven VIPs.

"Four areas, but we did not find bodies."

"We are about to search the Monastery. Keep looking." The major led his men into the ancient mausoleum carved high up into the mountain.

The soldiers crept through every nook of the rock tomb even though the dogs showed no interest. They were drawn to the outer terrace where drops of blood had dried on the stone.

The major stepped outside and looked down on Petra, which had become a beehive of activity. A large detachment of soldiers had begun searching, their flashlights illuminating hundreds of possible hiding places.

A forensic unit and coroner from the Aqaba police had erected a tent for a temporary morgue. Their officers gathered blood samples from the sites the dog handlers had marked.

Helicopters covered the vast area with their bright spotlights. Their rotor blades thundered inside the valley.

The major called the central command tent in the temple area. "Lieutenant, give me a sit rep. Have we found anyone?"

"Negative, sir. The bus driver reported seeing a helicopter fly out of Petra, but it didn't look big enough to carry seven

VIPs and the kidnappers. Based on the blood, there should be more bodies. The dogs have not found them."

"Four people were shot on the Monastery steps halfway up. I will concentrate my search there." The major signaled his men to gather as the dog handler stood nearby with the dogs. "We will search the area around the holy spring. Look for clues, anything that might help us find the tour group."

The soldiers followed the dogs back to where the blood had been found. The dogs trotted into a narrow cleft, their barks echoing off the rock walls.

"In here!" the handler yelled.

The major pushed past two soldiers and stopped behind the dogs that were barking and scratching at the rock where the path dead-ended.

"Well?" the major asked.

The handler pulled the dogs back so the major could see the pith helmet on the ground next to the mountain. "Look at this." He pointed at the helmet and then to the square indentation in the rock with the trident and inverted pyramid indents embedded in gold.

The major picked up the helmet and detected faint perfume. He shined his light on the square, and the gold gleamed. He scanned the surrounding area and found only solid rock. Then his radio crackled with another call.

"Major, we found tire tracks in a *wadi* at the south end of the city. The tracks lead into the desert. Looks like a Humvee."

"Send a helicopter to follow the tracks. A Humvee only holds eight, not big enough for the tour group and their kidnappers. Perhaps some left in the Humvee, and the rest flew out in the helicopter the bus driver reported."

The soldiers continued searching through the night, but no trace of the tour group was found.

Earlier in the day, a report of the attack reached the media after the bus driver called 191. It grew to international news when soldiers found blood but none of the VIPs.

Television and Internet news sites repeated the lead story: Sir Lady Samantha Starr and movie stars Jack Stone, Carlene Jensen, and Rod Rogan vanished with three air crew in Petra. Eight Royal Guard soldiers, a photographer, a flight attendant, and a tour guide were murdered.

46

MATT CALLED ROSS AT the SAS base.

Ross answered his mobile. "Hey, Matt, I guess you got my email about Sam. Her tour group vanished in Petra earlier today."

"No shit, it's all over the news! Have you heard from Interpol or the Jordanian authorities?" Tension tinged Matt's voice.

"Aye, a helicopter was seen leaving Petra, and they found Humvee tracks. Neither had the capacity to hold Sam's group and an unknown number of kidnappers."

"Could have divided the group, took the most valuable hostages in the chopper. Did they get a radar track on them?"

"The chopper flew under radar, and the Humvee vanished across the border. Sam's DARPA watch stopped sending a signal in Petra." Ross cleared his throat. "Uh, Matt, there's something else. They found evidence that six or seven people bled out, but they couldn't find their bodies."

"Sonofabitch! That means only one or two might still be alive. Do you think Nicolai attacked them?" Matt's voice telegraphed his anguish.

"He hasn't been spotted since your sister tossed him off the cliff in the Highlands. If she hadn't heard his voice on that mobile call to Lord Sweetwater during the royal ball at

Buckingham Palace, we wouldn't know he's still alive."

"That and the eyeball he sent her later."

"Aye, Nicolai's known for his eyeball collection."

"So who did this?"

"I think the same group that attacked her in Hong Kong and Agra is responsible. Could be the Black Sun, not sure. She said she found an ancient weapon, and they want it. Does Mike know about Sam?"

"He's out on a mission. I'll tell him when he gets back. What did she do with the weapon? She can't carry it with her on the airliner."

"She sent it to a university professor. Do you know who that might be?" Ross tried to sound hopeful.

"Professor Ben Armitage at Harvard. He's an expert on antiquities and a friend of our family. I'll call him. Maybe he knows who's behind Sam's kidnapping."

"Brilliant. Call me when you know something. I'll do the same."

Matt called Ben. The professor answered on the third ring.

"Matt? It's been a long time. How are you?"

"Not so good. Sam vanished with a small group in Petra today. Any chance you know who was after her?" Matt tried to keep his voice even.

"I heard about her on the news. I was hoping you called to tell me she's safe. She mentioned a group called the Black Sun, said they attacked her in Hong Kong."

"Who the hell's the Black Sun?"

"Prominent Nazis who belong to a secret cult that went underground after World War II. Their goal is to harness Earth's electromagnetic energy, which they call Vril, and use the power for world domination."

"What does that have to do with Sam?" Matt felt frustrated.

"She found what may be the prototype for a doomsday weapon called Poseidon's Sword and shipped it to me from Hong Kong. The weapon is thought to have been invented by scientists in Atlantis."

"Atlantis? Seriously?"

"I carbon dated it. It's eleven thousand years old. It almost burned down my house."

"Shit! Why does my sister have to be such a freaking danger magnet? A doomsday weapon? That's just great!" Matt tried to rein in his emotions. "But if you have the weapon, why do they want her?"

"I think they need her to activate it. The crystals lit up when she touched them. They were still glowing when I received the artifact next-day air freight."

"But that's just the prototype. Where's Poseidon's Sword?" Matt's tone betrayed his concern.

"Ancient scrolls say it's hidden at the intersection of powerful ley lines. Maybe they think she knows where it is."

"What the hell's a ley line?"

"Ley lines, also called dragon currents, are lines of concentrated electromagnetic energy that crisscross the Earth. Ancient temples were built on their intersections. In fact, Petra is located on one."

"Got it. Are you aware the women in our bloodline have psychic powers? Some call it the second sight. Sam started seeing visions a few months ago, usually in her dreams."

"Psychic power is filled with electromagnetic energy. Sam's energy must be the right frequency to switch on the weapon."

"Great, millions of people on the planet, but *my* sister has the exact frequency needed to activate an ancient weapon. What are the odds? Shit! Sorry, Professor. It's just that I'm really worried about her."

"I am too, but Sam has survived many dangerous

situations. Just because she disappeared in Petra doesn't mean the Black Sun took her. She may have evaded them. That city is two thousand years old. Maybe she found a secret passage. Eighty-five percent of the city is still undiscovered, buried long ago in a major earthquake. My money's on Sam, especially since her energy's in synch with whatever the ancients may have hidden there."

"I hope you're right. She seems to have vanished without a trace." Mike sighed. "Please call me if you learn anything new. Watch your back, Prof. They may come for you next."

"Will do, Matt. Keep me in the loop. I'll keep looking for anything that might help. And please, be careful."

47

MATT GAZED AT THE lights on the massive U.S. aircraft carrier anchored in the harbor in Naples, Italy and wondered if he should alert SOCOM about Poseidon's Sword and the Black Sun. *Either they'll help rescue Sam or bring a shit storm down on her.*

He called Ross and filled him in on everything Armitage had told him. Matt cleared his throat. "Um, there's something else you should know. My mom has psychic abilities, and Sam recently acquired them too."

"What exactly do you mean by *psychic abilities*?"

"They see visions, usually of future events. It runs on the female side of the family, but don't worry. They're not witches."

Matt felt it was important for Ross to have all the facts. "The professor thinks Sam may have eluded capture using her psychic talent to find a hidden passage."

"Nothing about Sam surprises me anymore. I hope the professor's right. If she hid with her group inside the mountain, her watch signal would've been blocked. But why didn't she come out when the soldiers arrived?"

"Who knows? I hope to hell they didn't get lost in there." Matt paced as he talked.

"If they did, we can find them with dogs, assuming we can locate the entrance. Are you aboard ship?"

"No, I'm calling from Naples. We ship out tonight. Then

I'm back on flight duty. You can reach me via email. Just be careful what you say."

"I haven't told anyone about Sam's discovery or the group that's after her."

"I'm debating whether to tell the captain of the *USS Lawrence Lee* about my sister and the search for an ancient doomsday weapon by some Nazi cult called Black Sun. Shit, what do you think?"

"Hold off. You're on the newest and largest nuclear-powered carrier in the U.S. fleet. Your skipper has the power to help us or make us wish we'd never been born. Let's sort this out. We don't want Sam in the crosshairs of the military, and we'd bloody well best not mention Nazis and doomsday weapons."

"You're right. We should be damn certain before we bring the military into the loop." Matt sighed.

"I managed to get a copy of the manifest for Sam's flight. Do you know anything about her two copilots, Lance Bowie and Pete Winston? Can she count on them in combat?" Ross's voice sounded tight with tension.

"Lance was her copilot last June when the bombs exploded onboard. He's former military. I think she said he flew fighters in the Air Force. He's solid. Pete's in the Air National Guard. He flew warthogs in Iraq. Yeah, Sam can count on both of them."

"The British movie star served in the Royal Navy. His father is Admiral John Stone, commander of the British fleet," Ross said. "He's pressuring the prime minister to send a SAS team into Jordan. He wants his son rescued. I don't know anything about the other celebrities, Carlene Jensen and Rod Rogan."

"Carlene Jensen's a Texas girl. She won a pistol-shooting championship. I could be wrong, but I think Rod Rogan's a typical Hollywood poser. You know, great with jokes and acting, but I wouldn't count on him in a fire fight."

"That means Sam has only four people she can count on. Wait a minute, what about the flight attendant?" Ross named Inga and sounded hopeful.

"When I saw Sam on a layover in Barcelona, she got me a date with Inga. She's Swedish and seems like the sort who'd remain calm in an emergency. She's a trained crew member and should be solid." Matt felt better after discussing things with Ross. "Try to let me know if you get sent in to look for Sam's group."

"I'll do what I can. Keep me in the loop from your end. Uh, Matt, one more thing, have you told Loren?"

"No, not yet. Mom's in Scotland with Duncan. Do you have time to stop by his castle to explain everything? My cell's battery is about to die."

"Aye, I'll take care of it."

Matt slipped his cell into his pocket.

Where are you, Sam? Somewhere safe, I hope.

48

"SAM, WHAT'S WRONG?" Lance spun me around by the shoulders.

I took a deep breath and tried to regain my composure. "Take a look." I handed him the night-vision binoculars and turned to Jack. "I hope to God you brought a flask with you."

"Sonofabitch!" Lance stood transfixed.

Jack glanced from Lance to me and pulled a large flask from a side pocket in his backpack. "One-hundred-and-eighty proof rum." He pulled out his phone to use the light.

I dug through my bag and pulled out the butane lighter. The rest of the group's cell lights blinked on as they tried to see the threat.

After slipping on my backpack, I took the night-vision binoculars from Lance and slipped them over my head. "Okay, I'll take that rum now."

I handed Lance the halogen flashlight. "Shine the light on them so I can douse them with the rum. Can't use the night vision. The bright fire would blind me. Sure hope this works."

Before Lance could protest, I ran toward the scary horde and unscrewed the flask's cap.

"Lance, what the hell's going on?" Pete yelled.

"Uh, keep everyone back. We're dealing with an insect problem." Lance aimed the flashlight at the horde.

"Must be some badass varmints," Rod said. "I heard the

captain scream. Nothin' ever scares her."

"Pete, don't let them get me!" Inga shrieked.

I stopped several feet short of the scorpions and checked the lighter. The blue flame shot up like a mini blowtorch. I poured a short fuse to the front line and doused them with rum as they scurried toward me.

"Die, you ugly bastards!" I flicked on the lighter.

No blue flame from the lighter. Scorpions rushed at me. I backed into Lance.

He yanked me behind him. "Give me the lighter."

We stomped the scorpions as he tried the lighter. This time it worked. I splashed the rest of the rum over the horde. Flames brightened the passage as we stepped back and watched burning scorpions trying to reach us.

"Is it working?" Pete asked.

"Yes, but the fire won't last long. Looks like the ones behind the flames are leaving," Lance said.

"I'd like to know where they're going so we don't run into them. Shine that light behind me so I can use the night vision."

When the fire burned out, I saw the scorpions scramble into a hole on the right side of the passage twenty feet ahead.

"Let me clean this up so we can get through here." Lance swept the dead scorpions to the side with the stock of his MP7.

When he finished, I whispered to him, "Sorry I reverted to frightened-girl mode when I first saw the scorpions."

"Don't sweat it. This was far worse than when I walked into a shed full of tarantulas in Texas. They were big mothers, but I knew they weren't dangerous. Yellow scorpions kill with one sting, and this was a shitload of 'em."

"We'd better move through before they return." I turned to the group. "All right, everyone, we need to get past a hole in the passage as fast as possible. Follow me single file on the left side."

"Lance, give Jack the flashlight." I held my MP7 butt down in case the scorpions rushed out.

Jack took his place behind me. "Bugger! Yellow scorpions! Are they dead?"

"These are, thanks to your rum, but I saw some scramble into that hole on the right." I hurried past the hole and checked the passage ahead. It looked clear.

"Get a move on, people! We need to get past this hole!" Jack waved the group forward and trotted up to where I had stopped to wait for them.

"Shit, look at all them dead scorpions! No wonder the captain screamed. Walk faster!" Rod's breath quickened, like he was about to hyperventilate.

"Holy shit! Nobody told me there'd be freakin' scorpions in Petra. This tourist crap sucks!" Pete pulled Inga behind him and bolted past the hole.

Lance and Carlene brought up the rear. Just as they edged up to the hole, a scorpion crawled out. Another was right behind it.

Lance shoved Carlene forward. "Run!" He swung the butt of his MP7 like a golf club and swatted the scorpions back into the hole. "Keep going, Sam. I'll catch up." He took a few more swings and then sprinted toward us.

"They're coming!" Lance yelled.

I jogged ahead using my night-vision gear. Jack wielded the flashlight and his cell, while the rest held their cell lights.

I rounded a curve and skidded to a stop. The walkway ended five feet above the fast stream from the cavern. I stepped back so my group wouldn't push me in when they rounded the corner.

"Everyone, stop! Water ahead!" I tried to block their path.

"Screw that, hundreds of those yellow buggers are coming for us!" Jack swerved around me and stopped at the edge. His light reflected off the rushing water.

Pete rounded the corner with Inga in tow. The rest of the group bunched up behind them.

"Lance, what's happening?" I yelled.

"Slowed down the first few with my golf swing, but then hundreds of 'em rushed at me. We don't have much time."

I ran my hands over the walls. No tingles. *Damn!* I studied the water. It was clear and only a few feet deep.

Carlene screamed. "Do something, Captain! They're almost here!"

I made a quick decision. "Check that your backpacks and weapons are secure and follow me into the stream."

I cinched my pack straps tight and slung the MP7 strap over one shoulder and under the other. The warm water from the hot springs felt good when I jumped in.

In seconds, we were funneling down the rapids. My night-vision gear was waterproof. *Thank you, Navy SEALs!*

We had no control as the stream swept us through the mountain. At least we were able to keep our heads above water. We were so busy trying to survive, no one screamed.

I whipped around a downward curve and was tossed into the air as the water plunged down a waterfall.

As I plummeted into the inky blackness, I tried in vain to see where I would land.

49

ROSS DROVE UNDER THE stone archway emblazoned with the MacLeod coat of arms. He followed the curving driveway to the ancient stone castle and parked his Aston Martin at the formal entrance. As he climbed the steps to the massive oak door, it opened.

"Welcome, Captain Sinclair. Laird MacLeod and Mrs. Starr are waiting for you in the great hall. May I take your coat?" The butler was dressed in his usual formal attire.

Ross slipped off his coat and handed it to him. "Thank you, Baxter. I can find my way." He walked across the foyer to the enormous room where Duncan and Loren sat at one end of the massive banquet table.

"Ross, it's good to see you." Duncan shook his hand. "Have a seat."

Loren's eyes were red from crying. She reached for Ross. "I need a hug."

Ross pulled her in, then held her chair, and sat across from her. "Sorry to meet under unpleasant circumstances."

Duncan was seated at the head of the long hand-carved oak table with Loren on his left and Ross on his right. "We've heard the news reports. I hope you know more about this than the television reporters."

"Aye, we think we know who was after Sam and why." Ross glanced around the great hall. "Every time I'm in this room, I feel like I'm in a giant's lair."

"That's exactly how I felt the first time I dined here." It was obvious Loren was trying to put on a brave face, but her voice trembled. "I suggested we sit in the great hall tonight. Something drew me to this room, and it was the last place Sam sat before she left Scotland."

Baxter poured a glass of soothing Bordeaux for Loren and placed crystal tumblers of single-malt whisky in front of Ross and Duncan.

"Matt told me that you and Sam have psychic dreams and visions." Ross sipped the aged whisky.

"Yes, the gift runs on the female side of the family and usually emerges in our mid-twenties. Sam started to acquire her ability when she was on vacation here."

"Hardly a vacation. I almost killed her." Ross sighed.

"Which brings us to her disappearance. What can you tell us?" Duncan looked concerned.

"A helicopter was seen leaving Petra shortly after we lost the signal on Sam's watch." Ross explained everything he had learned from the military-intel network, Interpol, Jordanian authorities, and Matt. "Your professor friend thinks she may have been drawn to a hidden passage into the mountain." Ross decided not to mention the missing bodies that had bled out.

Loren paused in mid-sip with a faraway look. She seemed frozen with her wine glass against her lips. Ross glanced from her to Duncan.

"Loren, what's wrong?" Duncan raised his voice.

She straightened and focused on Duncan. "Remember when Sam wanted to follow the secret passage that leads down to the sea?"

"Aye, my stable boy interrupted us with that package for Sam."

"And then we were whisked away after the eyeball was

discovered." Loren looked excited.

"Aye, but what has that to do with this?" Duncan looked puzzled.

"I feel compelled to go down that passage now. It must be important. Please, Duncan." She stood and glanced at Ross for support.

"I'm game for a stroll down to the sea." Ross stood and looked at Loren. "The climb back up may be a bit taxing. Can you manage in those heels?"

She glanced down. "Give me a minute to change. Be right back." She trotted away.

Duncan rang for the butler. "Baxter, fetch three torches and my Glock. My guests want to explore the escape passage down to the sea."

Loren returned in jeans and sneakers at almost the same moment Baxter walked in with the flashlights and pistol.

"Shall I come with you, sir?" Baxter asked.

"Not necessary. We'll be back in about an hour." Duncan took the Glock and handed a flashlight to Loren and another to Ross. "Let's go." He reached behind a portrait. "Follow me."

A section of stone swung open to reveal a dark, narrow passage.

Loren followed Duncan, and Ross trailed behind her. Once inside, Duncan pulled a lever. The door closed to complete darkness. They switched on the flashlights and walked single file. When they reached an intersection, Duncan turned left and led them sixty paces. He paused at the top of stone steps.

"Take care as you descend. The steps are steep and may be slippery, and the passage curves like a spiral staircase." Duncan started down slowly.

Ross watched Loren run her hands along the rock walls on the way down. What was she feeling for? After descending two hundred feet, they rested in an alcove.

"This is halfway down to the beach," Duncan said.

Loren shined her flashlight on the walls. The rock opposite the seaside wall had a dull area six feet above the floor. "My right hand tingles when I run it over this spot. It feels soft, like it's filled with dirt. Let's see what's under there." She turned to Duncan and Ross.

Ross used his pocket knife to scrape away the dirt. When most of it was out, he brushed the rest away with his handkerchief.

"Look at this." Ross shined his light on it.

At six-three, Duncan was the same height as Ross and easily looked inside. At five-nine, Loren had to stretch on her tip toes.

"A gold handprint! Let me try something." She reached up and pressed her right hand against the indented form.

Grinding reverberated in the rock alcove. Moments later, a stone door swung inward beneath the handprint. Loren shined her light through the opening. Before she could step inside, Duncan pulled her back by her waistband.

"Not so fast, lass. We don't know if it's safe." Duncan slipped his arms around her waist.

"Surely it's safe for *me. I* opened it."

Ross ducked his head inside and looked for signs of traps. "What is this place, Duncan?"

"There's no record of it in the family archives. This chamber could have been chiseled into the cliff a thousand years ago. What do you see?"

"I need a closer look." Ross hunched over to clear the low door.

Loren couldn't wait. "Ross? Is it safe?"

"Seems so. No way to be certain. It's quite spectacular!"

Loren grasped Duncan's hand. "I promise to be careful. Let's go." She tugged him forward.

Their lights illuminated a circular room with images carved into the walls and adorned with gold, moonstone, crystals, and jewels. The tableau incorporated an ancient-looking seafaring nation with circular canals, longboats in the harbor, and flying airships. Enormous pyramids bordered the city, and massive sphinxes guarded the perimeter.

The chamber door closed with a thud. They spun around and faced solid rock.

50

DUNCAN THRUST HIS HANDS on his hips. "We're trapped in a place Baxter doesn't know exists." He shook his head. "Look for a way to open the door."

Loren shined her light on the wall near the door and gasped. Three women with identical shapes and familiar facial structures stared back at her. One had gold hair and aquamarine eyes, another had obsidian hair and sapphire eyes, and the third had ruby hair and emerald eyes. Inlaid in the rock wall, their bodies were carved from moonstone. Each woman held a crystal pyramid.

"These women look like Sam, especially the one with the gold hair." Loren touched a crystal, and it filled with bright light.

"Touch the other crystals. Maybe the door will open." Duncan stood beside her.

When all three crystal pyramids lit, holograms displayed images of an ancient nation in the center of the chamber. One showed a nearby island in the throes of a volcanic eruption. Molten lava spewed as sparks and smoke clouded the sky. Longboats and airships rushed to leave the magnificent city on the neighboring island.

The volcano exploded, and half the mountain slid into the sea. A massive tsunami raced toward the nearby nation. The wave towered over pyramids that appeared to be taller than five hundred feet. In seconds, the city was buried beneath the sea. Nothing remained but the distant airships flying to safety. The images faded, and the lights extinguished.

Loren looked shocked. "I think that may have been Atlantis. I don't know why the three women look like Sam."

Ross pulled out his mobile. "I suggest we use our phone cameras to take pictures of everything on the walls. I'd also like to get a video of the holograms."

When they finished photographing, Loren activated the crystals again. They each took a video of the disaster as it played in front of them.

"All right, lass, time to open the door," Duncan said with a light tone. "We don't want to give poor Baxter a fright."

Loren ran her hands over the rocks. "I don't feel any tingly places, and I can't find another handprint." She stared at the door, paused, and looked down. "I wonder—"

She removed her shoes and socks before slowly pacing closer to the door.

"Here!" She dropped to her knees and tried to dig away the dirt.

Ross used his pocket knife and handkerchief again to access a gold footprint recessed into the rock floor.

"Okay, boys, let's hope this works." Loren stepped onto the footprint with her right foot.

A grinding noise heralded the door opening. Duncan shined his flashlight through the doorway. Baxter stood outside looking stunned.

"Good of you to come, Baxter. We found a hidden chamber. Have a look inside."

Baxter looked wide-eyed as he entered the ancient chamber.

"Loren, darlin', you'll be the last to exit," Duncan said. "The door seems keen on closing right after you." He waved

Ross outside and waited for Baxter to look around. "I want you right behind me, lass." He led her by the hand out of the chamber.

As soon as Loren stepped through the doorway, the heavy stone door swung closed and blended back into the rock wall.

"All right then, let's head upstairs. I think we'll work up a good thirst on the way." He wanted to keep the mood light until everyone had climbed the cliff stairs and was safely inside the castle. "After you, Baxter." Duncan waved the butler ahead.

Loren became breathless as they neared the top. "Good thing we didn't go all the way down to the sea."

"Aye, the climb would have been twice as far if we had," Duncan said. "Ross isn't out of breath. Must be the rigorous SAS training, right lad?"

"Aye, Duncan, as well you know." Ross stepped onto the landing behind them. "I could do with another drink while we sort this out."

Baxter's wife, Fiona, was waiting in the great hall with the whisky and wine. "My but you lot look like you've seen a ghost."

Duncan nodded. "In a way, we have. Best bring Loren a chocolate bar."

The three sipped their drinks in silence, each lost in thoughts.

Ross swirled the amber liquid in his glass. "I think Loren should call that Harvard professor Sam sent the weapon to and ask him to describe it for us. Could be related to that hidden chamber."

"Aye, lass, put your phone on speaker and call him." Duncan squeezed her hand and gave her a light kiss. "Don't mention what we found. We'll draw our own conclusions after we've heard what he knows."

Loren swallowed a piece of chocolate and called Professor

Armitage. He answered on the second ring.

"Hello, Ben, how are you?" Loren tried to sound casual.

"Ah, my dear, I heard about Sam. What can I do to help?"

"Tell me everything you know about the ancient weapon Sam sent you. Also, anything you know about anyone who might be after her or the weapon. We're trying to connect the dots before it's too late." Her voice quavered.

"I suggest you turn on the record feature on your phone. It may be hard to remember so many details."

Loren pushed the button. "Go ahead."

Ben described the obsidian pyramid and statues in detail, including how it worked and what happened to his roof. He shared the two names he had deciphered on the goddess statues and the age of the artifact, explained ley lines/dragon currents, and told her what he knew about the Black Sun.

Ben concluded, "I guess you know psychic power contains strong electromagnetic energy. Sam's energy was the right frequency to activate the weapon."

"So, the weapon really is from ancient Atlantis?" Loren asked.

"I believe it is. The evidence is quite compelling, especially in light of the discovery of a submerged city near Cuba. It has pyramids larger than the Great Pyramid in Giza and several sphinxes bigger than the one in Egypt. It all fits with the map on the artifact."

"Why does Sam look like the women on the obsidian pyramid?"

"I'm speculating, but I think her bloodline connects all the way back to Atlantis. You and Sam may carry the same electromagnetic frequency as your ancestors."

"That would explain how her touch activated the weapon. If you think of anything else, please call me on my cell. I'm in Scotland. Thanks a million, Ben."

"Happy to help. Please call me when you find Sam."

Loren glanced from Duncan to Ross. "What do we do now?"

Ross finished his whisky. "Now that we know you can open rock walls, I think we can assume the same about Sam. Maybe she escaped the Black Sun by hiding inside the mountain like the professor suggested. I need to be on the SAS team Admiral Stone sends to Petra."

"I know the admiral. I'll give John a call. You'd best go and prepare for the mission." Duncan stood and walked Ross out. "Thanks for stopping by. We'll get this sorted. Keep me in the loop."

"Aye, you do the same. Thanks for the whisky."

When Duncan returned to the great hall after calling the admiral, Loren showed him a map on her phone. "Ley lines in Scotland. MacLeod Castle sits on a major intersection."

Duncan shook his head. "Life is never dull around the Starr women."

51

I FELL INTO A dark abyss, landed in a deep warm pool, and fought my way to the surface. Gasping for air, I swam to the side and struggled to pull myself up on the ledge with the backpack and weapons weighing me down.

I collapsed on the smooth hard surface, slipped off my pack and MP7, and pulled off the pistol holster in case I had to jump in and rescue someone. My NV-binoculars helped me see in the dark, but the others would need light. Jack had my flashlight.

Jack surfaced and swam toward me. "Take my weapon." He handed me the flashlight and an MP7, pulled off his backpack, and shoved it onto the ledge. "Take the light and shine it on the pool."

"Help! All this heavy shit's pullin' me down!" Rod sputtered and coughed, struggling to keep his head above water.

Jack swam to him and took his weapon. "Catch this." He tossed it to me.

"I'm going down!" Rod sank.

Jack grabbed the strap on Rod's backpack and towed him to the ledge. "Here, take this." He handed me Rod's pack. "I'll push and you pull him."

As Jack shoved Rod from behind, I dragged him out of the water by his arms.

Rod coughed and gasped, catching his breath. "Thanks for savin' my ass."

"Happy to help." Jack sat beside Rod.

Loud splashes heralded the arrival of Pete and Inga as they dropped into the pool. Moments later, they joined us on the ledge.

Lance and Carlene splashed down.

"Hey! Somebody take this heavy-ass weapon." Carlene held the MP7 in front of her as she treaded water. "Lucky my titties are helpin' me float."

Lance took the weapon and tossed it to Jack, then boosted her up to Pete.

"Thanks, boys. It's good to be on dry land." Carlene sat down beside Rod. "You okay?"

"I almost drowned. Now I feel nauseous. So much for a fun day in friggin' Petra! If we ever get outta here, I'm never going on another tour."

Inga glanced at the flashlight. "I can't believe the light still works after being in the water. My cell phone's dead."

I stood the flashlight on its end and pointed it at the rock ceiling. "It's actually a mini dive light. I keep it in my handbag with my Leatherman tool and butane lighter. I like to be prepared, and I scuba dive when the layovers are long enough."

"Uh, Sam, I think we should check for yellow critters." Lance picked up the light.

"Good idea. You scan that end, and I'll look over there." I turned and pulled on the NV-binoculars. It didn't take long.

Lance motioned me away from the group. "No scorpions, but we have another problem. I shined the light across the hot spring and looked everywhere. There's no way out. We're trapped."

"Maybe not. Could be another hidden door, but I need to rest a bit before I start looking for it."

"Good thing it's warm in here. It may take a long time to dry out. Let's have a snack." Lance walked to his backpack and sat down.

I stood in front of the group. "All right, everyone, time for a little snack and some rest before we press on. Your backpacks will dry faster if you empty them. Try to get comfortable."

"Good idea, Captain." Rod started emptying his pack. "My ass is worn out. I've had more exercise in Petra than I normally get in a year. Let's chill awhile."

Everyone ate in silence and sipped their warm water. We sat close together for emotional support. No one spoke of our dead friends, but they had to be on everyone's minds.

"I'm ready for a nap. Snuggle next to me, honey buns." Carlene looked at Lance and patted the ground beside her.

"Right, we should pair up for warmth and safety." Jack moved toward me.

Inga grabbed his hand. "Sleep by me, Jack, I'm scared." She pulled him down next to her.

"I'm scared too. You're sleepin' next to me, Captain." Rod reached for me. "I feel safer when I'm with you."

"I'll stand the first watch," Pete said.

I motioned for him to join us.

"Don't bother. Nothing to watch for here. I'd rather have everyone rested."

I didn't think I'd be able to sleep, even though I felt exhausted from all the stress and drained by the heat of the hot spring.

The last thing I remembered was Rod snoring into my ear.

52

AFTER RETURNING FROM DUNCAN'S castle and receiving orders, Captain Ross Sinclair faced the seven SAS soldiers he had chosen for the mission, including his friend and second-in-command, Lieutenant Derek Dunbar.

"We have our orders directly from Admiral John Stone. His son, actor Jack Stone, served in the Royal Navy and is one of the missing VIPs in Petra. My girlfriend, Samantha Starr, is the pilot for their charter flight. She vanished with them."

"Sounds like déjà vu from last August. She did a lot of vanishing then too." Derek shook his head. "Don't forget to wear a helmet this time." His emerald-green eyes danced with mirth.

"Aye, and plenty of body armor. Took me two months to heal after the last mission involving Sam," a soldier said, rubbing the scars from his bullet wounds.

"Missions involving your girlfriend are more dangerous than fighting the Taliban," another soldier said.

Ross's Special Air Service team included top soldiers in the British Special Forces. His men were close and never missed a chance to tease their leader. He knew they would follow him through the gates of Hell and win the fight.

"If you're done busting my balls, we have a mission to plan. Unless we receive new information, we're operating under the assumption Sam led her people inside the mountain. We can't gain entry the same way she did. We'll need plenty of explosives. No telling how many rock doors we'll have to blast open to find her.

Ross pointed at a diagram of the Petra site. "We have the king's permission to do this as long as we don't damage tombs and historical areas. I intend to do whatever's necessary to rescue them and ask for forgiveness later."

"How did Sam enter the mountain?" Derek asked.

"Recent evidence I'm not at liberty to discuss in detail suggests Sam's body energy may be the precise electromagnetic frequency required to activate ancient door mechanisms." Ross kept his tone serious. "This is no joke."

"How reliable is your intel?" Derek asked.

"Solid enough to convince *me*." Ross paused. "Sam's copilots are both military men. They could be assets if we get in a firefight with the kidnappers."

He briefed his men on the Black Sun, the previous attack in Agra, and the unknown sniper. "Like last summer, there are multiple unknown players. Wheels up in fifteen. With the time difference, we'll be jumping in early daylight."

The team packed their backpacks, checked their weapons and parachutes, and boarded the military jet that would fly them to the drop zone over Petra.

ROSS LED HIS TEAM into the narrow crevice where the pith helmet had been found. At the dead end, his heart quickened when he spotted the gold square with the trident and inverted pyramid indents.

Looks similar to what I saw last night in the castle's chamber.

"This could be it, lads. Place the explosives a few feet below this symbol." Ross hoped Sam had survived the attack and was able to open rock doors.

A few minutes later, the blast revealed a dark passage. The team donned their night-vision gear and climbed over the rubble.

"Follow me, lads." Ross jogged down the passage as his men trailed in close quarters.

Thirty minutes later, they reached the waterfall and pool feeding into the stream. Ross nimbly led his team along the narrow path around the pool. When they reached the wide rock floor on the other side, they found entrances to three tunnels.

"Bugger! Check twenty feet into each passage for signs of foot traffic." Ross entered the left tunnel.

Moments later, Derek called out, "Here! Scuff marks in the one on the right."

Ross rushed into the tunnel and took the lead. A hundred yards in, he signaled a stop.

"Look at this, burned yellow scorpions, a lot of them. These buggers are deadly. Stay sharp in case there are more."

Ross slowed his pace. His senses were tuned to every sound.

The team walked past a hole on the right side.

"Ross, double-time it!" Derek yelled from the rear. "Hundreds of the yellow buggers rushed out the hole."

Ross broke into a run. When he rounded a corner, he almost fell into a stream where the path ended. "Halt!"

His men gathered around him.

"Look for a gold symbol marking a hidden door. It could be on the floor or walls." Ross searched for the path Sam must have taken.

"Ross, they're almost here!" Derek yelled as he turned and faced the horde.

"Light flares and burn the bastards," Ross commanded.

The men switched off their night vision before the white-hot flares ignited. Brilliant light whitened the passage. The flares burned the first scorpions and forced the horde back to their hole. The light confirmed Ross's suspicion that the stream was the only exit.

"Right, lads, prepare for a water egress." Ross tightened the straps on his pack and secured his weapons.

Soon the team was racing down the waterway that Ross hoped Sam's group had taken. They covered a long distance in just minutes. Ross slid around a sharp turn and shot out into the air. He glanced down into the dark abyss.

"Brace for impact!"

53

SORE AND HUNGRY, I sat up and checked my watch. *We slept all night!* The rest of the group stirred.

"Rise and shine, intrepid travelers," I said in a cheerful tone.

"What time is it?" Rod asked, rubbing his eyes.

"Time for breakfast. I'm hungry," Pete said.

"I'd kill for a latte." Lance took a sip of warm water.

"Fried eggs, ham, and grits would be better," Carlene said, rummaging through the goodies she had emptied from her pack.

"What the dickens is a grit?" Jack asked.

"Grits are a sickly yellow color and real slimy, but they taste good. Not sure what they're made from." Rod bit into an apple.

"Grits are made from cornmeal. Come to Texas, Jack, and I'll make you some." Carlene grinned and tore open the wrapper on an energy bar.

"First we have to find a way out of this bloody mountain." Jack paced as he ate an orange.

Lance leaned in and whispered, "Any ideas?"

"Good thing the wrappers were waterproof on these health snacks." I ate the last bite of mine. "My pack and my stuff are dry, except my leather purse is damp, the tissue is useless, and my phone is ruined. I should have bought a waterproof model."

I shoved all the stuff worth keeping back into my pack.

Lance sighed. "I meant do you have any ideas about getting out of here?"

"Oh, right, that was next on my list. I'll start feeling around for tingly places." I stood.

"Find us a way out of here and I'll make you tingle like you've never tingled before." Lance kissed the nape of my neck and winked.

"Uh huh, I bet you say that to all the girls." I walked to the wall and slid my hands along the smooth rock.

"Looks like our captain's doin' her magic shit again. We'll be out in the sunshine in no time. I got faith," Rod said.

I felt along the wall from the floor to as high as I could stretch. The rock walls met at right angles near one end of the pool. My hands found a spot in the corner that triggered faint jolts of electricity. No soft dirt, though, and no indentation.

I fingered the pendant hanging from my neck while I strained to solve the puzzle. The pendant's diamond pyramid shot a light beam into the corner, penetrating a tiny crack. A low door of solid rock swung open.

"Well, hot damn! You did it again, Sam." Lance picked up my flashlight and shined it into the opening. "Looks like the way out. Everybody, grab your gear and get moving."

Lance packed his backpack and pulled it on, slung the MP7 over his shoulder, bent through the door, and lit the way with the flashlight.

"Pack up all the good food and water. Don't forget the weapons. Let's go. Jack, I need you up front again to check the cave." I pulled on my pack, clipped the pistol holster to my jeans, and slipped the MP7 strap over my shoulder.

Inga strapped on her pack and carried a submachine gun as she followed Pete to the door. I was the last one through.

"Wait! I left my bracelet on the ground." Inga started back

through as the door swung back.

Just in time, I yanked her into the chamber by her backpack strap. She dropped the MP7 in the doorway. The rock door crushed it and left the butt sticking out toward her.

"Sorry, Captain, thanks for saving me." Inga stared at the mangled metal and took a deep breath.

We gathered in a circular room where a dark passage started on the opposite side. Two moonstone statues holding crystal pyramids faced each other on a stone pedestal in the center. The statues looked like the golden-haired goddess Solraya from the artifact I found in Hong Kong. They also looked exactly like me.

Focused on the passage out, the group didn't notice the faces on the statues.

The walls were covered with images of an ancient city bordered by huge pyramids and giant sphinxes. Longboats were moored in the harbor, and airships were flying around.

I felt a compulsion to touch the statues' crystals. When I caressed one, it filled with light and projected a hologram of the ancient city in the throes of disaster. A volcano on a nearby island exploded and half the mountain crashed into the sea. A tsunami raced toward the city and buried it underwater before the image faded.

"Whoa, awesome video!" Rod said.

"I wonder where that happened," Carlene said.

"It may have been Atlantis." I touched the other crystal.

When I did, it filled with light and projected a different hologram. Atlantis rose from the sea and pushed massive waves in every direction. The image faded.

"We'd better get moving before another door closes on us." I waved everyone forward. "Jack, lead the way down that passage. I'll bring up the rear."

Lance handed the flashlight to Jack and ushered the group

into the passage. The moment I walked through the opening, a door dropped down from a slot in the ceiling and sealed the room behind us. We followed the passage to where it ended in a hundred yards.

"Sam, come and find the door." Lance leaned against a side wall.

I squeezed through the group and searched the wall at the end. I felt a square indentation six feet above the floor in the center and wiped away a light coating of dirt. I found a square gold lock identical to the one at the end of the crevice near the holy spring.

"Finally, something easy!" I stuck my pendant into the lock, and the door opened into sunlight.

I hesitated while my eyes adjusted and everyone exited. When I pulled out the pendant, the door closed behind me.

I walked around a boulder. Was my imagination playing tricks on me? A private Boeing 727-100 airliner was parked a hundred feet below at the nearest end of a long, dry riverbed between the mountains.

The distinctive whine of the auxiliary power unit roared as it provided electricity and air-conditioning to the parked aircraft. A fuel truck pulled out from the far side of the jet and drove away.

Two armed guards walked around the aircraft in opposing circles. They met at the rear and entered through the aft airstairs.

I grabbed Lance and pointed at the jet. "I found us a ride out of here, but there might be some gun play."

54

LANCE LOOKED DOWN AT the Boeing 727 jet. "Why do you think we'll have to shoot our way in?"

"I saw two armed sentries. They entered the aircraft after the fuel truck drove away. We have to think of a plan in a hurry. Looks like they're leaving soon."

I scanned the area and tried to visualize a scenario that ended with us flying the jet.

Lance stood with his hands on his hips. "Sam, we can't take these people into a combat situation. Now that we're out of that damn mountain, hit the emergency button on your DARPA watch and wait for your Highlander hero to rescue us."

"I told you, there's no signal, and they don't have SAS or SEAL teams here. We're on our own, but I have an idea."

I asked Pete, Jack, and Carlene to join us and outlined my plan.

"Sam, there's no friggin' way we're using you as bait." Lance gave me his angry alpha-male glare again. "What if that airplane belongs to the Black Sun? They'll grab you and fly out of here."

"I saw the guards. They're Arabs, not Germans. My plan will work." I gave him my stubborn alpha-female stare.

Carlene touched Lance's arm. "Sugar, I think when it comes to bait, two babes are better'n one. Besides, I'm faster on the draw than Sam. Those A-rabs will be so focused on our bosoms they'll never expect us to pull pistols out the back of our pants. This'll work, darlin', don't you worry none."

Lance glanced from Pete to Jack. "The loud jet engine in the auxiliary power unit will help. What do you guys think?"

Pete scanned the airplane. "They've got the window shades down to keep the airplane cool. They won't see us coming, and that APU will cover any noise we make."

"Right, we'll hide behind the aft airstairs while Sam and Carlene trick the guards and the rest of our group waits up here." Jack checked his pistol and holstered it.

Lance looked at Carlene. "Are you sure you can pull the trigger? Have you ever shot anyone?"

"I shot my first husband when I caught him humpin' Becky Sue Harper. Probably would've killed him if the damn Glock hadn't jammed. Never seen anybody run so fast with a bullet in his ass." Carlene racked the slide on her sidearm and stuck it in her pants in the small of her back.

"Let's get moving. If they close the airstairs before we get in position, it'll be game over." I checked my pistol and shoved it in my jeans. "Show time."

I headed down the mountain with Carlene and the men following me.

55

ROSS LANDED IN THE hot-spring pool and swam to the ledge. He pulled himself out of the water and watched as his seven soldiers dropped in and swam to him.

"Right, lads, everyone good to go?"

"Aye," they said in unison.

Energy-bar wrappers, orange peels, apple cores, wet tissues, and other trash littered the wide ledge. Ross found a gold bracelet with *INGA* engraved on it.

"We're close, lads! A flight attendant from Sam's crew was here recently with several people." He held up Inga's bracelet. "We'll need a bright light to locate the exit. Switch off night vision before I light the flare." Ross pulled a flare from his pack. "Lighting flare now."

Solid rock stood before them.

The team searched for a gold symbol or signs of a door.

"Ross, I found something." Derek stood where the rock walls met at right angles.

Ross jogged over to the far end of the ledge. Derek pointed at the barrel of a weapon sticking out of the corner joint. Smoke from the flare flowed through the tiny opening in the rock.

"Somebody dropped a weapon right when the door closed. Either the tour group got their hands on weapons, or they're prisoners of armed kidnappers," Derek said.

"If the tour group escaped with weapons, they might shoot at us before they realize we're here to rescue them. So, as much as you might like to shoot Sam, don't. She'll stand down when she hears my voice."

The men chuckled.

The team placed explosives on the rock door and took cover at the far end of the ledge. When the smoke cleared from detonation, they entered the circular chamber. Ross recognized the images on the walls and the statues on the center pedestal.

Looks like the chamber under Duncan's castle. Sam must be opening doors like her mother did.

"Ross, there's a large gold trident set into the wall opposite where we entered." Derek pointed at a five-foot trident.

Ross studied the room. His team couldn't afford to waste explosives. How many stone doors would they need to blow open?

"Plenty of scuff marks on the rock floor in front of the trident. This must be the door." Ross planted the explosives.

The team retreated to the ledge by the pool. When the dust from the explosion settled, Ross led them through the circular chamber into the passage. A few minutes later, they reached a dead end.

Ross found a gold square identical to the one near the holy spring where they had entered the mountain.

"This must be the exit, lads. Be ready for a firefight when we blow the door. Hostiles may be nearby. And remember, don't shoot my girlfriend."

After setting the explosives, the team retreated to the circular chamber. The rumble of exploding rock reverberated through the passage.

Ross led the team through the rubble and into the sunlight. He crouched behind boulders and waited for his vision to adjust.

Sounds like jet engines spooling up, but that can't be happening here. My ears must be wonky from the explosions.

"Ross, there's a jet down there. Looks like it's about to take off." Derek pointed at the 727.

56

CARLENE AND I HAD crouched behind a boulder and waited for the men to get in position under the jet behind the airstairs that descended from the tail.

Our makeup and lipstick had survived the water. We did a quick primp, brushed our hair, and left our backpacks and MP7s behind rocks.

"Do we look good enough to pull this off?" I brushed off my jeans.

"You're not showin' enough titty." Carlene unbuttoned three of my buttons. "That's better."

"Thanks, now wait until we're close before you yell for help so they can hear you over the APU." I reached behind me to check my pistol.

A few minutes later, we stood near the aft airstairs. Lance gave us the thumbs-up signal. I took a deep breath and nodded at Carlene.

"Help! Anybody in there? We're lost. Help!" Carlene's high-pitched voice carried well.

Two armed men rushed down the stairs and halted with their AK-47s pointed at us. They wore turbans and looked Middle-Eastern.

"Your names? Where from?" the taller man asked in broken English.

"We're from America. We escaped our kidnappers in Petra.

Now we're lost. Please, help us." Carlene acted weak and dizzy.

"Water, please. Very thirsty." I spoke in a faint voice and pretended to swoon.

With a dramatic flourish, Carlene crumpled to the ground beside me.

When the men slung their rifles over their shoulders and bent over us, we reached up and yanked them down. Off balance, they fell forward as we rolled clear. We sat on their backs and pressed our pistols against their necks.

Lance rushed forward. "Move and you die." He pointed an MP7 at them while Carlene and I unwound their turbans.

We cut off strips for gags and used the rest to tie their hands behind their backs.

"Wait here with the prisoners while we storm the airplane." Lance signaled Pete and Jack.

The three men ran up the airstairs with their weapons ready to fire. I heard one shot, then silence. After a few tense minutes, Jack emerged.

"Mission accomplished. I'll guard the prisoners while you go get the others." Jack trained his MP7 on the captives.

"Carlene, if you grab the packs and a submachine gun, I'll climb up and fetch the rest of our group."

We trotted to the boulder where we left our stuff, and I slung an MP7 over my shoulder.

Carlene put on her backpack and slipped her left arm through the straps on mine. She held her MP7 ready to fire. "Thanks, Sam, see you on the airplane."

It wasn't long before I led Inga and Rod up the airstairs. We passed eight tied-up Arabs, including the flight crew, all looking angry. I noted one man had a bleeding shoulder wound.

A few rows farther, I stared into the face of the most wanted terrorist leader in the world.

Oh damn.

Lance walked up to me. "We've really stepped in it this time. Even if we fly to safety, his entire terrorist organization will be out for our blood. This isn't just their airplane. It's their friggin' command center, which is why our military couldn't find it. They keep moving. Dang it!"

"They won't come after us if they don't know we took it. We'll land at a U.S. military base and make sure our government takes all the credit and keeps our part a secret. Are the tanks full?"

"Yep, I'm guessin' we're good for about a six-hour flight. We could make it to Ramstein Air Force Base in Germany if we can get permission to fly through the airspace of several countries on the way. What the hell do we tell the air-traffic controllers? Maybe we should land in Aqaba."

"Do you trust an Islamic king to save us and arrest the terrorists? They were hiding in his country." I jumped when an explosion rattled the aircraft. "Time to go. Close the airstairs. I'll start the engines."

On the way to the cockpit, I grabbed a satellite phone.

It took a few minutes to get all three engines running. I transferred electrical power to the number-three generator, shut down the APU, and turned off the transponder so it wouldn't be as easy to track us.

Lance entered the cockpit. "We've got nine prisoners. Inga's never held a gun before, and I'm not sure about trusting Rod. If it's okay with you, I'll play copilot and flight engineer so Pete can help Carlene and Jack with guard duty." Lance grabbed the checklists.

"All right, let's get to it. Read the after-start and before-takeoff checklists." I released the parking brake and started taxiing.

As soon as the aircraft was ready, I picked up the mike.

"Everyone sit down and buckle up. We're taking off now."

I pushed the throttles up, and the jet accelerated on the dry river bed.

Where the hell do we go?

As we passed two thousand feet on the climb, I hit the emergency button on my watch.

"I want to get out of the airspace belonging to Islamic countries. We'll head for the Mediterranean Sea." I turned west when we were high enough to clear the mountains.

"I hope nobody sends their fighters after us." Lance scanned the sky.

The cockpit door flew open, and Pete rushed in.

"Carlene swears she saw soldiers in desert fatigues shooting at the airplane during takeoff. Couldn't hear them with the JT9s at full power. What if the king's protecting these terrorists?"

"Then he'll send fighters. One missile up our ass and we're toast." Lance shook his head.

I glanced over my shoulder at Pete. "How would the soldiers know to shoot at us? And why would they kill men under the king's protection? Check if a prisoner sent a message."

"Not possible, they're all tied up."

"The Black Sun in Petra wore desert fatigues. Maybe they saw us enter the airplane, but they couldn't get close enough before we took off," Lance said.

"Good, the Black Sun doesn't know where we're going." I scanned the bright morning sky.

"Hell, *we* don't know." Lance glanced at the gauges. "What altitude should I set for the cabin?"

"You flew in the military. What's the best altitude to sneak past the Israelis and Egyptians? I plan to blast through that short patch of Israeli airspace over the desert, then fly north over the Sinai along the border, and head out over the Mediterranean."

"When we clear the mountains, hug the deck and pray for a miracle."

57

"BLOODY HELL, HOW DID that aircraft get here?" Ross focused his binoculars on the jet.

"Must've paid off the right people. Best get a move on." Derek secured his weapon.

Ross turned to his men. "Double-time it down to that jet." He ran down the mountain.

The soldiers reached the dry riverbed and ran toward the jet moments before it started the takeoff roll. They were thirty feet from the left wing when the aircraft accelerated.

"Shoot holes in the left wing tank and the belly tank." Ross opened fire.

The SAS team shot at the fuel tanks before the airplane sped out of range. They could only watch as the aircraft climbed at a steep angle and turned west over the mountains.

Ross made a call on his SATCOM. "Joint Command, this is Highlander. Missing tour group's in private Boeing 727 that just took off from this location headed west. Track that airliner and arrange transport for my team."

"Highlander, expect evac in one hour and be advised we received an emergency signal from Sierra Lima Sierra Sierra. The signal came from that jet."

Ross knew SLSS was code for Sir Lady Samantha Starr. "Understood. Ask the Jordanians and Israelis not to shoot them down. We put several rounds into the fuel tanks. That

Boeing will have to land soon. Highlander out."

"What's the word from on high?" Derek asked.

"Sam activated the emergency signal on her DARPA watch as soon as she reached altitude. She's definitely on that jet and will be in Israeli airspace soon. I hope to God they don't shoot her down."

58

AFTER WE CLEARED THE mountains, I dove for the deck. The roomy seating configuration and low passenger count on the private jet made it far lighter than a standard airliner. The forward section held a communications center with sophisticated electronics.

"According to the flight manual, this little 727-100 is equipped with powerful JT9-17 engines like most of the bigger stretch 200s. I'll keep up the speed and blow through Israeli airspace before they have time to scramble fighters." I tried to sound more confident than I felt.

Lance had a map spread on his lap. "I programmed the NAV computer to take us on the shortest route across Israel to the Sinai, then straight north to the Med. This had better work."

"I'd better keep it at 1,500 feet in case they have radio towers along the way. We probably wouldn't spot one until it was too late to avoid a collision." I leveled off over the Israeli desert.

"Avoid populated areas and maybe they won't consider us a threat." Lance scanned the sky above us.

"We should stay off the radio. We can't tell ATC who we are or who owns this jet and risk the information becoming public."

"Yeah, but then how do we convince their military not to

shoot us down? And where can we land?" Lance studied the map.

I had flown to so many airports around the globe, I had a world map stored in my brain. "We'll land at the U.S. Navy base in Naples. We can avoid other countries and most of their airspace by staying overwater until we get to Italy."

"Good idea, but first we have to survive Israel and Egypt. Any ideas?"

"Do you remember the radio frequency from your Air Force days for an Airborne Warning and Control System jet?"

Lance's face lit up. "Friggin' awesome! Jeff's secretary said he was doing carrier landings in the Mediterranean. Carrier groups always have an AWACS for recon over the fleet. Let's hope they're operating somewhere near us."

"Is that a secure military frequency? Could we safely tell them the truth?"

"Radios are never 100 percent safe, but we should be okay."

"Not good enough. When you make contact, ask for a call number on SATCOM." I handed him the satellite phone.

Lance tried a radio frequency from memory. No response. He tried another.

"Uh, Lance, we're running out of time. We have company." I pointed at two Israeli fighters flying forward of our wings.

"Dang it! If we were higher, maybe I could contact the AWACS. Pretend were NORDO and start climbing while I keep trying." Lance dialed in another radio frequency.

NORDO was the term for no radios operating. I pointed at my ears and shook my head, hoping the Israeli pilot would understand. He signaled for me to follow him. I estimated we were about one minute from the Egyptian Sinai border and pretended not to understand his instructions as we zoomed up to ten thousand feet.

A stern military voice came through the radio speakers. "Aircraft calling AWACS, identify yourself."

"Hot damn! What do we tell them?" Lance glanced at the fighters. "I'll have to keep my head down. Can't let the fighter pilots see me talking into the mike."

"Say it's an emergency, and you're a U.S. Air Force pilot with American civilians aboard. Ask if they show us leaving Israeli airspace."

Lance replied, "I'm a U.S. Air Force Reserve captain." He repeated everything I suggested.

"We show you over Egyptian airspace five miles west of the Israeli border at angels ten. Confirm you have Sierra Lima Sierra Sierra aboard and state intentions."

Lance looked at me as I banked the aircraft in a right turn north toward the sea. "Sam, how do they know?"

"I hit the emergency button on my DARPA watch when we left the river bed. Tell him we need to communicate via SATCOM."

After Lance switched to the satellite phone, he quickly briefed them, asked them to keep it secret, and requested safe passage to the U.S. Navy base in Naples.

The Israeli fighters peeled off and vanished behind us.

Lance pointed. "Either their bugging out or they've decided to get on our six and blow us out of the sky. Dang!" He explained our situation to the AWACS officer.

"Boeing, squawk 0727. What's your tail number?"

Lance turned on the transponder and entered code 0727. "We're in an unmarked Boeing 727-100. No tail number. Requesting U.S. fighter escort to Naples."

"Understood, Boeing. Be advised four Egyptian fighters are headed your way. They're probably more concerned about the Israeli fighters that violated their airspace, but I'll relay your request to command."

"Hurry!" Lance checked the navigation computer and turned to me. "One hundred and thirty miles to the coast. I hope the Israelis are still on our ass so the Egyptians go after them."

"Not likely. Israel has enough problems without provoking a war with Egypt. You can bet they bugged out. Those Egyptian fighters are coming for us." I pushed up the throttles.

"Hold it just under the never-exceed speed and say a prayer."

59

COMMANDER JEFF ROWLIN, CALL sign *Bücker*, completed his checklist and waited for the signal to taxi to the catapult. He heard the air boss in his helmet speaker.

"*Bücker*, hold for armament. New mission." The air boss gave Jeff the coordinates and told him to proceed at maximum speed for the intercept. "Expect four fighters to join you on-site at angels ten as soon as we can get them armed and launched."

In a few minutes, Jeff's Boeing F/A-18E Super Hornet was loaded with missiles and ready to launch from CAT one. It wasn't long before he had the Egyptian coast in sight.

"*Bücker* has the airliner and four Egyptian fighters on target radar. Range sixty miles. Awaiting orders."

"Provide safe escort for the Boeing 727. Fire if necessary. Help is five minutes out."

Dang! May as well be five hours. This could be over in less than thirty seconds.

Jeff armed his missiles and prayed he wouldn't need them. Engaging four fighters alone was not supposed to be part of his carrier-currency training.

"Give me a frequency for the Egyptian fighters. I'll sweet talk 'em while I wait for backup."

The 727 and fighters were fifty miles from the coastline. Two fighters flew ahead of the Boeing's wings, and two fighters maintained firing position behind the airliner.

Jeff keyed his mike. "Attention, Egyptian fighters: *Bücker* thanks you for escorting our airliner to the coast. The *USS Lawrence Lee* sent me to escort the Boeing. Stand down and return to base."

Jeff glanced at his watch. Four minutes left.

"Negative, *Bücker*. Airliner must land in Egypt or we will shoot it down. Return to your ship."

"Stand down. You have no justification to shoot down an unarmed aircraft leaving your airspace. I have you on film."

Three minutes.

"We have orders. Airliner must not leave our airspace."

"The Boeing is under the protection of the U.S. military. Any hostile action will be considered an act of war. Call your commander."

Jeff watched the Boeing approach the coastline and checked his watch. Down to two minutes.

"*Bücker*, if the airliner reaches the twelve-mile limit offshore before we receive new orders, we must shoot."

"Stand down, or I'll be forced to engage. Let's not start a war over one airliner. Wait for new orders."

Jeff maneuvered behind the two fighters that held firing positions on the Boeing.

One minute.

The AWACS gave him a radio frequency to contact the Boeing. He selected COMM 2. "Boeing airliner, this is *Bücker*. Continue straight ahead to the sea. American fighters will protect you."

"Jeff?"

"Sam?"

Oh dang!

COMM 1 blared into Jeff's helmet. "Airliner is approaching twelve-mile limit. Tell them to turn back or be fired upon."

"Hold fire! American fighters have missile lock on you.

Stand down." Jeff selected missile lock and got tone on the fighter behind Sam's aircraft on the left.

As if on cue, four American fighters appeared and acquired their targets. The Egyptian fighters pulled up and bugged out.

"Thanks, gentlemen. Try not to cut it so close next time."

Jeff blew out a sigh. He switched the mike back to COMM 2. "Sam, what the hell?"

"Long story, ultra secret. Our military will get all the credit."

"Understood. Confirm there's a 767 parked in Aqaba."

"Affirmative. Are you here to escort us to Naples?"

"That's me rocking my wings in front of you. I'll take you to the *USS Lawrence Lee* where freshly fueled fighters will escort you to Naples."

"Thanks, Jeff, I mean *Bücker*. I'll stay on your six until you land on the carrier."

60

NO LONGER AFRAID OF being blown out of the sky, I throttled back to cruise speed and shadowed Jeff's Super Hornet over the Mediterranean Sea.

"Well, we made it out of hostile airspace." Lance blew out a big sigh. "So, what's the deal with Jeff's call sign?"

"It's short for *Bücker Jungmann*, Jeff's antique German biplane. *Jungmanns* are fully aerobatic and fly like a dream with instantly responsive controls. His airplane's a beauty."

"Sweet. I'm sure nobody in the Navy has ever used that call sign before. Jeff's one of a kind. I'm glad he's our chief pilot." Lance grinned.

"Me too. He's the best of the best. He totally saved our butts back there." I relaxed a little.

When I switched off the autopilot, I felt major changes in the feel of the 727. The right wing was a lot heavier than the left.

I glanced at the fuel gauges on the engineer's panel, and my breath caught. The quantities in the left-wing tank and center tank were much lower than the right tank and steadily decreasing.

"Lance, we have a fuel leak. Feed all three engines from the right tank and turn off the pumps in the left and center tanks."

Lance moved to the engineer's panel. "The soldiers Carlene saw must've shot holes in the tanks. We're not going to make it to Naples."

I pulled out the aircraft flight manual. "This baby has nose-wheel brakes in addition to the main brakes. With the light-weight configuration, a good headwind, and the carrier making maximum knots, we can pull this off. I'll touch down in full reverse thrust."

"Where? You're not talking about a carrier landing, are you?"

"Ditching an airliner in the open sea is rarely survivable. Look at the size of those rollers." I pointed down at the rough seas. "A carrier landing is our best chance, and it'll give the Navy an opportunity to recover all the intel and interrogate the terrorists."

"Dang, woman, life with you is never dull!" He sighed and shook his head. "Ask Jeff how long the landing deck is from end to end."

I called Jeff to explain our emergency and my plan.

"Sam, have you lost your friggin' mind?" Jeff said. "You can't land a 727 on a carrier. The skipper would never allow it."

"*Bücker*, our passengers and intel will guarantee your skipper makes admiral in record time. Now, how long is the landing deck from the approach end to the far edge?"

"It's 795 feet, but we only use half of that starting where the arresting cables are positioned."

"We'll fly short final at 110 knots. Judging by the seas, the headwind must be at least 20 knots. With the carrier making 40 knots or better, we'd have an effective ground speed of 50 knots or less when we touch down in full reverse. And we have the added benefit of nose-wheel brakes. I know I can do it, *Bücker*. I'm counting on you to sell this to your captain. Tell him to call AWACS on SATCOM for the info on us. In the meantime, I'll throttle back to save fuel."

"All right, I'll try. If he agrees, we'll have to clear the area near the island and at the departure end of the landing deck. You'll need the entire length, and we wouldn't want your wing tip to hit a parked airplane. Stand by."

After a brief wait, Jeff called. "Boeing, this is *Bücker*. Permission to land denied. Captain Kingston suggests landing near the carrier for rapid rescue. Sorry, Sam, I tried."

"*Bücker*, ask again. I promise I won't put his carrier at risk. You know I can do this."

"Stand by, Boeing."

A baritone voice with a British accent boomed over our radio speakers. "Attention Boeing approaching the *USS Lawrence Lee*: This is Admiral John Stone of Her Majesty's Royal Navy. Is my son aboard your aircraft?"

"Affirmative, sir. He's fine, but we're running short on fuel and awaiting permission to land on the U.S. aircraft carrier."

"May I have a brief word with him?"

"Make it quick. We're about to get very busy." I grabbed the mike and keyed the PA system. "Jack, report to the cockpit immediately."

Jack rushed into the cockpit.

I handed him a microphone. "Your dad wants to speak with you. Make it fast."

"Go ahead, Admiral." Jack sounded stiff and formal at first.

"Glad you're all right, Son. I have an important question: How good is your pilot?"

"I have complete confidence in her. She's top notch, Father."

"Tell her she can land on my aircraft carrier, *HMS Queen Victoria*, if the *Lawrence Lee* refuses permission. We'll find a way to make it work. See you soon, Son."

"Thank you, Father." Jack handed back the mike.

Lance grinned. "Well played, Admiral Stone! The man understands the game."

"What do you mean by that?" I asked.

"Admiral Stone knew the captain of the *USS Lawrence Lee* would be listening. He all but guaranteed we'll get permission to land there now." Lance smiled at Jack. "It's good to have relatives in high places. Thanks, Jack."

"My pleasure. Best I strap in and brace for the carrier landing. Do your magic, Captain."

"Thanks for the vote of confidence, Jack." He saluted me, and I returned it before he left the cockpit.

"Boeing, this is Captain William Kingston of the *USS Lawrence Lee*. Are you certain you can land safely on my ship?"

"Affirmative, sir. I can fly this Boeing like I was born in it. The aircraft is light, we have additional braking, and we'll be in full reverse thrust when we contact the deck. After we stop, I'll shut down engines one and three and leave the center engine running for the exit. Send your best men to escort the people off and strip the aircraft. When they're finished, I'll back off your ship to clear the landing deck for the fighters."

"Are you planning on going off the aft deck with the airplane?"

"No, sir, I plan to use an escape rope and jump out the forward galley door once the airplane is on a steady backward course. Do you have a SEAL team aboard that might be willing to catch me?"

"Affirmative. SEAL Team Six is standing by. You have permission to land. Deck is ready. Don't make me regret this. The air boss will take over now."

"Thank you, Captain Kingston, I promise to keep your ship safe."

"Boeing, this is Air Boss. *Bücker* is landing. You're number two. Rodeo will guide you in."

"Understand Boeing is number two for landing."

"Sorry, Sam, I'm flying on fumes. See you aboard. Good luck. *Bücker* out."

I grinned at Lance. "Rodeo is Matt's call sign. He used to ride broncos. This should be fun."

"Your fighter-pilot brother is stationed on the *USS Lawrence Lee*?"

As if on cue, Matt's voice filled our radio speakers. "Boeing, this is Rodeo. Ready to make Navy history, Sis?"

"Affirmative, Rodeo, lead us in. Expect 110 knots on short final." I spotted the carrier in the midst of the battle group. Our floating airport looked tiny, like a water bug.

"Dang, that ship looks small. It was a lot easier landing on a carrier in a flight simulator, probably 'cause I knew I couldn't die. This is gonna be tight."

I addressed the passenger cabin: "Attention Pete and Inga, prepare the cabin for a hard landing. Everyone put on life vests and pull your seat belts tight. Expect touchdown in five minutes."

"Want me to get you a vest?" Lance glanced around the cockpit and felt behind his seat.

"No way are we getting wet on this landing. I'm not about to mess up with my brother watching. Sit tight and give me flaps five and the landing checklist."

61

I GLANCED AT THE fuel panel on the engineer's station. "Left and center tanks are empty. Right tank is almost dry. We have gear down with three green lights, flaps forty, and speed one-ten."

"Boeing, call the ball," the air boss said.

I keyed my mike and focused on a horizontal row of fixed green lights intersecting a vertical array of red and yellow lights—a signal system called the meatball. "Boeing has the ball."

"Rodeo has you on speed, centerline, and glide path. Hold steady, Sis."

"Boeing is cleared to land." The air boss sounded matter-of-fact, like he cleared airliners to land on his ship every day.

"Damn it, we just lost number one!" I felt the airplane yaw and compensated with the rudder as I eased the number-two throttle forward.

"Boeing is below glide path," Rodeo said.

"We lost the left engine." I kept my voice steady.

"Boeing is back on glide path. Watch your speed, Sis."

"We're stabilized now, Rodeo."

"We're comin' up on five hundred feet. Speed looks good." Lance scanned the panel.

"Give the cabin six bells. I'm going to full reverse a few seconds before touchdown so we get max stopping power. I'll call it." My heart hammered against my chest as we neared the carrier.

How close do we have to get before the ship looks bigger?

"The friggin' deck is pitching. Better time this right, or we'll drive the gear up into the belly when we smash into the deck. Three hundred feet to touchdown." Lance clenched his jaw. "If we survive, we are damn well havin' high-adrenaline sex *this* time."

"*Seriously*? You're thinking about sex *now*?" I took a deep breath. "If we can keep at least one engine running, we'll make it. When I plant the nose wheel on the deck, stand on the brakes with me."

My throat was dry, and every muscle felt taught, like tightly tuned guitar strings. We were just seconds away, and the ship still didn't look any bigger.

"Two hundred feet." Lance was all business.

I waited until we passed 150 feet. "Selecting full reverse thrust now."

I was at the point of no return. There would be no chance of going around for another try or arresting the descent with power. We had to miss the fantail and glide to the landing deck.

Two engines roared in full reverse as I hauled back on the yoke. The runway was so short it vanished from view when I pulled the nose up for the flare.

"We lost number three." Tension cracked Lance's voice.

With only the center engine operating, the yaw from the dead left engine was balanced by the dead one on the right. I centered the rudder and nose as the main wheels slammed into the deck. If not for my five-point harness, I would have been thrown out of my seat.

I pushed the yoke forward and stood on the brakes as we rushed toward the end of the runway deck.

"It's gonna be close," Lance said. "We've got about two hundred feet left. There's the net."

The big Boeing ploughed into the net and ripped it from the deck. We stopped with our nosecone poking over the lip and our nose wheel five feet from the end.

"Lance, switch electrical power to the number two generator."

He leaned over the back of his seat to switch generators.

I selected idle thrust on the center engine as a fire light illuminated on the panel.

I keyed the radio. "Boeing has a wheel-well fire. Probably hot brakes."

"Boeing, deck crew is extinguishing the fire. Wheel chocks are in place. Open aft airstairs."

I turned to Lance. "One and three are secured. Tell Pete to open the aft airstairs."

I spoke to the air boss. "Opening aft airstairs. Need fuel in right wing tank for the evac. Advise SEALs my people have weapons and are guarding the prisoners."

"Understood, Boeing. Brake fires are out. SEALs are boarding."

I addressed the cabin: "Attention, SEALs are coming aboard. Hand over your weapons and follow their orders. We need everyone off as fast as possible."

Lance pulled out his knife and cut the escape rope out of the compartment near his side window. "I'll secure this to the handhold at the forward galley door."

"I'll prepare the cockpit."

While I set the cockpit controls, the terrorists and my people were swiftly led off the aircraft. A large group swarmed the airplane to strip computers and electronic devices from the command center.

"Excuse me, Captain Starr, I'm Lieutenant Joe Kernan

with SEAL Team Six. I understand your copilot will be backing the jet off the deck." A lean, muscular man with intense blue eyes stood behind me.

"Negative, Lieutenant, I'm responsible for the exit. I'll need a bungee cord to keep the throttle in full reverse when I leave the cockpit. And I need your team to wear as much padding as possible and position themselves at one-hundred-foot intervals along the landing deck starting two hundred feet behind the parked Boeing. The man closest to the fantail should wear a life vest in case I can't jump before I get to him and we go over the end."

"We don't need padding. A little lady like you won't hurt us when we catch you." His body looked like molded steel.

"The padding's for my protection. I break easily. Slamming into you would be like hitting a block of concrete. My body wasn't designed for high impact."

"Understood. Maybe you should let your copilot do it. He looks fit."

"I was responsible for bringing this jet aboard, and I'll taxi it off. I'd think you'd prefer catching a one-hundred-and-twenty-pound woman rather than a two-hundred-pound man. My way's safer for everyone." I locked onto his intense eyes and held my ground.

"You're the captain. I'll get my men ready and send someone with a bungee, helmet, life vest, and netting for you." He nodded at the pistol in my hip holster and held out his hand. "Give me the weapon."

I pulled off the holster and handed it to him.

"The combat knife too." He pointed at the sheath on my other hip.

"I might need this during the exit. Let me keep it for now." I offered my best smile.

A man stepped in the cockpit doorway. "Lieutenant, this

airplane is wired with explosives. We haven't found the detonator device. Captain Kingston wants the Boeing backed off the deck ASAP."

"Understood. Has the jet been fueled?"

"Yes, sir, and the men will finish the strip job in three minutes."

"My men will be ready." Lieutenant Kernan turned to me. "You heard what he said about the explosives. Not too late to change your mind."

"I'm good to go as soon as I get a life vest." I checked the fuel gauges and noted the right wing tank had sufficient fuel for the reverse-thrust exit.

"One more thing, Lieutenant, make sure my copilot is safely inside the ship. He tends to be stubborn when it comes to what he sees as a damsel in distress."

"I'll take care of it." He jogged out the door.

Moments later, a man handed me a life vest. "Put this on and wear this netting over it so it'll be easier for a SEAL to grab you. Here's your bungee cord and helmet."

"Thanks." I did as instructed and checked the lifeline in the forward galley.

The rope was secure with the door open. All I had to do was slide down the rope to the deck while the airplane was accelerating toward the fantail in full reverse.

What could possibly go wrong?

Inside the cockpit, I sat in the left seat and keyed the mike. "Boeing pilot is ready. Waiting for clearance to back off landing deck."

"Roger, Boeing, close the aft airstairs and stand by for clearance."

"I'll be off radio while I secure the stairs." I ran to the back, closed the aft airstairs, and glanced around on my way to the cockpit.

The airplane was empty. Wired explosives were exposed along the sides of the fuselage where the sidewalls had been torn off. Thank God I didn't see any blinking red lights or timers counting down.

62

HUSSEIN LAY IN A padded, sound-proofed ceiling compartment lined with silver reflective foil to block infrared sensors. He had scrambled into his secret hiding place when armed men rushed into the airplane while it was parked on the dry riverbed. He had felt the acceleration of the takeoff and the hard landing later.

The vibrations told him at least one engine was running now, and the private airliner seemed to be rocking. The tight space must have tricked his senses.

He pulled the remote detonator from his pocket and looked at it.

What to do? Are my leaders captive or safe? Where are we? Don't want to kill my people if there's no need, but our command center must not fall into enemy hands.

As Hussein contemplated his next move, he felt the airplane jerk and accelerate. He needed more information before he activated the detonator. He was not afraid to die for the right reason. He unlocked the hidden entry door and dropped into the empty cabin.

63

"BOEING IS CLEARED TO back off the landing deck. Chocks are pulled. SEALs are in position," the air boss said.

"Boeing starting reverse thrust."

I selected full reverse thrust on the center engine and secured the thrust handle with the bungee cord before I released the parking brake. The airplane rolled backwards and slowly accelerated as I centered the nose-wheel steering.

"Boeing is on a straight path to the fantail and accelerating," the air boss said. "Pilot is cleared to jump."

"Pilot exiting now."

I headed for the forward galley, but a man in a turban blocked my path. He held a detonator in his left hand and a knife in his right.

"Where are my people? What have you done with them?"

Out the corner of my eye, I saw the Boeing pass the first SEAL. *Damn!* That was my easiest way off while the speed was slow.

"Your people left the airplane. They're safe. Drop the detonator and I'll lead you to them."

"Liar! Where are we? What are you doing?"

We passed two more SEALs as the speed increased. Three SEALs and three hundred feet left.

"I'm repositioning the aircraft on the parking ramp. I must get back to the cockpit."

"Liar! I will send you to Hell. *Allahu Akbar*!"

He rushed forward and plunged his knife into my left breast.

"You first!" I yelled as I drew my knife.

We passed the fourth and fifth SEALs as I kneed his groin, shoved my knife into his gut, and drop-kicked him into the cabin. I ran for the open galley door and grabbed the rope on my way out.

One hundred feet to the fantail.

Lieutenant Kernan was my last hope as I soared toward him at almost fifty knots. He ran toward me and snagged my netting as I passed even with him. He pulled me close and wrapped his arms and legs around me as we hit the deck and rolled over and over.

The Boeing's main landing gear rolled off the after deck a second before we stopped at the edge of the deck with the lieutenant on top of me. The tail dropped straight down toward the sea as the airplane rotated into a vertical position.

The carrier must have been making better than fifty knots. For a second, the Boeing seemed to hang in the air with its nose pointed skyward and its belly facing us. Then it exploded, and one of the main wheels hurtled toward us as the carrier pulled away.

"Roll forward!" I pushed off with my leg to roll us over.

The wheel slammed into the deck where we had been a second before and bounced clear. Now I was on top of the SEAL.

"Roll aft!" he yelled as he rolled me back just in time to avoid another main wheel hitting the deck beside us.

I scanned the sky. No more giant wheels. Pieces of the Boeing fluttered down and disappeared in the sea.

The pain in my breast commanded my attention.

"Rolling around on the deck with you would be a lot more

fun if I didn't have a knife sticking in me." I gave him a light kiss. "Please take me down to medical."

He rolled off me and focused on the blood staining my life vest. "Shit!"

64

LIEUTENANT KERNAN SCOOPED ME into his arms and ran off the deck.

"Make way! Coming through!" he shouted inside the carrier.

In the medical facility, he gently laid me on an exam table and yelled for a doctor.

A woman in a white lab coat walked in with a nurse. "What have you brought me, Lieutenant?"

"Knife wound in the chest, left side." He stepped aside.

The hilt protruded from my life vest over the lower portion of my left breast. Blood soaked the four-inch-thick flotation panel while my body hummed with adrenaline.

"I'm Doctor Linda Carole. We need to cut the vest and shirt off, uh, Miss?"

She handed scissors to the nurse and picked up heavy gauze.

"Samantha Starr, but everyone calls me Sam."

"Nice to meet you, Sam." The doctor yanked the knife out and pressed gauze against the wound. "There, all done except for the stitches."

"I hope the wound won't leave an ugly scar." I tried to inspect the cut.

"Those double Ds saved your life. Good thing they're natural. The blade would have ruined an implant."

The doctor talked as she stitched. "The scar won't be visible to anyone except your boyfriend, and I'm sure he won't care."

It was then I noticed the SEAL lieutenant staring at the floor with an anguished look.

"I'm sorry, Sam, this was my fault. I should have been with you on the aircraft."

"No way, Lieutenant! I'm responsible for what happens to me on my airplane. A small army of men missed finding my attacker. We all thought the airplane was empty when I closed the airstairs. I guess we'll never know where he was hiding."

I was so focused on his sad eyes, I forgot I was topless.

Captain William Kingston walked into the room and froze. He turned his back. "Please, excuse me, Miss Starr. I came to check on you and find out what happened."

Doctor Carole bandaged the wound and handed me a hospital gown.

"Any allergies? I need to give you antibiotics. Can you take Percocet for the pain?"

"No allergies. I need a pain med approved for pilots."

"I can give you 800-milligram Motrin." She handed me pills with a glass of water. "When was your last tetanus shot?"

"I had one in Scotland two months ago after I was shot twice."

"You do get into trouble, don't you?" She shook her head. "I'm sure our captain can find a good place for you to rest."

She turned to the skipper. "She's decent now."

"Miss Starr, how are you feeling?" Captain Kingston asked.

"I feel like the 727 ran over me. I'm sure I'd feel a lot worse if Lieutenant Kernan hadn't caught me and protected me with his body. That was a wild roll across the deck."

I smiled at the lieutenant and drank the water.

"Why were you so late jumping from the airliner?"

"An Islamic terrorist blocked my exit and stabbed me in the chest."

"What? Where did he come from? The airplane was empty."

"I don't know, maybe a secret compartment. He had a combat knife and a detonator."

"How did you escape?"

"I kneed him in the groin, stuck my knife in his gut, and kicked his terrorist ass into the cabin."

I saw the lieutenant smile.

The skipper grinned too. "Lieutenant Starr told me you have combat skills. I thought he was joking."

"Matt's twin is a SEAL and taught me all sorts of moves. I've been getting a lot of practical experience lately, which reminds me, I'd appreciate it if you would keep our involvement a secret. We'd like the Navy to get full credit so we don't have to worry about repercussions from the Al Ghazi terror network."

"No problem." He looked at the doctor and nurse. "Miss Starr's presence aboard and everything she said is top secret."

He turned back to me. "We'll have Navy Intel create a cover story for you and your people. They'll debrief you on the Petra incident and your escape in the Boeing. Anything else?" Captain Kingston looked pleased.

"When you make admiral soon, please remember to be good to my brothers, Lieutenant Kernan and his team, and Commander Jeff Rowlin."

"That's an easy promise to keep. They're all good men and a credit to the Navy. Now, with Doctor Carole's permission, I'd like to get you settled in the vacant admiral's suite so you can rest."

The captain offered me his hand.

"The patient is good to go, Skipper. See to it she has plenty of fluids available."

"Thanks, Doc." My legs felt like rubber.

I wobbled as I saw Lance, Pete, and Jeff in the open door. They looked frantic until Captain Kingston caught me.

"Sam, are you all right? We heard you were wounded somehow." Lance moved closer.

"Yeah, Sam, what happened?" Jeff asked.

"A terrorist stabbed me in the chest when I left the cockpit."

"Sonofabitch!" Pete said. "How did they miss him when they searched the airplane?"

Lance turned pale and focused on my chest. He swallowed hard. "Dang it! I knew I shouldn't have left you alone on the airplane."

The doctor touched his shoulder. "She's fine. Just a few stitches in her left breast. You probably won't even notice the scar."

The bad-boy glint returned to Lance's eyes. "I'll be the judge of that, Doc."

"Since when? I thought she was dating the Scottish badass," Jeff said.

"I hope I'll still be dating Ross. He'll be angry about Petra. He warned me not to go. And there's no telling what he'll think about my carrier escapade."

"Which is why you should be dating *me*. I'll massage antibiotic cream onto your wound several times a day, and I won't scold you about your misadventures." Lance grinned.

Jeff glared at Lance. "Cool down, fly boy. We have a rule in the Navy: No friggin' in the riggin', and that applies to civilians too. Right, Skipper?"

"Affirmative. Sam's in no condition for that anyway. Tomorrow, I want everyone in a debriefing session with Navy Intel. They'll devise a good cover story for the group and arrange transportation. Gentlemen, keep a tight lid on everything, including the stabbing."

Captain Kingston took me by the arm. "Time to get you settled. Can you walk?"

"Yes, sir, I have my sea legs now. Are you able to accommodate the rest of my people?"

"Everyone has been assigned bunks. Most of them are in the wardroom now eating lunch. If you're hungry, I'll send lunch to the admiral's suite. Ready?"

"Lead on, Captain."

"Excuse me, Skipper," Jeff said. "I've finished my operational currency training, and I'd like to attend the debriefing tomorrow. I'm Sam's chief pilot at Luxury International, and I'll be taking her place for the remainder of her charter flight."

"I'll have someone notify you when they schedule it, Commander Rowlin. Now, let me take your pilot up for a well-deserved rest."

The captain ushered me out the door.

65

WHEN I WOKE, MATT was sitting on the edge of my bed. His aqua-blue eyes twinkled with delight as he smiled and wedged a pillow behind me. I sat up, and he put a meal tray on my lap. The roast beef smelled delicious.

"Thanks, I'm hungry." I didn't hesitate to dig in.

"I thought you had nerves of steel when you rode those wild broncos in the Texas rodeos, but now I realize it goes way beyond that. Brother, you're freaking fearless landing on this ship every day. I've done some scary stuff, but nothing compares to the terror of landing on that deck."

He rubbed the back of his golden-blond buzz cut. "I'd love to let you think I'm Superman, but the truth is my fighter was designed to land on the deck. An airliner is another story. My squadron was so impressed with your shit-hot landing they made you an honorary member of our fighter wing and gave you a call sign."

Matt pulled a bomber jacket from a bag. BOMBSHELL was embroidered on the left breast along with their fighter wing designation. His handsome face beamed with pride as he handed it to me.

"This is so cool! Thanks, Matt. I love it." I hugged him.

"While you were deep in slumber all day, your VIPs entertained our fighter pilots. Carlene Jensen is an amazing singer, and I loved her comedy skit. Rod Rogan was hilarious too. Jack Stone explained how they shoot the impossible action scenes and radical stunts. I had no idea actors were such fun people." Matt poured water into my glass.

"Sounds like my group is having a grand time. Captain Kingston told me to expect a debriefing with Navy Intel tomorrow. How much should I tell them?"

"Now that you're the captain's new best friend, I'd tell them everything. The military can help you and make sure that doomsday weapon doesn't fall into the wrong hands."

"How do you know about that?"

"I talked to Professor Armitage after you vanished in Petra."

Doctor Carole walked into my cabin. "How's my patient feeling?"

"Sore as hell, but good otherwise. The food here is excellent." I patted my mouth with the linen napkin and smiled. "I guess admirals travel in style. This suite sure is luxurious."

"The ship's captain is our god, and the admiral is his god." She checked my pulse, blood pressure, and temperature. "Do you need another pill for the pain before I change your dressing?"

"No, I took one before my meal."

"I'll have to ask Lieutenant Starr to step outside."

"No problem, Doc. See you later, Sis." Matt kissed my cheek and left.

"Now, let's have a look at your wound."

I ached all over as I pulled off the hospital gown.

"Your wound looks good. No infection," she said after changing my dressing. "The stitches should be removed in seven to ten days."

I stifled a yawn. "Thanks, Doc. I feel like going back to sleep even though I slept all afternoon."

"Your body suffered major trauma. Rest is the best medicine. Sleep as long as you can. You'll feel a little better tomorrow, but you'll be sore for quite a long while."

66

THE NEXT DAY, WE gathered in a conference room for the debriefing with Navy Intelligence. Captain Kingston sat at the head of the table with the intel officer at the other end. The three VIPs from my group sat on one side, and my crew and Jeff sat opposite them.

Carlene grinned at me. "Hey, Sam, how're you feeling? We've missed you."

"I'm banged up and bruised all over from my kamikaze roll on the deck. I heard you entertained the fighter pilots. Good job!" I gave them a thumbs-up.

The captain cleared his throat. "I think you all know your lives depend upon keeping silent about taking the Al Ghazi airplane. No one can ever know you were on that airplane or this ship, understand? My crew will keep your secret. As far as the world is concerned, Navy SEALs rescued you from Petra and returned you to Aqaba where you continued your charter flight. You'll never give the press any details about your rescue. Any questions?"

Rod raised his hand. "I got one: Who the hell keeps attacking us and why?"

"Yeah, they killed Hal and Tawnee," Carlene said. "Did you catch them and shoot their criminal asses?"

Captain Kingston and the intel officer exchanged glances. "I'll let Commander Robert Metz of Naval Intelligence answer that." He nodded at the officer with the dark-blond crew cut.

"A group of mercenaries have branched out into kidnapping high-value celebrities for large ransoms. The three of you, along with Captain Starr, would net them a big payday. I suggest you arrange for extra security in the places you're scheduled to visit. As you know, Captain Starr was injured when she jumped from the Boeing. Chief Pilot Jeff Rowlin will take her place." He glanced at Jeff and me. "Isn't that right, Commander Rowlin?"

"Yes, sir, and I'll take the necessary precautions to ensure the safety of my passengers and crew. I cancelled the leg to Dubai. The film festival would be over by the time we landed. I understand you're sending us to Aqaba via Naples later today." Jeff gave me a meaningful glance.

"If we send you straight from the ship to Aqaba, Jordanian authorities will know you were here and that you took the airplane. Instead, you'll land at our Navy base in Naples disguised as military personnel. Then you'll change to civilian clothes and board a Navy transport to Aqaba."

"What about Sam? Is she coming with us?" Lance knitted his brows.

Commander Metz shook his head. "Captain Starr needs to recuperate. We'll arrange transport for her."

He pushed a button on a recorder. "Now, let's start with the celebrities. Mr. Stone, please give us an account of everything that happened after you disembarked the tour bus in Petra."

As the actors recounted our ordeal in Petra, I noticed the astonished looks of the Navy officers, including Jeff. Jack's account was straightforward, but the others couldn't resist embellishing. The size of the scorpions grew with each new telling. Rod was last, and he insisted they were as big as rats. My crew listened and smiled.

"All right, that covers the celebrity interviews. Anything else you'd like to add before you're excused?" Commander Metz asked.

"I'd like Navy SEALs to accompany us to Aqaba, you know, for security reasons and to help us sell the cover story." Carlene gave Commander Metz her million-dollar smile.

"Good idea!" Inga nodded.

"Arriving with a SEAL team would give credibility to the cover story," Lance said.

Captain Kingston nodded. "I agree. I'll make it happen."

Commander Metz stood and faced the celebrities as he switched off the recorder. "Thank you for your cooperation. Follow Ensign Marsik, who'll take you to the wardroom for lunch."

Ensign Marsik waited by the door as the actors walked around the table to me.

"We're not leaving until we hug our captain. She saved our butts several times." Rod gave me a gentle hug, followed by the others.

"Be careful. I'll miss you all." I waved good-bye and watched them leave.

"Next up, I'd like to hear from the flight attendant." The commander switched the recorder back on.

Inga gave a professional account of her experience, hugged me, and left the conference room.

My turn.

67

"ALL RIGHT, MISS STARR, let's discuss what's really going on. I'll move you over to the empty side so your brother can join you." Commander Metz pulled back my chair and helped me around. "Your fellow pilots are military men. Secrets aren't an issue."

Matt knocked and walked in.

"Lieutenant Starr, have a seat next to your sister," the captain said. "We're ready to hear her story."

Commander Metz switched on the recorder.

"The women in my family line have psychic abilities, mostly visions during dreams, but sometimes while awake. In Hong Kong, I saw a vision of an ancient island civilization that Harvard Professor Ben Armitage, a friend who's an expert in antiquities, thinks was Atlantis. Later, I saw the catastrophic destruction of Atlantis on a hologram and saw it rise again on another hologram in a hidden chamber in Petra."

"Our Navy discovered Atlantis during the Cuban Missile Crisis in the '60s," Captain Kingston said. "One of our subs almost hit a massive pyramid underwater near Cuba. We kept it secret for years, but recently two scientists leaked the information. They posted pictures of the submerged city on the Internet." He smiled. "Go on."

I told them about all my visions, the curio shop in Hong Kong, and the artifact. "Professor Armitage thinks it's the prototype for Poseidon's Sword, a possible doomsday weapon invented by scientists in Atlantis. It almost burned down his house when he tinkered with it."

"Odd they call it Poseidon's *Sword*," Captain Kingston said. "The god of the sea carries a trident."

"I think sword may have been meant as a metaphor for something far more deadly than a trident," Commander Metz said.

"I agree. Their technology is amazing." I showed them the pendant I found in Agra.

As they passed it around the table, I told them about the German-accented kidnappers and the unknown sniper who killed them at the Taj Mahal. I concluded with my account of Petra, including how my attackers were also shot by unknown snipers.

"So this pendant opened the mountain in Petra?" The commander held it out to me.

"Yes, and it opened a door on the other side of the mountain where we exited. Watch this." I activated the diamond pyramid.

"Whoa, what's that? It's as bright as a laser." Commander Metz leaned back from my outstretched hand.

I handed him the pendant. "Here, touch the diamond. It isn't hot."

"How did you do that?" Captain Kingston asked, looking amazed.

"Sam's psychic energy is the right electromagnetic frequency to activate it, just like she did with the weapon prototype," Matt said. "Professor Armitage thinks my family's ancestors are from Atlantis." Matt put his arm around me and smiled proudly.

Lance joined in. "The Dragon Master in Hong Kong told her to follow the dragon current and warned her about the Black Sun. We've since learned that dragon currents are ley lines, and the Black Sun is a Nazi cult bent on world domination."

"How did the Black Sun know Sam would get the weapon prototype?" Captain Kingston said. "I'd like to know how they found her in that curio shop at just the right time."

"They couldn't have known I was going there. *I* didn't know I was going to that shop until the day I went. Unless—"

"Unless what?" Captain Kingston asked.

"It's possible there's a written prophecy about me. The Dragon Master told me my destiny lies hidden in one teardrop on the cheek of time in a rose-red city as old as time. He might have omitted the part about the curio shop since I was already there."

"The teardrop is the Taj Mahal, and the rose-red city is Petra," Lance said.

"Any idea who your guardian angel snipers might be?" Commander Metz asked.

"Not the SAS—I asked them. I doubt it's the Dragon Society. I got the impression their sole mission was to give me the prototype. Could be a rival group to the Black Sun. Both times, I couldn't see the snipers. They must've been too far away." I hung the pendant around my neck.

Matt turned to me. "What about Nicolai? Could he be working with the Black Sun?"

"Who's Nicolai?" The intel officer looked confused.

"Nicolai Vasiliev is a psychotic Russian giant who nearly killed me last summer in Scotland. He's former Spetsnaz and a skilled assassin. I don't think he's connected to the Black Sun. They all seem to be German." I glanced from Commander Metz to Captain Kingston.

"We can't let that Nazi cult get a weapon of mass destruction," the captain said. "And we should look for a rival group that wants the weapon. They could be shadowing you to protect you until you find it. I'll see to it all the resources of the U.S. intelligence community focus on solving this puzzle before it's too late."

"We need to keep my sister safely hidden somewhere. The Black Sun and who knows how many other groups are hunting her." Matt's voice was filled with worry.

"I'll stay with Ross in his castle. He can protect me."

Matt shook his head. "That's the first place they'll look. He can't fight a small army alone."

Lance nudged Jeff. "Pete can cover the copilot duties for the rest of the charter flights. We don't have any more extended legs. I could take Sam to my cabin on Possum Kingdom Lake in Texas. Nobody will look there."

"You don't know that." Matt's face reddened. "They've had little trouble tracking her so far. If they follow you to that cabin, you'll be toast."

"Everybody calm down. Lance, I appreciate your kind offer, but I'm going to Scotland. I'll stay in Duncan MacLeod's castle in Craigervie. He has loads of secret passages and places to hide me. Don't forget he and his butler, Baxter, were Special Forces soldiers in the SAS. Ross and his team can help protect me there. And Mom can nurse me back to health."

The captain cleared his throat. "Eh, Miss Starr, we'd like to keep this situation under American control. The Brits don't know about the weapon and the Black Sun."

"Ross knows, which means his commanders probably know. The UK appreciates what I did for them last August. They'll do whatever's necessary to protect me."

Matt nodded. "That's true. And Ross knows everything we know. In fact, he may know more because he followed Sam's trail into the mountain in Petra. He may have seen the ancient chamber she encountered."

"What? Ross was in Petra? Is he okay? I didn't know he

went looking for me."

"His team parachuted in the morning after your group vanished. He saw the 727 take off and knew you were aboard because you activated the emergency button on your DARPA watch. He sent me an email," Matt said.

"His soldiers are probably the ones who fired at the airplane during takeoff. Wish I'd known." I turned to the captain. "I understand America wants custody of the weapon when it's found, but I'm not about to go looking for it in my condition. After I'm healed, I'll help our military find it. Okay?"

"We'll work something out with the Brits. Commander Metz will communicate with you daily. I'll arrange transport for you. You'll be in disguise during transit. Is that acceptable?" The captain gave me an encouraging smile.

"Thank you, Captain Kingston. I appreciate all the help you've given me. I promise to keep Commander Metz in the loop." I smiled and sighed. "I guess we should say our good-byes now, in case we don't connect again before our flights depart."

The captain gently kissed my hand. "Miss Starr, it has been my pleasure."

Commander Metz took my hand. "I'll see you before you leave." He walked out with the captain.

Matt hugged me. "I'll wait for you outside and walk you to your cabin."

I turned to the three brave men I had the privilege of working with.

"Jeff, thanks for saving our butts back in Egypt. Sorry for leaving the 767 in Aqaba and bringing the Black Sun down on our tour group." I hugged him and planted a kiss on his cheek.

"Hey, don't worry about it. You didn't know that would happen. Stay safe in Scotland and let me know how you're doing if you can communicate without compromising your security."

Pete hugged me. "Be careful, Sam." He walked out and left me alone with Lance.

Lance stepped closer. "When you jumped out of the 727, did your jaw hit the deck? Maybe you chipped a tooth or hurt your mouth?"

"No, I wore a helmet. My body is severely bruised, but my head and mouth are okay."

"Good." Lance pinned me against the wall and kissed me with a passion so intense it felt like I was in a fighter doing multiple snap rolls.

When he pulled back, he looked into my eyes. "Sam ... if you need me, anytime, anywhere, call me, and I'll be there. Please, stay safe."

His liquid-green eyes looked into my soul as he held the door open for me.

Matt peeked into the room. "Sam? You coming?"

"Huh?" I felt weak in the knees. "Uh, um, yeah."

Texas men. Damn.

68

I STOOD IN PRIMARY Flight Control, or Pri-Fly as the pilots called it, the glass-enclosed part of the island tower where the air boss controlled air traffic departing and arriving on the ship.

The air boss pointed at a twin-engine propjet. "Your people are about to launch on the COD."

"COD?"

"Carrier On-board Delivery. That one's a C-2A Greyhound with twin turboprops. They're ready in the catapult." He turned and spoke into his boom mike. "COD is cleared to launch from CAT two."

I watched the C-2A roar to full power. The catapult instantly flung the COD into the sky. The airplane climbed and banked toward Italy.

"I guess they didn't have room for me on that flight." I watched the airplane vanish in the clouds.

"The skipper has something more exciting planned for you." The air boss gave me a knowing smile. "You'll arrive in Naples long before your friends."

Matt tapped my shoulder. "The skipper said I'd find you here." He held up a G-suit with *Bombshell* sewn on the left breast. "Think this'll fit?"

My spirit soared. "Seriously? A ride in a fighter?"

He grinned. "Yep, I'm taking you to Naples in an F/A-18F.

That's a two-seat Super Hornet. Let's get you suited up. We launch in twenty."

He led me out of Pri-Fly, and I waved good-bye to the air boss. He smiled and saluted.

Minutes later, I looked like a real fighter pilot in the G-suit. Matt briefed me on ejection protocol and everything else I needed to know. I felt like a little kid at Christmas. Everyone who saw me broke into a big smile.

My doctor approached with a concerned look. "Sam, are you sure you want to fly in the fighter? The G-forces from the CAT launch and fighter flight might pop your stitches."

"No way am I missing a chance to fly a Super Hornet! I can get stitched up again in Naples. It's only a breast wound." I gave her a pleading look. "Please, Doc, this is a chance of a lifetime for me."

"All right, but only if your brother promises to take it easy on you and not do anything crazy." Her voice had a stern tone.

"Don't worry, Doc, I'll keep my baby sister safe." Matt put his arm around my shoulders.

Doctor Carole smiled. "It was a pleasure meeting you, Sam. Try to stay out of trouble. Remember, your body needs time to heal." She saluted us and walked away.

Commander Metz walked in. "Sam, we have a military Gulfstream jet waiting for you in Naples. They'll take you to Edinburgh where you'll transfer to a helicopter for the flight to the SAS base in Dundee. Wear the flight suit and helmet when you transfer to the Gulfstream and again when you board the helicopter. Captain Sinclair will meet you when you land at the SAS base. Any questions?"

"How should I communicate with you?"

"Use this encrypted satellite phone. It will work almost anywhere except underground." He handed me the phone. "My number is taped on the side. Put it in one of the zippered pockets in your jumpsuit. Call me when you're secure at MacLeod Castle."

"Thank you, Commander Metz. I'll call you when I arrive in Craigervie." I kissed his cheek.

He smiled at the unexpected affection. "Have a safe trip, Miss Starr."

Matt led me out to the flight deck and pointed at a nearby fighter. "There's our ride. Ready to rock 'n' roll, Sis?"

"Hoo yah! Let's hit it." I fastened my helmet and climbed the boarding ladder.

It wasn't long before I heard the air boss in my helmet. "Rodeo and Bombshell, cleared to launch from CAT one."

Our jet vibrated at takeoff power. In an instant, we sprang from zero to 165 mph and kept accelerating. The Gs pinned me against the seat with a distorted grin as we shot into the sky.

"Hot damn!" I screamed.

"Rodeo is cleared to angels twenty. Give her a good ride," the air boss said in a fatherly tone.

Matt repeated his clearance to the air boss, pulled the stick back, hit the afterburners, and blasted us straight up into the wild blue yonder. In seconds, the massive aircraft carrier looked like a tiny speck on the sea.

At twenty-thousand feet, Matt leveled off. "It's all yours, Sis. We have room to play until we get closer to the Italian coast."

I whipped the Super Hornet into some lightning-fast aileron rolls and giggled. "Oh my god, Matt, this is amazing! I've never flown anything like this."

"Want me to show you all the cool stuff it can do? That is, if you're feeling okay."

"Hell yes, brother dear, give me a ride I'll never forget."

And he did. We danced across the sky in a high-performance aerial ballet. Matt talked me through the combat maneuvers, then took over as we hooked up with an airborne tanker for inflight refueling, another thrill.

As we approached Naples, Matt gave me one last surprise. "Sis, you'll make the landing. It'll be our secret. I'll talk you through it, just like I did for your carrier landing in the 727."

"Wow, you really are fearless." I laughed. "Okay, Rodeo, let's do it."

"Damn straight, Bombshell. Make your big brother proud."

The Hornet felt squirrely in my hands compared to a Boeing airliner, which felt as steady as flying a house. The Super Hornet's sensitive controls responded to the slightest touch. My hands sweated in my flight gloves as I concentrated on the glide path and extended centerline of the runway.

"Looking good, Sis. Hold steady. Watch your airspeed. Your pitch is perfect. Add a little power. Good. Hold this attitude. When you get close to the runway, flare it just a little."

I eased back on the stick as we neared the pavement, and the main wheels kissed the runway.

"That was shit hot, Sis! Lower the nose gear and ease it into reverse. Perfect. Okay, I'll taxi it to the ramp and complete the after-landing checklist. Good job!"

Matt parked on the ramp and shut down the engines.

"Thanks for giving me a flight I'll never forget, Matt. That was a dream come true. I don't think I'll ever stop smiling."

"My pleasure, Sis, you're a good stick. Too bad Dad wouldn't let you join the Navy. You would have made a great fighter pilot."

"That's assuming my nerves could survive all the terrifying carrier landings. Aerial combat must seem like a cakewalk compared to landing on a pitching flight deck at night in bad weather. You're the man!"

"I admit my job has its moments." He pointed to his right. "Looks like your Gulfstream is ready to depart. Don't go inside the terminal. They want you to board directly from here."

Matt opened the canopy, and we climbed down the ladders the ground crew had positioned.

"I guess this is good-bye. I love you, Sis. Stay safe." He saluted me.

I saluted Matt. "I'd like to hug you, but I'd blow my cover. I sure am proud of you. Give my best to your skipper and tell him how much I enjoyed the flight. Stay safe, Matt. Love you." I swallowed a lump in my throat as I walked away with my small travel bag.

As I approached the boarding stairs with my helmet on, the copilot met me and grinned at the call sign on my flight suit.

"Welcome aboard, Bombshell." He led me up the airstairs and motioned for me to sit in the plush cabin.

I buckled my seat belt as he retracted the stairs and closed the forward entry door. The pilot started taxiing when the copilot entered the cockpit. Moments later, we were on the takeoff roll. I took one final glimpse of the Super Hornet as we flashed past the ramp. After we were airborne, I removed my helmet.

Hope I get a warm reception from Ross.

69

ROSS WAS WAITING FOR me when I exited the helicopter at the SAS base in Dundee, Scotland. He saluted me to continue the ruse. I returned his salute and followed him inside. He led me into his office and locked the door.

I pulled off my helmet and fluffed my hair. "Ross, I missed you." I reached for him.

He focused on the name sewn over my left breast. "Bombshell?"

"It's my call sign. Matt's fighter squadron gave it to me after my carrier landing."

"The name fits." He pulled me against him and kissed me with a fierce passion.

Memories of our first tryst in his office flooded back. He swept his desk clean with one hand and held me with the other. He unzipped my flight suit as I unbuttoned his shirt.

In seconds, he stripped me and laid me across his desk. As he worked his way down, kissing my lips, neck, and nipples, he stopped cold when he kissed my left breast.

"Sam, you're bleeding!" He reached for tissues and blotted the blood.

I tried to see the underside of my breast, which was impossible without a mirror. "Did the stitches come loose?"

Ross dabbed the wound and looked closer. "Two stitches broke. What happened? This looks like a stab wound. I'll call the medic." He leaned over me to reach for the phone.

I grabbed his hand and pulled him to me. "I popped the stitches hours ago when I flew a fighter with Matt. Right now I need you more than a medic. Call him later." I kissed him.

Ross looked at my body and gasped. "Sam, you're covered with bruises. Are you sure—"

I wrapped my legs around him. "You have the medicine I need, Doctor Sinclair. Now get busy."

"Aye, Sir Lady, I'll have you smiling in no time."

Later, the medic applied Steri-Strips and a new dressing. "This should hold you until you heal." He glanced at Ross. "No rough stuff, Captain Sinclair."

"Don't blame Ross. I was like this when I arrived." I smiled at my sexy boyfriend.

"Right, so why did you wait so long to call me?" The medic sounded accusative.

"I had more important matters to deal with first. Isn't that so, Captain Sinclair?"

Ross smiled. "That will be all, Sergeant. Thank you."

The medic smiled and left us alone.

"I have black combat fatigues and a helmet for you to wear until I have you safely inside Duncan's castle." Ross handed me the uniform. "Here, see if this fits."

I put it on. "A bit baggy, but close enough." I tried the helmet.

"Good, but stuff that long blond hair inside. This should pass muster in the dark."

Ross wore a uniform identical to mine. "We're taking a Lynx to MacLeod Castle. It will look like we're relieving soldiers on guard duty."

I grabbed my little bag containing my precious flight suit and bomber jacket. It wasn't long before we landed on Duncan's lawn. We saluted the soldiers who met the helicopter

271

and entered the ancient stone fortress.

Duncan and Mom were waiting for us in the great hall. Fires blazed in the massive hearths, and red velvet drapes covered the soaring windows.

I pulled off my helmet and rushed to my mother. "Mom, it's so good to see you! I missed you."

She hugged me. "I was so worried. Are you all right?" She looked me over.

The uniform hid my bruises and bandaged breast. "I'm fine, just a bit sore from a fall yesterday." I smiled at Duncan. "Good to see you too."

He kissed my cheek. "We're relieved you're here, dear. You must see what's beneath the castle, but only if you feel up to the steep stairs down the cliff."

"I'm good. Show me now." I glanced at Ross. Would he object?

Ross smiled and offered me his hand. "I'll go down with you. You'll want to see this. It's a lot like the circular chamber inside the mountain in Petra."

Duncan rang for Baxter. "We'll need four torches. Sam wants to see the secret chamber."

While we waited, I checked in with Commander Metz on the satellite phone.

Baxter returned with the flashlights, and Duncan led us down the secret passage's stone steps to the North Sea. Halfway down, we stopped in a small alcove two hundred feet above the sea.

"Sam, put your right hand on that handprint." Mom pointed her flashlight at it.

I pressed my hand against the gold and heard grinding as the stone door opened. She hugged me.

"See? I knew she could do it." Mom grinned at Duncan and Ross.

"Did you open this the first time, Mom?"

"Yes, come and see what's inside." She motioned to me.

Ross stepped in front of me. "This is one time where the men must enter first. As soon as you and your mother are inside, the door will close." Ross ducked his head.

Mom and I followed Duncan through the door, which closed behind us. I recognized the three goddesses on the wall and scenes from Atlantis.

Mom pointed at the crystal pyramids held by the triplets. "You'll be amazed when you touch the crystals." She seemed giddy.

When I did, a hologram appeared in the center of the room. Three baby girls with the same features as the three women appeared and grew older in a high-speed sequence that ended when they reached the same age as the goddesses. They stood back-to-back atop a huge obsidian pyramid, each holding a brilliant crystal. The scene ended in a blinding flash.

I noticed everyone's shocked looks. "Is something wrong? Is this what you saw last time?"

"Not even close," Ross said.

Duncan looked at my mother. "Loren, darling, your face is pale. Are you all right?"

She blinked and took a deep breath. "I think I know who the three women are. Let's go upstairs. I need a drink and some chocolate."

"Mom? What's wrong?"

"I'll explain upstairs." She pointed at the footprint as she clutched Duncan's arm. "Sam, place your bare foot on the gold to open the door."

We climbed the steps and headed for Duncan's study. Baxter provided glasses of Merlot and chocolate cake for Mother and me and whisky for the men.

"Sorry, Baxter, I think I need whisky this time." Mom

watched him pour her a double.

"I should have made the connection when Professor Armitage told me the names of two of the goddesses, but I assumed the images were women from the ancient past." She drank half the whisky.

"My best friend, Sheila Conor, looked so much like me, people thought we were sisters. She gave birth to triplets on the winter solstice two years after Sam was born. Her daughters, Solraya, Luna, and Blaze, had identical features, except for their hair and eye colors, like the women in the secret chamber. Twenty-three years ago, Sheila was lost in a plane crash in the Himalayas."

I was stunned. "I remember you told me she had the same psychic powers as you."

"Yes, we had so much in common, and her blond triplet looked like you." Mom sighed.

"Professor Armitage couldn't decipher the name of the fire goddess. It must be Blaze." I sucked in a deep breath. "What happened to the babies?"

"They were with their parents when the plane crashed. Everyone assumed they were killed, but their bodies were never found. There was one survivor—a flight attendant."

"Do you know her name? Maybe she could tell us something that could help us find the girls," Duncan said.

"Richard Conor's company, Gold Trident Industries, should have the information on file. I'll call them." She pulled out her cell.

"Holy cow! I've been following gold trident symbols. I found them on the artifact in Hong Kong, on the Taj and pendant in Agra, and inside the mountain in Petra. We assumed the three women were a vision from the past, but they could be a prophecy of the future." I took a long drink.

"If they're alive, we have to find them. I have a feeling

they're in grave danger." Mom scrolled through her phone directory and found the number for the American headquarters of Gold Trident Industries.

The offices were open because they were five hours behind Great Britain. Mom spoke with the CEO, Richard's younger brother, Tim Conor, and soon had the information we needed.

"I can't believe this. The lone survivor, flight attendant Suzanne Berglind, married a man she met when her part of the airplane slid into his base camp on Mount Everest. She lives in England now. Her husband is Lord Colin Covington. They have a large estate near York."

"I know Lord Covington. I'll arrange a meeting, and we'll get this sorted." Duncan glanced at his watch and reached for the phone.

"Laird Duncan Macleod calling Lord Covington with a matter of great urgency. Aye, I'll hold." After a brief wait, Duncan said, "Colin, good of you to take my call." He explained his request and paused. "Aye, tomorrow afternoon. May we land a helicopter on the lawn? Good. See you then."

I looked at Ross. "I want to go too."

"You'll have to wear the SAS uniform and ride in a military helicopter with me. We'll land at the nearest military base and drive in. Duncan and Loren will fly there in a private helicopter."

I nodded. "That's fine with me as long as I get to go. I have questions that need answers."

"Please explain us to the Covingtons," Ross said to Duncan and Loren. "We can't let Sam be seen in public without her military disguise."

My mother stared at me. "Oh, my God! I know why the Black Sun wants you. You're a carbon copy of Solraya, and your touch activates the weapon. They think *you* are the blond triplet known as the Golden Goddess."

"The Dragon Master addressed me as Solraya Twin. I believe they think I'm her non-related twin—a woman with the same appearance and psychic power, but not her sister. Lucky me."

I drained my wine glass as the color drained from my face.

70

NICOLAI PACED ON THE terrace of Sweetwater's Caribbean island home as he spoke into the satellite phone. "What do you mean she vanished in Petra? Find her!" He roared with rage.

"Relax. My men killed everyone who was hunting her. She's hiding somewhere in the mountains." Lord Sweetwater sounded confident.

"Send team back to find her." Nicolai reached for his glass of Zyr.

"Petra is crawling with Jordanian soldiers and SAS teams. They'll find her. We're listening to her boyfriend's and relatives' phone calls. We'll know something soon."

"I am tired waiting. I must have revenge."

"You've only been there three and a half weeks. Be patient."

"I am not patient man. I will not wait much longer."

71

AN HOUR BEFORE DAWN, Captain Jeff Rowlin boarded the Luxury International 767 parked in Aqaba, Jordan. At six-five, he ducked his head out of habit from spending a week on the Navy ship.

Lieutenant Joe Kernan of SEAL Team Six followed him in and stood in front of the seven crew members and sixteen passengers. The two flight attendants and thirteen passengers, who had been waiting at the Hotel Royal ever since their friends and coworkers vanished in Petra, were aboard with the returning actors and crew.

The lieutenant held a mike close to his mouth. "Keep the window shades down. It's easy to see inside a lighted airplane at night. We helped your pilots do a careful inspection of the aircraft, including scanning for bugs and tracking devices. We found five."

He paused when the passengers gasped. "You're safe now. We also searched and scanned the luggage before it was loaded. Remember to stay vigilant. Captain Rowlin wants to depart for Paris as soon as my team disembarks. Any questions?"

Carlene raised her hand and batted her lashes. "Can we keep you until we leave Paris? I'd feel a lot safer with SEALs looking after me."

Inga smiled sweetly. "I agree with Carlene. We need you.

Can't the Navy spare your team for another day?"

"Yeah, we need armed protection. Ask Captain Kingston." Rod looked like he needed a boatload of Xanax to calm his nerves.

"You'll be safe with Captain Rowlin. Our COD is ready to depart. Good-bye and have a safe flight." He saluted, handed the mike to Jeff, and joined his team on the ramp.

Blond and blue eyed, Jeff looked like a Nordic sea captain, minus the beard. "Hello, I'm Captain Jeff Rowlin. As you know, Hal and Tawnee were killed and Captain Starr was injured in Petra. I'm replacing her for the duration of your charter flight. The Dubai flight was cancelled. I arranged for private security guards to meet our airplane in Paris and stick with us until we depart. We'll keep you safe."

"Maybe Jack should ask Admiral Stone to send a SAS team with us." Rod looked concerned.

"No time for that. We're leaving. Buckle up and wave good-bye to Jordan." Jeff entered the cockpit.

Lance and Pete followed Jeff as Inga closed the forward entry door. Lance slid into the right seat, and Pete sat in the jumpseat behind them.

"That's one nervous group of passengers. No joking on the PA. Let's give them a nice calm flight." Jeff adjusted his seat and buckled his harness.

"A normal flight will be a welcome change." Lance tapped in the flight info for the navigation computer. "Looks like west over the Mediterranean, then northwest past Sicily to Paris for noise abatement."

"Yep, pre-dawn over the sea and dawn patrol into Paris. Should be easy," Jeff said.

Pete glanced at Lance. "I guess we should warn Jeff about Carlene ... she's not as harmless as she looks."

"What do you mean? She's barely five feet." Jeff glanced

from Pete to Lance.

"He means she's an insatiable man-eating vixen. I have the scars to prove it."

Jeff laughed. "You've got to be kidding. You're complaining about hot sex with a movie star?" Jeff shook his head.

"Lance is serious. She may be tiny, but she's aggressive as hell. Don't say we didn't warn you." Pete tightened his harness.

The flight crew completed the checklists. Soon the charter was on the takeoff roll at Aqaba International Airport. After the initial climb, Jeff turned the big airliner toward the Mediterranean Sea.

Later, he felt uneasy as he glanced at the Egyptian coast and thought about what had happened two days earlier.

Air traffic control called on the radio. "Luxury 813, fog is building around Paris. Reduce speed to 280 knots."

Lance answered the call. "Luxury 813 is reducing speed to 280 knots."

As their airliner crossed the pale pre-dawn sky over water midway between Tripoli and Sicily, two unmarked L-39 fighter jets appeared forward of their wings.

"Uh, Jeff, we've got company." Lance studied the fighter on his side.

"I see them—L-39s. No flags. Looks like R60 air-to-air missiles on the outer pylons."

Lance pulled out his mini binoculars. "They've got 23-millimeter twin-barreled cannons too. A friend of mine has an L-39, told me all about it and the weaponry on the ones used by the military in Third-World countries. They're not as fast as a 767. They never would've been able to intercept us at our normal speed."

"Too bad we can't outrun their missiles," Jeff said in a calm tone.

Pete pointed. "The one on the left is holding up a sign:

FOLLOW US OR DIE. NO RADIO CALLS."

72

"USUALLY STUFF LIKE THIS only happens when Sam's with us."
Lance shook his head.

Jeff pulled a SATCOM from his flight bag and handed it to
Pete. "Duck down so they can't see you and call the AWACS
aircraft. It's already set to their number. Tell them to send
fighters."

Lance glanced at Jeff. "What do we do in the meantime?"

"We play along. Turn on the seat-belt sign and tell the
cabin crew to strap in." Jeff followed the fighter on his side as
it banked to the left and descended toward Africa.

Pete put the SATCOM on speaker so Jeff could hear the
military's response. "Luxury 813, we scrambled the fighters.
Remain over water. F/A-18s en route, ETA fifteen minutes.
Enemy aircraft too close to your airplane for long-distance
missile shots from the fighters."

"We'll be over the coast in fifteen. No way are we landing
in Muslim-controlled territory." Jeff throttled back to 250
knots to give the American fighters time to arrive.

"Unable to pursue into foreign territory after recent Egypt
incident. Stay over water. Do not cross the coast."

As the airliner neared Africa, Lance wiped his brow, and
Jeff cracked his knuckles.

American fighter pilots were known as highly skilled
predators of the sky, and Jeff was no exception. His mind

reeled with scenarios to defeat the enemy.

"Lance, is the fighter on your side directly in line with our wingtip?" Jeff checked the L-39 on his side.

"Looks like it, and we're only thirty miles from the coast. The Super Hornets won't get here in time."

Jeff throttled back to 230 knots.

The L-39s slowed for the 767 to catch up. Their pilots needed to remain close to the airliner to preclude a long-distance missile shot from an American fighter.

"Luxury 813, AWACS has you approaching the coast. Fighters two minutes out. DO NOT CROSS THE COAST."

Jeff checked the positions of the L-39s and saw he was seconds from crossing over land.

"Screw this! No way will I let terrorists take us!" He reverted to fighter-pilot mode and pushed the throttles to full power. "They aren't expecting us to accelerate. Time to splash two tangos."

Jeff knew he had to take out both fighters simultaneously or the remaining L-39 would shoot them down. With absolute precision, he slammed his wingtips into the tails of the fighters before they could react. The big Boeing crushed their tails and glass canopies as its wingtips raked across the L-39s.

As the fighters fell into the sea, Jeff checked his controls. He adjusted the throttles and banked the 767 hard to the right, away from the coast.

He grabbed the SATCOM. "AWACS, this is *Bücker*. Splashed enemy fighters. Need escort to prevent retaliation."

"How did you do that? Never mind. F/A-18s are closing on you. Continue north across the sea. I'll patch the fighters into your SATCOM."

Jeff held the SATCOM close to his mouth. "Understood. *Bücker* is on frequency."

"*Bücker*, this is Rodeo. We have your Boeing in sight.

Where are the L-39s?"

"Splashed 'em, took out their tails with my wingtips. Close in tight and check my wings."

"Hoo yah, *Bücker*, splashing two fighters with an unarmed airliner! You just made aviation history. Uh, left wingtip's gone, sheared off the outer three feet or so. The rest of the wing looks good."

"Hot damn, *Bücker*! This is Jersey. Your right wingtip's gone too. Looks like it broke off about three feet from the end. The good news is the wings look symmetrical."

"That's why all right-thinking pilots say, 'If it's not a Boeing, we're not going.'"

"Heads up, *Bücker*, enemy fighters approaching your six. Rodeo has missile lock on the one on my side."

"Jersey has tone on the other one. Continue north, *Bücker*. We'll splash the tangos."

Seconds later, Rodeo reported, "Enemy fighters down. *Bücker* is clear."

"Thanks, Rodeo and Jersey. Not sure how I'll explain my wing damage. I'd better land at the Navy base in Naples and keep this quiet. As far as the world is concerned, you guys shot down *all* the L-39s."

"Rodeo suggests you call Commander Metz on the SATCOM. He'll take care of it."

"Good idea. In the meantime, I'll tell ATC we have radio problems that require a landing in Naples."

"We'll shadow you to the Italian coast, *Bücker*. You now have legendary status with the Navy. Nobody will ever top this. You're shit hot, man!"

Lance grinned. "He's right about that, Jeff. Your ballsy maneuver will be recorded in the annals of aviation history."

"I'm just happy it worked." Jeff blew out a sigh.

"Oh, and thanks for savin' my butt, again. Sam was right

about you. She told me if she was flying a fully armed Super Hornet and you were in a Piper Cub with a BB gun, you'd still find a way to take her down." Lance laughed.

"Yeah, thanks, Jeff. Guess we can't blame Sam for this one." Pete patted Jeff's back.

"The jury's still out on that. The terrorists don't know she isn't aboard." Jeff adjusted the elevator trim. "Lance, call Inga and check on the cabin."

Lance called Inga on the intercom and reported back, "Inga said all's well in the cabin."

"Good, I'll have some explaining to do when we land in Naples. We'll need a good cover story, and we'd better pray the passengers didn't see those L39s." Jeff glanced at Lance.

"I hope the Al Ghazi network isn't after Sam. She's got enough enemies without them," Pete said.

"If they're onto her, they'll be after us too. I think the hijacking was a fishing expedition. They wanted to land us on a terrorist airfield so they could find out if we knew what happened to their leaders. We'd better watch our backs for a good long while."

"Dang, our job's not supposed to be *this* stressful." Lance shook his head.

Lance answered a call from ATC and told them the radios were intermittent, and they were diverting to Naples.

Jeff called Commander Metz on the SATCOM. "We've got big problems. Meet us in Naples."

73

THE SPY HELD THE mobile phone to his ear. He zipped his jacket and gazed across the bay as he gave his report to Lord Sweetwater.

"Navy SEALs rescued her group in Petra and brought them to Aqaba. Her charter to Paris made an unscheduled landing at the U.S. Navy base in Naples, but we aren't sure she's on the flight."

"I'll send a team to Naples. They can grab the crew and find out where she is," Sweetwater said.

"Loren Starr and Laird MacLeod are taking a private helicopter to an estate in York today for a luncheon with Lord and Lady Covington." He raised his collar against the brisk wind.

"I'll send the team watching MacLeod Castle to York. They may get a chance to snatch Mrs. Starr. She must know where her daughter is. Good job."

74

WERNER STOOD ON THE balcony of his top-floor suite in the centuries-old Highlander Inn in Craigervie, Scotland. He gazed down at the angry North Sea under a gray mid-morning sky. Foamy waves crashed into the rock cliff and splashed plumes of salty spray. He turned his back to the cold, wet wind to protect his mobile against his ear.

"I used the tail number on the helicopter in Petra to find them. The pilot feared his employer more than death. The promise of millions and a ride to South America loosened his tongue. After he talked, I disposed of him."

"Our enemy's name?"

"Lord Edgar Sweetwater, British billionaire arms dealer. Lives on a big estate northeast of London. He has a sniper team shadowing the Golden Twin."

"Why?"

"Sweetwater wants Poseidon's Sword. He thinks she will lead him to it."

"How does he know Samantha Starr's travel plans?"

"He has a high-tech spy facility in Dundee. They tap into all her phone calls and text messages."

"Where is she now?"

"Sweetwater is not sure. We have a parabolic listening device focused on their spy facility. They tracked her charter flight to the U.S. Navy base in Naples and also have a team watching MacLeod Castle near Craigervie where her mother is staying. I sent a team to Naples, and I have another team here near the castle. Sweetwater sent a team to Naples too."

"Destroy the rival teams first, then take the crew in Naples and interrogate them. Do the same with her mother in Craigervie."

"British Special Forces are guarding the castle. It will be easier to take the mother when she visits the Covingtons in York today. They are landing a private helicopter at the estate."

"I'll expect good news soon."

"*Jawohl*, Master."

75

AS JEFF PACED BY the conference-room window of the Navy base, he heard a turbo-prop aircraft in reverse thrust. He looked out and saw the COD taxi to the ramp.

"Commander Metz just arrived. I hope he has a plan to keep our involvement with the L-39s secret. Too bad they don't have a hangar big enough to hide our Boeing." Jeff gazed at the tarps covering the outer wings of the big airliner.

"Good thing the passengers were asleep with the shades down when we hit the fighters. Inga said it happened so fast, no one in the cabin saw the collision." Lance poured a cup of coffee.

"They woke when they felt us hit something, but they didn't know what happened. She told them we hit a flock of birds." Pete checked his watch. "Commander Metz will be here any minute."

Right on cue, the Navy intelligence officer walked in. "Good morning, gentlemen. I wasn't expecting to see you again so soon. Lieutenant Starr told me you had some trouble today." He poured a cup of coffee and sat at the table.

Jeff briefed the commander on their encounter with the L-39s. "My main concern is keeping this a secret and getting our airplane repaired without questions about the damage."

"I took care of it. Boeing is a military contractor, and my brother is one of their top engineers. New wing tips will arrive soon with a maintenance crew. Repairs will be made with no questions asked." The commander sipped his coffee.

"A bigger concern is why Al Ghazi targeted your airplane. They can't possibly know who took their command center or what happened to their leaders."

"What if the Egyptian fighter pilots knew who owned the 727 I escorted out of their airspace? They could have sent word back to Al Ghazi," Jeff said.

"You were in a U.S. Navy fighter identified by your call sign. The Egyptians couldn't have made a connection to your airline or flight crew. It plays in perfectly with our soon-to-be-released story that our Navy took the Al Ghazi command aircraft."

Lance sighed. "Then this was a fishing expedition to see if our people knew anything about their 727. The sooner you release that story, the better it will be for us."

Pete joined in. "Are we certain the L-39s belonged to Al Ghazi? What if it was the Black Sun trying to capture Sam? They probably don't know she isn't with us."

"The enemy fighters were leading you to a terrorist camp in northern Africa run by Al Ghazi. We confirmed that this morning by satellite."

"So it's what I suspected: They were just taking a chance we might know something," Jeff said.

"Even if you didn't know anything, they probably planned to use your people as bargaining chips to get their leaders back." The commander took another sip.

"The president will make an announcement on national TV today confirming our Navy captured the terrorist leaders and their command center." Commander Metz nodded at Jeff. "You should be in good shape after that. I arranged hotel accommodations for your passengers and crew. Your airplane will be ready to depart late tomorrow."

Lance cleared his throat. "Uh, Commander, have you heard from Sam? How's she doing?"

"I talked to her last night after she arrived at MacLeod Castle. Said she got one hell of a ride to Naples yesterday—popped a couple stitches in the F/A-18F with Matt, but said it was worth it."

Lance grinned. "Well, hot damn! She's always wanted to fly a fighter. I'm glad she got the chance."

"I've arranged a security detail to watch over your crew and passengers until you leave tomorrow. They'll wear civilian clothes to keep a low profile." The commander made a call on his cell. "The security team's coming here. I want you to meet them."

Jeff glanced at Lance and Pete. "Commander, is there any chance you could provide weapons for the three of us? We're all military trained."

"Wish I could. It was tough enough getting permission from the local *carabinieri* for the security team." The commander turned when he heard a knock on the door. "That's the team now. They're military police in plain clothes."

Six men with hard eyes walked in and stood at attention. Commander Metz introduced them to Jeff, Lance, and Pete.

"There's a tour bus outside for your passengers and cabin crew. You'll ride in the van with the security team." Commander Metz escorted them to the waiting vehicles. "I'll meet you and the survivors of the Petra tour group this afternoon for lunch."

76

CLOUDS RACED ACROSS A gloomy fall sky as Loren looked down at the vast Covington estate twenty miles northeast of York. The helicopter made a wide circle over a stately stone castle perched on a wide hill surrounded by a thousand acres of grassy fields and woodlands. It landed sixty yards from the castle on a level, well-manicured lawn bordering a cobblestone driveway that wound down the hill.

Duncan helped Loren out of the helicopter as the blades spun down. They ducked as they strode across the grass to where Ross and Sam parked a black Range Rover they had borrowed from a nearby military facility.

Duncan leaned into Loren. "Colin's castle has been in his family for six centuries."

"It looks impressive from the outside. I can't wait to see what the interior is like."

"It was recently restored and refurbished. Suzanne described it as an elegant blend of ancient history and modern convenience. We'll soon see if we agree." He took her arm as they climbed the stone steps with Ross and Sam.

"The timing worked out perfectly, arriving together as planned," Ross said.

When the butler opened the door, they stepped into an elegant foyer with stone floors covered in red Axminster carpet and magnificent crystal chandeliers hanging twenty feet above.

"His Lordship and Lady Covington are waiting to receive you in the drawing room." The butler led them into an expansive semi-circular room with towering windows and a lavish cream and green Aubusson carpet covering the stone floor. The green silk wall coverings matched the draperies and silk-covered furniture. Two crystal chandeliers glittered above.

"Lord and Lady Covington, thank you for seeing us on such short notice," Duncan said when the attractive couple in their mid-forties stood to greet them.

"It's our pleasure." Lady Suzanne Covington smiled warmly. "Let's dispense with the formalities. Please call us Colin and Suzanne."

"Sorry about having to keep your curtains drawn, Suzanne. We can't risk anyone seeing my daughter, Sam." Loren gestured at Sam, who stood beside her dressed in black combat gear.

Sam removed her helmet with the dark visor. "Colin and Suzanne, I appreciate your discretion. My presence in your country must be kept secret. As you can see, I'm under military protection. I can only tell you that it's to ensure my safety."

"We understand. Our three daughters, Kristin, Kathleen, and Kerri mean everything to us." Suzanne led her guests into the dining room. When everyone was seated, she asked, "How may we help you?"

Duncan took the lead. "Loren was close friends with the Conor family. Until recently, she thought the entire family perished in the crash. New information has come to light that leads us to believe the triplets may have survived."

"What new information?" Suzanne raised an eyebrow.

"Unfortunately, the details must be kept secret for Sam's safety." Duncan shook his head. "Sorry. It's complicated."

Colin glanced around the table as lunch was served. "It's clear you took great care in coming here. This must be quite important. We'll keep this secret and give you what help we can, won't we, darling?"

"Yes, of course. What do you need?" Suzanne sipped her ice tea.

Loren swallowed a bite of chicken cordon bleu and activated the record function on her cell phone. "Tell us everything you can remember about the plane crash in the Himalayas. The smallest detail could help us."

Suzanne described the sequence of events during the crash and her rescue as though it had happened the day before. "The babies' survival pod broke loose and was flung out the broken cabin toward a distant green area shrouded in white mist. That was the last time I saw them."

Duncan raised his eyebrows. "Weren't the mountains covered in snow?"

"Oh yes, it was freezing cold." Suzanne took a small bite of chicken.

"Then how do you account for the green area?" Duncan asked.

She swallowed her food and took a sip of ice tea. "No idea, but I'm certain I saw it. Colin, darling, was your team aware of a green oasis in the midst of the frozen mountains?"

"I'm afraid not, dear, but if you say it was there, I believe you." Colin turned to Duncan. "Suzanne's not the sort who imagines things or exaggerates. She's steady as a rock and quite brave."

"Suzanne, your memory of the event is quite vivid, which is an immense help to us," Sam said. "Do you know why the airplane crashed?"

"One of the engines exploded, and we lost altitude. Richard Conor ran to the cockpit. The pilot turned to avoid the higher peaks. Then the electrical power went off, and the other engine stopped. Mr. Conor told me we were in a dead zone and to strap in for the crash. Soon after that we slammed into a mountain peak."

"Could be an electromagnetic dead zone caused a small climate anomaly that created the green oasis." Ross smiled at the elegant blonde. "Thanks to Suzanne, we know what to look for."

"I hope you find the triplets alive and well. Please, let us know how this turns out." Suzanne offered Ross her hand.

Ross kissed it. "If we find them, I'll tell them you made it possible."

Suzanne looked from Sam to Loren. "You both bear an uncanny resemblance to Sheila Conor."

"We weren't related, but people used to think we were sisters." Loren sighed. "Sheila was my best friend. I miss her."

Duncan dabbed his mouth with a linen napkin and stood. "We won't keep you. Thanks for the hospitality." He shook hands with Colin, kissed Suzanne's hand, and helped Loren put on her coat.

After the good-byes, Sam pulled on the black SAS helmet and followed Ross to the military Range Rover parked in front. Duncan and Loren walked across the lawn as their pilot started the helicopter's engine.

Duncan leaned close to Loren. "That went well. We're no longer looking for a needle in a haystack."

"A green area in the frozen Himalayas ought to be easy to spot." She squeezed his hand.

"If it was obvious, someone would've found it long ago." When Duncan leaned over to kiss her, he collapsed and released her hand.

Loren stared in shock at the crimson stain spreading across the left side of his camel-colored leather jacket.

She dropped to her knees and held his head. A rocket-propelled grenade streaked past her and hit the helicopter. The shock wave from the explosion knocked her onto her back.

She lay stunned as two men in ski masks and combat fatigues grabbed her and dragged her to a helicopter. After they strapped her into a seat, she felt a needle prick.

Loren descended into a black, soundless void.

77

AN EXPLOSION BEHIND US rattled our windows as Ross drove the military Range Rover down the long driveway. Black smoke rose from the flaming helicopter as Ross swapped ends in a bootlegger turn and raced toward the wreckage.

"I see another chopper taking off. Somebody's on the ground. Hurry!" I tried not to panic.

"Call 999 for an ambulance and fire truck." Ross skidded the car to a stop beside a body.

I finished the call and jumped out. "Oh my God, it's Duncan! He's been shot!" I knelt and checked for a pulse.

"Looks like he took one in the left lung. He's having trouble breathing. I've seen this before." Ross took off his insulated nylon jacket and folded it. "Duncan, take in a deep breath and then blow it out hard."

Duncan's eyes opened as he struggled to take a breath. When he exhaled, I heard the air hiss from his wound.

Ross pressed his jacket against the wound as a compression bandage.

"Sam, hold this down." Ross pulled out his mobile. "I'm calling the base. It'll take too long for the ambulance to drive this far out in the country."

Ross made the call and pocketed his phone. "A medevac helicopter's on the way."

The Covingtons rushed out with a blanket, towels, and

first-aid kit.

"Duncan's been shot." I reached up to them. "Hand me a towel and cover him with the blanket."

"Suzanne called emergency services. They'll be here in fifteen minutes." Colin squeezed my shoulder.

Duncan gasped and coughed up blood. He looked deathly white.

"A military chopper's on the way with paramedics. We're too far out to wait for the ambulance." Ross pointed at the sky. "There it is."

Suzanne covered Duncan with the blanket and glanced at me. "Where's your mother?"

I fought back tears, looked at the burning wreck, and bit my lip.

Ross pulled me aside to make way for the paramedics. "Sam, your mother's alive. They shot Duncan so they could take her. I promise we'll get her back."

I looked back at the burning helicopter. "The pilot, we've got to save him!"

He grabbed my arm. "Forget it. He's dead. We're going with Duncan to the hospital."

I turned to Colin and Suzanne. "I'm sorry."

"We're fine. We'll drive to the hospital and check on Duncan after we deal with the authorities." Colin hugged me. "Don't worry, the SAS will rescue your mother."

We were airborne with Duncan in less than a minute. The paramedics worked on him all the way to the hospital helipad where a surgical team whisked him away to the operating room.

Ross walked to the nurses' desk, pulled off his helmet, and took out a card. "Nurse, please give this to the doctor who operates on Laird Duncan MacLeod. Ask him to call my base in Dundee with an update on MacLeod's condition."

The nurse looked up at his handsome face and smiled. "Of course, sir, happy to do it."

Ross pulled on his helmet and returned to my side.

I felt sick with worry. "Ross, I don't think I could bear it if Duncan dies or anything happens to my mother. What are we going to do?"

Ross held me and didn't seem to care how it looked to the public, two soldiers in combat fatigues and helmets embracing.

"Ready, Captain Sinclair?" a paramedic from the helicopter asked.

"Aye, let's go." Ross took my hand and followed the paramedic to the helipad.

I stopped. "Wait, we can't leave Duncan."

"There's nothing more we can do. The Covingtons will be here soon. They'll see to it Duncan's properly looked after. My job is to keep you safe. We're leaving." Ross pulled me into the helicopter.

We switched to the Lynx at the military base and continued back to Dundee.

Derek was waiting for us when we landed. "We found six dead mercs near MacLeod Castle, no IDs."

I was shocked. "Were they Germans?"

"No, they looked like typical mercenaries." Derek opened the door for us.

We entered a large room with flat-screen monitors covering the walls. Ross's team stood when we entered.

"At ease, gentlemen." He turned to Derek. "What do we know about the helicopter that took Loren Starr?" Ross pulled off his helmet and reached for a cup of coffee.

Derek stood in front of a map of Great Britain. "The chopper stayed below radar most of the time. It showed up here, here, and here." He pointed at places on a northerly flight path. "Looks like they might be headed to a remote place in the

Highlands."

A short, young man entered. "Captain Sinclair, there's a call for you from the DSF. Line one."

"I'll take it here, Burnsie." Ross punched the lit button and put the phone on speaker. Director of Special Forces Brent Barnes spoke in an English accent.

"Captain Sinclair, is Samantha Starr safe?"

"Aye, sir, she's with me. Her mother was kidnapped at the Covington estate by persons unknown, and Laird Duncan MacLeod was shot in the chest."

"How's MacLeod doing?"

"He took a bullet in his left lung. He's in surgery."

"Any progress on finding Mrs. Starr?"

"We're working on it. They may have taken her to the upper Highlands."

"The Americans offered their help. We'll get satellites looking for that chopper. Send a team in as soon as we locate them, but keep Samantha under wraps. She's your top priority."

"Aye, sir, I'll keep her safe." Ross hung up, glanced at me, and focused on the map.

I sat in a chair, closed my eyes, and tried to relax. My mind filled with an image similar to Stonehenge, but it was in the Highlands. The view was as if I were in the center of a hilltop circle of standing stones. I recognized the panoramic view of the surrounding hills.

A tall man with spiked blond hair and cold blue eyes stood close. His intense scrutiny shocked me into opening my eyes.

I gasped, and everyone turned to me.

"I think I know where they took my mother."

78

JEFF SAT AT AN OVAL oak table at the outdoor café across the street from the Napoli Hotel with the Petra tour group and Commander Robert Metz.

The commander, dressed in pressed jeans and a polo shirt, tapped his knife against a glass to garner everyone's attention.

"I wanted to gather the Petra group for lunch with your new captain away from the other flight attendants and passengers in the hotel. I have some disturbing news, and it's time to bring everyone into the loop because this may affect all of you."

He glanced around to check if anyone else was seated near the building. The other customers dotted small tables along the sidewalk border.

"What I'm about to tell you must not be repeated outside this group."

Jeff glanced at Lance and Pete and sucked in his breath. "What's happened now?"

"Sam's mother was kidnapped today, and her boyfriend, Laird Duncan MacLeod, was shot in the chest. He survived surgery, but the doctor said it'll be a while before he recovers. Their helicopter pilot was killed."

Lance's jaw dropped. "Commander, what about Sam? Is she safe?"

"Sam's safe, and please call me Bob." Bob took a sip of

Vino Nobile di Montepulciano, Caterina Dei.

"Bob, how did they find out where Sam was hiding?" Carlene looked concerned.

"They might not have known she was at Duncan's castle. Could be they were watching to see if she would come."

"So how did they get her mother and not her?" Rod asked.

"They snatched Loren when she was visiting an estate in England. She and Duncan flew there in a helicopter." Bob glanced around the café to check the locations of the security team.

"How does this kidnapping affect the Petra group?" Jeff asked.

"We think they took Sam's mother to find Sam. They might take members of this group too if they think you know where Sam is, but I doubt they'll come looking for you in Italy. They must think your flight went to Paris as scheduled."

The guard leaning against the wall near their table crumpled to the ground with a bullet hole in his forehead. The other guards rushed to the table and went down in a hail of bullets.

"Everybody under the table!" Jeff shouted.

Customers screamed and jumped over the low stone border of the café. Jeff and Bob urged their group to huddle close to the building as they tipped the table over for a shield.

"Grab the weapons!" Bob snatched a pistol from the nearest fallen guard.

Jeff, Jack, Pete, and Lance took weapons from guards who were unconscious or dead. In all the chaos, no one saw Carlene snatch a pistol.

"Surrender to the Black Sun or die!" a man shouted in a German accent from behind a parked vehicle.

Jeff pointed at the picture window behind them. "Check the reflection. I see four shooters."

In the next instant, a barrage of submachine-gun bullets shattered the window.

"Don't shoot, we surrender!" Rod screamed, raising his hands above the table.

Inga did the same as sirens blared in the distance.

A large black van screeched to a halt in front of the café. "Toss out your weapons and put your hands on your heads. Now!" one of the Germans yelled.

Jeff and Lance shoved their pistols into the waistband of their jeans at the small of their backs. Bob did the same with his weapon.

Jeff nodded at Pete and Jack. "Toss your weapons over the table."

They hesitated before tossing the pistols. Carlene crouched low against the table. No one noticed her tiny form. All attention was on the armed Germans as the group slowly stood up.

"Hand over your weapon, Commander! The Black Sun Master wants you alive, but I will do what I must."

Bob slowly pulled the pistol from his back and tossed it at the leader as the sirens grew louder.

"Everybody in the van!" The leader motioned toward the waiting vehicle and glanced up the street.

Carlene popped up from behind the table and shot the leader and one of his men in their foreheads. Jeff and Lance pulled their pistols and opened fire on the remaining two gunmen as the group dove for the ground.

Bullets sprayed from a submachine gun as the German holding it fell dead with his finger on the trigger.

Jack crouched behind the table. "Carlene! Bloody hell, woman!"

"Told you I never miss, sugar." Carlene held her pistol ready to fire again as the van burned rubber around a corner.

"Help, I'm hit! I knew this would happen. The brother always gets it." Rod clutched his bloody left shoulder. "I feel faint. This is the end. Tell my mama I love her." He swooned.

Carlene rushed to his side. "Let me see." She checked the wound and slapped his face. "It's just a graze, you big baby! You won't even need stitches. Stop your whinin' and sit up."

Rod sat up and pouted. "But I'm bleeding, and I feel dizzy."

"Suck it up, Rod. Our guards need medical attention. They have real wounds." Carlene gave first aid to one of the surviving MPs.

Three vehicles filled with *carabinieri* slid to a stop in front of the café. The police officers surrounded Jeff's group. Bob showed the lead officer his military ID and explained what happened.

Ambulances joined the scene. Paramedics stabilized the wounded Navy men and shuttled them to a hospital.

Bob made a call, conferred with the Italian policeman in charge, and rejoined the group.

"This changes everything. We're going back to the Navy base. Pack your bags. The bus will be here in ten minutes. I'll notify the rest of the passengers and cabin crew." Bob led them across the street to the hotel with the *carabinieri*.

79

I LOOKED UP AT Ross and tried not to sound like a crazy person. "I had a vision and saw one of the Germans. I think he has Mom in the center of ancient standing stones on a high hill in the Highlands."

"What did the surrounding area look like?" Ross seemed excited.

"It was remote, and the nearby hills were a drab brown. Probably not much color there in October. And I didn't see any houses. The west coast was at least ten miles away." I hoped my description would jog someone's memory.

Derek snapped his fingers. "Sounds like the Druid ruins in Northwest Sutherland. My family used to picnic there in the summer when I was a wee lad."

"That makes sense. Druid sites were built over intersecting ley lines." I nodded at Derek. "Could be they brought Mom there to use the power of the Vril on her."

Ross turned to Corporal Burns. "Burnsie, I want both Super Lynx helicopters ready with full armament in five."

The young corporal snatched up the phone and called the hangar.

Ross stood in front of his team. "Gentlemen, we'll do whatever it takes to bring Loren Starr back alive."

I stepped forward. "You have to take me in case they move her before we get there."

Ross looked at me with a pained expression. Before he could answer, the telephone rang.

Corporal Burns answered it. "Aye, sir, he's right here." He passed the phone to Ross. "It's the DSF for you, Captain. Sounds serious."

Ross answered the call from Director Barnes, but he didn't put it on speaker this time. He listened for a few minutes. "Aye, sir, understood. On a brighter note, she's had a vision of what may be her mother's location. We were about to leave."

With Ross still on the phone, Corporal Burns fielded a call from Duncan's hospital. "We're happy to hear that. Thanks for the call."

I saw Ross's jaw tighten and assumed his commanding officer had issued new orders.

He responded, "Right, basically a modified replay of last summer. It'll be tricky, but we can do it, sir." He hung up and took a deep breath. "Burnsie, who just called?"

"MacLeod's doctor. He said Duncan survived surgery and is expected to recover."

"That's good news." Ross glanced at me and addressed his men. "The DSF has given us a top-secret mission. Every word I say from this moment is classified."

Ross told us what happened to my crew on the way to Paris and described the attack in Naples. "Things are heating up. The Americans are demanding we hand over Sam for their safekeeping. Translation: They want to make sure they get Poseidon's Sword."

He trained his deep-blue eyes on me. "Decision time, Sam, your country or your mother?"

"I love my country, but family comes first. I intend to rescue my mother with or without help."

"That's what I was counting on. We have a covert op to rescue your mother and keep you both safe. The tricky part is we can't communicate with anyone outside our base because our government is telling the Americans you went rogue to look for your mother, and we don't know where you are. The entire Scottish police force will be searching for you. SAS teams with SEAL observers will join the hunt. Sound familiar?" He removed my watch.

"Burnsie, I need you to deactivate the automatic tracking feature on this watch, but leave the emergency button functional." Ross handed him my DARPA watch.

I thrust my hands on my hips. "What *automatic* tracking feature?"

"Sorry, lass, we're all trying to keep you safe. DARPA installed it." Ross shrugged.

"So we're back to the fun and games of last August with our favorite elusive American? Are her twin brothers joining in again?" Derek nodded at me.

"The DSF didn't say anything about Sam's brothers." Ross faced his team. "We need to go dark and rescue Loren fast. Gear up."

I blocked Ross. "What about me?" Oh boy, his tough alpha-male look again.

"You'll come dressed like us, and you'll do exactly what I tell you. Put on your helmet."

"Soldiers carry weapons. If you want me to blend in, I should be armed."

Ross crossed his arms and looked down at me. "What do you have in mind?"

"A combat knife, pistol, and submachine gun will do nicely."

"I'll give you a knife and a pistol with extra mags. Let's go." He held the door for me.

I didn't argue. The submachine gun was the bargaining chip that got me what I really wanted. I strapped on the thigh holster with the pistol and the sheath with the combat knife, and shoved extra magazines in the cargo pockets of my jacket.

The insulated jacket, Kevlar vest, and other layers of combat attire shaped me like a five-foot-nine-inch fire plug. With the helmet hiding my hair and face, there was no danger of being recognized as female.

Ross inspected me. "I want you glued to my left hip unless I say otherwise."

Corporal Burns handed my watch to Ross. "All set, she's good to go."

Ross gave me the watch, and I strapped it on.

I climbed into the Lynx and sat beside him. "How long will it take to get there?"

"I'm not sure because we have to fly an indirect course below radar. Try to relax." He draped his arm around me after the helicopter lifted off.

"If Mom's in the open at the Druid ruins, how will we take them by surprise?"

"Long-distance sniper shots. If that isn't possible, we'll fly in fast from opposite directions and take them out before they have time to mount a defense." Ross squeezed my shoulder.

"I don't like it. What if your men hit my mother?"

"Not bloody likely."

Derek winked at me with the thumbs-up sign. I tried to relax. *These men are the best of the best.*

Nearing the target, the two Lynx helicopters took opposite courses—ours west toward the ocean and the other inland to the east. We eased north until we were five miles west of the ancient site. The other Lynx hovered five miles east of the target.

My heart rate accelerated as I watched snipers train their high-powered scopes on the Druid ruins. When we flew closer, I focused my binoculars on the standing stones.

Deserted.

When we hovered ten feet above the center stone, I spotted something glistening in the sunlight. My binoculars zeroed in. *Fresh blood!*

80

FROM THE PICTURE WINDOW in the Navy base's conference room, Jeff watched a Boeing C-17 Globemaster III land and taxi to the ramp.

He faced the three actors who had endured the Black Sun attack earlier that day. "Transport home has arrived for the non-Petra members of your entourage. It won't be what your people are used to, but at least it'll be a non-stop flight."

Jack clutched Inga's hand and gave her a peck on the cheek. "What about Inga? Is she leaving now?"

"FAA regulations require one flight attendant for every fifty seats on a commercial airliner, even if most of the seats are empty. That means we need Inga and one more flight attendant when our 767 is repaired. Landon and Arial volunteered, so we decided we may as well keep the crew together. Bob wants the passengers from the Petra group to stick together." Jeff turned and watched the other passengers enter the C-17.

Lance stood and stretched. "According to Bob, the mechanics and parts for our airplane were on that transport. They'll have us ready to go tomorrow."

Bob walked in, still in civilian clothes. "I wanted to make sure everyone, except the Petra group and crew, got on that C-17."

Carlene turned from the window. "What do you have

planned for us, Bob?"

"What happened at the café proved it's not safe to send you home until we neutralize the threat. The Black Sun may continue to target your group until they find Sam."

"Are you saying we have to hide at this Navy base?" Rod looked ready to bolt.

"You could have been killed today. The only way to keep you safe is move you to a secure military facility that the Black Sun doesn't know about."

Jack crossed his arms. "I'm not going to an American black site. I'll fly back to England where the British military can protect me."

Rod looked confused. "I don't want to go to no black site."

"A black site's a secret place that has nothing to do with a person's color," Bob said. "The point is to secure you where the Black Sun can't find you."

Jeff stepped closer to Bob. "I need to get my crew home as soon as our airplane's ready. If you think it's safer for the actors to remain in military custody, that's your call."

"You and your crew are as much at risk as the actors. Get a ferry crew to fly the empty airplane back to Florida. We want to keep you and the Petra group together."

"Bob, I appreciate your concern, but we have a small airline. Sam is laid up with injuries, and two of our captains have broken bones from an auto accident. If I can't bring my crew home, the airline will have to cancel flights and lose big money."

"You'd be putting future flights and passengers at risk if the Black Sun continues to target this crew to locate Sam." Bob's voice remained steady and calm.

Lance stepped forward. "How much time are we looking at before a military solution is achieved?"

"It's too soon to know. Our intelligence network is

searching for the Black Sun's operations base. Once we locate it, we'll eliminate the threat. Then you can go home."

Jeff shook his head. "No offense, but I remember how long it took to find Osama bin Laden. We can't wait ten years. We'll give you two days. Then we're taking our 767 home."

Carlene stood between Lance and Jeff. "Forget about sending me to a black site. I'm stickin' with the Texans."

"Me too," Rod said.

"Let them stay with the crew and book me a flight back to England," Jack said.

Bob glanced around the room. "How about a compromise? Everyone stays here for two days, and then we'll assess the situation. A lot can happen in that time. Please work with me."

Everyone turned to Jeff.

"Okay, Bob, this is a reasonable alternative to the black site. Let's see how things play out."

Jeff shook Bob's hand.

81

OUR PILOT DROPPED US off near the standing stones so we could get a blood scraping. I waited until the sample was collected before touching the blood-stained stone. A vision made me scream and fall back on the cold, damp ground.

Ross crouched down. "Sam, what happened?"

I flipped up my visor to wipe my tears.

"The bastards pulled off the fingernails on Mom's left hand!" I bit my lower lip and sobbed.

"Sorry, lass, at least her injuries aren't life threatening. Did you see where they took her?" Ross pulled me close.

I took a deep breath. "No, only what happened here."

A frigid northwest wind whipped through as I sat against the center stone and closed my eyes. My body tingled from the ley lines' energy in the standing stones as I emptied my mind and waited.

The vision that came was so dark I didn't realize at first what I was seeing. A cave with a cathedral ceiling brought back memories of my recent summer vacation in the Highlands.

I shivered and opened my eyes to Ross.

"Mother might be in the same cave where the boys were held in August."

Ross motioned Derek over. "Are you sure, lass? That place was cordoned off after the kidnappings."

Derek's jaw dropped. "Loren's in the cave where Mike and

I captured the guards?"

"I'm not positive, but it's the perfect hiding place. No one's allowed inside, so no one will look there." I gave Ross a pleading look. "It can't be far from here."

"They'll hear us in the helicopters. We'll have to hike up and call in the choppers after we rescue Loren." Ross signaled for the Lynx to pick us up.

Our pilot was the one who had flown Derek's team to the cave in August. The second helicopter followed us as we hugged the terrain during the short flight southeast over the Highlands.

We flew around the mountain and approached low, landing in a remote valley near a dirt road that led up to the cave.

Soldiers from the second Lynx leaped out, and their chopper flew east down the valley. The plan was to refuel the helicopters at the airport in Inverness while the teams attempted a rescue mission.

When I leaped out of our Lynx, Ross grabbed my arm.

"Where do you think you're going? Get back in."

"You might need me. Besides, I have to pee. I can't hold it in cold weather."

Ross clenched his jaw and glared at me. He waved the chopper away so it wouldn't draw the attention of the men who might be in the cave.

"My job is to keep you safe. You're not going into combat. I'll assign one of my men to look after you. We'll collect you on the way back."

Ross called a soldier over. "Chris, stay with Sam. Hide her in the trees near the dirt road and keep her safe."

"Aye, Captain, I'll protect her."

I leaned into Chris. "We'll follow them a little ways up the road. Then I'll cut into the brush so I can pee. Wait for me on the dirt road and don't expect me to do my business in thirty seconds like you men do."

"So how long do you need? Two minutes?"

"I'll need plenty of time to loosen my holster and sheath straps so I can pull down my pants, do my thing, dry off, pull up my pants—you get the idea. Give me ten minutes. Otherwise, I'll stress over you finding me with my pants down."

"*Ten* minutes? Really?" Chris looked baffled.

"At least. I have to find a good place to squat first. Don't rush me. We have plenty of time before the teams return."

"All right, lass, but don't stray too far. If anythin' happens to you, Ross will skin me alive."

We followed Ross up the road until he stopped to gather his men for a quick briefing.

I trotted into the trees where I accomplished my pee-pee mission in record time. I sneaked up to catch Ross's conversation with Derek at the end of the briefing.

"Sam and Loren aren't going to be happy about being held in a MI6 safe house under guard. Loren will want to be at Duncan's side, but she won't be safe until we find the Black Sun's base and neutralize them," Ross said.

"Aye, the DSF said they attacked the people from Sam's Petra tour in Naples, which proves they'll target anyone who might know where Sam's hiding. Her family, crew, and passengers are in danger."

I slipped away and ran for the narrow trail I had taken on the motorcycle with Charlie in August. The timing would be close, but my way was shorter. If I ran hard, I would get there first. Failure was not an option. I bolted up the mountain.

Charlie and I never told anyone about the back entrance to the cave. It was too narrow for men to crawl through, and its opening into the cavern was hidden by rocks we had rolled into place after our escape.

Before I entered the cave, I took a couple of minutes to catch my breath so I wouldn't make noise while crawling inside. This time would be even scarier without night-vision gear. I couldn't let my claustrophobia stop me. Mom needed me. I blocked the fear from my mind and focused on the mission.

Time was short, so I forged ahead into the pitch-black cave on my hands and knees. My only consolation—only one passage. I couldn't get lost.

In minutes, I found the end and moved a rock enough to see inside the lighted cavern. Two guards sat at the far end. Mom was tethered beneath my vantage point, four feet above the cavern floor.

Gunfire erupted outside.

The guards jumped up and pulled their weapons.

"Hans, stay with the prisoner. If they make it past me, kill her."

A guard ran into the passage to the main entrance.

Hans focused on the dark passage leading outside, instead of my mother, who was tied to a bracket fixed to the stone wall.

Ross's team was probably seconds away from charging in.

The guard had a Kevlar vest, so I rested my pistol on a rock, took careful aim, and put a bullet into the back of his head before he could turn around.

I moved the bigger rocks and dropped down beside Mom.

"Don't worry, Mom, I'll get you out of here!"

"Sam!"

I cut her loose with my combat knife, coiled the rope, and shoved it into my cargo pocket.

"You have to be quiet and do exactly what I say. When I boost you up into that opening, crawl as fast as you can until you're outside. I'll be right behind you. Go!"

I boosted her into the passage, then grabbed the dead

guard's cell phone, turned it off, and pocketed it.

Inside the narrow passage, I moved the rocks back in place to obscure the exit.

82

EARLIER, ROSS SCANNED THE summit fifty feet above the cave. No enemy helicopter. He sent a man around the west side to climb to the top and check for guards while the teams hid in the forest. There were no vehicles, and the only sound was the cold wind rustling the trees.

The climber called Ross. "No guards up here. The summit above the cave has a level area where our helicopters can land later."

"Their chopper may have dropped them off there. Guards could be hiding in the shadows inside the cave entrance. The helicopter that took Loren had room for four men plus her and the pilot. Drop a rock in front of the cave to see if we can lure them out," Ross whispered into his mike.

Secure in rappelling gear and hidden behind boulders above the cave, the soldier dropped a big stone. It bounced and rolled close to the entrance.

Two guards stepped out and looked up. Ross's team took them out with head shots and hid their bodies behind the trees.

"Team Two, hold your positions in the trees. Derek and I will wait on either side of the entrance. Let's see if anyone else comes out before we sneak inside."

Ross and his men waited.

A third guard ran to the entrance and stopped. When he cautiously stepped out to look for the missing guards, Ross kicked the weapon out of his hand. He tried to yell a warning, but Derek reached around from behind him and slit his throat.

A gunshot reverberated from inside the cave.

"Team Two, guard the entrance. Team One, follow me." Ross and Derek rushed through the long winding cave to the cavern entrance where Ross almost tripped over a dead guard.

"Looks empty. Where is she?" Ross said.

Team One arrived and spread out to search every dark corner.

Derek paused at the bracket fixed into the rock wall. "Ross, over here."

Ross joined him. "What?"

Derek pointed at blood drops and a brass casing beneath the bracket. "Someone cut her loose and shot the guard."

"So where in bloody hell is she? There's only one way out." Ross looked exasperated.

"Maybe not. Remember Petra. Call Chris so you can ask Sam."

Ross jogged outside and called Chris.

"Uh, sorry, Captain, I can't find her. She stepped away for a pee and never came back. I've been hunting for her ever since. She seems to have vanished like she did last August."

"Get your sorry arse up here. Now!" Ross took a breath and tried to calm down. *Think.*

He decided to call Laird Moncreiffe. "James, I need to speak to Charlie. It's an emergency."

"Hang on, I'll get him."

The excited voice of the twelve-year-old boy came over the phone. "Hello, Captain Sinclair."

"I have a bit of an emergency where you and Sam rescued the kidnapped lads in that cave. Is there another way out of the big cavern?"

"Aye, there's a narrow passage above the bracket in the

stone. We rolled rocks in front of the opening to hide it from the kidnappers. Your men are probably too big to crawl through it, but if you turn left out of the main entrance and hike around the mountain, you'll find it."

"Thanks, Charlie, you've been a big help." Ross pocketed his phone as he ran through a mental inventory of his men. Even the shorter ones had broad shoulders and barrel chests. He jogged back to the cavern.

"Sam has vanished. I called Charlie. He said there's another passage above the bracket."

As Ross searched for an opening, a puff of air blew past his face. "Here!"

He pulled out rocks and dropped them on the cavern floor.

Derek shined a flashlight into the passage. "Looks too narrow for us. A woman would fit through there. Maybe Loren remembered Sam telling her about this secret passage."

"No, Sam crawled through there, shot the guard, and rescued her mother. That brass you found was from a 9-mil Sig like the one I gave Sam."

"Why would she do this?" Derek looked perplexed.

"I don't know. Last August, her brothers told me she always has a good reason for everything. It can't be that she didn't trust us to rescue her mother. This has to be about something else. We need to double-time it east around the mountain to where this passage exits." Ross led his men out of the cavern.

Chris ran up to him. "Ross, I'm so sorry."

"Stay here and watch the cave in case they come back." Ross ran east into the trees.

His teams fanned out and found the passage's exit in fifteen minutes. No sign of Loren or Sam, though.

Derek jogged up to Ross. "There's a hiking trail on the other side of these boulders. It leads down the mountain."

"That must be where they went. Let's go."

83

"HURRY, MOM, WE HAVE to get down this mountain before they find the secret passage!"

She stumbled over roots, rocks, and ruts in the trail, but she kept going.

Fifteen minutes later, we ran out of the trees across from the old church I had used to hide the children in August. I had hoped the same van was still there, but the driveway was empty.

I took a moment to catch my breath. "Come on, Mom."

We ran to the church, and I used my combat knife to jimmy the ancient lock.

"Mom, run into the bathroom and wash your hands so your wounds don't get infected. I'll wait by the door. Hurry!" I looked out the door and saw a lone horse grazing in a pasture.

I rushed to the ladies room where Mom was drying her hands. She grimaced when the paper towels brushed her left fingers.

"I'm sorry you're hurting, but we have to escape this valley fast. Let's go!"

We headed for the pasture.

When a brisk wind funneled through the valley, I grabbed Mom's arm. "Is your short coat warm enough?"

"Yes, it's heavy wool. I think I'm too scared to be cold anyway." She squeezed my arm.

Midway along the dirt road, we found the pasture gate. I whistled, and the horse walked near us. We lured him closer with handfuls of long grass from along the fence.

Mom held his halter and petted him while I tied the rope I had saved from the cave to the rings on his halter. I positioned him beside the wood fence for easy mounting and helped Mom up behind me.

"Hang on, Mom, we're going to that isolated grass-strip airport where I took the Cub in August." I urged the horse into a canter.

When we neared the hangars, Mom said, "It looks deserted, no vehicles or sounds of activity."

"Probably because it's a weekday." I pulled the lead ropes, and the horse slowed to a trot.

"Should we be worried about security guards?" Mom asked.

"No guards. A remote grass airport in the Highlands with small general aviation airplanes wouldn't be considered a target for terrorists." I glanced over my shoulder for Ross's men but saw no one.

We trotted past the open T-hangars in search of a fast airplane. A Swearingen SX300 stood proud in the center hangar. I tied the horse to a support pole between the hangars and helped Mom down.

We entered the hangar, which was shaped like a T with the widest part open and the sides and back enclosed. The aircraft was backed in for the tail to fit in the narrow end.

I forced open a lockbox on the wall with my combat knife, took the aircraft keys, and unlocked the canopy. Not many pilots had the skill to fly this high-performance two-seat rocket. My late father had owned one, and it flew like a fighter.

I was relieved to see the aircraft's fuel tanks were full, a common practice to prevent condensation. The GPS navigation unit in the instrument panel made planning the flight easy when I switched on the battery power and checked for the nearest airport to York with the runway length and facilities necessary to execute my plan.

I pulled off my helmet and stashed it behind the seats.

"Climb in, Mom. This is like the one Dad had. Sit in the left seat. It's designed for the pilot to fly from the right side. I'll be right back. I need to check something."

I walked outside where she couldn't see or hear me and pulled out the mobile phone I had taken from the guard in the cave. I turned it on and punched in a number I had memorized recently.

When I finished the brief call, I selected the only number programmed into the phone. A man with a German accent answered.

"Hello, my name's Samantha Starr. I think you're looking for me. I'd like to make a deal." I told him my plan, and he agreed. I left the phone turned on atop the wheel chocks I had moved to the side wall in the hangar.

After I untied the airplane, I strapped in and found a logbook in the map compartment. I left a note for the owner there and wrote one for Ross, which I tore out and pocketed.

The 300-hp Lycoming engine started on the first try. I checked the wind sock and taxied for a takeoff to the northeast. We thundered down the grass runway and shot into the sky.

I continued straight over the valley until we reached a safe altitude to clear the peaks. The Lynx helicopters were low in the distance as I turned south and hugged the mountains. I set the cruise speed at 250 knots and headed for England.

I had to fly under radar and avoid obstacles. The sun was nearing the horizon. It would be a race to complete the flight before nightfall.

"Sam, I'm afraid to ask …. Did Duncan die?"

"Duncan survived the surgery and is expected to recover. I'm taking you to see him. He's at the York hospital."

"Oh, thank God! I was so worried about him."

"Mom, I'm so sorry about your hand. They tortured you to find me. This was my fault." I bit my lip.

"No, dear, this was the fault of evil men. I'm okay, and my nails will grow back eventually. Why are we acting like criminals? Where's Ross?"

"Ross was ordered to hold us in a MI6 safe house. I guess the Brits and Americans are fighting over custody of me. Both countries want Poseidon's Sword. If we had gone with Ross, you wouldn't be allowed to see Duncan. He needs you. For now, we're keeping our location a secret." I turned to avoid a radio tower.

My mother sighed. "How did we get into this mess? Poor Duncan. He must be in a lot of pain."

"My crew and passengers from the Petra tour were attacked too. Fortunately, they survived unharmed, but the Black Sun won't stop targeting them until they find me."

"What can be done to end this safely? Can't the military stop them?"

"They need to find their home base so they can take out the leaders—cut off the head of the snake. Until the military is able to do that, this will never end."

I flew without position lights, hoping I could complete the low flight undetected. My destination was the Leeds-Bradford International Airport twenty miles from York. The GPS indicated its only runway was 7,382 feet, perfect for my plan.

It was dim twilight when I saw the Runway 14 lights in the distance. I set the radio to the tower frequency and heard an airliner was cleared to land on Runway 14. They were low enough that our airplane would be lost in the ground clutter on the radar as we merged with their blip.

I seized the opportunity and intercepted their approach path at a position slightly above and behind the airliner. Mom kept quiet as we piggybacked the jet.

I stayed above it until the jet touched down so I could avoid the wake turbulence. The private terminal was on the opposite side of the runway from the airline terminal.

I had plenty of airspeed when I shut down the engine, did a side-step maneuver, and glided to a silent landing on the parallel taxiway. I popped open the canopy, turned into the ramp, and coasted to a stop near the private aircraft terminal.

No one noticed our silent landing on the taxiway in the dim light. I put the aircraft key in the map compartment and pulled on my helmet.

"Okay, Mom, we need to get out fast." I jumped out and helped her down.

Colin and Suzanne Covington were waiting for us inside. I handed Mom my folded note for Ross.

"Make sure Ross gets this. My life may depend on it."

I nodded at the Covingtons. "Thank you. Please leave right away for the hospital."

I hugged Mom. "Go with them. I have to stop the Black Sun. I love you."

"Wait! Where are you going? Sam, come back!" Mom yelled.

I ran outside to the Gulfstream G650 idling on the ramp.

Inside the corporate jet, the steward took my weapons and helmet, scanned me for electronic signals, retracted the airstairs, and closed the entry door.

As the airplane taxied to the runway, a tall blond man waved me to a seat beside him.

"Welcome aboard, Samantha, or should I say Golden Twin? My name is Werner. Buckle up."

The Gulfstream jet roared down the runway and lifted off.

84

EARLIER, ROSS AND HIS men paused at the base of the mountain where the hiking trail ended. An old stone church stood nearby. The valley was cold and silent.

"Surround the church. They must be hiding inside." Ross ran to the door.

The team circled the church and guarded every window. Derek backed up Ross at the door.

Ross pointed to where the old lock had been forced open with a knife. "Ready?"

Derek nodded.

Ross yanked the door open, and they rushed inside.

"Check the pews. You take that side." Ross pointed to his left.

They covered the small church sanctuary in thirty seconds. Ross pointed at the restrooms.

Derek checked the men's room while Ross searched the ladies' room.

"I found paper towels with blood stains in the bin," Ross said when they met in the hall. "Look for hiding places while I check the office." Ross walked behind the altar.

Moments later, Ross returned to the sanctuary.

"The office is empty and appears undisturbed. They were here, though. What are we missing?"

Derek looked deep in thought with his hands on his hips.

His emerald-green eyes brightened. "Call Charlie. Ask him what he and Sam did the last time they were here."

"They never said anything about this place."

"Aye and they never told you about the secret passage in the cavern. Could be there's a lot they didn't mention. Probably thought it wasn't important after everythin' was over."

"I doubt my mobile will work in this valley. I'll step out and call him on the satellite phone."

Charlie sounded eager to help. "Aye, Sam used the computer in the *kirk* to send the email to Emily. Then we borrowed the van to take the lads to the barn, but Sam returned it before she went to the airport. I don't think the church ever knew we borrowed it."

"What airport?"

"There's a grass airport in the valley on the way to Inverness. She rode the motorcycle there and took the airplane."

Ross heard distant helicopters. "Thanks, Charlie. Stay close to the phone in case I need you again."

He contacted the lead Lynx. "Land in the valley near the stone church. We're all here, except Chris."

Five minutes later, Ross and his teams boarded the helicopters. He sent the team in the second Lynx to pick up Chris and ordered the lead Lynx to land at the grass airport.

It wasn't long before Ross's team was on the ground searching the airport.

He spotted a horse tied between two T-hangars.

"Derek, help me check that empty hangar." Ross ran beside his second-in-command.

The mobile phone was in plain sight on the wood wheel chocks. Ross checked its call log and called Corporal Burns on his SATCOM.

"Burnsie, find out who these two numbers belong to, but

don't call them." Ross recited the numbers. "Get back to me ASAP."

Derek stood beside Ross. "The aircraft's tail number is on the wheel chocks, NX70SX."

"Any clues on the aircraft type? I noticed the Piper Cub Special she took last time has been repaired and is parked in its hangar."

"No idea, but Burnsie can use the tail number to find the aircraft type and owner."

Ross's SATCOM rang. "Who did she call?" His face brightened as he listened. "What about the other number? Right. I'll hold while you look up the owner and airplane type for NX70SX."

Ross turned to Derek. "Burnsie said the first number she called was Lord Covington's phone. She must be taking Loren to visit Duncan. The other number was a burner phone like this one. No name."

Burnsie spoke on the SATCOM. "A Swearingen SX300. It's a two-seat American homebuilt airplane made from a kit designed by a Texan named Ed Swearingen. It's all metal and flies like a fighter. Top speed is close to 300."

"Do you have the owner's phone number?"

"I called him. He said the private airport is owned by a group of pilots who share the expenses. Each member has a key to the fuel pumps. His airplane is parked in T-hangar number seven."

"Not anymore. Sam took it. We can't tell anyone about this. If we put out an alert for that tail number, the Americans will take her."

"What are your orders, Captain?"

"Find airports near York that have long enough runways for that airplane. She's probably trying to fly under radar. It must be very small if it only has two seats. We'll head back to base and refuel. Then I'll take a team to York. Oh, and Burnsie, we're bringing back four DBs for identification."

Ross's team gathered around him, and he made a radio call. "Team Two, take the bodies from the cave back to base for ID and fly at normal altitude. We're heading back."

Team One boarded the Lynx, and Ross sat beside Derek as they flew to the base at maximum speed.

"I hope the Americans aren't watching Duncan's room," Ross said. "Sam will arrive about an hour before we can get there. Our advantage is being able to land on the hospital roof. That will save time."

"Mayhap she heard us talking about the safe house. That would explain why she took Loren. She knew her mother would want to be with Duncan. No telling what mental condition she's in after the torture." Derek winced.

"I don't know. I'd like to think Sam trusts me enough to talk to me first about her concerns. I have a sick feeling this is about something much bigger. Wish I knew who else she called." Ross shook his head.

85

THE MOMENT THE LYNX touched down on the York hospital roof, Ross and his men jumped out. He had called ahead for Duncan's room number.

Ross addressed his men inside the stairwell where the walls muted the sound of the thumping blades. "Derek and I will go to room 610. Will, secure the hallway outside the room. Steve, guard this stairwell for the extraction."

Ross ran down the stairs and slowly opened the door to level six. All clear. He waved his men forward to room 610. Edging the door open, he saw Loren sitting beside Duncan's bed, her eyes red from crying. Lord and Lady Covington sat near the window.

"Hello, everyone." Ross glanced around the room as Derek checked the bathroom. "Where's Sam?"

"Oh, Ross, thank God you're here! You have to save her. Sam sacrificed herself to protect us. She left about an hour ago in a private jet." Loren stood and pulled the note from her pocket. "It's all in this note." She handed it to Ross.

Ross read aloud:

Ross, I'm sorry for the trouble I've caused. All the attacks were because of me. The Black Sun thinks I'm the Golden Twin. They won't stop targeting people I care about until they have me. Find their base, or this will never end. I had to do this to help you destroy them.

I'm leaving England with their leader in a Gulfstream G650 from the Leeds-Bradford International Airport. Don't know where they're taking me, but Germany is a good guess. I'll activate the emergency signal at an opportune time, assuming they don't take my watch.

Ross, you're my only hope. I'm counting on you to find the Black Sun and rescue me. Please understand I had to protect all the innocent people I put at risk. I would never betray you. This was the only solution. I knew you'd never let me do it if I told you. You're a good man, and I'm grateful you're in my life. Please don't be angry. If this doesn't go well, I'd hate for you to remember me in a bad light.

Mother might be able to help you. She needs to calm herself and allow a vision to enter her mind.

Godspeed.

Love, Sam

Duncan's voice was weak. "Ross, kill those Black Sun bastards and save Sam."

"Aye, Duncan, I'll find them. Loren, tell me about the men who took you."

"They're German, and their leader, Werner, is a merciless monster. He's tall and fit with a blond crew cut and cold blue eyes. I think he enjoyed ripping off my fingernails." Her voice quavered. "They wanted Sam, and now they have her."

Ross touched her shoulder. "Have you had a vision about Sam?"

"No, I've been too upset. I feel calmer now that you're here. Let me try again." She closed her eyes, took a deep breath, and released it slowly.

After a few moments, she straightened, gasped, and opened her eyes. "I didn't see Sam, just the man who ripped off my fingernails."

"Where is he?" Ross tried to remain calm.

"I don't know. I only saw his evil face." She bit her lip. "Does anybody have some chocolate?"

"Here, honey, I always carry some in my purse." Suzanne handed her a truffle.

"Thank you. Chocolate soothes me." Loren peeled back the wrapper and took a bite.

Ross called the DSF on his SATCOM. "Sir, I need military flight tracking on a Gulfstream G650 that left Leeds Bradford about an hour ago. The Black Sun has Samantha Starr on that airplane. We think they're going to Germany. Loren Starr is safe at the York Hospital with Duncan MacLeod. My team is with them at the hospital."

Ross looked at the expectant faces in the room. "DSF Brent Barnes is arranging the tracking. He'll call back soon with the info and a plan of operation."

"Sounds like we may be going to Germany." Derek glanced at his watch.

Ross paced. "It's a big country. We need to know where they're taking her after they land."

Duncan pressed the electric control on his bed to sit up. "Maybe Loren can help you with the location."

Ross stepped closer to Duncan's bed. "Sorry, my brain was so focused on the mission, I forgot to ask about you, old friend."

"The doctor said I'll be good as new in a few weeks. Please see to it Loren's hand is tended to. She refuses to leave my side."

Derek checked her hand. "I'll find someone to get this looked after." He nodded at Ross and left the room.

Suzanne whispered something to her husband, and he nodded.

"Captain Sinclair, you and your men are welcome to use

our private jet," Suzanne said.

"Yes, our Gulfstream is set up for ten passengers at Leeds Bradford," Colin said.

"Would you like us to call our pilots? They live nearby," Suzanne said.

"One moment. Let me take this call." Ross answered his SATCOM.

"Aye, sir, understood. Her mother has visions about her. When they arrive at their destination in country, Loren may be able to tell us where they took her." He checked the time. "Our Lynx is standing by on the roof. We can be at the airport in five minutes."

He listened again. "Right, we'll head for Germany and jump over the target as soon as we know where it is. The Germans will want in on this. Understood. We'll do a joint op with their GSG-9 counter terrorism unit. Thank you, sir."

Ross faced the Covingtons. "Thank you for your generous offer, but we're going on a military jet. We'll need to parachute in to save time."

86

WE FOLLOWED A CURVING road up the hill in Werner's black Mercedes. Towering above us, the unlit castle looked sinister. The triangular-shaped fortress had three circular towers, one at each junction of the triangle.

"What a magnificent castle! Is that where we're going?" I tried to sound excited.

"Are you familiar with Wewelsburg Castle?" Werner seemed taken aback.

"No, but I love castles. The histories and designs fascinate me."

"Ah, this one has a dark history. It was built in the early 1600s, but the Nazis used it for occult purposes. It holds more secrets than you. In fact, it is designed to expose your secrets." He gave me an evil smile.

"Werner, I came with you willingly. Remember our agreement?"

"Then you intend to answer all our questions? Tell us whatever we wish to know?"

"I can only tell you what I know. I may not have the knowledge you seek, but I'll certainly do my best to give you the answers you want."

"If you do not have an answer, you can ask your special twin or all three triplets."

"They aren't here."

"Do not toy with me. I know the prophecy. They do not need to be here. I am a citizen of the Black Sun. My people have mastered the power of the Vril. You cannot deceive me. Do not test me again, or the result will be extremely unpleasant for you."

"I'm sorry. I didn't mean to offend you. Please understand I'm in the habit of dealing with the unenlightened. You clearly deserve to be treated as an equal. Mea culpa." I looked into his icy-blue eyes and smiled.

The driver turned onto a narrow access road beside the moat and switched off the headlights before slowly driving around the castle. When he stopped near the north tower, we stepped out into the cold night air.

"Ah, my dear, the moment of truth has arrived. You will soon meet Master. First, one more scan." He waited while the driver ran the scanner over me.

"She's clean." The driver pocketed the device.

"Come with me." Werner opened the access door to the north tower. "I'm taking you down to the vault, a circular room designed with special acoustics."

Our footsteps echoed off the stone steps as we descended into a round room where twelve pedestals lined the perimeter, each with a wall niche above it holding a lit candle.

A swastika with ornamentally extended arms was centered on the domed ceiling. Beneath it, a wide circular area was recessed two feet into the floor with a gas-fed flame burning in the center.

A frail man in his seventies with round wire-rimmed spectacles waited opposite the entrance. His pale, blue-gray eyes focused on me in my black combat attire.

"Ah, the Golden Twin, Samantha Starr, welcome. I am a master of the Black Sun. You will call me Master. I must say your choice of clothing is a bit odd. Not at all what I expected."

His gravelly voice resonated in the acoustics.

"The British SAS made me wear this so the Americans wouldn't recognize me. I'm honored to meet you, Master." I did a half curtsy.

"You came with Werner in exchange for us to stop targeting your coworkers and family."

"Yes, the attacks have become tiresome. I'd rather work with you and perhaps find a solution that will satisfy everyone."

Master stepped closer and scrutinized my face. "Are you from Atlantis?"

"No, my ancestors are from Atlantis. I was born in America."

"Good, you are telling the truth. It would be unwise to lie to me. Who raised the triplets?"

"The Dragon Society found and raised them. They too are aware of the ancient prophecy."

"Where is Poseidon's Sword?"

"I was closing in on it when your men interfered in Hong Kong, Agra, and Petra. A trail of clues intended for me alone was laid thousands of years ago."

"Not the triplets?"

"The clues were intended for the Golden Twin. Surely you know that. The Dragon Master is holding the triplets prisoner as incentive for me to locate Poseidon's Sword."

"Where are they?"

"The Dragon Master has hidden them in a remote part of the Himalayas. He brought them there blindfolded. They don't know exactly where they are, so they can't direct me there."

"What is the purpose of Poseidon's Sword?"

"It is a weapon of mass destruction for which there is no countermeasure."

"Ah, yes, but what was your ancestor's plan for it?"

"World domination, of course."

"That wouldn't help them in this day and age unless part of their civilization survived the destruction of Atlantis and is hiding, waiting to rule the world." He stepped closer. "Where is the remnant hiding?"

"I don't know."

I could feel his breath on my face. His stare pierced my eyes.

"I think you do. The vault will reveal your secrets." He motioned to men who had entered after me. "Chain her to the floor in the pit."

I spun around and flipped the nearest man into the pit. He landed on the eternal flame and screamed when his clothing caught fire. Spinning heel kicks took out two more soldiers. The remaining one drew his weapon.

Werner rushed forward. "Hold fire, you fool! We need her alive."

I side-stepped the soldier's charge and flipped him into the wall.

Master focused his power on me.

I collapsed, writhing in agony from an unseen force.

87

DEREK WALKED IN WITH a young nurse pushing a medical cart. "Pam, this is your patient, Loren."

Pam moved close to Loren. "Let me see." She looked at the swollen, blood-scabbed fingers. "I'll clean and dress your hand and apply a local analgesic."

"Derek, the DSF said Sam's flight already landed at a private airport near Paderborn, Germany," Ross said. "By the time police arrived, everyone was gone. He's sending a military transport with jump gear for us. We'll head for Germany and parachute over the target. We're counting on Loren telling us where they took Sam if she doesn't activate her emergency signal." Ross glanced at Loren.

Her voice was tense with pain from Pam's treatment. "Ross, you can count on me. I'll find her."

Loren paused while Pam applied an antibiotic ointment that contained a strong pain killer.

"Ah, much better. Thank you, Pam." She looked up at Ross and Derek as the nurse bandaged her hand. "Gentlemen, I'm counting on you. Please save my daughter."

"This isn't just a military op for me. I love Sam and want her back safe. My men joke a lot about last summer, but they care about her too. We'll save her. That's a promise." He kissed her cheek, saluted Duncan, and nodded farewell to the Covingtons.

Ross jotted down a phone number and handed it to Loren. "Call me the moment you know where she is."

Ross gathered his team into the Lynx and flew to Leeds Bradford International Airport. A military jet transport taxied to the ramp moments before they landed in the Lynx.

Inside the Boeing C-17, they checked their parachutes and gear as the jet took off and raced toward Germany at maximum operating speed.

88

I HAD LIED MYSELF into a corner. I had no idea if the triplets survived the crash, and if they did, who raised them. I said the Dragon Society had them because the Dragon Master warned me about the Black Sun. I wasn't sure if my lineage traced back to Atlantis. If people from Atlantis were in hiding, I had no idea where. Maybe the Atlanteans raised the triplets.

My watch signal wouldn't penetrate the underground vault. I had to figure a way to trick them so I could activate the emergency button in a place where the signal would work.

My eardrums had ruptured, and my nose and ears were bleeding. I choked from blood running down my throat.

Master's voice sounded far away. "The location of the remnant, Samantha?"

"Yes." I coughed up blood.

"I want to tell you, but I need to connect with the triplets and use our combined powers to find them. The vault is blocking my communication with them."

89

ABOARD THE BOEING C-17, Ross received a call from Loren on his SATCOM.

"I saw a circular pit made of stone blocks, and the overhead dome had a giant swastika in the center. There were twelve pedestals along the perimeter of the outer circle, each with candles burning in alcoves above them."

Duncan's weak voice rasped, "Have Burnsie research German castles near Paderborn for a room that fits Loren's description."

Ross made the call and recited the details to Corporal Burns. "Burnsie, every minute counts on this one. I'll hold."

Two minutes later, Burnsie came back on. "Captain, it's Wewelsburg Castle on a hill near a village with the same name. It was closed last year for a two-year renovation."

"Thanks, Burnsie." Ross ran to the cockpit.

The pilot looked over his shoulder as Ross said, "Drop us over Wewelsburg. Our target is the castle on the hill near the village."

"I'll send a warning to the jumpmaster when we're five minutes out. Good luck, Captain."

Ross returned to his team and called the DSF. "Sir, her mother thinks she's in Wewelsburg Castle."

"I'll get right back to you."

90

MASTER STUDIED MY FACE for a sign of treachery. I hoped the pain masked my deceit. He turned to his men.

"Take her to *Obergruppenführersaal*. Chain her over the Black Sun." He stepped back and supervised the men as they unchained me and dragged me upstairs.

"The museum calls this room the SS Generals' Hall. It holds great significance for us. Do not fail me again." Master looked at me with merciless eyes.

I glanced around as I was dragged to the center of another circular room where a dark-green sun wheel was set into the pale marble floor. The ominous room was encircled by twelve columns joined by a groined vault, twelve window and door niches, and eight tall windows.

"The center of the sun wheel is pure gold. It is the symbol for the Black Sun. You will soon feel its power." Master pointed down. "Chain her over it."

I managed to tap my wrist against the marble floor at the perfect angle to activate the emergency button before they chained my arms and legs in the position of Da Vinci's Vitruvian Man in his most outstretched pose. I took a deep breath and tried to calm down.

"Now you will contact the triplets and answer all our questions or suffer the consequences of disobedience." Master looked down at me.

"I need a few minutes of absolute silence. No interruptions." I closed my eyes and tried to empty my mind.

I saw a vision of my mother sitting with the Covingtons and Duncan in his hospital room. Where was Ross? I had been certain he would track me there. *Damn.*

Master interrupted my vision. "Have you connected with the triplets?"

"Yes, but you broke the connection. Now I must try again. Silence, please."

If the triplets are alive, maybe I can make a telepathic connection with them. They should be old enough to have the same psychic abilities their mother had. Maybe they can help me somehow. If not, I'm dead.

I closed my eyes and concentrated on the names Solraya, Luna, and Blaze in the remote chance they would hear my desperate plea. A few minutes of silence passed.

"Enough! You are stalling for time. Your boyfriend will not find you. Neither will the Americans. Tell me the location of the remnant or suffer my wrath."

I ignored him and tried to stay focused. The triplets were my only hope. Pain seared through my upper back, which was directly over the Black Sun symbol. I struggled to maintain my mental concentration on the three names.

"That is a taste of what is to come if you do not answer me. Tell me the remnant's location now, or I will make you beg for death."

I remained silent. My body filled with excruciating pain, like being electrocuted from the inside out.

I gritted my teeth and kept summoning the triplets, hoping the painful energy flowing through me would strengthen my telepathy. Slowly, I was losing consciousness.

Three familiar faces were the last thing I saw.

91

THE DSF SPOKE TO Ross on his SATCOM. "I received intel that Sam activated the emergency signal on her watch ten minutes ago. Her GPS is accurate within three feet. She's in the north tower in the SS Generals' Hall. The Americans picked up her signal at the same time. A SEAL team led by her brother was on ready alert at Ramstein Air Base in Germany. They'll probably arrive first because of the short distance. GSG-9 is coming from Hannover. Looks like you'll arrive last by a few minutes. I'll notify the Americans you're coming so they don't shoot you. Bring her back to Great Britain, Captain."

"Aye, sir." Ross acquired the tactical frequency from the DSF so his team could communicate with Mike Starr's SEAL team and the German GSG-9 unit.

Minutes before his team jumped, he called Sam's brother. "Mike, it's Ross. My team's about to parachute down to the castle. Give me a sit rep." Ross heard gunfire when Mike keyed his microphone.

"My six-man team is pinned down in the trees by snipers on the north tower. Sam's in the SS Generals' Hall near ground level. Snipers inside the southeast and southwest towers are targeting the ten-man GSG-9 unit on the south grounds. Enemy shooters on lower levels are firing into the trees at all of us. Our best guess is about two-hundred tangos."

"Derek, Steve, and Will are with me. Two hundred tangos

against twenty special operators sounds like a fair fight. Hang tight. We'll come in dark and take out the snipers. Alert the GSG-9 leader. ETA six minutes."

Ross finished the radio call seconds before the green jump light illuminated.

Adrenaline pumped through him as he and his men dived from the aft cargo door into the cold night sky toward Wewelsburg. They opened their high-performance black chutes at three thousand feet and glided to the targets. Flashes of gunfire from the towers and surrounding grounds looked like strobe lights.

Ross and Derek focused on the primary target: the north tower where Sam was held captive a few levels below the top. They circled three hundred feet above the snipers and dropped grenades straight down. Steve and Will did the same over the other two towers.

The SAS team held their rifles ready to fire as they circled ever lower and waited for the smoke from the grenades to clear. Ross spotted one man moving on the north tower and shot him. Bodies littered the ramparts. Ross landed and stood guard while Derek slipped off his chute and stuffed it under a nearby body.

"Southeast tower's secure at top," Steve reported. "I entered through a hole I blasted in the roof."

"Southwest tower's secure at top. Snipers inside are dead," Will reported.

Ross radioed Mike. "Snipers neutralized. All tower roofs secure. Derek and I are going in."

"Call me when you're outside the SS Generals' Hall where they're holding Sam," Mike said. "The majority of Black Sun soldiers are guarding entrances to ground levels of the castle and towers where they're under attack by my SEALs and GSG-9."

Descending the winding staircase, Ross and Derek encountered enemy soldiers around every turn. In a brief firefight, Ross and Derek took out the remaining soldiers guarding the door to the SS Generals' Hall.

Both men were grazed: Ross on his left shoulder and Derek on his right thigh. They ignored their minor wounds and pressed on.

"Good thing this castle's a museum. There's a sign over the door for the SS Generals' Hall." Derek pointed.

"Derek and I are outside the target room. Area's secure," Ross reported.

"Hold fire. I'm coming in," Mike said. "My men are keeping the enemy busy."

Moments later, Ross, Derek, and Mike stood together, opened the door, and peered in.

They had to turn off their night-vision gear and wait for their eyes to adjust.

"Bloody hell! Looks like an electrical storm in there." Ross shielded his eyes.

A whirlwind of electromagnetic energy was firing thousands of brilliant blue-white lightning bolts all over the room from the center. The men inside had been scorched. Grotesque corpses lined the outer circle.

Ross squinted as he scanned the room. "I see her! She's chained to the floor in the center."

Mike looked relieved to see his sister. "She's not burned. It's like she's protected by an invisible Faraday cage."

"An invisible what?" Derek asked.

"I'll explain later."

"How do we rescue Sam in that electrical storm?" Ross asked.

"I'll try to talk to her and find out how it works. She must know something if she's the only one who survived." Mike whistled loudly and yelled, "Sam! The Black Sun soldiers are dead. Ross and Derek are with me. How do we get to you?"

"Mike?" Sam's voice was weak.

"Yes, baby sister, it's me. Tell us how to save you," Mike shouted.

"Wait!" She sounded frantic.

The crackling tornado roared a few seconds longer, then vanished. The room fell dark and silent.

"Okay, it's safe now. I need wine and chocolate," she said in a barely audible tone.

Ross scanned the dark room with a flashlight.

The scent of charred flesh fouled the air.

Derek nudged Mike. "I think you'd better tell us what you know about this."

"An Englishman named Michael Faraday invented the Faraday cage in 1836. The cage protects its contents from electrical currents."

Mike stopped beside Sam. "Well, obviously there's no cage around her. It's as though an invisible force field protected her."

92

THE TRIPLETS WERE STILL patched into my mind. They saw what I saw. When Mike, Ross, and Derek approached to unchain me, the triplets watched them through my eyes.

"Ask them to clean off the greasepaint. We want to see their faces so we can recognize them if we ever meet."

"Sorry we don't have any wine or chocolate, lass. I'll get some for you soon." Ross kissed me. His words sounded so far away.

When they unchained me, I sat up and wiped the blood away from my nose and ears with my sleeve.

"Ross, I need you to clean your face—Mike and Derek too. It's important. I need to see your faces right away. Please." I choked and spit up a little blood.

They exchanged concerned glances, shrugged, and began wiping off the greasepaint.

I noticed Derek's thigh. "You're wounded!"

"Just a minor graze. No worries." He smiled and leaned in close.

I touched Derek's face. "Derek, thank you for coming to my rescue."

His emerald-green eyes twinkled. "Sam, you know I specialize in damsels in distress. Thanks for giving me so much practice."

"Ah, Derek is quite handsome. We like his sexy green

eyes."

Next, I touched Mike's face and noticed blood seeping from his left temple. "Mike, you're bleeding too!"

"It's nothing. My helmet got the worst of it. You know I have a hard noggin', Sis."

"I love you, Mike. I couldn't bear it if anything happened to you."

"Love you too, Sis. Glad you're safe now." He hugged me and smiled.

"Oh, I like this one. He's so good looking!" Blaze said.

"Too bad there isn't two of him. I love his blond hair," Luna said.

"Actually, Mike has a twin brother named Matt who looks a lot like him," I told the triplets.

"Good, then maybe we'll both be happy some day," Luna said.

I reached for Ross and kissed him. "I love you, Ross. I'm sorry about leaving you back in the Highlands. Please forgive me."

"I understand, Sam. You did what you thought you had to do. You know I love you, lass. I'm so glad to have you back in my arms. I saw the blood. Are you hurt?" Ross looked me over.

That's when I noticed his shoulder was bleeding. "Ross, you're wounded too!"

"Relax, lass, it's just a wee scratch." He gave me a reassuring kiss.

"Ross gives good kisses," Solraya said.

"His eyes are the same color as mine," Luna said.

"We'll have no problem remembering these three," Blaze said.

"And Mike's brother, Matt," Luna said.

"I'll be forever grateful to you three," I said. "The pain was terrible. Thank you for saving me."

I closed my eyes and saw Solraya's face.

"How could I not save someone who looks exactly like me?" Solraya said. *"We'll leave you now with those handsome men, but expect to hear from us again."*

The triplets vanished from my mind.

93

"SAM? ARE YOU ALL right?" Ross squeezed my shoulders.

"My eardrums are ruptured, and my insides feel like they were electrocuted. My captors tore open my stitches, and I hurt all over. Other than that, I'm fine."

"What caused the electrical storm in here?" Mike asked.

"I'm not sure," I lied. "The Black Sun Master had unusual powers. He tormented me, causing a lot of pain without even touching me. I think he used the Vril. The Dragon Master warned me about it."

Mike called his men to check on the battle. "Give me a sit rep." He listened a few moments. "Good work, my sister's safe. We'll bring her out now." He looked at Ross. "The castle's secure."

Ross scooped me into his arms. "Time to take Sam to a military medical facility." He carried me down the short flight of stairs to the outside.

"There's a Chinook inbound to fly us to Ramstein Air Base." Mike scanned the sky. "Here it comes now." He pointed at the helicopter. "Plenty of room for your team, Ross."

Ross called Will and Steve. "Meet us at the Chinook. We're hitching a ride to Ramstein."

The big helicopter landed between the north tower and the forest where the SEALs and SAS soldiers boarded. I closed my eyes as cold air from the rotor wash hit my face.

Ross lifted me inside and held me on his lap. "From now on, lass, I intend to keep you close." He gave me a light squeeze and kissed me.

I rested my head on his broad shoulder, grateful to be free of the torture chamber. The helicopter seemed a lot quieter, thanks to my ruptured ear drums.

We didn't try to talk during the short flight to the American Air Force base. I was content in his arms, finally safe.

A medical team stood ready to whisk me from the helipad.

"This woman's safety is my responsibility," Ross said to the medics. "I'll carry her to the ambulance."

Derek and Mike walked beside us as Will and Steve followed.

"Sis, I need to meet General Ryan for a debriefing. Are you okay with that?" Mike looked into my eyes with concern.

"You're not going anywhere until your wound is looked after." I pulled his face close and kissed his cheek. "I mean it. Same goes for Derek and Ross."

"Well okay, little miss bossy pants." Mike grinned and kissed the top of my head.

When we arrived in the examining room, the doctor said, "We'll need to remove her clothes for a complete examination. The soldiers should wait outside."

"The soldiers are wounded." I pointed at Mike, Derek, and Ross. "That one's my brother, he's my friend, and this one's my boyfriend."

Ross glanced at Mike and Derek. "The two lieutenants will go to another treatment room, but I'm not leaving," Ross said to the doctor. "My orders are to protect her at all times." Ross crossed his arms with a don't-mess-with-me look.

It was then the doctor appeared to notice Derek, Ross, and I were wearing identical uniforms.

"I see. Nurse, take the lieutenants next door. Captain, take off your shirt while we remove her clothing."

It wasn't long before I was stripped down to my panties, and an intern was dressing Ross's shoulder graze. The doctor grimaced when he saw my severe bruises and torn stitches.

"Let me see what I can do about these stitches." After re-stitching my wound, he examined me. "Why is there blood in your ears and nose?"

"My eardrums ruptured. I'm not sure if the blood in my nose is from that or something else."

Wish I could curl up in Ross's arms and sleep for a long time.

The doctor checked inside my ears and nose. "Fortunately, it looks like it's just your eardrums. How did this happen?"

Ross interrupted, "She can't answer that. It's classified."

The doctor sighed. "I'll clean your ears and give you something to prevent infection. As long as you protect your ears and avoid infection, they should heal in a couple months."

"That's good news. Thanks, Doc." I gave him my best smile.

After I was patched up, cleaned up, and well medicated, I dressed in fresh blue hospital scrubs just in time to meet a four-star general accompanied by Mike and Derek.

Mike handed me a chocolate bar and kissed my forehead. "Hey, Sis, feeling better? This is General James Ryan."

Mike turned to the general. "Sir, this is my sister, Sam, and that's her boyfriend, Captain Ross Sinclair."

The general kissed my hand and saluted Ross. "Miss Starr, we're glad to have you home safe. It appears the threat from the Black Sun has been neutralized. However, while you're in a weakened state, it might be best to keep you in a secret facility until we have time to investigate other groups and confirm the threat is indeed over."

"Thank you, General, I appreciate your concern for my safety. Please understand my wounds extend beyond the obvious physical damage."

I played the emotional trauma card to ensure I would be allowed to recuperate with Ross, Mom, and Duncan in Duncan's castle. After the torture I had endured, I didn't need to fake it.

"Ross and his Special Forces team are willing and able to protect me while I heal in Scotland with my mother at Duncan MacLeod's castle. All government agendas will have to be put on hold during my recovery." I popped a piece of chocolate like a pill and let it melt in my mouth. *Now that's what I call good medicine.*

Mike superseded the general's objections. "Sir, I can assure you based on my own experience that nobody can make my sister do something she doesn't want to do. She's a loyal American. Give her time to heal and everything will turn out the way you want."

General Ryan looked into my determined eyes. "As you wish, Miss Starr, I'll arrange transport to Scotland for you as soon as the doctor clears you for travel." He glanced at the doctor.

"A good night of sleep and she'll be ready to go," the doctor said, looking at me. "I'll send you off with a bottle of antibiotics for your ears. Start the pills right away."

"Thank you, Doctor." I smiled and faced the general. "Thank you for granting my request, General Ryan. I appreciate your consideration."

The general nodded. "All right, Doctor, let's get Miss Starr settled in a room where she can rest."

Fifteen minutes later, I was in a private room. The bed felt wonderful.

Ross pulled off his combat gear. "Derek, work out a

schedule with Steve and Will. I want one man on guard duty at all times. I'll be in here with Sam."

Mike leaned down and kissed my forehead. "I have to go, Sis. Have a good rest."

Ross slipped into the bed and gathered me against his bare chest.

Finally, dreamland.

94

THE FOLLOWING EVENING, COMMANDER Bob Metz walked into the Officers' Club and found the table where the Petra group waited with Captain Rowlin.

"Good evening, everyone, I have good news. The Black Sun is no longer a threat. They were defeated last night, and Sam was rescued. She's safe in Duncan's castle with her mother, Duncan, and Ross." Bob waved at a waiter and pointed at the wine list.

"You said Sam was rescued. Rescued from what?" Lance asked.

"She handed herself over to the Black Sun so she could lead us to their base of operations."

Jeff looked outraged. "How could you send her out on a mission like that? She was in no condition for a dangerous op."

"Nobody sent her. She slipped away from Ross and made a deal with the Black Sun to go with them if they agreed to stop targeting her people. She assumed they would take her to their headquarters. We found her when she activated the emergency signal on her watch."

"Sounds a lot like what she did last August when she sacrificed herself to save the boys." Lance shook his head. "That woman can't stay out of trouble."

Pete filled his glass with Pellegrino water. "Yeah, she keeps the Brits and our military busy. Rescuing her is a full-time job."

"Sam's a brave woman who saved us many times." Carlene glared at the men. "Cut her some slack. She probably saved the whole world by helping the military stop the Black Sun."

Rod lifted his glass of Champagne. "Damn straight! Sam sacrificed herself to keep us safe. They could have killed her. She deserves a medal or something."

"She already has one from last summer." Lance grinned. "Simmer down, people. We're all proud of Sam and grateful for what she did. I just wish she could have a normal life."

"I guess she'll need a couple of weeks for her wound and bruises to heal. Did she say when she'll be able to return to work?" Jeff asked.

Bob hesitated. "Uh, she'll need at least two months. The Black Sun tortured her and ripped apart her stitches. Her eardrums were ruptured, and she experienced severe psychological trauma."

Everyone stared at Bob in shock.

"Bloody hell! What did those Black Sun bastards do to her?" Jack asked.

"She said they used the power of the Vril to torture her, whatever that means. She didn't want to talk about it." Bob placed his order with the waiter.

Lance looked crushed. "Sounds like a lot more than ruptured eardrums. Do they know if she'll recover?"

"She'll heal from the physical injuries, but psychological trauma is hard to predict. She's in good hands. Ross and his team are protecting her. Duncan has round-the-clock medical staff at his castle, and Sam's mother is there too. Sam's surrounded by people who love her. They'll nurture her back to health."

"Well, that's good to hear. Sorry to change the subject, but is our airplane ready to go?" Jeff asked.

"Yes, the repairs are finished and the tanks are full. Do you mind giving the mechanics a ride back to the States?" Bob sipped a glass of 2006 vintage Querciabella Chianti Classico.

"No problem. We'll leave after dinner. Are the mechanics ready to depart?" Jeff sipped his coffee.

"I believe so. They're having dinner at that table." Bob pointed.

"Excuse me a moment." Jeff walked over to chat with the mechanics.

Carlene turned to Lance. "Sugar, are we stopping in New York like we originally planned?"

"Yes, you'll get a new airplane and crew in New York for your return trip to LAX. Jeff is taking our airplane back to home base in Florida because the wings need to be repainted, and the crew needs time off." Lance patted her hand. "The new crew will take good care of you."

"Why don't I fly down to Florida with you, and then you can come home with me to Texas?" Carlene batted her lashes. "I'll charter a little jet. It'll be fun. What do you say, sugar?"

"I'll have to take a rain check on that, darlin', but thanks for asking." Lance kissed her hand.

Carlene hid her disappointment and batted her lashes at Jack. "What about you, Jack? Want to come out to Texas? I'll fix you some grits."

"Sorry, baby, I'm taking a charter flight home to England. I've had enough adventure to last me a long time." Jack swirled the whisky in his glass.

"I'll miss you, Jack," Inga said and kissed his cheek.

"Not as much as I'll miss you." Jack hugged her.

"Carlene, if I come to Texas, will you teach me to shoot straight?" Rod asked.

"Count on it, sugar. I'll take you to my private shooting range. We'll have a good ole time."

Pete downed his soft drink and checked his watch. "Sorry

we can't take you back to LAX. I've enjoyed hanging out with all of you. Thing is, we're a bit shorthanded. Besides Sam, we've got two pilots out with broken bones, and this crew needs a duty break."

Jeff returned to the table. "The mechanics said the wings are in good shape. A little paint and she'll look like new."

"Sounds good." Lance stood. "I'll head out and do the walkaround."

Pete slid back his chair. "I'll go with you."

Bob stood and shook their hands. "It was an honor sharing combat with you, gentlemen."

"You've been a huge help to us, Commander," Jeff said. "I can't thank you enough."

"It was my pleasure. Have a safe flight home." Bob saluted Jeff.

Forty-five minutes later, Luxury Flight 813 was on the takeoff roll. Bob watched the big Boeing vanish into the night sky.

95

Black Sun Base
Antarctic

THE SUPREME MASTER OF the Black Sun addressed his council.

"I regret to inform you the life energy of two hundred of our brethren has extinguished. We have lost the Master of Wewelsburg."

A hush fell over the cavernous room five-hundred feet beneath the ice.

"This small inconvenience will not deter us from our ultimate goal. Our enemies think they have defeated us. We will wait and watch. When the time is right, we will seize the Golden Twin and take command of Poseidon's Sword.

"In the meantime, we have a team in Massachusetts watching Professor Ben Armitage. The Golden Twin sent him an artifact from the curio shop in Hong Kong. He may prove useful."

96

LORD EDGAR SWEETWATER CALLED his instrument of wrath, Nicolai.

"Did you find her?" Nicolai asked with an edge.

"She's in Scotland at Macleod Castle, recuperating from injuries she suffered at the hands of the Black Sun. A joint military op wiped out their base of operations in Germany and rescued her."

"Why did Black Sun want her?" Nicolai asked, suspicious.

"Case of mistaken identity. She bore a strong resemblance to a woman they were hunting," Sweetwater lied, not wanting Nicolai to know about Poseidon's Sword.

"Send jet to island. I will deal with her and others in Scotland."

"No, Nicolai, the castle's under constant military guard. Stick with our plan. I pulled some strings and arranged a job for you as a maintenance man at the Harry Potter theme park in Orlando. My pilot is bringing the documents for your new identity as a Florida resident. When she brings the brats there, you'll be in perfect position to execute the mission."

"When are they coming to Orlando?"

"In two months as originally planned. You'll start working there in two weeks. A man will meet you at the Orlando airport and give you keys to a car and apartment. He'll provide whatever weapons and other items you request."

Sweetwater detailed his plan for the kidnappings. "Taking them out of the country will be easy with my clever scheme."

"*Da,* is good plan. I will be ready."

As if reading his mind, Sweetwater said, "You gave me your word you wouldn't mess with them until I arrive. Together we can introduce them to my special dungeon."

"While I wait, I will tell them my plans and fill them with terror."

"Fine, just see that you wait."

97

MY TIME IN SCOTLAND was coming to an end. Mother and Duncan had healed nicely. My stitches had long since been removed, and my bruises faded about the same time. My hearing was back to normal, thank God, but it would be another two weeks before I could resume pilot duties.

The upside of two months in Scotland was plenty of hot sex with my Highlander hero and quality time with my mother, Duncan, Scottish friends, and my golden colt, Zeus. The downside was frequent nightmares. Emotional trauma from the Black Sun's torture had taken its toll.

Alone for the moment, I sat in the lotus position on the stone floor in the northeast tower of Duncan's castle. I wanted to contact the triplets, but had been unable to since Wewelsburg. I was disappointed they hadn't contacted me since then and was beginning to think I'd imagined them.

I hadn't told anyone about my telepathic communication with them or that they saved me from the Black Sun. I didn't know how to explain what happened. As time passed, I wondered if they had been a hallucination brought on by extreme pain.

Mom interrupted my solitude. "Sam? Charlie and Emily are here. Come down to the study."

Charlie Moncreiffe and Emily Brown were extraordinary children. His bravery and her cleverness had saved me a few months ago during my Highlands adventure. I adored them.

I untangled my legs and stood. "I'm looking forward to my trip with them. They're so cute together, aren't they?"

"Adorable. I want to squeeze them every time I see them."

"Well, it's a good thing you don't, or they would never come here again." I followed Mom down the winding staircase.

The children stood when we walked into the room. Twelve-year-old Charlie was muscular and fit from playing soccer and hiking in the mountains. His hazel eyes twinkled with mirth as he smoothed his unruly auburn hair.

Eleven-year-old Emily stood three inches shorter than Charlie. Her long brown curls framed a lovely face dominated by intelligent blue eyes.

I exaggerated a curtsy. "Ah, Sir Charles Moncreiffe and Dame Emily Brown, always a pleasure."

Emily giggled and Charlie bowed.

"The pleasure is ours, Sir Lady." Charlie kissed my hand.

"I smell fresh chocolate-chip cookies. Shall we dispense with the formalities?" I swept my hand to the table set with three glasses, a pitcher of milk, and a large platter of cookies.

After inhaling two cookies, Charlie wiped his mouth with a linen napkin. "Are you all set for our trip to Florida?"

"I'm packed and ready to roll. Don't forget I promised your parents I'd see to it you both use plenty of sunscreen." I savored a warm cookie.

"You'll have no problem with me. I don't want more freckles." Emily glanced at Charlie and blushed.

Ross walked in. "Hello Charlie, Emily, the helicopter will land in five minutes. Put on your coats and make sure you have everything ready to load aboard."

I stood. "Enjoy your cookies while I slip out and smother my boyfriend with kisses."

They snickered.

After a blazing five minutes with Ross and teary good-byes with Mom and Duncan, I pulled on a heavy leather jacket and climbed aboard beside Ross. Charlie and Emily already were buckled in. The mid-December sky looked bleak.

"The corporate jet is waiting for you at Edinburgh Airport." Ross wrapped his arm around me and warmed me up with a long tender kiss.

More giggling from the children.

I looked across at them. "I hope you remembered to bring your VIP dragon keys."

They reached into their backpacks and held up their prized possessions—silver keys with dragons perched on them. The inscriptions read: "Free Lifetime Entry to the Wizarding World of Harry Potter," with their names on the other side.

Charlie leaned in to Emily. "Should we give it to her now?"

"Aye, may as well." She grinned and reached into her bag. "When we told Daniel what a big fan you are, he convinced Universal Studios to make this for you."

Emily handed me a similar key with my engraved name and a solid gold dragon clutching the key.

"Wow! Thank you. I'm excited about touring the park. I know you both already saw it with Daniel, but you missed the new Diagon Alley. We'll have a great time." I admired my VIP key and showed it to Ross.

"You never told me you're a Harry Potter fan." Ross raised his eyebrows.

"The subject never came up. I've read the books and seen all the movies. My mother's a fan too. It's an extraordinary series. Have you read them?"

"No, lass, I don't read children's books."

"Well, I guess I'm just a big kid at heart." I kissed the gold dragon and tucked the key in my shoulder bag. "I need this fun distraction before I get sucked into a dangerous mission with the military. Besides, I promised Charlie and Emily I'd go with them. You know I always keep my promises."

"Aye and the Americans were quick to agree because they're eager to get you back on U.S. soil."

"What do they expect from me? I have no idea where Poseidon's Sword is hidden or if it exists. I found some clues at the Taj Mahal, Petra, and here, but that's all."

"Lass, you have the power to activate the crystals that project the holograms."

"So does my mother, but they don't know that." I looked out the window as we approached Edinburgh Airport. "We're almost there. I'll miss you."

"Call me when you land in Florida."

We landed near Starr Corporation's Citation X. Ross and I shared another kiss before he ushered us into the jet and checked on the pilots. Satisfied, he waved good-bye and walked across the ramp.

Our two months together had solidified our relationship. My heart ached when I looked out the window and saw him standing beside the helicopter.

It wasn't long before we were airborne and headed to Florida. The children loved the soft leather seats with individual entertainment centers.

"What's the Starr Corporation?" Charlie asked. "I saw the name on the airplane."

"It's an international aerospace company my father started. He invented several high-tech components for civilian and military aircraft. The company also has a space division that supplies parts for the International Space Station. After Dad died in a plane crash five years ago, my mother became the majority shareholder. The company's fleet of corporate jets is available for our family's private use." I sipped on a mint iced tea.

"Why didn't you work as a pilot for your father's company?"

"I could have, but I wanted to earn my own way in the world." I sunk back into the sumptuous leather. "Do you have any idea what you want to do after you finish with school and university? Maybe help your father run his shipping empire?"

"I'm not sure, maybe a Special Forces soldier like Captain Sinclair. His missions are so exciting." A dreamy look softened his face.

"You definitely have the courage. You proved that last summer. And your combat skills are quite impressive for your age. Just remember that job has a huge downside."

"What do you mean?" Charlie tilted his head.

"I mean you might get killed. Plenty of good men die in combat. Sometimes it's a matter of luck who lives and who dies." I sighed. "I worry about Ross."

"Aye, but the same thing can happen crossing a street. You never know. Better to do what you love."

"My dear young man, you are wise beyond your years." I toasted him with my glass.

Emily checked the website for her Magic Club on her laptop. "Johnny, Sally, Kenny, and Dolly are in the chat room. They wished us a fun trip."

The flight attendant interrupted Emily's Internet chat with a delicious prime rib dinner.

After eating, we snuggled up with blankets and watched a Harry Potter movie. I dozed off at the end and woke in Orlando.

98

THE HARRY POTTER THEME parks in Universal Studios and Islands of Adventure opened for us at dawn the next morning. We had both parks to ourselves until 9:00 a.m. No lines. No crowds.

The park always opened early for VIPs and special tours, but this was the first time since their trip with Daniel that the park was restricted to our private use. Charlie and Emily wanted to see the new Diagon Alley in Universal first.

"Ooo, it looks just like the street in the movies." Emily's face lit up.

"Let's stop at Ollivander's Wand Shop. I want a magic wand." I opened the door.

Wand boxes lined the shelves of the cluttered shop from floor to ceiling.

The elderly proprietor greeted us. "Welcome, young wizards and witches. How may I help you? A wand perhaps?"

Charlie pointed at me. "We already have wands. Can you find one for her?"

Emily giggled. "Trust us, no one needs a wand more than she does."

"That's true. A magic wand might solve all my problems." I stepped forward.

"Well, my dear, in this store the wand chooses you. Let's see if I can divine a match." He pulled out a box. "Here, try this one. Top of the line."

I lifted the wand from the box and waved it. Boxes flew off the shelves, and one even exploded. Charlie and Emily cackled as smoke rose from the debris. The lights brightened, and boxes rattled on the shelves. After a blast of cold air whistled through, everything returned to normal.

"Perfect. I'll take it."

I glanced at Charlie and Emily, snickering and whispering.

"Shall I wrap it for you?"

"No, I'll hang on to it. I might need it before the day is over." I winked at the shopkeeper and pulled out my wallet.

We continued along Diagon Alley to Weasley's Wizard Wheezes, Madam Malkin's Robes for all Occasions, Wiseacre's Wizarding Equipment, and Quality Quidditch Supplies. My favorite shop was the Magical Menagerie—basically a pet shop for wizards and witches. A live variety of beautiful owls, furry animals, and reptiles filled the cages.

After a brief walk down Knockturn Alley, we strolled to our primary destination—the roller coaster inside Gringotts Bank. It was run by goblins reining tight control over the valuables in their subterranean vaults. I flicked my wand at the dragon atop the bank, and it breathed fire at us.

"That dragon looks angry. We'd better go inside." I led the way.

"The goblins are glaring at us," Emily said as we walked past the creepy bank tellers.

We walked through the strange bank and boarded the rail cart that was supposed to carry us deep underground.

I sat between the children as the ride descended on steep rails into the spooky depths and zoomed around sharp corners. Charlie maintained his manly composure while Emily and I squealed at each new thrill. Another fire-breathing dragon took us by surprise.

"That was brilliant!" Charlie grinned as he exited.

"It might be even better than the Forbidden Journey ride inside Hogwart's Castle at the other park." Emily bubbled with enthusiasm.

I checked my watch. "Let's head for Kings Cross Station and board the Hogwarts Express."

"Right, we'll go to platform 9¾ and take the train to Hogsmeade in Islands of Adventure. Let's ride the Dragon Challenge roller coaster when we get there." Charlie checked his map.

"You'll love it, Sam. The twin roller coasters are inverted and cross paths along the route," Emily said.

"Alrighty, let's go." I led them to the train station.

It was a short ride to the Wizarding World of Harry Potter. Charlie led us straight to the giant roller coaster where we screamed with glee. The ride ended too soon for me.

"Wow, I've never been on one like that before! Let's go again after we take the ride inside the castle." I handed them their backpacks and pulled on mine.

"The entrance to Hogwarts Castle is this way." Charlie forged ahead down the deserted street.

We stored our backpacks in the lockers, as required by security, and entered the replica of the famous castle known as Hogwarts School of Witchcraft and Wizardry.

As we toured the castle, the realism amazed me. "It looks exactly like the one in all the Harry Potter movies. I feel like I'm in the real place."

I couldn't stop smiling. As the wizards in the paintings spoke to me, I forgot about the terror I'd endured two months ago. The castle was ours.

Our castle tour ended at the entrance to the Forbidden Journey ride. With me in the middle again, the locks clicked tight on our seats. The ride simulated following Harry on flying broomsticks as he out-maneuvered an angry dragon above the castle and then zipped us through the forbidden forest where giant spiders chased us. We flew through exciting scenes from the movies, as though we were inside the story with Harry.

When the ride tapered to a stop, our seats swiveled to the exit platform. A giant man with a maniacal grin stood before us holding a weapon.

Nicolai!

We struggled to escape, but our seats remained locked, trapping us.

"I have waited too long for revenge. Now you are mine." Nicolai laughed as he shot us with darts.

His ugly, distorted face seemed to melt as I lost consciousness.

99

NICOLAI LOADED HIS VICTIMS into a cart and closed the lid. He wheeled the cart down a maintenance ramp to the rear of a panel van, transferred the threesome, and sped out the maintenance exit.

Thirty minutes later, he drove through the general aviation gate at the Orlando International Airport and pulled up to a private jet parked on the ramp.

The forward entry door was open.

He carried Sam up the airstairs into the cabin where the window shades were pulled down. He dropped her on a seat, rushed out, and slung a child over each shoulder.

In a few seconds, they were aboard with the door closed. A catering truck pulled away from the aft door moments before the jet engines started.

The private jet taxied to the runway and soon was on the takeoff roll. It climbed into the bright morning sky and turned toward the Atlantic Ocean and Europe.

Twenty minutes later, Nicolai called Lord Sweetwater on a satellite phone.

"We got away clean. Plan worked perfectly. We land in nine hours and transfer to boat under cover of darkness. I will call when we dock at island."

"Good job, Nicolai. I told you this would be worth the wait.

Remember your promise. Do nothing to them until I arrive. I will pay you a bonus of five million pounds. You can enjoy your revenge and live a life of luxury wherever you choose."

"*Da,* I will wait, but not long."

Nicolai slid the satellite phone into his pocket and glanced out the small passenger window at the vast Atlantic Ocean.

100

CORPORAL BURNS RUSHED INTO Ross's office. "Captain, Sam and the children have vanished. The security guard who was overseeing their visit said they never came out of Hogwarts Castle. That was three hours ago. They've searched everywhere and can't find them."

"Are they certain they didn't leave on their own?" Ross asked.

"Their backpacks are still in the castle's lockers. They wouldn't leave them behind."

"Bloody hell! I hope to God you remembered to reinstate the automatic tracking feature on her watch before she left Scotland."

"Aye, sir, I just checked. The watch is over the Atlantic Ocean heading toward Europe. No way to know if she's still wearing it."

"Burnsie, get me the FBI in Orlando. Maybe a security camera at the airport shows her boarding a flight. Hurry!" Ross followed the corporal into the communications room.

The corporal checked his computer for the local FBI field office in Orlando and dialed the number.

After a brief conversation, he handed the phone to Ross. "Agent Robert Gosk for you, sir."

Ross explained the situation. "How quickly can you check if security tapes show a young blond woman, a twelve-year-old boy, and eleven-year-old girl boarding a private jet at the Orlando airport?" Ross listened a moment. "Right, I'll hold."

Ross paced while he waited. "Burnsie, call Sam's brothers. Maybe one of them will answer their mobile."

"Aye, Captain, calling now."

Ross listened to Agent Gosk before saying, "You're sure? And the destination? Good work, sir. You may have saved three lives with your fast response. I'll be there when they land."

Corporal Burns looked up from his phone. "Captain, I couldn't reach Mike Starr. He must be on a SEAL mission. I have Matt on line two."

Ross punched the button. "Matt, someone took Sam and the children from the theme park in Orlando today. They're on a private jet headed to Rome. Airport security cameras recorded a man fitting Nicolai's description carrying Sam and the children onto the aircraft. They appeared to be unconscious."

Ross's voice tightened. "If they were already dead, he wouldn't have bothered taking them aboard."

"Damn it! I was afraid something like this might happen. Can you have your team on site before the airplane lands?"

"Aye, we have plenty of time to coordinate with Interpol and local police before the flight is due. Air traffic control has been alerted to notify us if the flight changes destinations. I'll be waiting for Nicolai when his jet lands in Rome."

"I hope it won't be too late to save them. He has plenty of time to carve them up during the flight over the Atlantic."

"I don't think he'll do it in flight—too messy, and he'll want them awake for the torture. He must have something special planned for his revenge and drugged them so he could move them easily."

"I hope you're right about him waiting, Ross. I wish I could be in on the kill. I'm aboard ship, and we just weighed anchor.

Send me an email after you nail the bastard."

"Count on it. Sam will never be safe as long as Nicolai is alive. He won't get away this time." Ross hung up and turned to Corporal Burns. "Burnsie—"

"Already done. Interpol Agent Farinati in Rome on line one."

Ross arranged a joint op with Interpol and Italian police. He looked up when Derek entered the room.

"Burnsie told me what happened. The team's ready." Derek looked determined.

"Good. My next call is to the DSF to commandeer a military jet for us." Ross glanced at Corporal Burns.

"DSF for you on line two." Burnsie pointed at the lighted button.

Barnes was eager to help save Samantha and the two heroic Scottish children beloved by the British people. "Take the team to Edinburgh. I'll send a C-17 for you. Save the children and Samantha, Ross. Bring them home to British soil. Leave the giant psychopath's body for the local authorities."

"Understood, sir. We'll solve the problem permanently." Ross hung up.

"Captain, the Lynx is ready when you are," Burnsie said.

"Right, I'll suit up. Keep an eye on her watch signal. Make sure it agrees with the flight were tracking." Ross jogged to the ready room.

Five minutes later, the Lynx lifted off with Ross and his team bound for Edinburgh Airport. The C-17 landed forty minutes after the helicopter. His team left Edinburgh in plenty of time to beat the private jet to Rome.

After his team disembarked at Fiumicino-Leornardo da Vinci Airport, Ross directed the C-17 to a nearby military air base. He didn't want to spook Nicolai, who might flee if he saw a British military transport on the field.

Ross shook hands with Agent Farinati. "Thank you for helping us on such short notice, sir. Nicolai's a formidable opponent. Keep the cops out of sight and off their noisy radios. If he smells a trap, he'll kill his prisoners."

An attractive Italian man with thick gray hair, Richard Farinati was eight inches shorter than Ross. Richard looked up at him. "Captain Sinclair, Interpol wants Nicolai alive so we can tie him to Lord Edgar Sweetwater. He may be our only way to close the link."

Ross gave Derek a meaningful look before saying, "I understand, Agent Farinati. We'll do our best."

The SAS team selected hiding places around the area where the jet would be directed to park. A sniper was positioned on the roof of the general aviation terminal. The police hid inside the building.

Ross checked his watch and whispered, "Five minutes to touchdown. I see landing lights in the distance. Hold fire until they exit the jet."

A few minutes later, a corporate jet landed and taxied to the ramp. An Interpol agent dressed as a ramp employee directed the airplane to park in front of the private terminal and chocked the nose wheels.

Ross's team waited while the pilots completed their checklist. The copilot opened the entry door and lowered the stairs. The cabin lights brightened, but the window shades prevented a view of the interior.

The pilot donned his uniform jacket and hat and walked down the stairs carrying a small box. He stopped a few feet from the airplane when Agent Farinati approached as a customs agent.

Ross could hear Agent Farinati's voice in his headset. "Good evening, Captain, are you ready to clear customs?"

"Do you need to check this? It's a package for SAS Captain

Ross Sinclair. Have you seen him?"

"Right this way. He's waiting for you inside." Agent Farinati escorted the pilot into the terminal.

The copilot headed for the building too. The ramp was silent except for a passenger jet shutting down its engines on the other side of the airport.

Ross heard Agent Farinati's voice again. "Captain Sinclair, come inside."

Ross keyed his mike. "Derek, I'm needed inside the terminal. Stay on target. Nicolai's waiting to see if the coast is clear." Ross kept in the shadows and entered the building from the street side.

Agent Farinati waved him into a side office with an angry expression. "Look at this."

Ross picked up the box which was designed to allow the lid to be lifted off without disturbing the gift wrapping.

Please, not Sam's eye. Ross inhaled and pulled off the lid. Sam's watch was pinned in the center. Beside it, a tiny note mocked him: I win. *Do svidaniya.*

Agent Farinati almost spat his words. "The pilot claims he was hired in Orlando to bring this box to Rome and give it to you. He swears there were no passengers."

Ross pocketed Sam's watch, handed the box to the Interpol agent, and keyed his mike. "Derek, take command of the airplane. The pilot swears it's empty. I'm on my way." Ross rushed through the terminal to the ramp.

Derek met him at the entry door. "The interior's empty. Let's check the cargo hold."

Ross walked with him and opened the cargo door. He felt a sick feeling of utter defeat when he looked inside.

The hold was empty.

101

ROSS HIT SPEED DIAL on his phone. "Burnsie, we've been duped. The jet was empty. Call FBI Agent Gosk in Orlando and ask him to look at the security tapes again. We need to know how they got off that airplane. Also, get a list of private jets that left soon after the one we tracked."

He pocketed his phone and faced Derek. "The pilots have to know something. Nicolai was seen carrying his victims onto this airplane."

"Time for a serious chat with the pilots. Best call the C-17 to return for us." Derek headed for the terminal as Ross made the call.

Agent Farinati was holding the pilots in a conference room. He and Derek looked up when Ross entered.

Ross focused on the captain. "If you want to live, you'd best answer my questions truthfully. Money won't do you any good if you're not alive to spend it."

"I know my rights. You can't touch me." The pilot crossed his arms and sat back.

Ross slammed his fists on the table and leaned into the pilot. "Terrorists have no rights. A British military transport will land here in fifteen minutes. I'll charge you and your copilot with kidnapping and terrorist acts against British citizens. When I take you aboard, no one will ever see you again. That's a promise."

"You can't do that. I'm an American citizen. The Interpol agent won't let you take us."

Agent Farinati quoted a law under an international treaty among cooperating nations. "That law gives Captain Sinclair the right to take you into military custody as an enemy combatant. Your only hope to avoid rendition is telling us the truth."

The copilot's eyes widened with panic. "Hold up a minute, I'm no terrorist. I'll tell you exactly what happened if you promise not to put me on that military plane."

"You have my word." Ross sat across from him. "Let's hear it."

"A tall man with a Russian accent chartered the jet with cash. He said the flight was time critical. We were ordered to fly to Rome and deliver the little box to you. He told us secrecy was essential and to keep the cockpit door closed and not look out the windows when he called a few minutes before he brought us the box. He said we'd know when to close the entry door by watching the indicator lights to see when the caterers closed the galley door."

"So you didn't see him carry the three people aboard?" Ross focused on his eyes.

"No, I did as instructed. It felt like he got on the airplane twice. It was only a few minutes before the galley-door light went out. I opened the cockpit door. The cabin was empty except for the little box. I retracted the stairs and closed the entry door while the captain started the engines. That's all I know, honest to God." The copilot looked too frightened to be lying.

Ross glanced at his watch and scrutinized the pilot. "Last chance. The transport will be here in a few minutes. What hasn't he told us?"

The pilot hesitated. "I want the same deal he got."

"All right. Talk." Ross searched the pilot's eyes for a sign of deceit.

"The answer to your puzzle is obvious. The Russian carried the people aboard in plain view of the security cameras so the authorities would think they were on the flight. Then he put them in the catering truck and left. I suggest you track where that catering truck went." The pilot shot Ross a smug look.

"Did he tell you that was his plan?" Ross watched his face.

"No, I figured it out. That Russian had crazy eyes. I had as little contact with him as possible. I just wanted to get the hell out of there in case he decided to kill us."

Ross's satellite phone rang. It was FBI Agent Gosk. Ross stood. "They're all yours, Agent Farinati. I have to take this call."

Ross stepped out as Agent Gosk said, "We found the catering truck in a private hangar, and the driver, a long-time employee named Robert George, had been murdered. A Gulfstream jet left the hangar ten minutes after the other jet took off. It flew to Bergen, Norway. The local authorities have a forensics team searching it. I'll keep you informed."

"Thank you, Agent Gosk. My team will fly to Norway now. You can always reach me on this satellite phone." Ross pocketed his phone as the C-17 parked nearby.

Derek joined him. "Did they find out where he took them?"

"Aye, gather the team." Ross jogged to the C-17 to give the pilot their new destination.

As they taxied for takeoff, Ross made a call. "Burnsie, track down the location of Lord Edgar Sweetwater and tell the DSF we need him held for questioning. Nicolai took Sam and the children to Bergen. We're headed there now."

"Aye, Captain. Nail the bastard. I'll locate Sweetwater."

102

AS PLANNED, NICOLAI ACCOMPLISHED the transfer from the private jet to the waiting boat via a black panel van before the bribed customs agent inspected the airplane. The aircraft manifest showed four new Harley Davidson motorcycles and leather riding gear, but no passengers.

Nicolai rigged the empty van to speed off the end of a deserted pier. He had opened the windows, so it sank quickly.

He secured his three unconscious victims in the cabin of the ocean speedboat and leaned over to check their breathing and pulse. Not certain of the exact dosage, he gave Sam another shot with twice as much tranquilizer as the children. It wouldn't be any fun if the boy and girl died en route.

The vessel's navy blue made it invisible on the water at night. Once he cleared the harbor, he set the powerful inboard engines at seventy-five percent throttle and switched off the running lights. The high-speed smuggler's craft would cover the distance to Sweetwater's private island in four hours, well before dawn.

A five-point harness secured Nicolai as he monitored the radar and autopilot. Unusually mild December weather with a clear night sky and calm winds helped him race across the North Sea. The enclosed cockpit kept him warm and dry.

By the time Nicolai reached the dock on Lord Sweetwater's isolated island between the Orkney and Shetland Islands, he felt fatigued from his long day and night of kidnapping.

He pulled on night-vision goggles so he wouldn't need lights. Satisfied his prey was still unconscious, he tied the bow and stern lines to the dock.

Nicolai strode up the steep steps to the imposing stone mansion forty feet above the sea and unlocked the heavy door with the key Sweetwater had provided. Inside, he found the control room and switched on the generator and furnace.

Soon the generator provided electrical power, and the oil-fired furnace sent heat into the duct work. His prey would be kept healthy until Lord Sweetwater arrived.

Nicolai carried Sam inside, dumped her on a twin bed in a downstairs servant's room, and tied her wrists to the metal headboard. He returned with a child slung over each shoulder, plopped them side by side on the other twin bed, and tied their wrists on the head bar. He locked the door with a key.

When he walked back to the boat, cold damp air slapped his face, while brisk wind tussled his black hair. The weather was turning. He stepped aboard to retrieve his gear and lifted a heavy canvas equipment bag and a duffel bag onto the dock.

The bow faced the sea inside a partial breakwater made of natural rock. Nicolai started the engines and set the high-tech autopilot to navigate past the rocks and run a straight course east. He set the throttles at half power and stepped onto the dock as the boat strained at the lines.

His Spetsnaz combat knife easily sliced through the heavy dock lines. He watched until the expensive boat cleared the rocks and raced out to sea. Satisfied the island appeared deserted as usual this time of year, he returned to the dark mansion.

He dropped his duffel in the foyer and carried his equipment bag down the stone steps to the specially designed dungeon. Flipping up his night-vision goggles, he switched on the light and admired the layout of the ancient torture chamber Sweetwater had replicated when the home was built. His heart thumped faster as he scanned the floor brackets, wall brackets, and ceiling chains for securing prisoners.

So many temptations! Who to have fun with first? Must wait for Sweetwater.

A heavy wood table on the center of the stone floor was the perfect place to display his instruments of horror. His stainless steel tools sparkled and clinked as he pulled them out of the canvas bag and lined them up across the table. He ran his fingers over them, smiling in perverted admiration.

Is good. I will rest now. Plenty time to play with them later.

Nicolai switched on his night vision and climbed the dungeon stairs. He picked up his duffel and chose a king bed in a guest suite on the second floor. Wind and rain pelted the windows as he fell into a deep sleep.

103

THE C-17 CARRYING ROSS and his team from Rome landed at Bergen, Flesland Airport and taxied to the general aviation ramp where the Gulfstream jet from Orlando was parked. It had been four and a half hours since the private jet landed.

British Interpol Agent Melody Stark waited for Ross beside the crime-scene van. After brief introductions, she delivered the bad news.

"A black panel van was seen driving away from the aircraft before customs cleared it. The pilots are dead and the customs agent arrived too late to see what happened. We've got every police officer and CCTV camera searching for that van. So far, no trace. Sorry, Captain Sinclair. Wish I had more for you." Melody shook her head.

Ross sighed. "Did the forensics team find anything?"

"A long blond hair. Nothing else."

"Samantha Starr has long blond hair." Ross thrust his hands on his hips and closed his eyes to think. "Has anyone checked the harbors?"

"Yes, there were the usual fishing boats and oil-rig tenders. One fisherman on his way to port claims he saw a dark cigarette boat headed out to sea. No way to know who owns it or who might have been on it. He didn't see a name on the stern."

"What about the helicopters flying back and forth to the oil rigs? Has anyone asked the pilots if they saw the cigarette boat?" Ross tried to sound hopeful.

"I thought of that too. The last chopper pilot landed three hours ago. He claims he didn't see any fast boats, just the usual fishing trawlers."

"Sounds like a dead end." Ross sighed. "I'll ask my commander if he can get satellite imaging on the cigarette boat. Thank you for your assistance, Agent Stark." He walked back to his team.

Derek patted Ross' shoulder. "I can see the news isn't good."

"Nicolai managed to spirit them away without a trace. Time to call Loren. Maybe she has received another vision about Sam." Ross dialed the number on his satellite phone.

After Ross explained everything, Loren said, "I'll close my eyes and try to see her. Hold on."

Ross paced in front of the C-17 with the phone against his ear.

Loren came back on. "I can't see anything, Ross. Maybe she's still unconscious or—"

"Don't even think that. Sam's alive, and we're going to find her. Keep trying. Let me know when you have something. I'm taking my team back to Scotland." Ross called the DSF and asked him to task a satellite to look for the cigarette boat.

Halfway home to Scotland, the DSF called Ross. "We have satellite footage of a dark cigarette boat leaving the Bergen harbor twenty minutes after the jet from Orlando landed. He must have turned off his running lights on the open sea because the next satellite pass showed nothing. Sorry, Ross."

"What about Lord Sweetwater? Where is he?" Ross tried to sound calm.

"He's at his estate outside London. He had a dinner party tonight for thirty guests. If he's involved, he didn't get his hands dirty."

"He has Nicolai for that, although I'm sure he still insists he's never heard of him." Ross couldn't conceal the bitterness in his voice.

"MI5 is keeping an eye on Sweetwater. If he makes a move, we'll know about it. Return to base and stay ready to deploy."

"Aye, sir, and be advised we have Sam's mother trying for another vision like she had when Sam was in Wewelsburg, but there's no guarantee."

Ross pocketed his phone and tried not to think about what Nicolai might be doing to Sam and the children.

104

CHARLIE WOKE WITH A pounding headache and a growling stomach. Confused, he glanced around and saw Emily tied beside him and Sam on the opposite bed. Memories of Nicolai and the darts twisted his gut with fear.

He nudged Emily with his foot. "Emily? Wake up."

Another nudge. Nothing. He looked over his head at the rope that bound his wrists to the head rail and thought. He swooped his feet over his head to the wall and pushed the bed away so he could drop his feet to the floor and stand behind the head rail.

After several minutes of careful tugging on the knot with his teeth, he was free. He untied Emily and began loosening the rope around Sam's wrists. He was almost finished when he heard Emily's confused voice.

"Where are we? My head hurts." She sat up and rubbed her forehead.

"Nicolai drugged us and took us prisoner. We have to escape before he comes back."

Emily wobbled over to Sam's bed and touched her face. "Is Sam okay?"

"She's still drugged. I can't wake her." Charlie shook Sam's shoulders. No response.

Emily lightly slapped Sam's face, but she remained still. "What are we going to do?"

Charlie tried the door. Locked. He studied the old-fashioned keyhole. "I think I can pick this. We have some locks like this at our house. Ben and I practiced picking them when we pretended to be detectives."

He removed a picture from the wall, pulled the hanging wire from the frame, shaped it, and wiggled it around in the lock until he heard the latch release.

Glancing at Emily, he eased the door open and peeked out. The hallway was deserted. The mansion was silent except for the oil-powered generator and furnace inside and the howling wind and rain outside. He closed the door.

Looking up at the ground-level window at the top of the wall, Charlie realized they were below the first floor.

"Right, we'll lean the bed frame against the wall like a ladder and make it look like we escaped out the window. I'll leave it open a little bit. Then we'll carry Sam to the first floor and find a safe place to hide her until she wakes up. We'll leave this door locked so he thinks we're outside."

"We'd best hurry. I'll help you." Emily pulled the mattress off the bed. "The storm is making so much noise maybe he won't hear us moving around."

They braced the twin bed frame against the wall with the mattress and box spring. Charlie climbed up to the window and opened it.

"Wow, it's cold and rainy out there. We're definitely not in Florida anymore."

He climbed out, pressed footprints in the moist ground to the rocks, backtracked in his prints, and climbed down after partially closing the window.

"Hand me the sheet. I need to dry myself off and wipe my feet so I don't leave tracks in here." He rubbed the rain out of his hair, cleaned his feet and the floor, and shoved the sheet under the mattress.

Emily studied Sam's sleeping form. "It'll be easier to carry her if we wrap her in this wool blanket. You lift her arms, and I'll get her feet."

They slid Sam's cocoon into the hall. Charlie locked the door with the pick and motioned for Emily to wait while he checked the stairway.

"Let's go. Be quiet. We don't know where Nicolai is," he whispered.

While Charlie pulled Sam up the stairs, Emily lifted and pushed. They stopped at the top to catch their breath. He tiptoed into a large room with leather couches and chairs. A cordovan sofa was positioned with the back close to a row of tall, narrow windows.

Charlie pointed. "We can hide her behind that big leather couch by the windows. Hurry!"

They silently slid Sam across the stone floor in the blanket and stashed her behind the sofa, draping the bottoms of the velvet curtains over her. After checking from several angles, they were satisfied Nicolai wouldn't spot her.

They froze when a brisk north wind rattled the windows.

Emily clutched Charlie's arm and whispered, "What do we do now?"

"Help me find the kitchen. We can arm ourselves with knives and find food. I'm starving."

"The kitchen is probably down on the servant floor. Let's go."

They crept back down the stairs and found the kitchen, pantry, and cold storage cellar. Charlie selected a large carving knife and sharp steak knives. Emily stuck a small square of cheese on the tip of a steak knife to prevent tearing her pocket.

Charlie looped oven mitts through his belt for knife holsters and positioned one on each hip. He loaded the mitts with his weapons and added a butcher knife and meat cleaver.

They gobbled down some cheese and sausage and gulped plenty of water.

Emily snatched a couple of chocolate bars from the pantry. "Grab a water bottle for Sam. We'll leave her some cheese and chocolate."

She wrapped the cheese in a hand towel with the chocolate.

They crept up the stairs and deposited the meat cleaver, butcher knife, and water bottle beside Sam with the sharp sides pointed away from her. Emily left the food atop Sam's belly over the blanket.

After peeking out the windows on all sides of the castle as the wind whipped away the fog, Charlie realized they were trapped on an island. The boat dock and helipad were empty and wet from rain.

Emily's eyes widened. "We're trapped. Please don't let him kill me."

"Maybe there's a secret passage below. Let's look." He took her hand and led her down a different stairway.

Emily gasped when he switched on the light. Instruments of torture taunted them from a table. The walls and floor anchored brackets with metal clasps. "This is where he plans to kill us."

Charlie recognized an instrument like the one kidnappers had used to cut off the pinky fingers of his friends last summer. He slipped it into the mitt on his left hip.

Emily grabbed his hand. "Let's get out of here."

Charlie switched off the light and started up the stairs. He froze on the bottom step when he heard Nicolai yell, "*Sooka!*"

"I hope he runs outside to look for us," Charlie whispered.

Emily squeezed his hand as he listened.

The front door slammed.

"Quick! Follow me."

He ran up the steps and bolted the door.

105

"WE NEED TO HIDE until Sam wakes up. I wish this mansion had secret passages like the ones Sam told us about in Laird MacLeod's castle." Charlie grasped Emily's hand.

"Maybe it does. In mystery books, the entrance is always behind a big painting or a bookcase." Her eyes brightened. "Let's check the study."

They ran to the first-floor study and felt around the bookcases.

Charlie jerked his head at the sound of a window shattering on the other side of the house. He struggled to dislodge the iron poker from the fireplace tool stand, but it just moved like a lever.

"Whoa, part of the bookcase opened to a secret passage! Quick, run inside!" Charlie pushed Emily inside.

Nicolai shouted threats as Charlie searched for the lever that closed the bookcase. Emily found it recessed into the wall and pulled it. The bookcase closed, and dim electric lights illuminated spiral stone steps descending beneath the study.

They rushed down to where the stairs ended at a long passage carved into the rock and ran a hundred and fifty yards to a cavernous chamber overlooking a lower level with a long dock.

Deep beneath the island, the water along the pier was calm. Large wooden crates were stacked on their level and below near the dock.

"This looks like an underground warehouse. What's in the boxes?" Charlie tried to open a crate, but it was nailed shut.

"How can boats get in here? There's no opening to the sea." Emily looked around the vast cavern.

"Could be a secret submarine base." He looked down at the dock area. "Those are cargo cranes like the ones at my dad's shipyard. I bet they used them to unload these boxes."

"I wish the submarine was here. We could escape." She glanced around. "What do we do now?"

Charlie pointed at a ladder bolted to the far wall. It led up to a small landing with a door. "Let's see what's behind that door."

They climbed the forty-foot ladder and entered a tunnel carved into the rock. The lighted passage ran straight for thirty feet, then curved sharply and opened onto a wide ledge on a cliff.

A three-foot diameter signal light covered with a heavy glass dome was bolted to the center of the rock ledge. A short spear-shaped finial rose from the dome's center. Forty feet below, waves crashed against the cliff.

Emily walked around the light and peered over the edge. "That's a long way to fall."

Charlie tugged her back. "Don't stand so close. The ledge is slippery, and it's really windy."

"Nothing down there anyway. Let's look for a path up the cliff." Emily turned around and screamed.

"Hello, brats. Where is blonde?" Nicolai blocked the tunnel entrance.

Charlie stepped in front of Emily and brandished knives from the oven mitts like small swords. His hands trembled as he focused on the Russian giant's dark evil eyes.

Nicolai laughed and stepped onto the ledge. "I am mighty

bear. You cannot kill me. Drop knives."

He crossed his arms with a smug look on his scarred face. "Jump and die, or come with me. Maybe I let you live."

One of Nicolai's long legs on his six-foot-eight frame kicked the knife out of Charlie's left hand, and Emily screamed again.

106

I WOKE TO GLASS shattering. Primal instinct kept me still. It took a few moments for the fog of confusion to lift. *Where am I? How did I get here?* I was wrapped in a wool blanket crammed behind a leather couch. Floor-to-ceiling windows beside me revealed a bleak landscape with an angry sea.

Something was poking my side. I discovered a meat cleaver, a butcher knife, and a water bottle. I felt something on my stomach—a block of cheddar and two chocolate bars in a towel.

The children must have left these for me.

The next sound filled me with terror.

Nicolai roared like a lion. "I will punish you for locking door. No escape from island. You will beg for death soon."

Island? Please no.

A cold wind blew under the couch as the psychotic giant rampaged through the room smashing vases and overturning furniture. He paused near the leather couch as if listening. I held my breath and heard him run from the room.

The house fell silent except for the wind funneling through the broken window. I felt weak and dizzy.

Better eat the cheese and drink the water.

Within minutes, I felt stronger as the dizziness faded. I tore open a chocolate bar and bit into it as I stood. If Nicolai was telling the truth, Charlie and Emily could hide from him, but they couldn't escape the island.

Why did he leave? He must've seen them outside. Must save Charlie and Emily.

I rolled up the sleeves on an extra-large wool sweater that hung to my knees over my jeans. *Nicolai must've put it on me.* I hefted the meat cleaver in one hand and the butcher knife in the other and jumped through the broken window to the ground five feet below.

Yep, this was an island. On the high ground, I could see in every direction. Muddy kid-sized footprints led from a low window to the west across the rocky ground. A cold northwest wind assaulted my face as I ran across the island, desperate to find the children before Nicolai.

I almost had reached the edge of the cliff when I heard Emily scream. Did it come from beyond the cliff? I ran and peered down the cliff as she screamed again.

Nicolai had trapped Charlie and Emily on a ledge fifteen feet below me and was waving his combat knife at them.

"Drop blade or I cut off your hand." He took a step toward Charlie.

I leaped off the cliff and landed on Nicolai. The force smashed his face against the glass dome and jarred the knives out of my hands.

Pain seared my chest. I had cracked a rib, maybe more. Gasping for air, I grabbed the meat cleaver and clutched a handful of his thick black hair. I lifted his head and pressed the weapon against his carotid artery.

I wasn't ready for what I saw. Neither were the children.

Charlie gasped while Emily fell to her knees and vomited.

The pointed finial had pierced Nicolai's left eye socket. Blood and eyeball goo streaked down his left cheek. Blood gushed from his crushed nose, and his other eye was open but lifeless. I dropped his head when I heard an approaching helicopter.

"We have to get out of sight fast." I pulled Emily to her feet.

"This way." Charlie pointed at the tunnel entrance.

We ran inside and stopped where a long ladder led down to a level above a dock area.

Emily clutched my side as her little body quivered.

I winced from pain as I hugged her. "Emily, you're safe now. Charlie and I will protect you. Forget about Nicolai so we can escape. Can you do that?"

Charlie hugged her too. "It'll be okay, Emms. We've got you covered."

She sniffled and inhaled a deep breath. "We'd best get down that ladder."

"Good girl, I knew we could count on the president of the Magic Club. I'll go first so I can catch you if you slip. Charlie will follow."

Once we were down, I glanced around the huge cavern. "This looks like a submarine base for a smuggling operation. Judging by the size of the crates, they're probably full of illegal weapons."

I found a crowbar wedged between two crates and pried open a lid. "Whoa, I think that's a Stinger missile."

"Can we use it on the bad guys?" Charlie touched it.

"We don't have the launcher, and I doubt we could lift it anyway."

Emily tugged my sweater. "Sam, what are we going to do?"

I glanced around. "Does that passage lead back to the mansion?"

"Aye, it ends at steps up to the study," Charlie said. "I found the lever that opens the bookcase."

Emily nudged Charlie. "It was my idea to look for a passage in the study in the first place."

"You're both brilliant. Thanks for hiding me and leaving the goodies. Now we need to get back to the house before that helicopter lands. It's our ticket out of here."

I hefted the crow bar. "Let's go."

107

LORD EDGAR SWEETWATER WAS quite pleased with himself for outsmarting MI5 and Scotland Yard again.

After MI5 interrogated him during his lavish party the previous night, three black Enstrom 480B helicopters lifted off from his estate outside London early in the morning. The pilots were Sweetwater's size and dressed in matching uniforms. Two helicopters carried passengers dressed like Sweetwater. He rode in the third one.

The helicopters scattered low over the terrain to stay under radar. The one carrying Sweetwater landed at the safe house the Russian assassins had used when they hunted Sam and Charlie last August.

The pilot refueled the helicopter while Sweetwater changed into a pilot uniform.

"It's full of fuel, Lord Sweetwater. Are you certain you want to continue on alone?"

"I'll enjoy the stick time and the solitude. There's a vehicle for you in the barn with the keys in the ignition." Sweetwater walked to the helicopter parked behind the barn.

Unlike most helicopters, the Enstrom was designed for the pilot to sit in the left front seat. Sweetwater fastened the five-point harness and tugged the straps before running through the checklist.

Once airborne, he headed to his private island where the

stone mansion and underground facilities had been built to his specifications. He was especially proud of the ancient-looking dungeon where he enjoyed torturing those who crossed him.

His heart quickened in anticipation of torturing the Scottish brats in front of Samantha to force her to divulge the location of Poseidon's Sword. Only then could Nicolai have the children. She had to be kept alive to activate the weapon, but that didn't mean they couldn't employ a little creative pain therapy on Samantha.

Sweetwater approached from the south, landing into a north wind on the helipad up the hill from the mansion. He buttoned the heavy raincoat up to his neck and waited for the rotor blades to wind down. His pilot cap shielded the light rain when he stepped out. Just in case, he decided to refuel the helicopter before entering the castle.

Sweetwater switched on the fuel pump and inserted the nozzle into the tank. He stamped his feet to get his blood flowing as the meter counted the gallons down. He glanced at the house, expecting to see Nicolai walking up the path.

Where in hell is he?

Annoyed, he called Nicolai on his mobile. Nothing.

Oh right, no reception on the island. If he started without me, I'll shoot the bastard.

Sweetwater pocketed the phone and finished the fueling. *Nicolai should be doing this damn task instead of me.* The thought of him enjoying the torture without him angered him so much he rushed down the stone path, slipped on a wet rock, and slid on his backside.

When he entered the mansion, he was boiling with rage.

108

THE STUDY COMMANDED AN excellent view of the helipad. I had watched the pilot fuel the helicopter and fall on his ass on his way down.

I turned to Charlie and Emily. "It's just the pilot. He's probably here to pick up Nicolai. Stay out of sight while I deal with him."

"I'll help you." Charlie drew a knife from his oven-mitt holster.

"Thanks, but I've got this. He's short and pudgy, and he fell on the stone path—no match for a black belt."

I walked down the hall and hid behind a pillar near the foyer. My cracked rib wouldn't stop me from kicking butt. Plus, I had a crow bar.

I heard the pilot slam the door and shout, "Nicolai, get your bloody arse up here!" He tossed his hat across the room.

His voice! Our meeting at Buckingham Palace flooded my mind. I stepped out and faced the balding man with sinister eyes.

"Lord Edgar Sweetwater, isn't it? Nicolai can't hear you." I walked within kicking range.

His fleshy face betrayed his shock. "You!"

He stepped back and started unbuttoning his raincoat. "Well, thank goodness you're all right. I'm here to rescue you from that giant psychopath. Gather the children and let's go.

My helicopter is ready."

"Nice try, but I know you hired Nicolai. You're done." I stepped forward.

Sweetwater pulled out a Walther PPK pistol like James Bond's. I kicked it out of his hand and swung the crow bar so hard against his face his head banged into the stone wall and knocked him unconscious. Blood gushed from his broken nose.

"Charlie, come here!" I gasped in pain, picked up the Walther, and shoved it into the back of my jeans.

He ran into the foyer with Emily trailing. They gawked at the man crumpled on the floor.

"Good job!" Charlie cocked his head and focused on the man's bloody face. "Huh, he looks a lot like that English billionaire we met at the palace."

"Yep, you're looking at Lord Edgar Sweetwater—billionaire scumbag and arms dealer. Help me tie him up." I looked around for something to bind him.

"Let's chain him in the dungeon. The wrist and ankle clasps will do nicely." He tugged an ankle to check Sweetwater's weight.

Emily gripped the other ankle. "I'll help."

"Lead the way." When I wrapped my arms around his chest under his arms and lifted his torso, pain tore through my ribs.

We struggled on the dungeon steps and dropped him twice. Finally at the bottom, Charlie switched on the light.

"This is where they were going to torture us." Emily pointed at the stainless steel implements glinting on the table.

I sucked in my breath and glanced around. "Shall we clamp him to the wall or the floor?"

"The floor would be easier for us." Emily pointed at a set of cuffs attached to floor brackets. "How about right here?"

"Good idea." I dragged him over the smooth stone and spread his arms to meet the metal clasps.

I clicked the cuffs into place over his wrists while the children did the same with his ankles. I checked all the bonds.

"That should hold him. Help me check his pockets." I found his mobile phone. "When we get upstairs, I'll call Ross. Let's go."

The children started up the stairs as I switched off the lights.

Emily looked back after mounting a few steps. "What if he dies down there?"

"Evil people like him don't die easily." I realized the same could be true of Nicolai and ignored the knot in my gut. "Trust me, he'll be alive when the police arrive." I herded them up.

Charlie paused near the front door. "Forgot something in the dungeon. Go ahead. I'll meet you at the helicopter." He ran back to the stairs.

Emily clutched my arm with a panicked look.

"Relax, honey, we're not leaving without Charlie. I'll call Ross." I punched in his number, but nothing happened. Oh, no signal bars.

"Is it ringing?" Emily sounded anxious.

I tilted the phone at her. "See, no signal here. I'll call on the helicopter's radio when we get high enough."

We waited in silence until we heard high-pitched screams rising from the dungeon.

109

WE ALMOST RAN INTO Charlie in the hall leading to the stairs. His strange expression wasn't fear.

"I'm okay, let's go."

I noticed a blood stain on a mitt holster where the pointy end of the clippers pressed against it. Our eyes locked, and I nodded.

Sweetwater's money might buy him a light sentence, or his slick lawyers might find a way to save him. With Nicolai dead, there might not be any evidence other than his arrival at the mansion and his submarine cavern.

This was Charlie's payback for what Sweetwater had cruelly robbed from Charlie's eight friends in that cave in the Highlands last summer. It was about honor and justice. Sir Charles Moncreiffe was only twelve, but he was a true knight in word and deed.

I touched Charlie's shoulder. "I understand. I did the same thing to the guards in the cave last summer. Let's go."

Emily looked confused and grabbed Charlie's hand. "What did you do?"

"Nothing he didn't deserve. Come on, we're leaving." He led her to the front door.

I peered out the window before opening the door. We ran to the helipad and disconnected the tie-down straps.

I opened the right door. "Good thing this is the high-density seating model. Emily, slide onto that bench seat in the back. Stay on the right and buckle up. Charlie, you sit on the right front in the copilot seat."

"This is brilliant. I didn't know you flew helicopters," Charlie said.

"I'm not a big fan of fling-wing death traps. Oops, did I say that aloud?" I patted his back.

"Don't worry. My brothers had one like this a few years ago and taught me to fly it. It's been a while, but I'll get us there in one piece." I walked around and opened the left door.

I slipped the Walther under the left chest strap of my tightened five-point seatbelt harness. My cracked rib radiated pain as I ensured they were belted in before I started the turbine engine.

While waiting for it to warm up, I studied the panel and checked our location on the GPS. After selecting a direct course to the SAS base in Dundee, I began the liftoff.

We were only a foot or two above the ground when the children screamed as the helicopter tilted sharply to the right. I tried to compensate as I glanced over and spotted Nicolai's hideous face outside the right door.

He wrenched the door open as the right skid slammed onto the helipad. He harnessed the momentum to pull the helicopter over and rolled clear as we crashed onto our side. The thundering rotor blades hit the concrete and sprayed razor-sharp shards.

I shut off the engine, mortified the fuel tank would burst into flames.

I turned to the children. "Are you okay? We have to get out fast!"

The children looked up behind me.

Emily screamed, and Charlie yelled, "Look out, Sam!"

Nicolai glared down at me through the pilot door and

yanked it open. "I have you now, *Sooka.*"

His mangled eyeball magnified his monstrous appearance.

I emptied the Walther into his face and chest as time seemed frozen. He fell backwards and dropped out of sight as I unbuckled my harness and climbed up out the door.

Nicolai lay motionless in a pool of blood.

"He's definitely dead this time, guys. Hurry and climb up here before the chopper explodes!" I reached in through the open door.

Charlie pushed Emily up to me, and I pulled her out. *Ow, my ribs.*

Charlie climbed out, and we sprinted down the path. Seconds later, the helicopter exploded into a fireball and knocked us to the ground.

We stared at the intense flames as we caught our breath. A brisk wind carried the scent of burning jet fuel and charred flesh.

The explosion numbed our hearing. Everything sounded distant as the barrel of a pistol was pressed against the back of my head.

"No one move or I'll blow her brains out," Lord Edgar Sweetwater said in a bitter tone.

110

EARLIER, ROSS PACED IN the operations center as Corporal Burns researched properties owned by Sweetwater or his corporation.

"Burnsie, at the ball after the royal awards ceremony in August, Sweetwater invited Sam and me to vacation on his private island near the Orkneys. Find out exactly where it's located. A fast boat probably could get there from Norway in four or five hours."

Ross nudged Derek and pointed at a map of the North Sea. "The Orkney Islands are there. Look at the distance from the coast of Norway. Think that's where Nicolai took them?"

Derek frowned. "Maybe. Sweetwater gave MI5 the slip today. Nobody knows where he is."

"Got it!" Corporal Burns handed Ross a printout and pointed at the map. "It's right there."

Ross stared at the map. "That has to be where he took them." He patted Burnsie on the back. "Tell the Lynx pilots wheels up in five. I'll get the teams ready."

Sweetwater's island was two hundred miles from the SAS base, which wasn't a long flight in a Super Lynx helicopter. Ross would send two helicopters with four-man teams in each. He would lead one team and Derek the other.

111

"PUT YOUR HANDS TOGETHER behind your backs and sit still."
Sweetwater slipped flexicuffs over my wrists with his left hand
and yanked them tight while his right hand pointed the pistol
at my head.

"Sit still while I cuff the brats." His broken nose made him
sound nasal. "Now walk ahead of me into the house, children
first."

Blood dripped from the stub where Charlie had clipped off
his left pinky finger.

"How did you get loose?" I tried to distract him with
conversation.

"Nicolai released me. The fool rushed out when he heard
the helicopter. He should have waited for me to get the
weapons."

"Where did you get the pistol?"

"A hidden wall safe. I also keep a satellite phone in there.
Too bad you didn't find the safe. You used all your bullets on
Nicolai. I'm in control now."

He glanced at his watch. "Hurry inside! I don't want us to
miss our ride."

My heart sank. "You called your submarine."

"It docks in fifteen minutes. You have until then to tell me
what I want to know, or the children will die." He urged us
through the door in the study's bookcase. "Take the passage to

the sub base."

When we reached the platform above the dock, he secured us to support columns. He was careful to stay out of range of my kicks.

He lifted devices that looked like bombs from a large crate, placed them next to support columns throughout the sub base, and set the digital timers.

"Now that I've taken care of housekeeping issues, I'll start with Charlie. He has too many fingers." Sweetwater retrieved the clippers from the mitt on Charlie's left side.

"Wait! If you harm either of the children, I'll never tell you anything, and I'll find a way to kill you before my last dying breath." I spoke with a tone of absolute conviction.

Sweetwater stared at me, apparently detecting the fire in my eyes. He stepped away from Charlie. "Tell me where Poseidon's Sword is hidden."

"I was gathering clues when the Black Sun disrupted my search. You know I haven't found it yet. Here's something you may not know. I care far more about these children than an ancient weapon, so I'll make you a good deal. If you leave the children here unharmed, I'll go with you to help you find the weapon. You'll never find it without me." I managed to keep my voice steady.

"I know about the triplets. I can use one of them to find the weapon." He smiled and stepped closer to Charlie.

"The triplets were killed in a plane crash in the Himalayas twenty-three years ago," I lied. "I'm the only one who can locate and activate the weapon. You need me."

His eyes revealed uncertainty as a submarine surfaced alongside the dock.

"Ah, my new stealth sub, 184 feet with an anti-magnetic steel hull. The special hydrogen/oxygen fuel cells allow for silent running underwater." Pride filled Sweetwater's voice.

A hatch opened on the deck forward of the superstructure, followed by an inner hatch beneath it.

"Time to go," Sweetwater said. "I'll take your deal."

"Disarm the bombs first." I saw the red LED timers counting down.

Six minutes until detonation.

Sweetwater cut the rope binding me but not my plastic cuffs. "Get moving down the steps to the dock."

"Not until I see you disarm the bombs."

Two men with machine pistols emerged from the hatch and stood on the deck.

Sweetwater gripped a small electronic device in his left hand. "This will disarm all the bombs simultaneously when I press the button, which I won't do until you're in the submarine."

Five minutes left.

I slowly walked down the steps to the dock as my ribs throbbed from the awkward angle of my arms behind my back.

"I'll step onto the deck, but I won't go below until I see you activate the disarming switch."

"Keep moving. I'll keep my word." Sweetwater pushed me toward the sub.

I glanced at the nearest bomb before I stepped onto the deck.

Four minutes.

112

TEN MINUTES EARLIER, THE lead Lynx circled the burning helicopter. Ross spotted a body engulfed in flames beside the wreckage on the helipad. He tapped the pilot's shoulder.

"Hover close to the ground and we'll jump out. Pass the word to the other team."

The two teams jumped from the helicopters and surrounded the mansion. After shattering windows for entry, they cleared the ground floor.

Ross and Derek headed downstairs and found the dungeon.

Ross turned on the lights while Derek stood ready to fire. It was empty.

Derek picked up something and held it out to Ross. "Look what I found."

"A bloody pinky finger. Keep it. We'll run the DNA." Ross shook his head.

"I hope it doesn't belong to Sam or one of the children." Derek wrapped the finger in his handkerchief and put it in a zippered pocket.

"Best we find them quickly." Ross and Derek conducted a quick check of the servant level and met the team in the living room.

"The home is empty, but we found muddy footprints from the door to a bookcase in the study," a soldier said. "Some were child sized."

"Must be a hidden passage. Show me the tracks." Ross followed his soldier into the study and examined the muddy tracks. One set tracked to the right side of the fireplace and then merged with the others at the bookcase.

The fireplace poker handle was wet with blood. Ross pulled it and the bookcase opened. "Could be whoever lost their finger pulled this."

He left two men in the mansion and led the other five down the secret passage.

When they arrived at the submarine base, Ross saw the children tied to a column and Sam standing on a submarine deck with Sweetwater and two armed men.

Ross and Derek shot the two gunmen before they had time to react.

Sweetwater held a pistol to Sam's head as he focused on Ross and his men. "Hold your fire or I'll kill her."

While Sweetwater was distracted by the SAS soldiers, Sam stomped on his foot, dropped to the deck, and rolled into the water on the far side of the sub. She disappeared beneath the surface as Sweetwater turned and fired.

Ross shot him in the left shoulder, and Sweetwater dropped an electronic device. It slid across the deck into the water as he dived through the hatch.

"Hurry, Captain Sinclair! The bombs are set to explode!" Charlie shouted.

Ross spotted the bombs against several columns. Red digital numbers counted down from two minutes.

"Bombs! We have less than two minutes. Free the children and take them out!" Ross ran to the dock as the submarine submerged. He frantically searched for Sam, knowing the water was cold, and her hands were cuffed.

"Help!" Sam had surfaced on the far side of the submarine

pen. She struggled to keep her head above water.

Ross peeled off his heavy gear, dived in, and reached her just as she slipped under the surface. He yanked her up and pulled her across to the dock.

Sam coughed up water when he deposited her on the pier and cut off her cuffs. Her eyes widened when she focused on the nearest bomb.

In a weak voice, she said, "Thirty seconds. Leave me—"

"Bugger that! You're coming with me."

Ross slung her over his shoulder and heard her gasp in pain as he sprinted through the passage. When they reached the spiral steps, he took them two at a time. Ross closed the bookcase a second before the bombs exploded.

"Everyone into the choppers!" Ross carried Sam to the lead helicopter.

Derek had directed most of the soldiers to board the second Lynx to make room for Sam and the children in the lead chopper. Aboard, he wrapped wool blankets around Sam and Ross, who were shivering. The children snuggled into blankets from the house.

The ground shook as the far side of the island dropped into the sea.

Ross tapped the pilot's shoulder. "Get us out of here! Stay well clear of the house."

The helicopters lifted off and cleared the island's eastern coastline when the house exploded and dropped into a massive water-filled crater. Fissures appeared like spider webs. The island disintegrated to half its size. All traces of the mansion, helipad, and submarine base were gone.

Derek nudged Ross. "Nothing's ever easy when it involves Sam, is it?"

Ross shook his head. "This woman could keep our military busy for years."

He remembered to check her hands. Thank God all her fingers were intact, but her expression was tight with pain. "Sam? What's wrong?"

She sucked in her breath. "Cracked ribs."

"Sorry about the rough handling, lass. There was no time." Ross stroked her cheek.

"That's okay. Thanks for saving me—again." She kissed his cheek.

Ross glanced at Charlie and Emily. "Derek, did you check the children's hands?"

"Aye, they're fine." Derek smiled at the children.

Sam nudged Ross and whispered, "Did you find a severed finger?"

"Aye, Derek has it in his pocket. Who—"

"Tell him to drop it into the sea. I'll explain later. Please." She squeezed his arm.

Ross saw the desperation in her eyes and turned to Derek. "Pull that bloody digit out of your pocket and hand it to me."

Ross passed it to the pilot. "Drop this out the cockpit side window."

Sam looked relieved.

"What happened to Nicolai?" Ross whispered against her ear.

"I gouged out his left eye, shot him full of holes, and burned him to a cinder. He's definitely dead this time." She snuggled against Ross and closed her eyes.

Ross processed the information and glanced at Derek. "You heard?"

"Aye." Derek locked eyes with Ross and grinned. "That's one dangerous girlfriend you've got there." He chuckled.

Ross shook his head and shrugged.

113

ROSS DIRECTED THE LYNX pilot to drop us off at MacLeod Castle and tasked Derek with reporting the rescue after returning to base.

Baxter opened the castle's door when he heard our helicopter. "Welcome back Miss Starr, Captain Sinclair, Charlie, and Emily." He held the door open and smiled.

Duncan and Mom were waiting behind Baxter to greet us.

"Sam, Ross, you're wet! Duncan, get a change of clothes for Ross. Sam, let me help you into dry clothes." Mom checked us over like a mother hen. "Are the children wet?"

"We're dry, but we could do with a snack," Charlie said.

"Baxter, take the children to sit in front of the fire in the study. Have Fiona bring them hot chocolate and biscuits while Loren and I tend to Sam and Ross. We'll be down soon for whisky, wine for the ladies, and chocolate." Duncan ushered Ross upstairs.

Ten minutes later, Duncan and Ross entered the study the same time as Mom and I. Ross and I sat on either side of the children on the big leather sofa. Ross wore Duncan's jeans and a heavy wool sweater. The children were finishing mugs of hot chocolate.

Baxter had left a bottle of forty-year-old Glenfiddich single-malt whisky and two crystal glasses on a tray on the coffee table. Duncan poured two doubles.

Baxter returned with a tray of chocolate confections for the children with two large glasses of milk. Moments later, he brought a bottle of Merlot and two glasses.

I was comfortable in Mom's jeans and sweater with my hair dry. Baxter poured wine for us as Mom sat across from Duncan in the leather chairs that flanked the sofa.

"All right, then, who would like to tell us about what happened in Orlando?" Duncan glanced from me to the children.

Charlie raised his hand. "I'll start, and Sam can fill in the part when we were separated."

He gave a glowing review of our tour through the Harry Potter theme parks, followed by a detailed description of our terrifying abduction by the scary Russian up to the point when I jumped off the cliff onto Nicolai. "Sam can tell you the rest."

Everyone was silent as they sipped their drinks and turned to me.

"I woke to the sound of Nicolai's angry tirade." I related the events leading up to Ross's arrival with the teams but omitted the severed finger. "Except for a cracked rib or two, I came through in good shape. Your turn, Ross."

Ross downed his whisky and recounted his rescue mission, ending with, "I winged Sweetwater, but he escaped in a submarine, and all evidence of his illegal arms operation is now at the bottom of the North Sea. So is Nicolai. We have no hard evidence they were working together, only the testimony of Sam and the children. A slick lawyer will get him out of that." Ross shook his head.

"You brought Sam and the children home safe and sound. That's the most important thing," Mom said. "If you hadn't been there—"

"But he was, and we're okay." I gave the children a reassuring smile. "One of these days, Sweetwater will get what's coming to him."

"Aye, I'll see to it," Ross said with a determined look.

"Good, because Sweetwater will be after them with a renewed vengeance," Mom said.

"Aye, especially since he lost his pinky finger. I can't stand the thought of that horrible man getting away with all the bad things he's done." Fear cracked Emily's sweet voice.

Mom and Duncan exchanged glances, and Mom turned to me. "What about his finger? Sam, you never mentioned—"

Charlie and I locked eyes.

"Forget about the finger, Mom. It's not important, and we'll never mention it again."

Emily's face flushed from her slip of the tongue.

Duncan patted Emily's hand. "Although there isn't enough evidence to prosecute him, that doesn't mean he'll escape punishment." He glanced at Ross. "Justice can be served many ways."

"Aye, his days are numbered." Ross nodded at Emily. "Not to worry, lassie."

The thundering blades of a helicopter interrupted our conversation.

"That might be Charlie's dad. I called him when you arrived," Duncan said.

Moments later, loud pounding erupted on the front door. Baxter hurried to open it.

Ross and Duncan stood as a herd of footsteps thudded on the stone hallway.

Eight U.S. Delta Force soldiers accompanied by DSF Brent Barnes entered the study.

Ross's commanding officer, DSF Barnes, stepped to the front. "Sorry, Ross, my orders came directly from the prime minister. The Americans want Miss Starr under their protection."

Barnes looked at me. "Samantha Starr, these men will escort you back to the United States. Say your good-byes quickly."

"No, I can't go now. I just got here, and my ribs are broken. *Ross* rescued me. I was on *American* soil when I was kidnapped. I'm safer here." I spoke nervously in fast short sentences.

"Your president and our prime minister negotiated this arrangement. We have no choice. You must go with the Delta team. You have one minute to say good-bye." Barnes was all business.

I softly hugged Loren, Duncan, and the children.

I gave Ross a long kiss and said, "I'll miss you, Ross. I love you." I snuck in one final kiss before the soldiers stepped forward.

"Time to go, Miss Starr." The Delta captain handed me a warm military jacket and whisked me out of the castle with his team.

I sat in shocked silence as the Chinook carried me away from MacLeod Castle.

Excerpt from Book Three

Winter Solstice
2015

LIEUTENANT MIKE STARR AND the five members of his SEAL team waited in their RHIB on the Arabian Sea. Their black-ops mission in Pakistan had gone well. The terrorists were minus several key players now.

A dense mantle of cloud cover obscured the jeweled sky and cloaked the men in inky darkness. Steady rain pelted the sea, making it difficult to discern sounds.

Mike's blond buzz cut was hidden under a black hat, and his face was swathed in greasepaint. He scanned the water with night-vision binoculars as he waited for the nuclear submarine to surface.

Dark shadows shifted behind the veil of rain.

"I think I see something." He adjusted the focus on his binoculars. "There!"

Narrow black dorsal fins three feet high knifed through the water, bearing down on them.

A heavy downpour shrouded the pod of orcas until they were about twenty yards away. The killer whales were twenty to thirty feet long, many of them longer than the rigid hulled inflatable boat.

He stiffened. "Heads up, guys! Orcas are zeroed in on our boat."

"Relax, they're just curious," a laid-back teammate said, shielding his eyes from the rain.

Mike rested a hand on his weapon as he took a closer look at the whales. "Holy shit, a woman's riding one!" His eyes widened as he sat up straighter.

"Lieutenant, your brain's waterlogged," the same man said, rolling his eyes. "We're a long way from Sea World."

Another teammate shook his head and laughed. "Poor guy probably hasn't been laid in a while. He's imagining women now."

Mike stabbed his finger at one of the onrushing orcas. "Look! She's right there and coming closer."

His men stared, speechless.

A huge killer whale glided alongside the boat.

A woman sheathed in a black bodysuit straddled the beast with her arms wrapped around its dorsal fin. Long red hair cascaded over her bowed head.

She struggled to lift her head. Her fluttering lids opened and her eyes found Mike's. "Mike, please save me," she said, her voice a weak whisper.

His jaw dropped. *How does she know my name?*

A SEAL punched his arm. "Lieutenant, get your ass in gear and pull her in!"

"Yeah, let's not upset her killer-whale buddies," another teammate said as he checked his weapon.

Mike pulled the woman into his arms. Her limp body slumped against him, her head on his chest.

He tilted her chin up and brushed the hair away from her face.

Her emerald eyes fluttered open again.

Good god, she looks like my sister!

"Who are you?" He searched her face for a clue to help him remember her.

She managed to whisper one word before she passed out: "Blaze."

Coming Soon: *BLAZE*, Book Three in the
Samantha Starr Series

Available Now: *DEADSTICK DAWN*, Book One in the
Samantha Starr Series

ACKNOWLEDGMENTS

My highest praise goes to my Lord and Savior, Jesus Christ, who is the guardian of my soul.

Many thanks to Dottie Littlefield, Suzanne Berglind, Fred Lichtenberg, Leslie Borghini, Tina Chippas, George Bernstein, and Richard Brumer for their helpful critiques.

Special thanks to my brilliant beta readers, June Piper and William N. Wolfe, and to my special advisor Barbi Leonard.

I am sincerely grateful to my editor extraordinaire, Susan Bryant, whose keen insight and attention to detail is invaluable.

American Airlines B787 Captain Jeff Rowland has my deep gratitude for helping me with the accuracy of the airliner flight scenes, since I've been out of the cockpit for over twenty years.

Thank you to Dr. Ira M. Fine, M.D., and Leslie Gosk, R.N., TNCC (retired) for help with the accuracy of medical scenes and to Fire Inspector Thomas Hughes for sharing his expertise.

Special recognition goes to the Islander Grill & Tiki Bar at the Palm Beach Shores Resort. Owners Niko and Mel Bujaj, manager Larry Wertz, and the friendly staff have always provided a warm welcome, delicious food, superb live music, and encouragement for my writing; and the resort's general manager, Sherry Smith, has always been supportive. I can't thank them enough. My books are available in the resort gift shop.

The covered deck at the Hilton on Singer Island is my creative writing nirvana. Thanks to Executive Chef Oscar Carranza for his delicious food and expert advice on martial arts, and to the wonderful managers and staff who provide me with such a pleasant writing and dining experience.

ABOUT THE AUTHOR

S. L. Menear worked as a water-sports model before traveling the world as a flight attendant with Pan American World Airways. After earning her commercial pilot license, Sharon left Pan Am to work as a flight instructor, charter pilot, and commuter airline pilot until she became qualified to work for a major airline.

US Airways hired Sharon in 1980 as their first female pilot, bypassing the flight engineer position. The men in her new hire class gave her the nickname, Bombshell. She flew Boeing 727s and 737s, DC-9s, and BAC 1-11 jet airliners and was promoted to captain in her seventh year.

Sharon also enjoyed flying antique airplanes, experimental aircraft, and Third World fighter airplanes. Her leisure activities included scuba diving, powered paragliding, snow skiing, surfing, horseback riding, aerobatic flying, sailing, and driving fast cars and motorcycles.

Like some of the airplanes featured in *DEADSTICK DAWN* and *POSEIDON'S SWORD*, Sharon has owned and flown a Piper PA-11 Super Cub, Bücker Jungmann, SIAI Marchetti SF-260, Swearingen SX-300, Glasair III, and many other exotic airplanes.

A rare eye disease sidelined her from flying and high-adrenaline activities. Her new passion is writing action thrillers.

The first novel in the Samantha Starr Series, *DEADSTICK DAWN*, won the 2011 Royal Palm Literary Award for Best Unpublished Thriller and was published in 2013.

DEADSTICK DAWN and *POSEIDON'S SWORD* are available in soft cover and ebooks at Amazon.com, BarnesAndNoble.com, and on request at bookstores.

S.L. Menear's web site: www.SLmenear.com
Facebook page: www.Facebook.com/slmenear